Swans in Space 1

STORY & ART by
Lun Lun Yamamoto

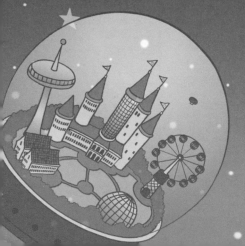

HOW TO READ MANGA!

Hi there! My name is **Instructor,** and this is the very first volume of **Swans in Space!**
It is a comic book originally created in the country of **Japan,** where comics are called **manga.**

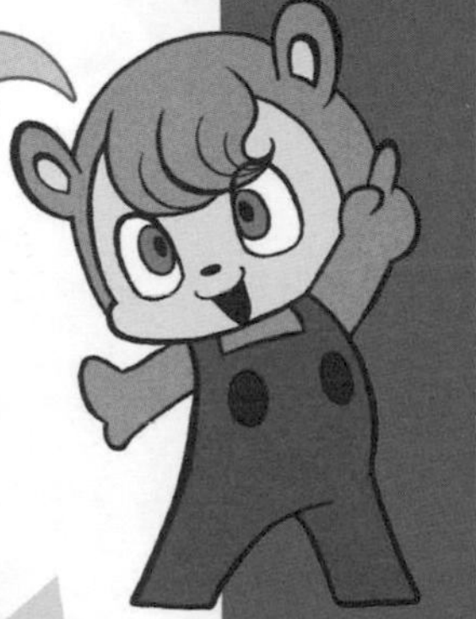

A manga book is read from **right-to-left,** which is **backwards** from the normal books you know. This means that you will find the first page where you expect to find the last page! It also means that each page begins in the top right corner.

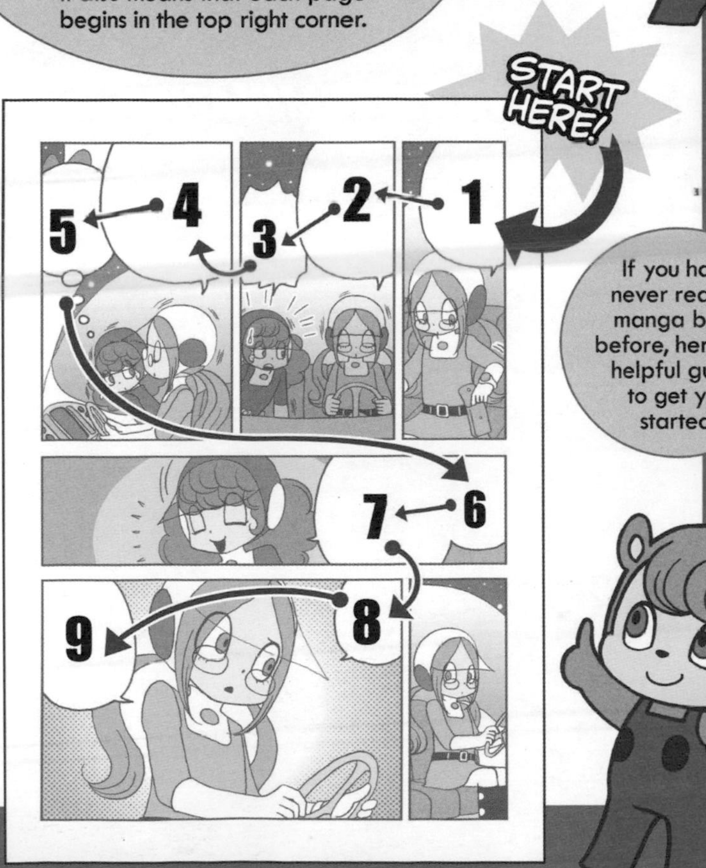

START HERE!
1
2
3
4
5
6
7
8
9

If you have never read a manga book before, here is a helpful guide to get you started!

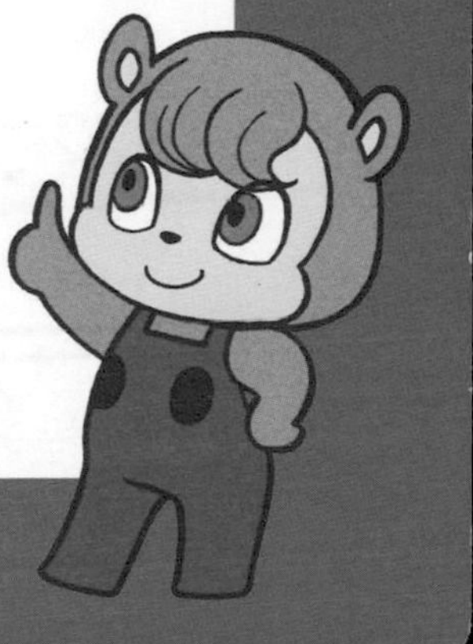

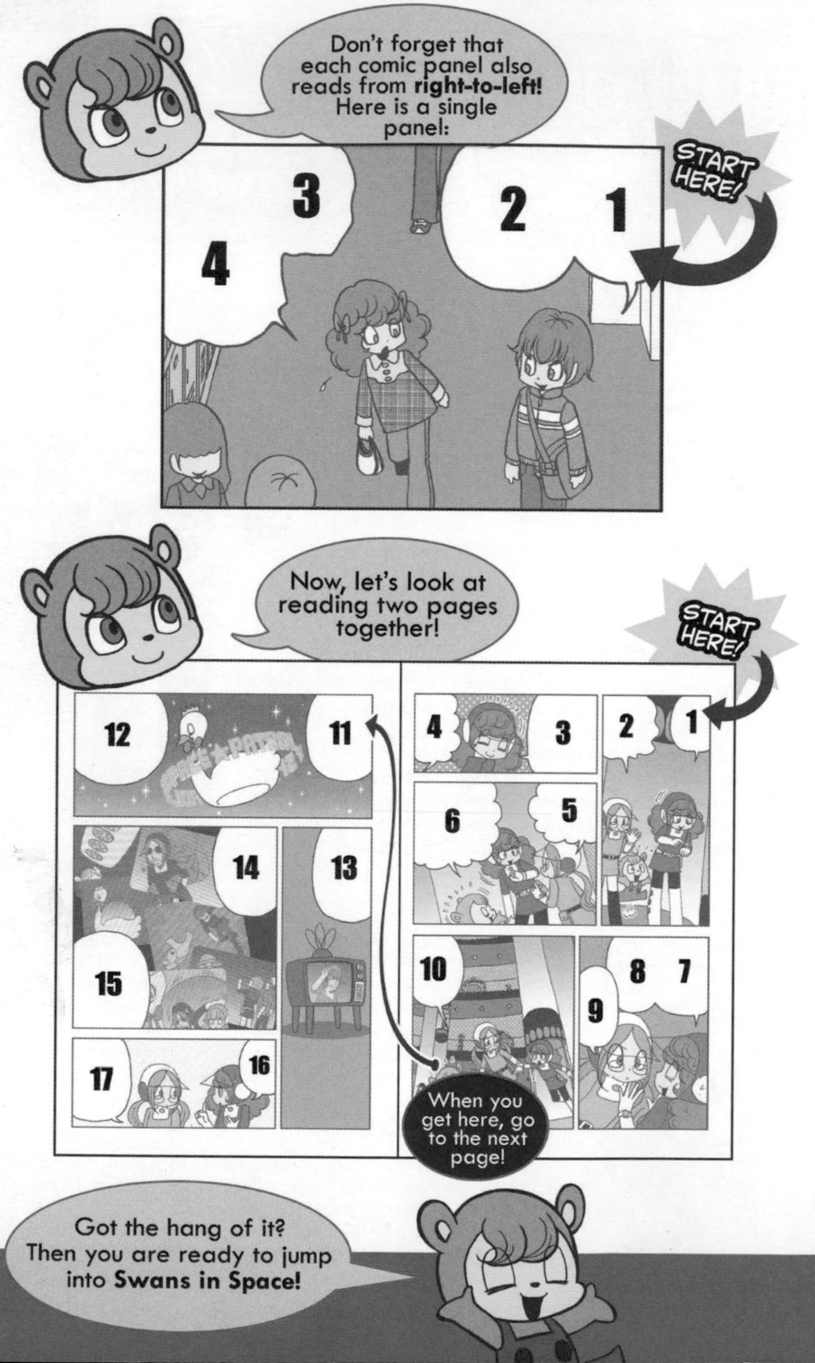

Don't forget that each comic panel also reads from **right-to-left!** Here is a single panel:
START HERE!
1
2
3
4
Now, let's look at reading two pages together!
START HERE!
1
2
3
4
5
6
7
8
9
10
When you get here, go to the next page!
11
12
13
14
15
16
17
Got the hang of it? Then you are ready to jump into **Swans in Space!**

SWANS IN SPACE

CHARACTER INTRODUCTIONS

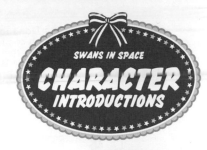

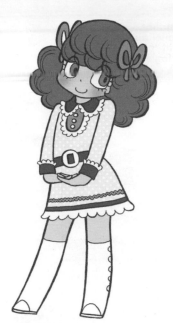

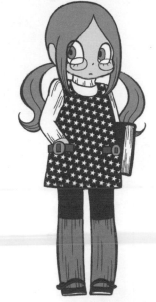

CORONA HOSHINO

A sixth grade student at the Cosmos Institute, Corona is an honor roll student who has high grades and does well at sports. Corona is the acting student council representative for her class, and her classmates often call her "Class President." A perfectionist to a fault, Corona's world is turned upside-down by Lan.

LAN TSUKISHIMA

One of Corona's classmates. A hardcore "Space Patrol" fan, Lan lives at her own pace. Lan does not particularly stand out in her class, as she can usually be found off on her own, reading a book. A rather lazy girl, Lan enjoys snacking on junk food.

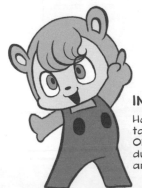

INSTRUCTOR

Hailing from the planet Omora, he acts as instructor to the trainees of the Space Patrol's Earth division. Obsessed with games, he often slacks off where his duties are concerned, but it is said that he is a kind and reliable father to his son.

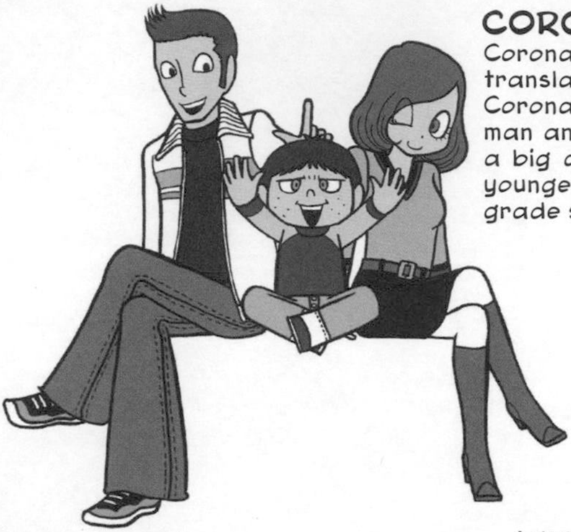

CORONA'S FAMILY

Corona's easy-going mother is a translator and works from home. Corona's father works as a stunt man and hopes to some day become a big action star. Subaru, Corona's younger brother, is an energetic first grade student.

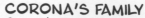

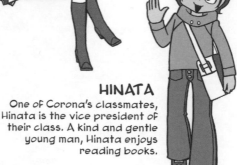

HINATA

One of Corona's classmates, Hinata is the vice president of their class. A kind and gentle young man, Hinata enjoys reading books.

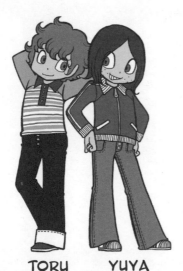

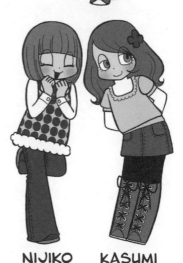

TORU   YUYA

The troublemakers of Corona's class. They are always up to no good.

NIJIKO   KASUMI

Corona's friends. Interests include fashion.

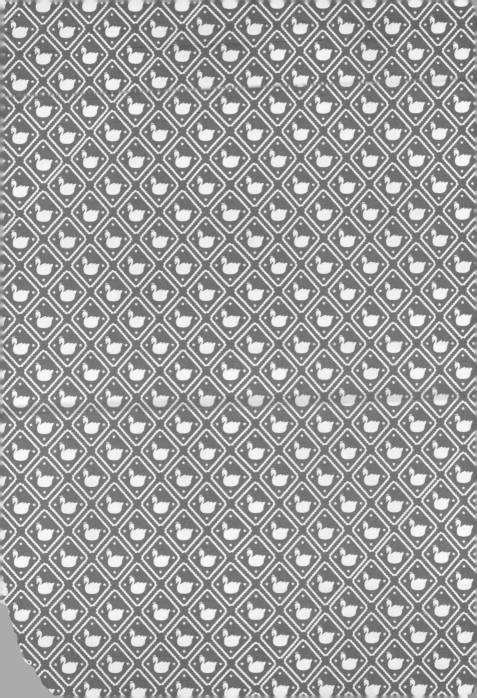

SWANS IN SPACE

CHAPTER 1
THE GIRL ON MY MIND

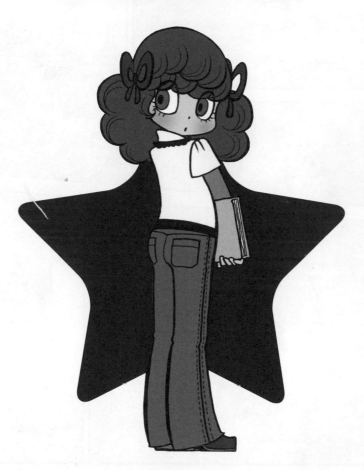

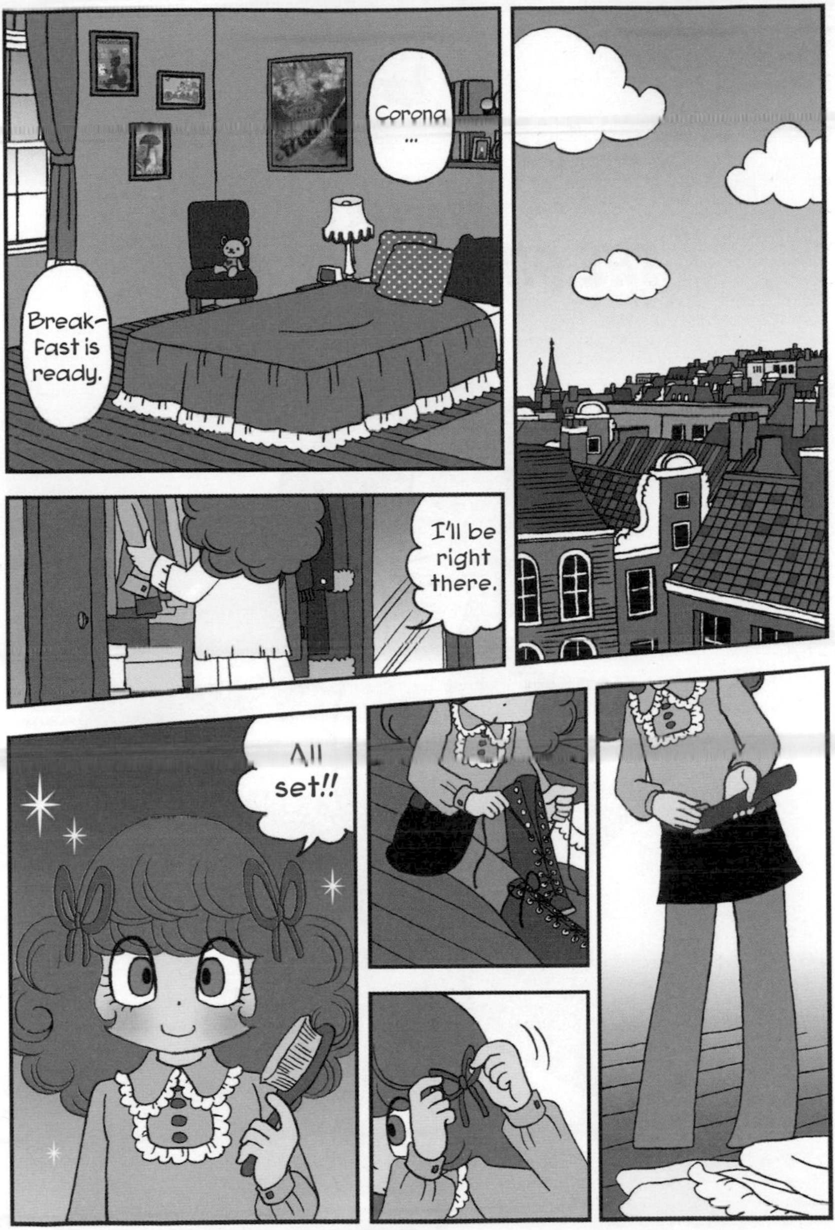
Corona ...
Break-fast is ready.
I'll be right there.
All set!!

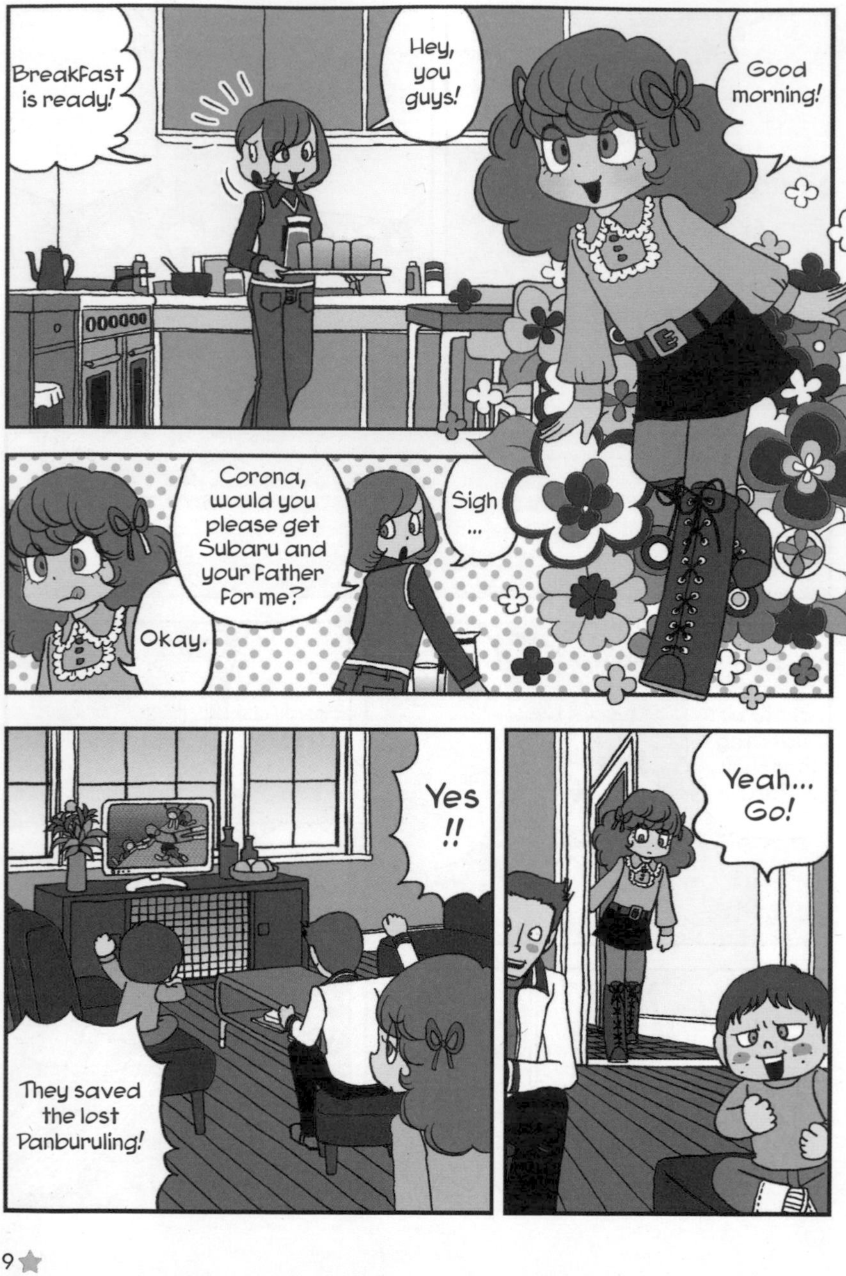
Good morning!
Hey, you guys!
Breakfast is ready!
Sigh ...
Corona, would you please get Subaru and your father for me?
Okay.
Yeah... Go!
Yes !!
They saved the lost Panburuling!

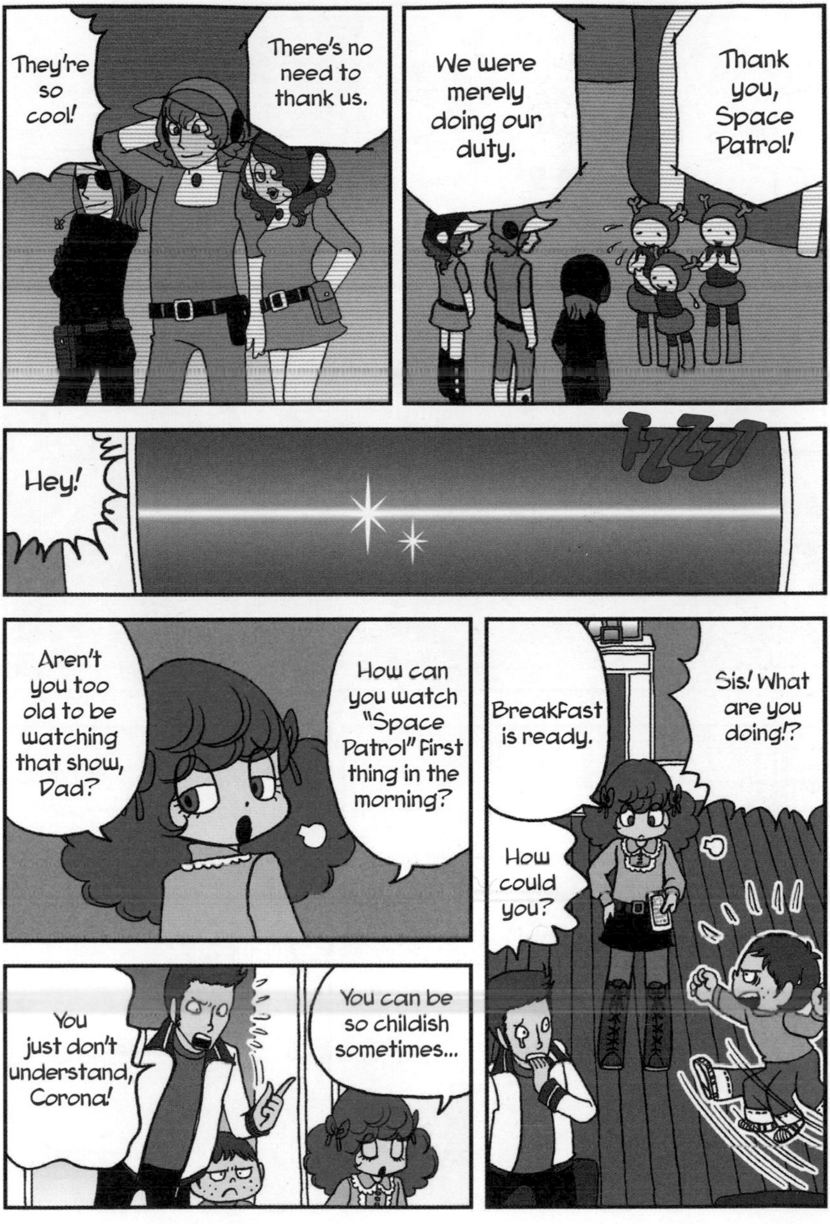
Thank you, Space Patrol!
We were merely doing our duty.
There's no need to thank us.
They're so cool!
FZZZT
Hey!
Sis! What are you doing!?
Breakfast is ready.
How could you?
How can you watch "Space Patrol" first thing in the morning?
Aren't you too old to be watching that show, Dad?
You can be so childish sometimes...
You just don't understand, Corona!

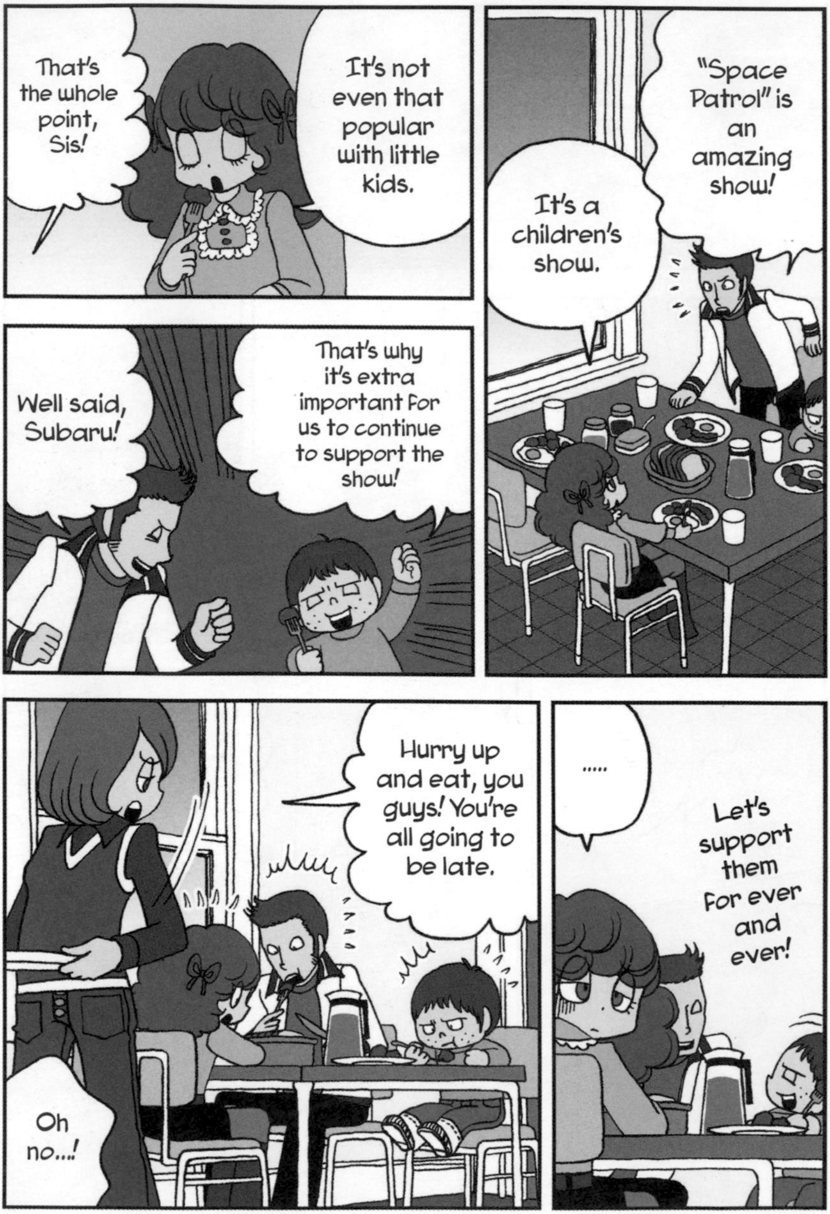
"Space Patrol" is an amazing show!
It's a children's show.
It's not even that popular with little kids.
That's the whole point, Sis!
That's why it's extra important for us to continue to support the show!
Well said, Subaru!
.....
Let's support them for ever and ever!
Hurry up and eat, you guys! You're all going to be late.
Oh no...!

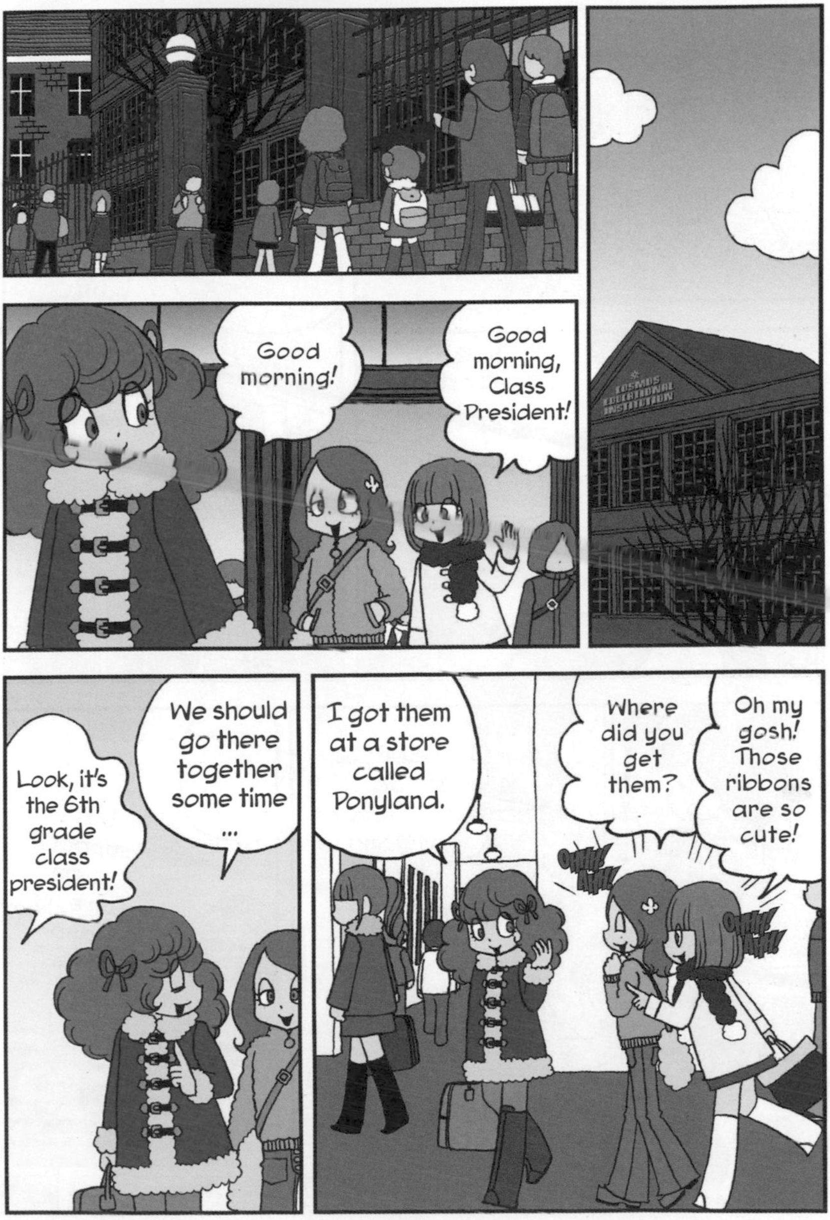
COSMOS EDUCATIONAL INSTITUTION
Good morning, Class President!
Good morning!
Oh my gosh! Those ribbons are so cute!
Where did you get them?
I got them at a store called Ponyland.
We should go there together some time ...
Look, it's the 6th grade class president!

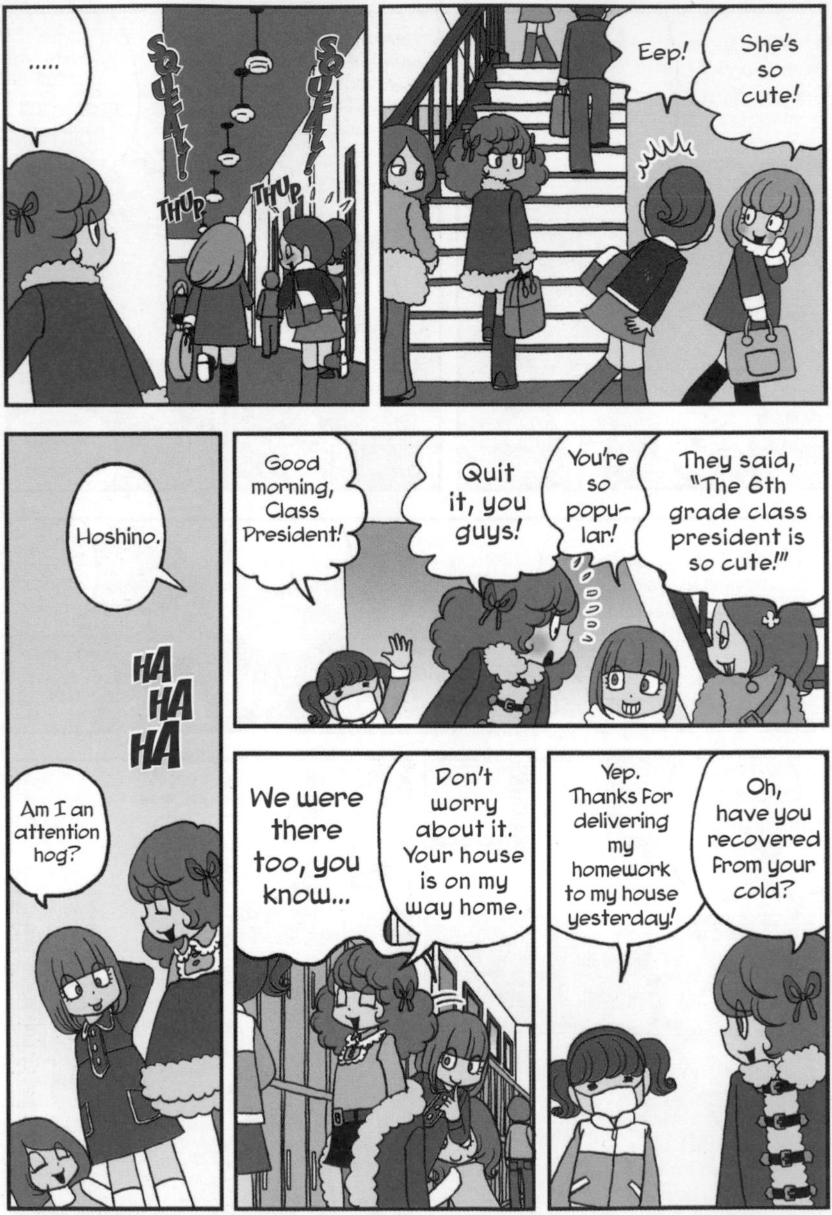
She's so cute!
Eep!
SQUEAK!
SQUEAK!
......
THUP
THUP
They said, "The 6th grade class president is so cute!"
You're so popu-lar!
Quit it, you guys!
Good morning, Class President!
Oh, have you recovered from your cold?
Yep. Thanks for delivering my homework to my house yesterday!
Don't worry about it. Your house is on my way home.
We were there too, you know...
Hoshino.
HA HA HA
Am I an attention hog?

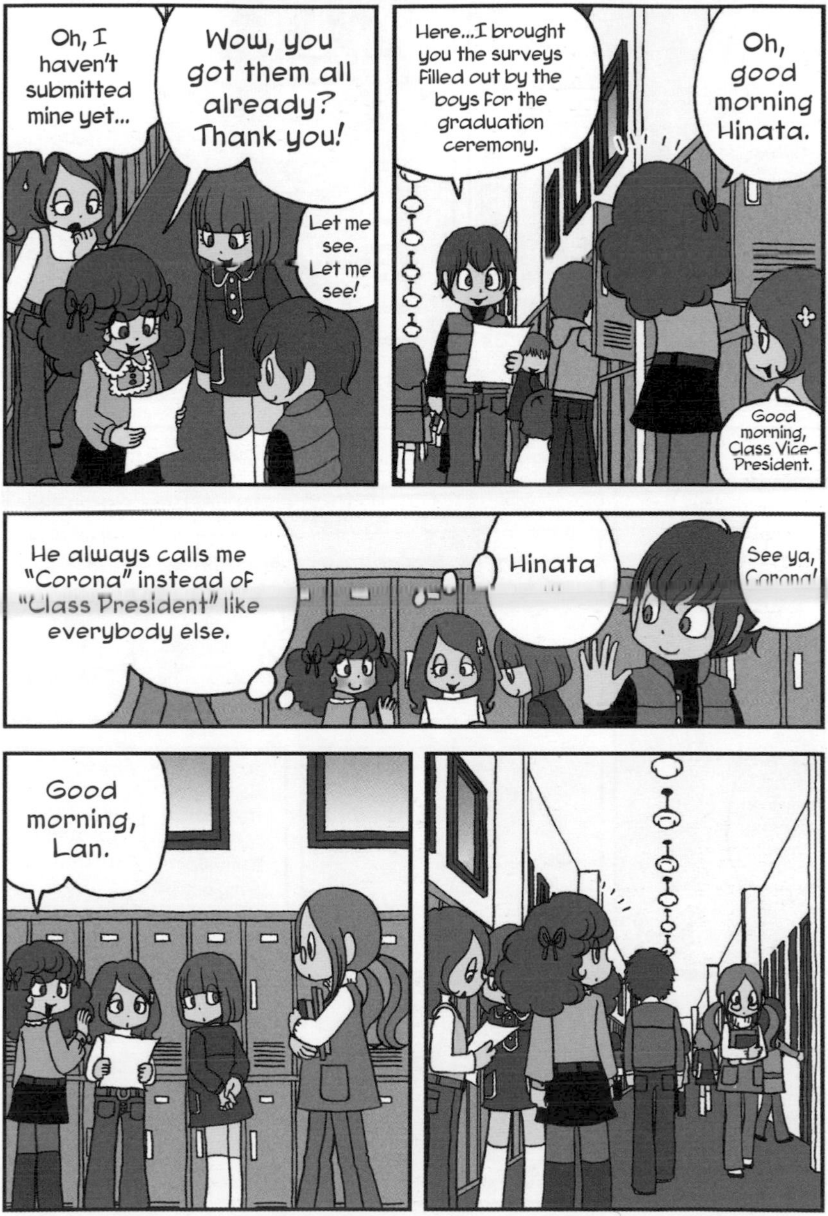
Oh, good morning Hinata.
Here...I brought you the surveys filled out by the boys for the graduation ceremony.
Good morning, Class Vice-President.
Wow, you got them all already? Thank you!
Oh, I haven't submitted mine yet...
Let me see. Let me see!
See ya, Corona!
Hinata
He always calls me "Corona" instead of "Class President" like everybody else.
Good morning, Lan.

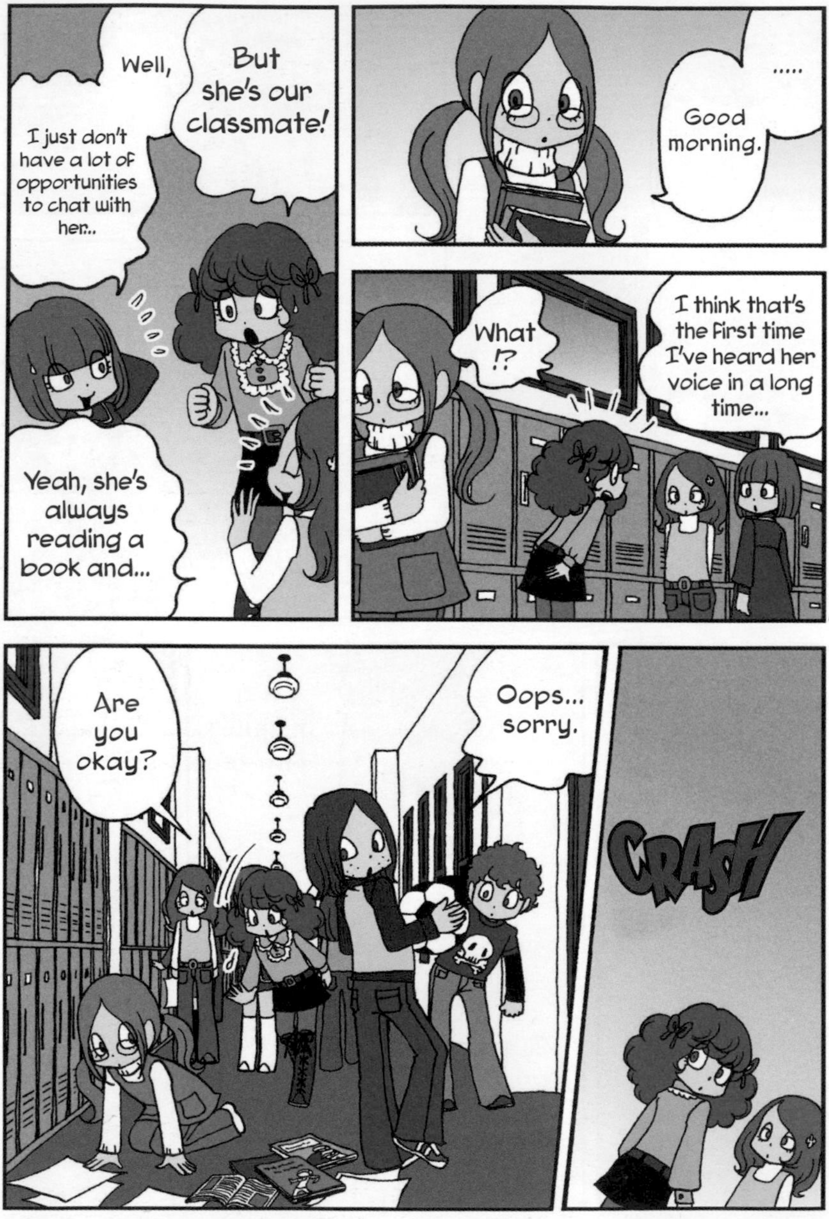
.....
Good morning.
I think that's the first time I've heard her voice in a long time...
What!?
But she's our classmate!
Well, I just don't have a lot of opportunities to chat with her...
Yeah, she's always reading a book and...
CRASH
Oops... sorry.
Are you okay?

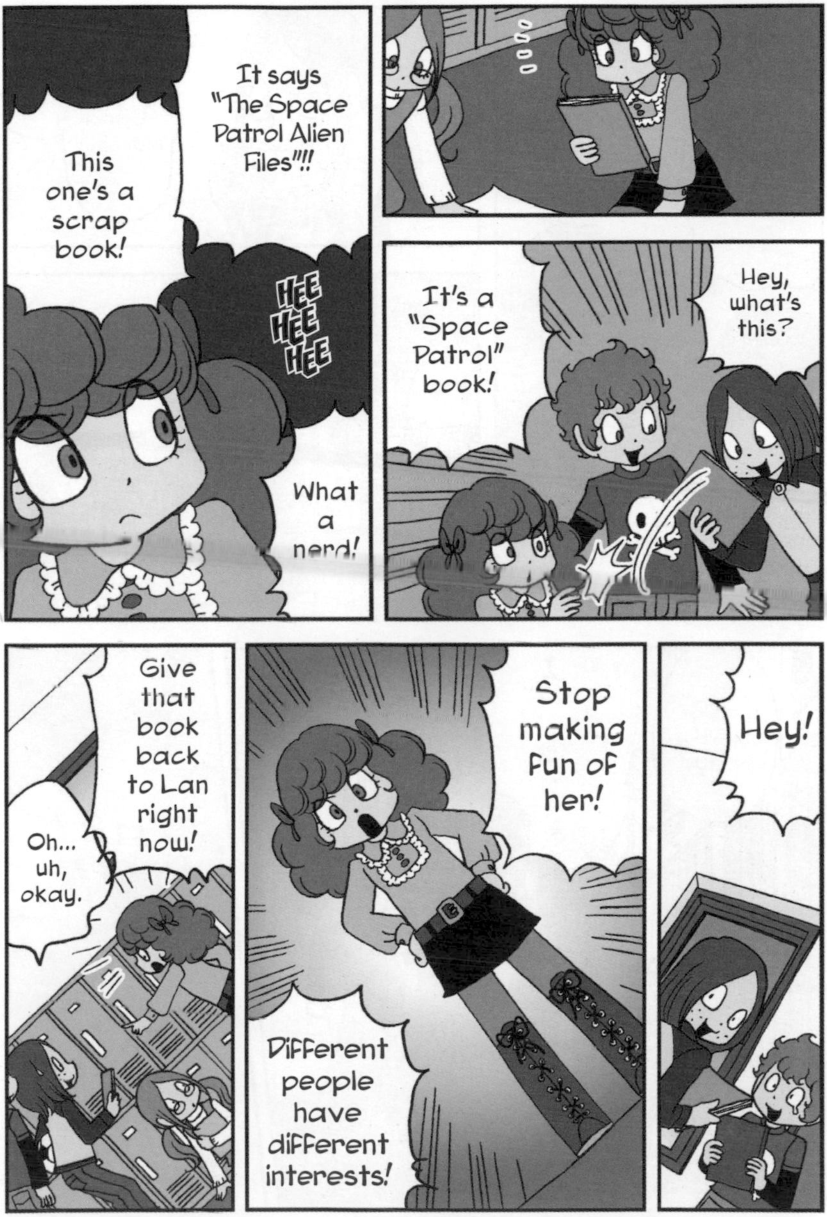
Hey, what's this?
It's a "Space Patrol" book!
It says "The Space Patrol Alien Files"!!
This one's a scrap book!
HEE HEE HEE
What a nerd!
Hey!
Stop making fun of her!
Different people have different interests!
Give that book back to Lan right now!
Oh... uh, okay.

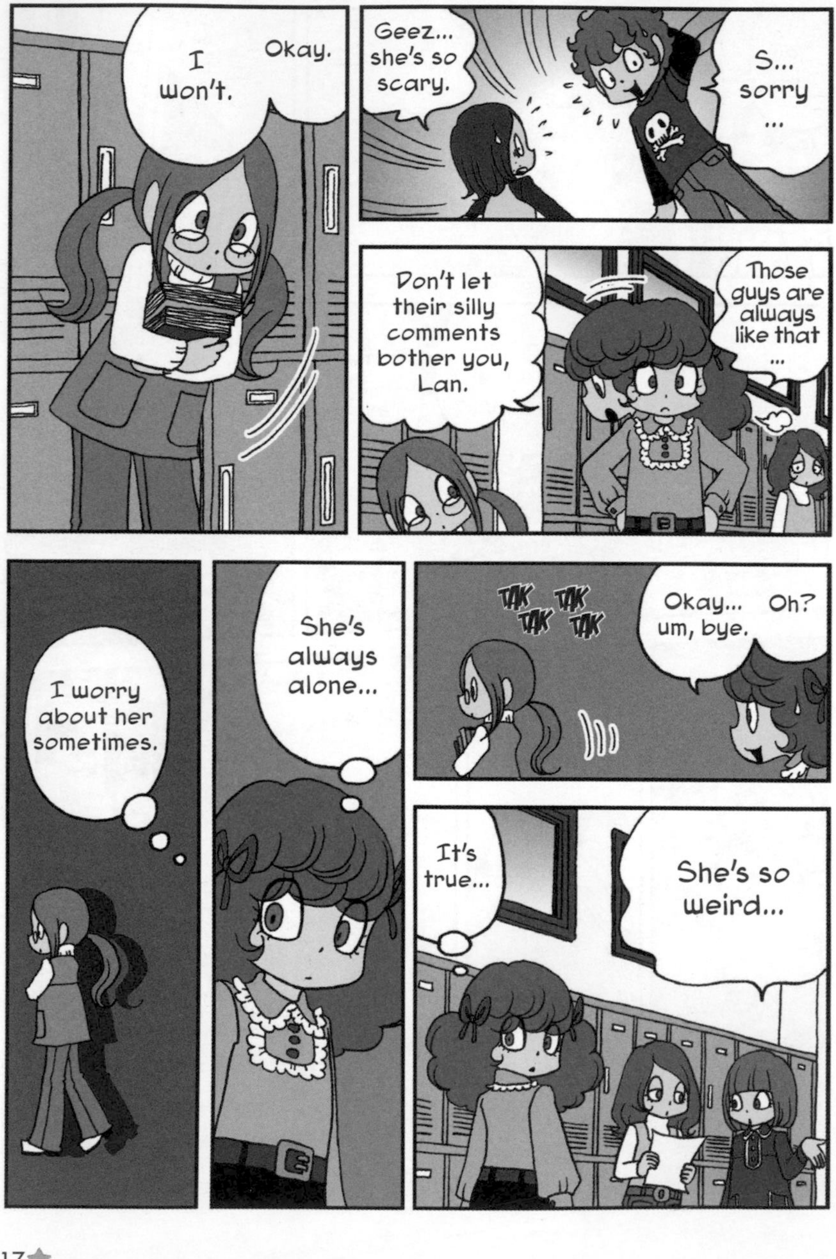
S... sorry ...
Geez... she's so scary.
Those guys are always like that ...
Don't let their silly comments bother you, Lan.
Okay.
I won't.
Oh?
Okay... um, bye.
TAK TAK TAK TAK
It's true...
She's so weird...
She's always alone...
I worry about her sometimes.

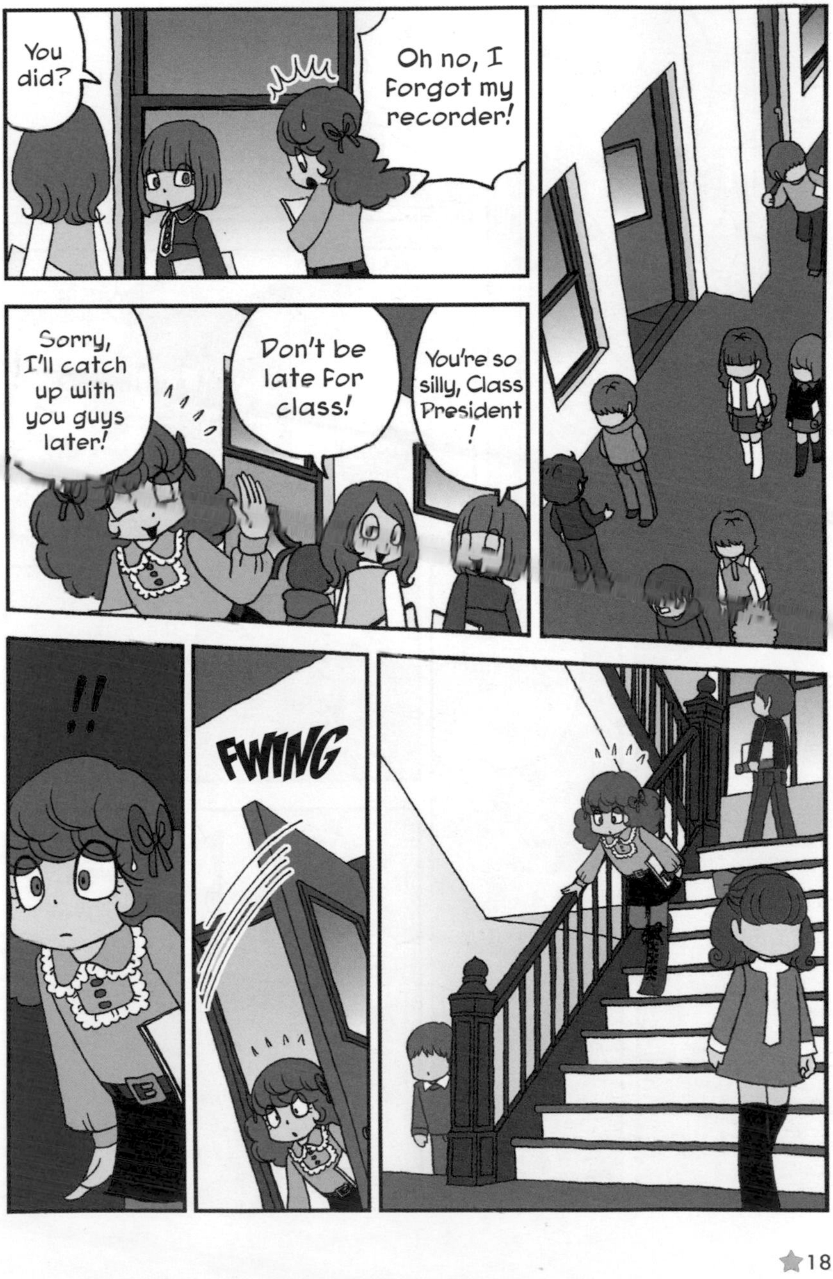
Oh no, I forgot my recorder!
You did?
You're so silly, Class President!
Don't be late for class!
Sorry, I'll catch up with you guys later!
FWING
!!

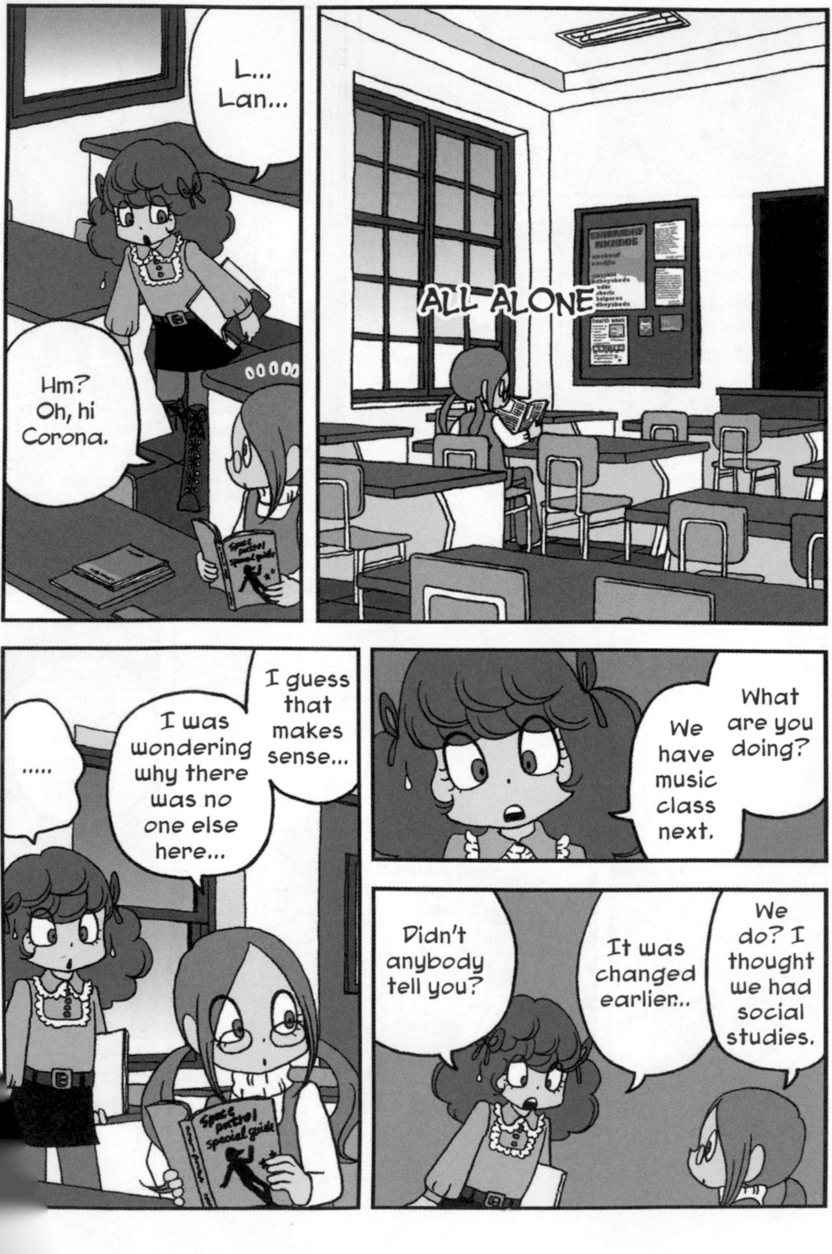
ALL ALONE
L... Lan...
Hm? Oh, hi Corona.
What are you doing?
We have music class next.
We do? I thought we had social studies.
It was changed earlier..
Didn't anybody tell you?
I guess that makes sense...
I was wondering why there was no one else here...
.....

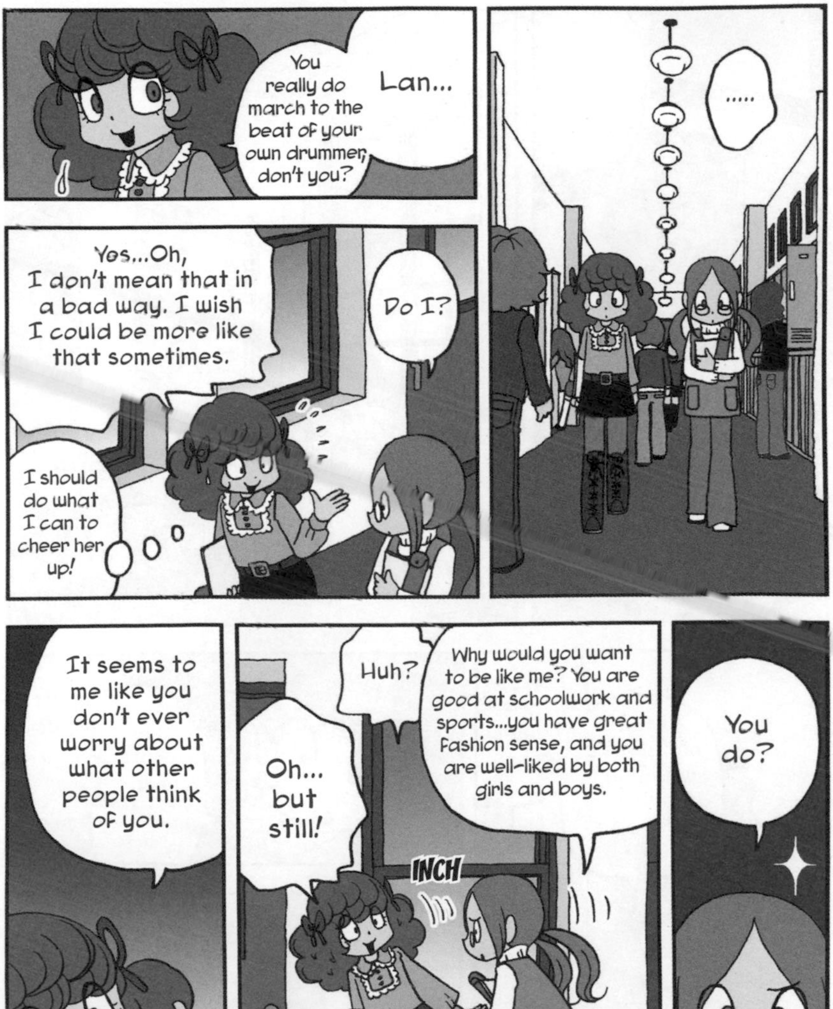
.....
Lan...
You really do march to the beat of your own drummer, don't you?
Do I?
Yes...Oh, I don't mean that in a bad way. I wish I could be more like that sometimes.
I should do what I can to cheer her up!
You do?
Why would you want to be like me? You are good at schoolwork and sports...you have great fashion sense, and you are well-liked by both girls and boys.
Huh?
Oh... but still!
INCH
It seems to me like you don't ever worry about what other people think of you.

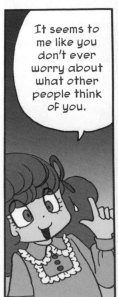

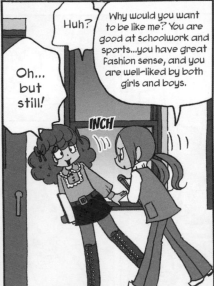

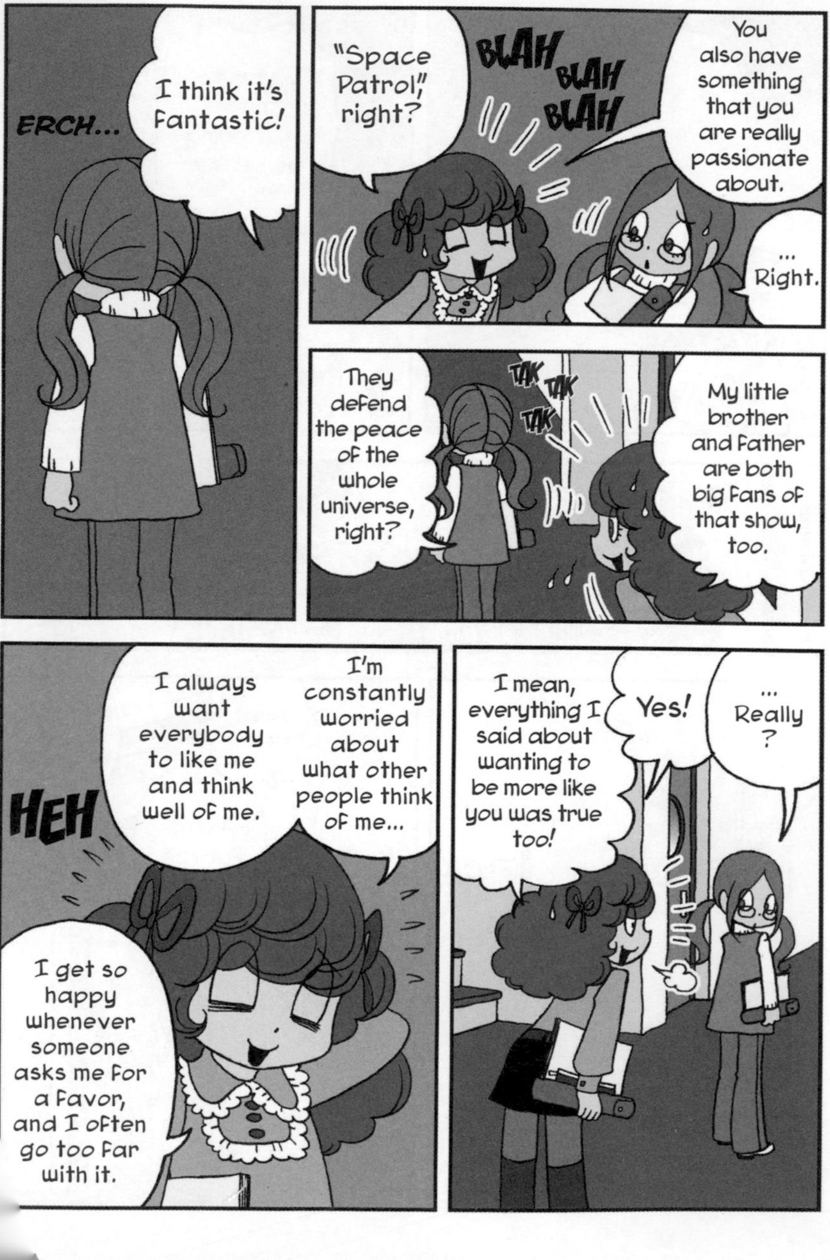
You also have something that you are really passionate about.
BLAH BLAH BLAH
"Space Patrol," right?
... Right.
My little brother and father are both big fans of that show, too.
TAK TAK TAK
They defend the peace of the whole universe, right?
I think it's fantastic!
ERCH...
... Really?
Yes!
I mean, everything I said about wanting to be more like you was true too!
I'm constantly worried about what other people think of me...
I always want everybody to like me and think well of me.
HEH
I get so happy whenever someone asks me for a favor, and I often go too far with it.

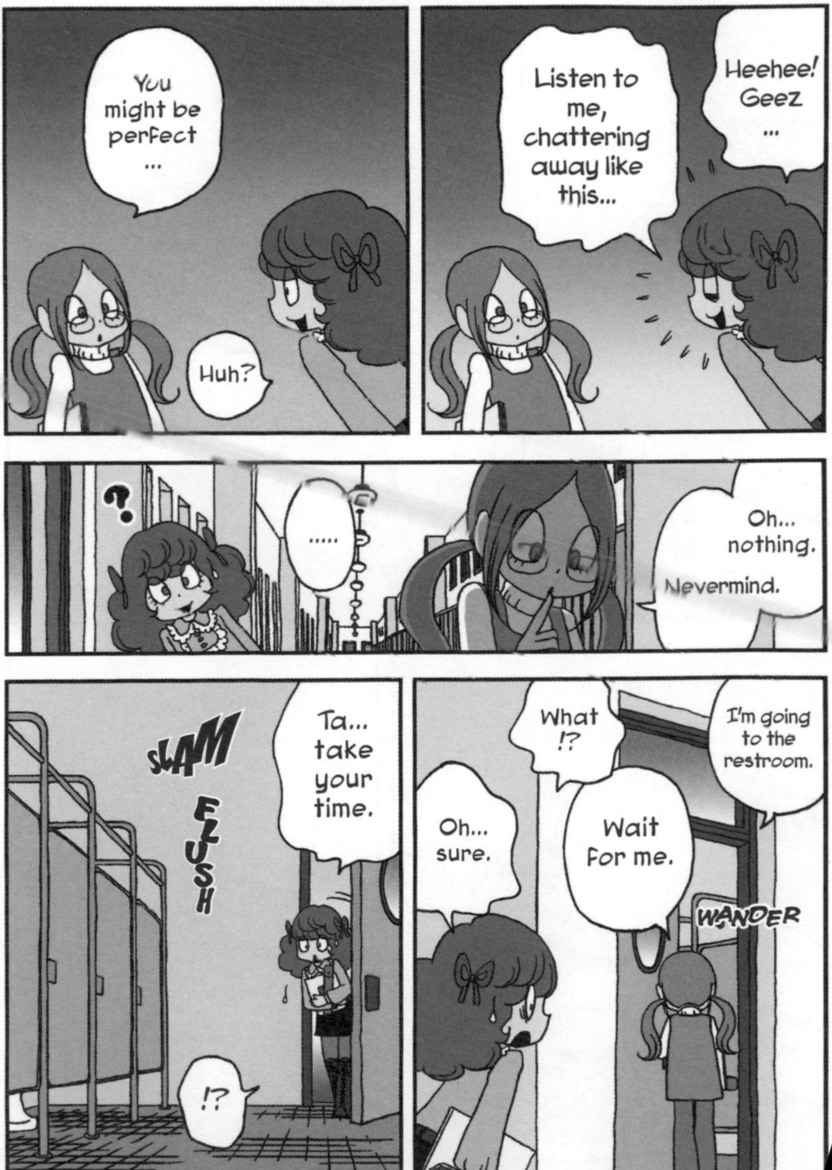
Heehee! Geez ...
Listen to me, chattering away like this...
You might be perfect ...
Huh?
Oh... nothing.
Nevermind.
.....
I'm going to the restroom.
What !?
Wait for me.
Oh... sure.
WANDER
Ta... take your time.
SLAM
FLUSH
!?

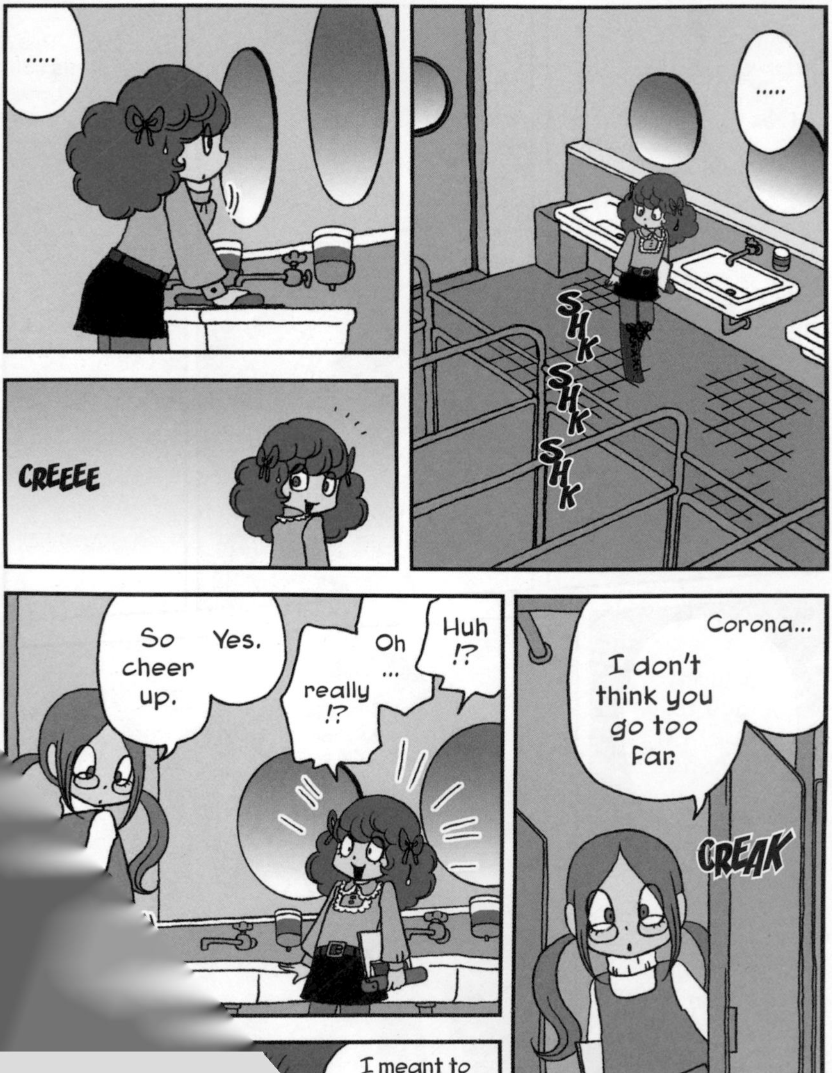
.....
SHK SHK SHK SHK
.....
CREEEE
Corona... I don't think you go too far.
CREAK
Huh !?
Oh ... really !?
Yes.
So cheer up.
I meant to cheer her up...but she's cheering me up instead?

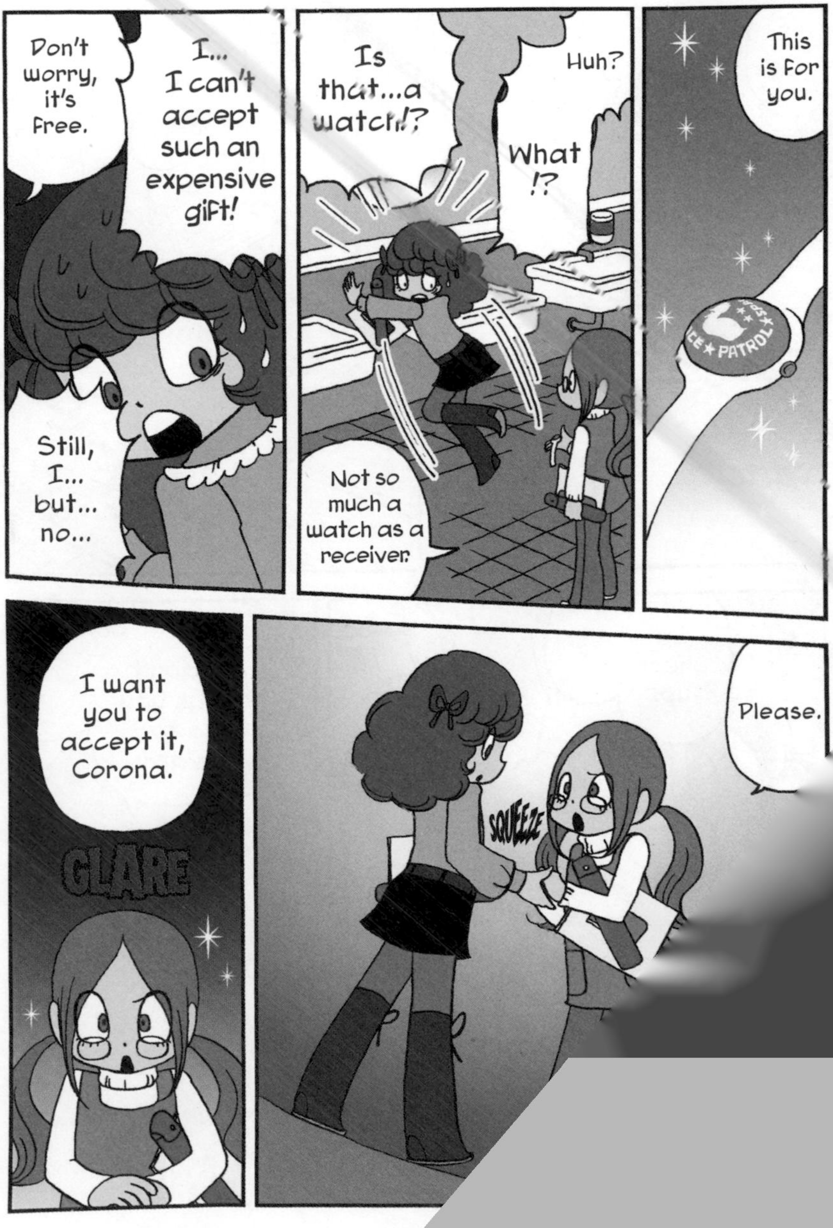
This is for you.
Huh?
What!?
Is that...a watch!?
Not so much a watch as a receiver.
I... I can't accept such an expensive gift!
Don't worry, it's free.
Still, I... but... no...
Please.
SQUEEZE
I want you to accept it, Corona.
GLARE

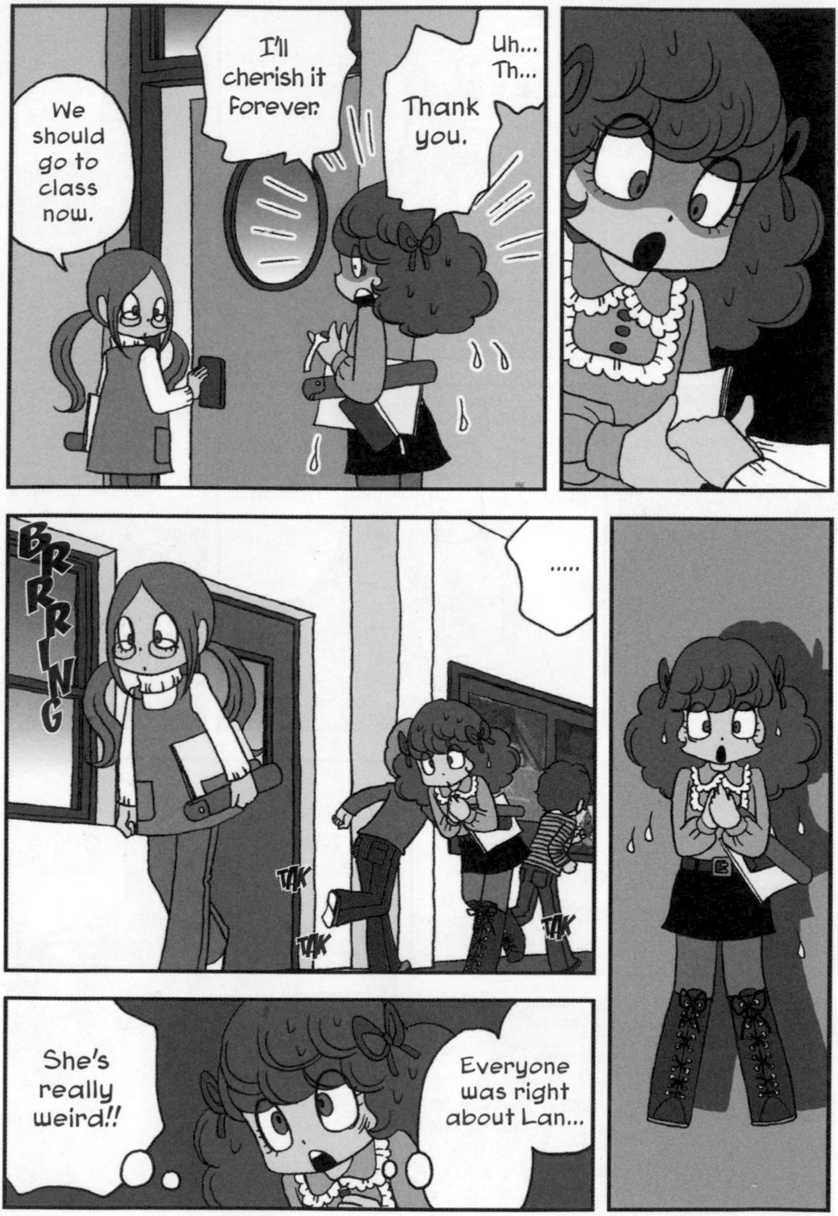
Uh... Th...
Thank you.
I'll cherish it forever.
We should go to class now.
.....
BRRRING
TAK
TAK
TAK
Everyone was right about Lan...
She's really weird!!

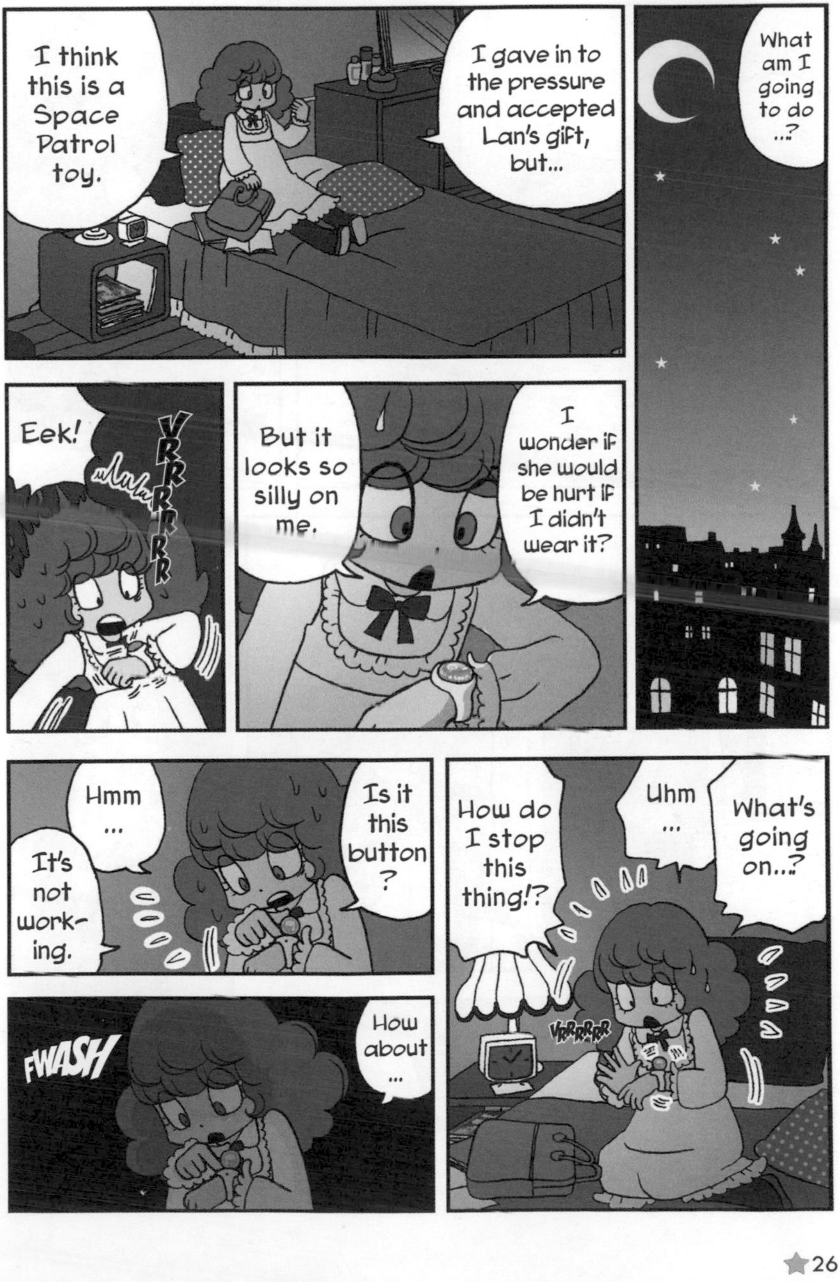
What am I going to do ..?
I gave in to the pressure and accepted Lan's gift, but...
I think this is a Space Patrol toy.
I wonder if she would be hurt if I didn't wear it?
But it looks so silly on me.
VRRRRRR
Eek!
What's going on..?
Uhm ...
How do I stop this thing!?
VRRRRRR
Is it this button ?
Hmm ...
It's not work-ing.
How about ...
FWASH

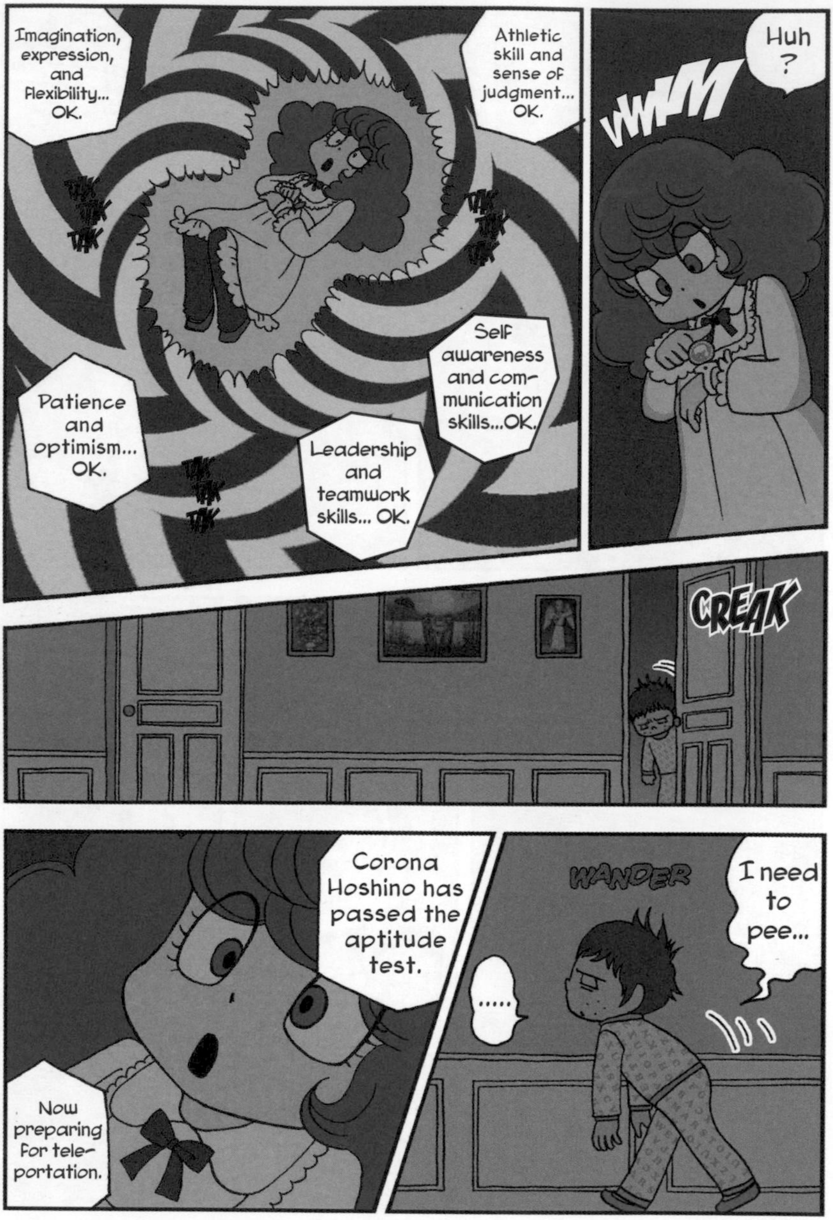
Huh?
VWWM
Athletic skill and sense of judgment... OK.
Imagination, expression, and flexibility... OK.
TAK TAK TAK
TAK TAK TAK
Self awareness and communication skills...OK.
Leadership and teamwork skills... OK.
Patience and optimism... OK.
TAK TAK TAK
CREAK
WANDER
I need to pee...
......
Corona Hoshino has passed the aptitude test.
Now preparing for teleportation.

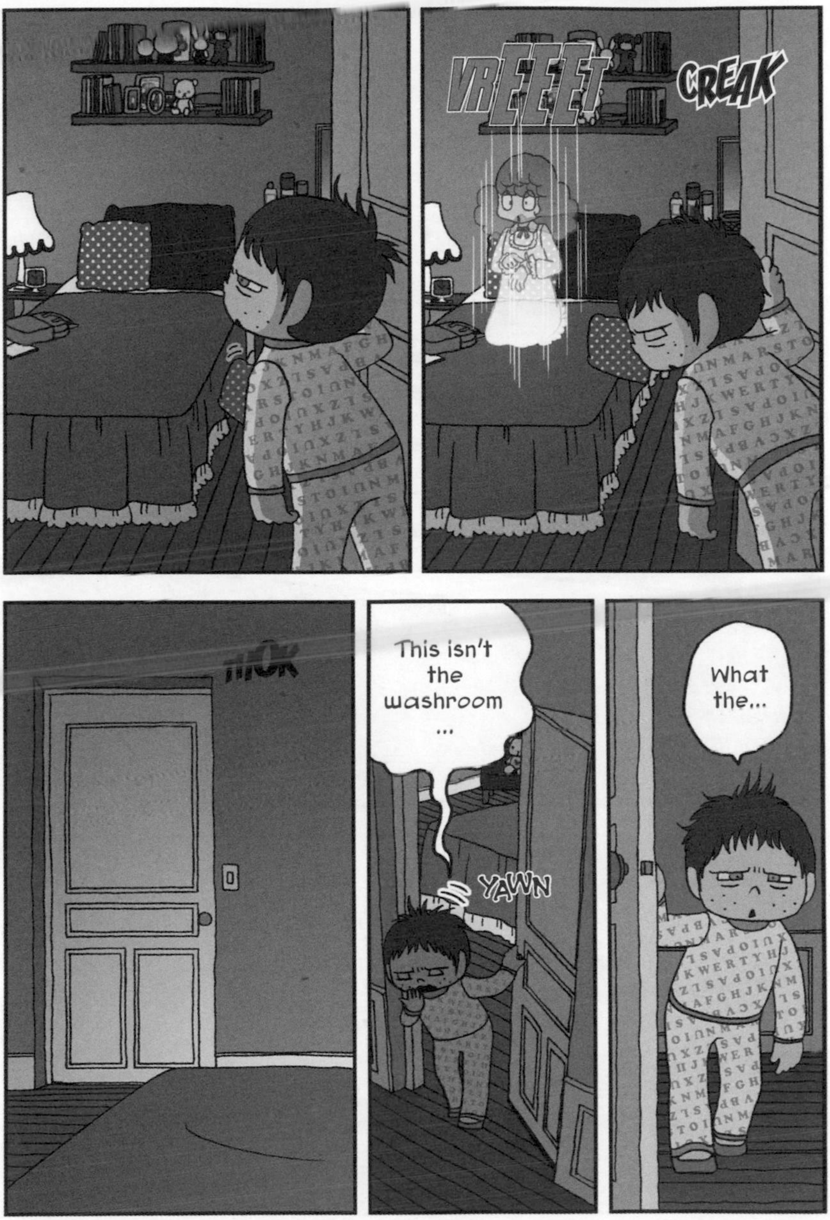
VREEEET
CREAK
What the...
This isn't the washroom ...
YAWN

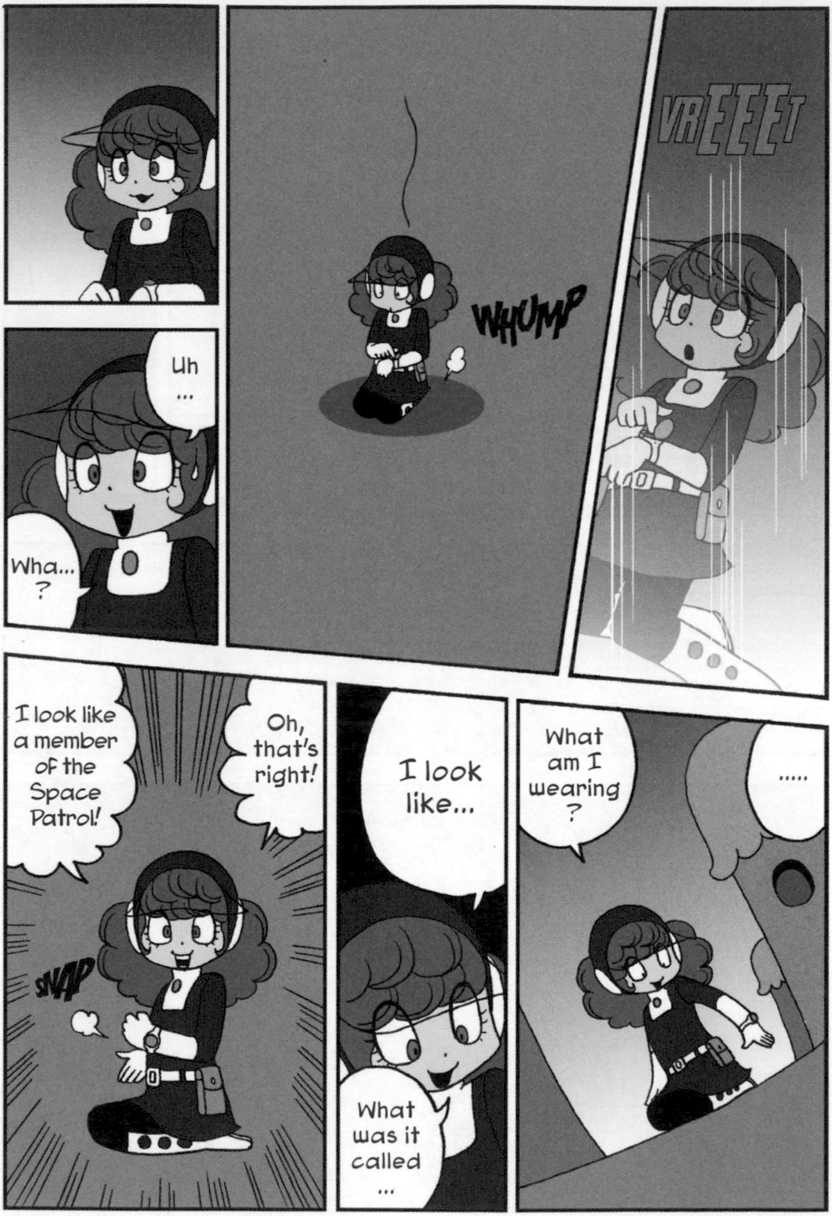
VREEEET
WHUMP
Uh ...
Wha... ?
.....
What am I wearing ?
I look like...
What was it called ...
Oh, that's right!
I look like a member of the Space Patrol!
SNAP

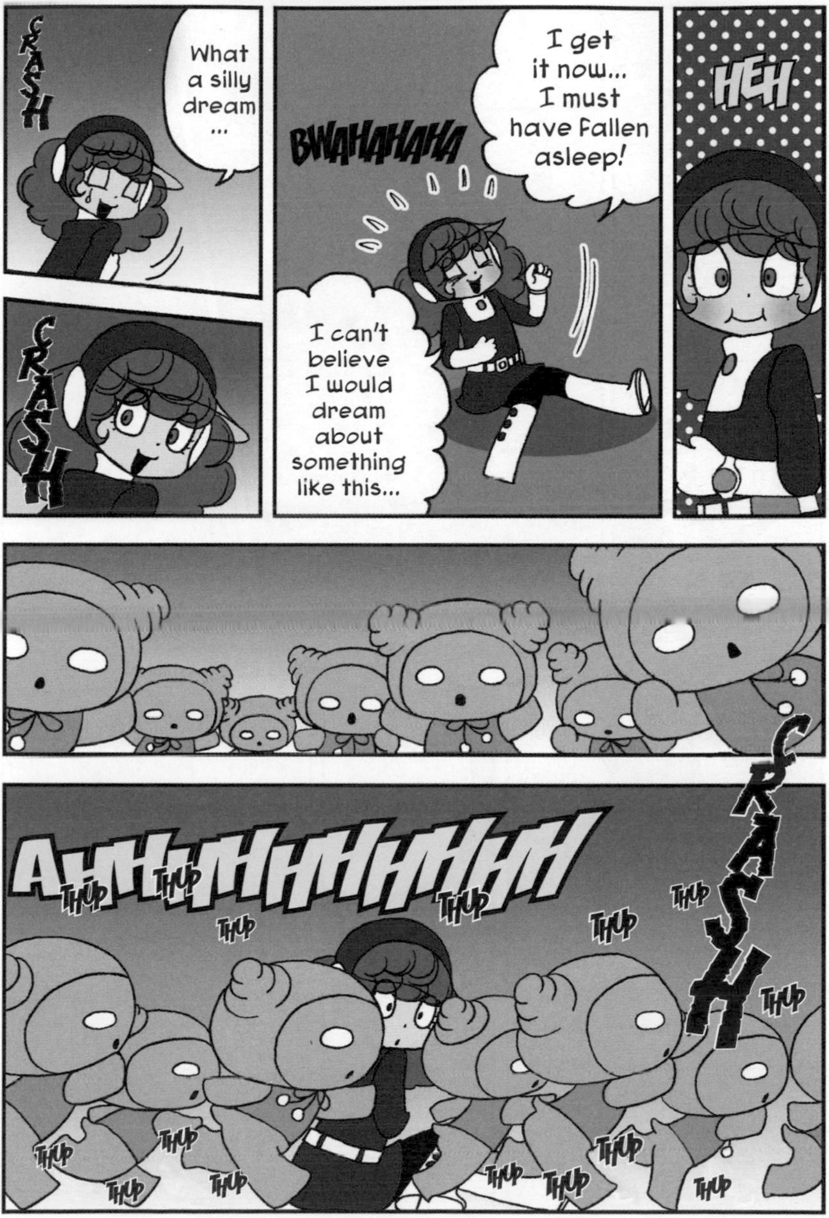
HEH
BWAHAHAHA
I get it now... I must have fallen asleep!
I can't believe I would dream about something like this...
CRASH
What a silly dream ...
CRASH
CRASH
AHHHHHHHHHHHH
THUP THUP THUP THUP THUP THUP THUP THUP THUP THUP THUP THUP THUP THUP THUP THUP

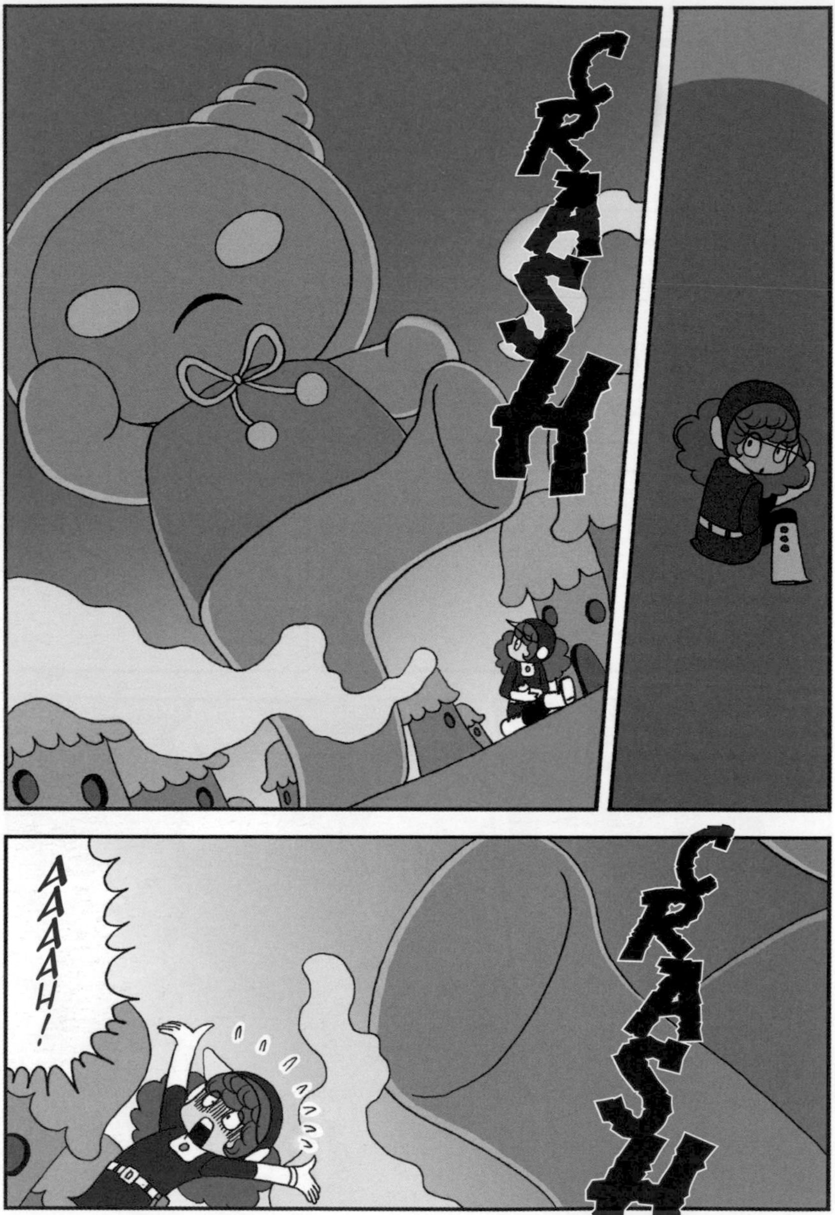
CRASH
CRASH
AAAAAH!

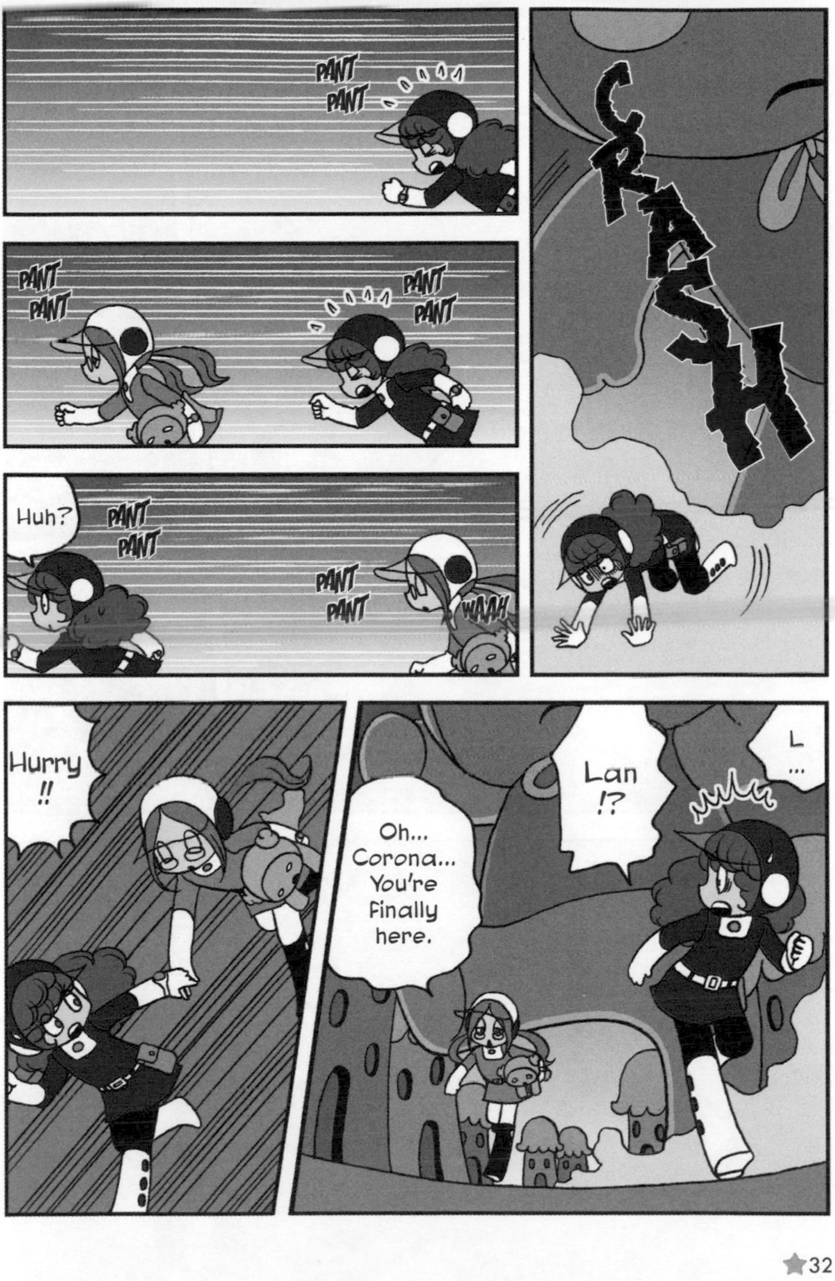
CRASH
PANT PANT
PANT PANT
PANT PANT
Huh?
PANT PANT
PANT PANT
WAAH
L...
Lan!?
Oh... Corona... You're finally here.
Hurry!!

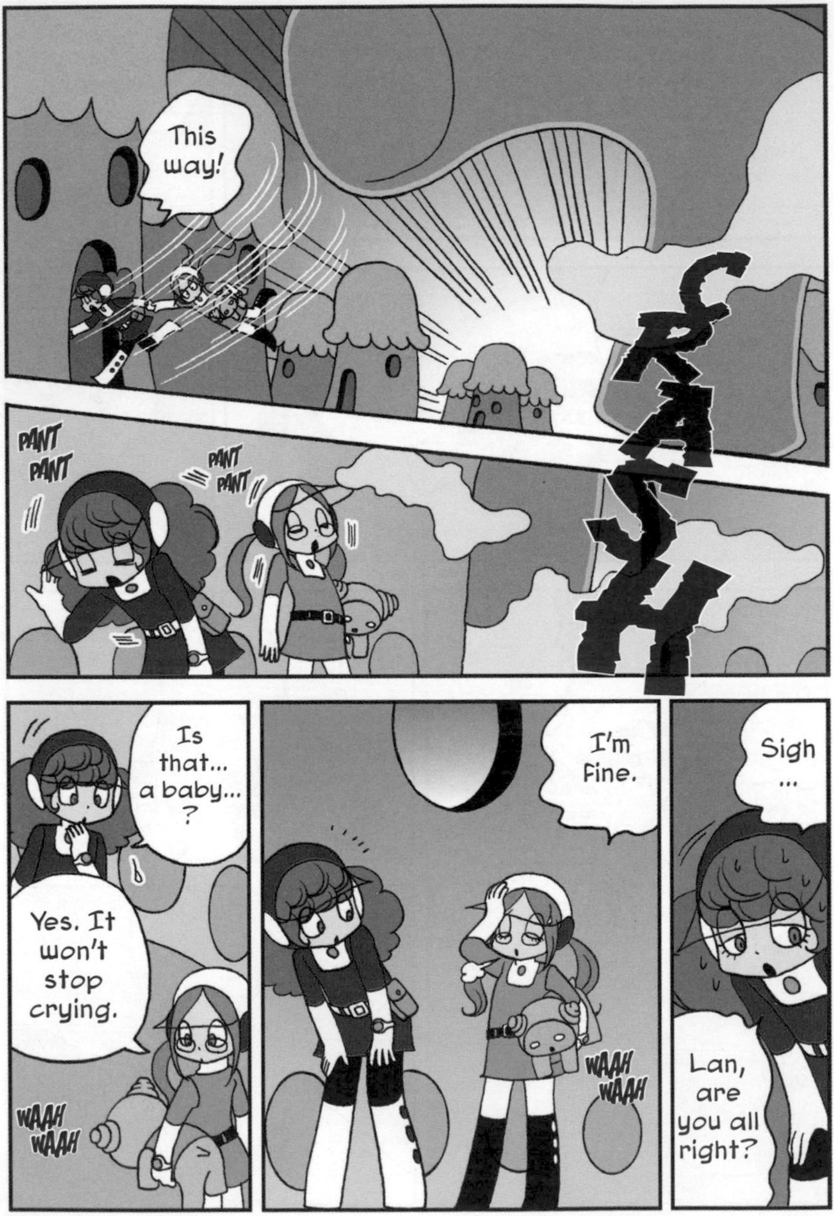
This way!
CRASH
PANT PANT
PANT PANT
Sigh ...
Lan, are you all right?
I'm fine.
WAAH WAAH
Is that... a baby... ?
Yes. It won't stop crying.
WAAH WAAH

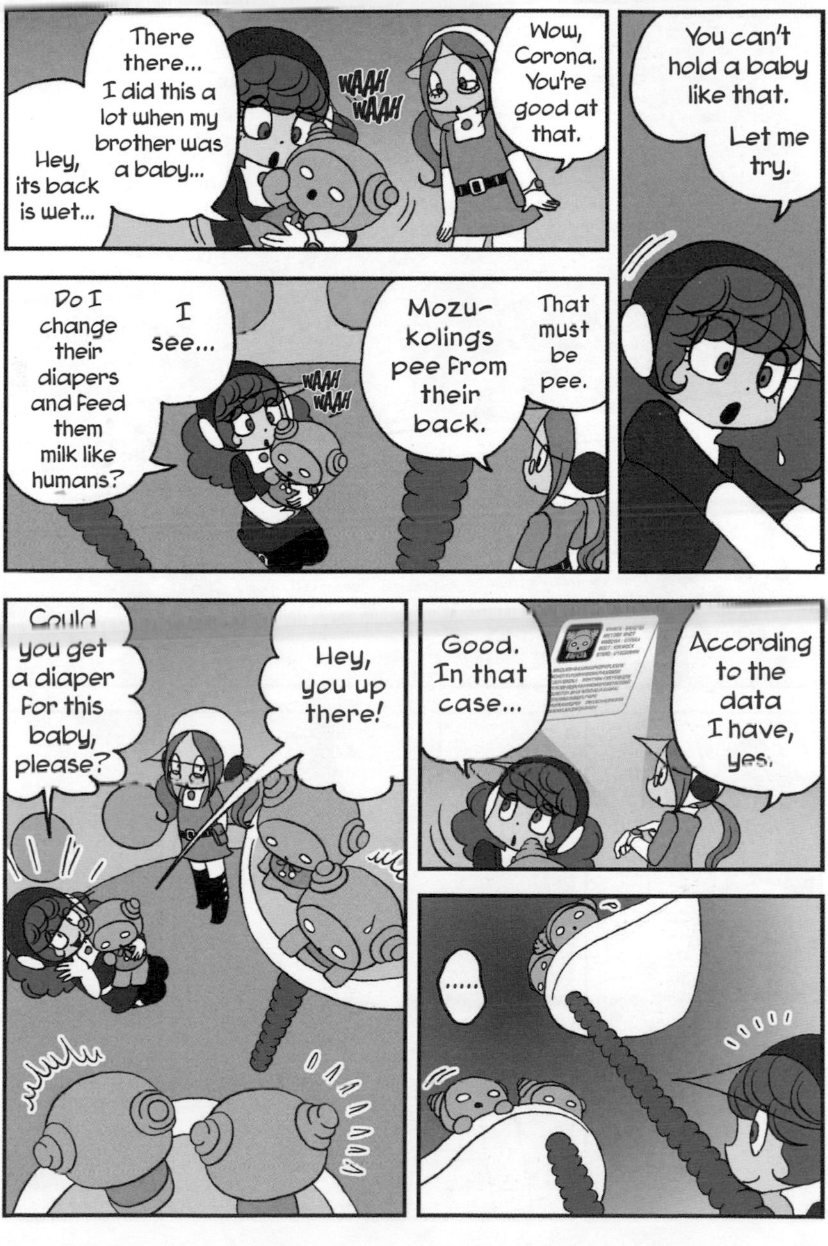

You can't hold a baby like that.
Let me try.
Wow, Corona. You're good at that.
WAAH WAAH
There there... I did this a lot when my brother was a baby...
Hey, its back is wet...
That must be pee.
Mozu-kolings pee from their back.
WAAH WAAH
I see...
Do I change their diapers and feed them milk like humans?
According to the data I have, yes.
Good. In that case...
......
Hey, you up there!
Could you get a diaper for this baby, please?

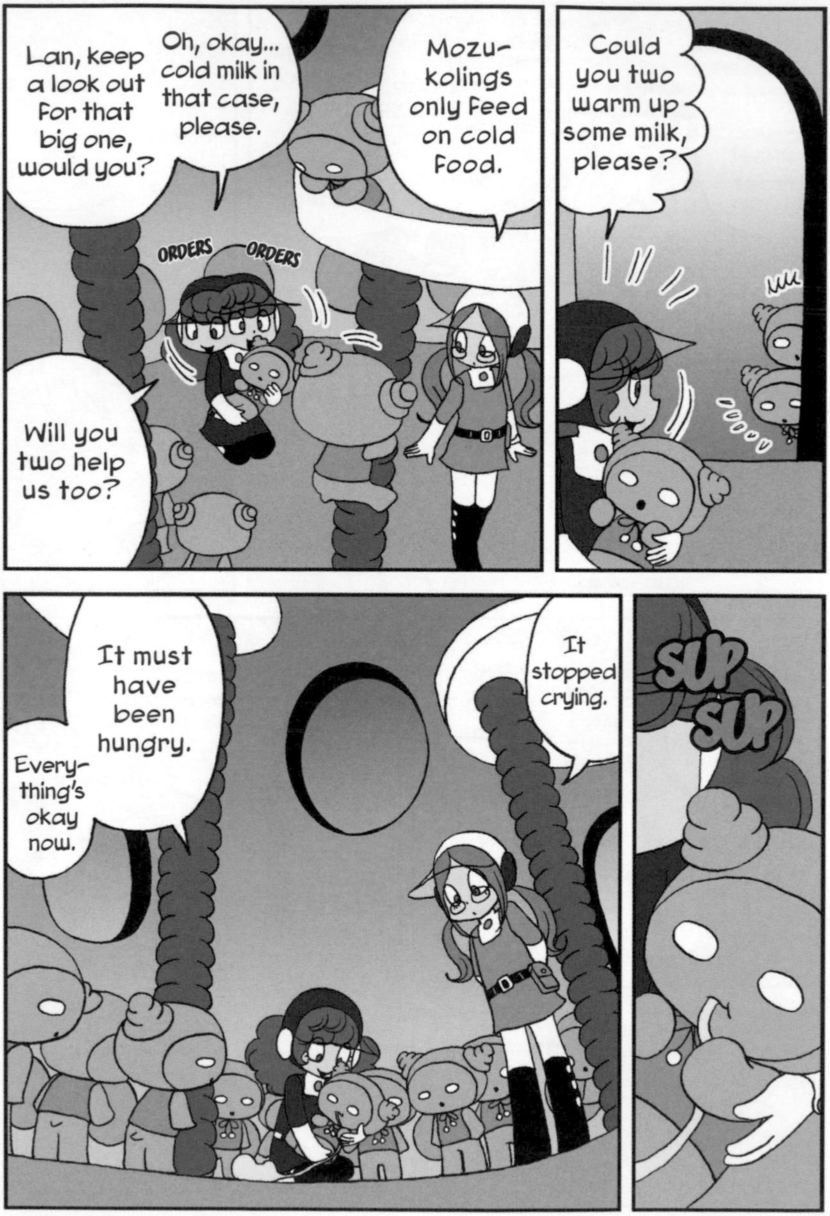
Could you two warm up some milk, please?
Mozu-kolings only feed on cold food.
Oh, okay... cold milk in that case, please.
Lan, keep a look out for that big one, would you?
ORDERS
ORDERS
Will you two help us too?
SUP
SUP
It stopped crying.
It must have been hungry.
Every-thing's okay now.

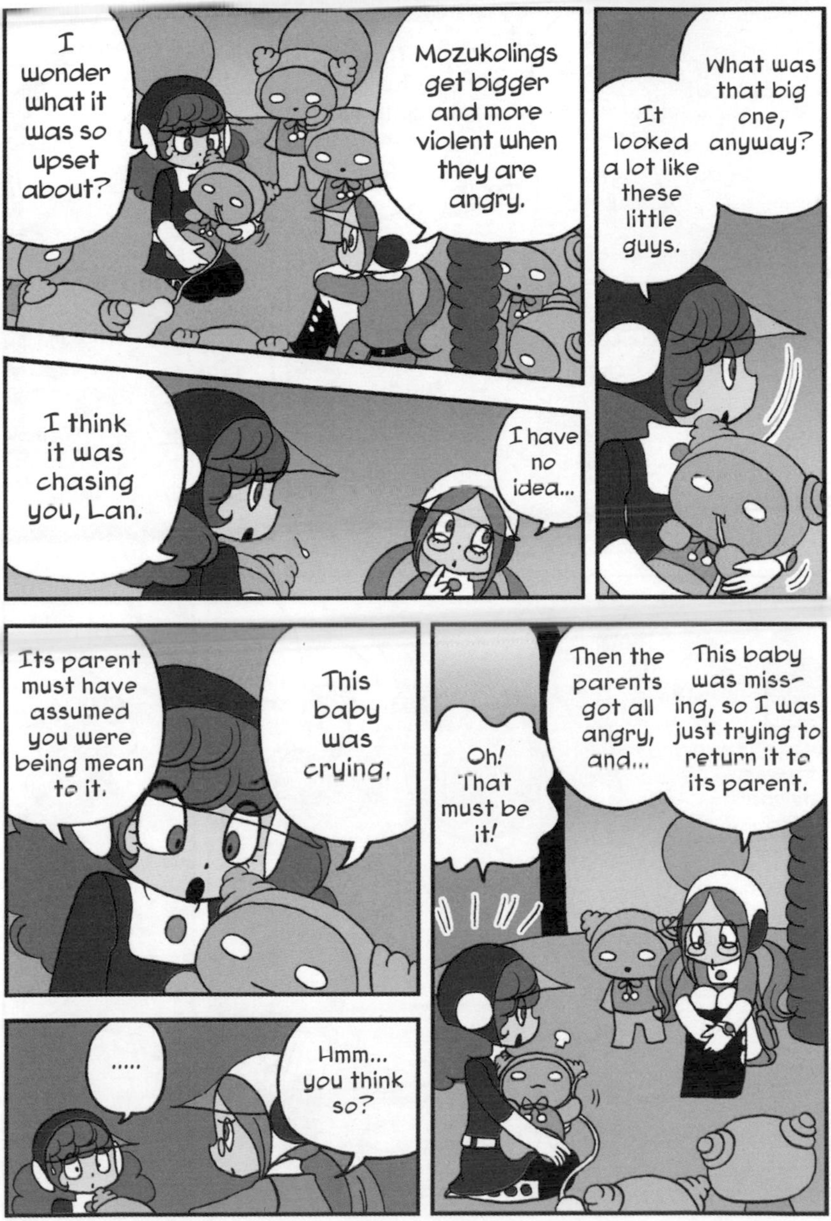
What was that big one, anyway?
It looked a lot like these little guys.
Mozukolings get bigger and more violent when they are angry.
I wonder what it was so upset about?
I have no idea...
I think it was chasing you, Lan.
This baby was miss-ing, so I was just trying to return it to its parent.
Then the parents got all angry, and...
Oh! That must be it!
This baby was crying.
Its parent must have assumed you were being mean to it.
Hmm... you think so?
.....

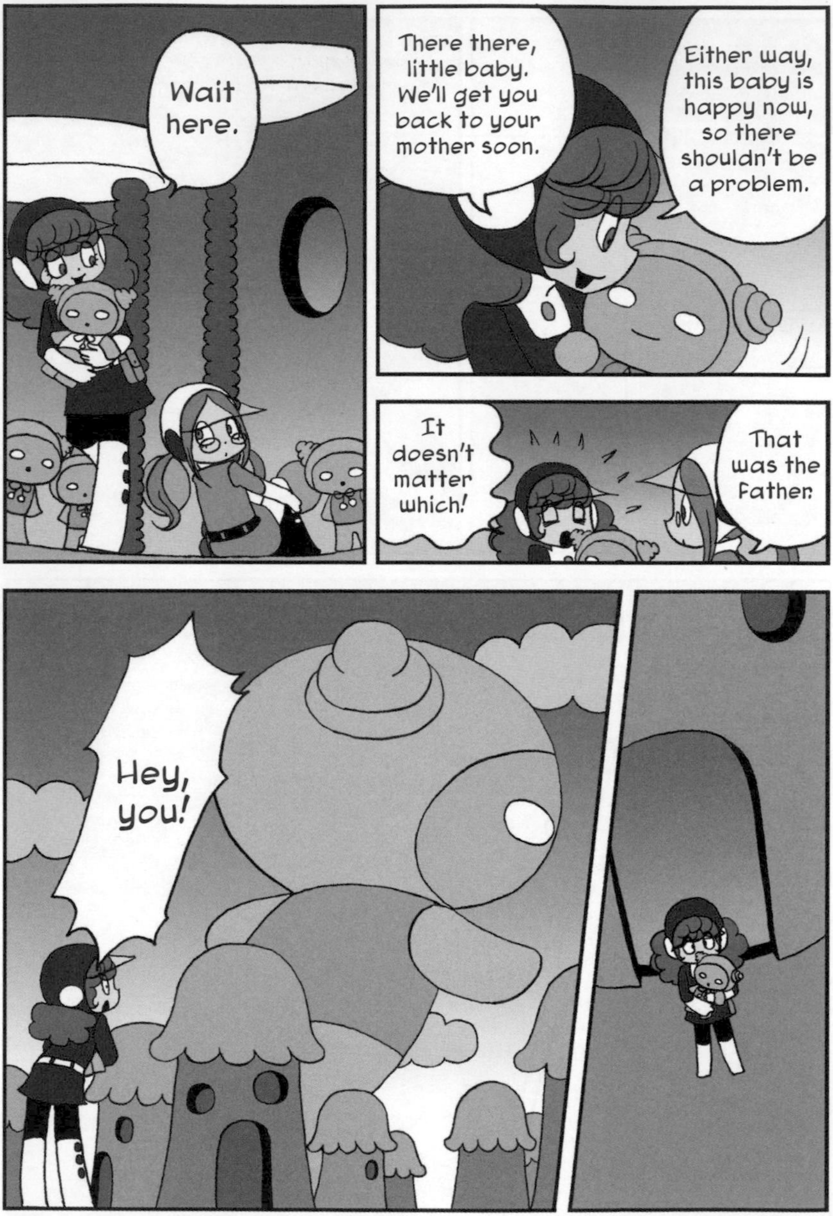
Either way, this baby is happy now, so there shouldn't be a problem.
There there, little baby. We'll get you back to your mother soon.
That was the Father.
It doesn't matter which!
Wait here.
Hey, you!

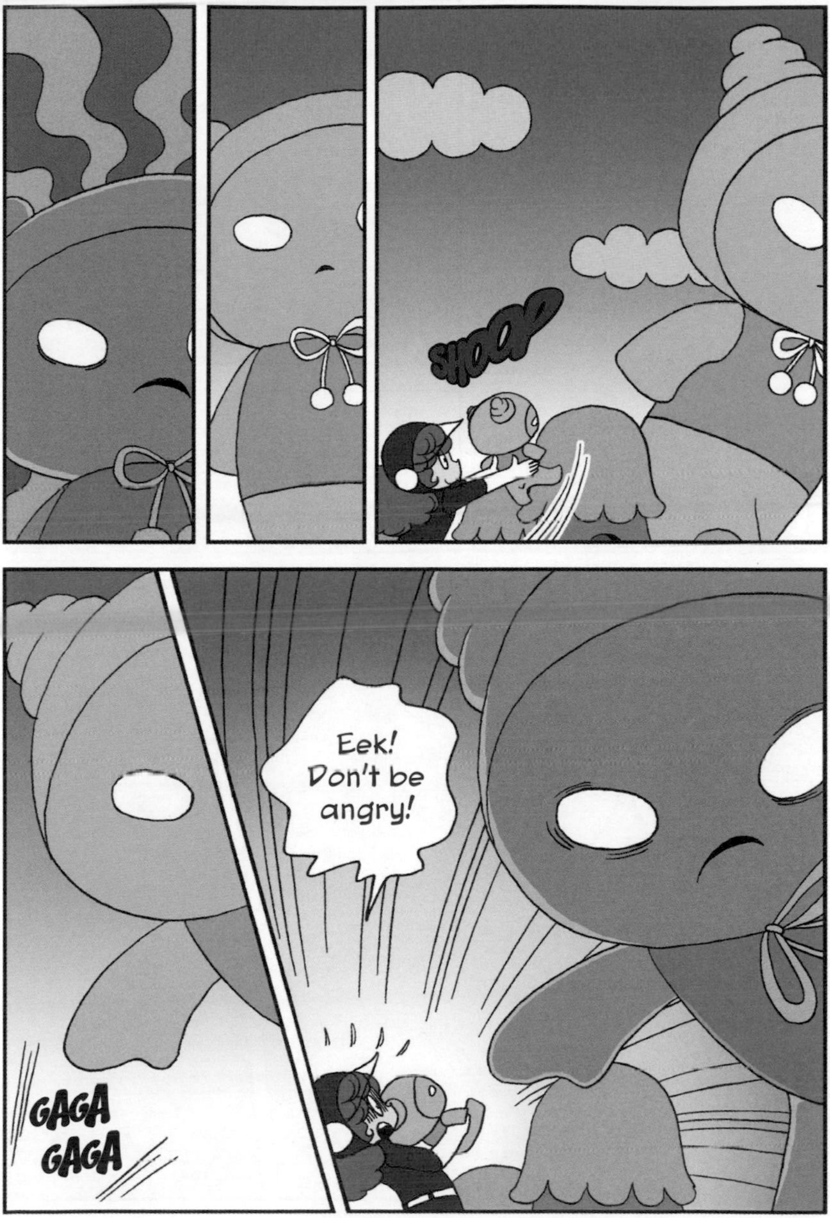
SHOOP
Eek! Don't be angry!
GAGA GAGA

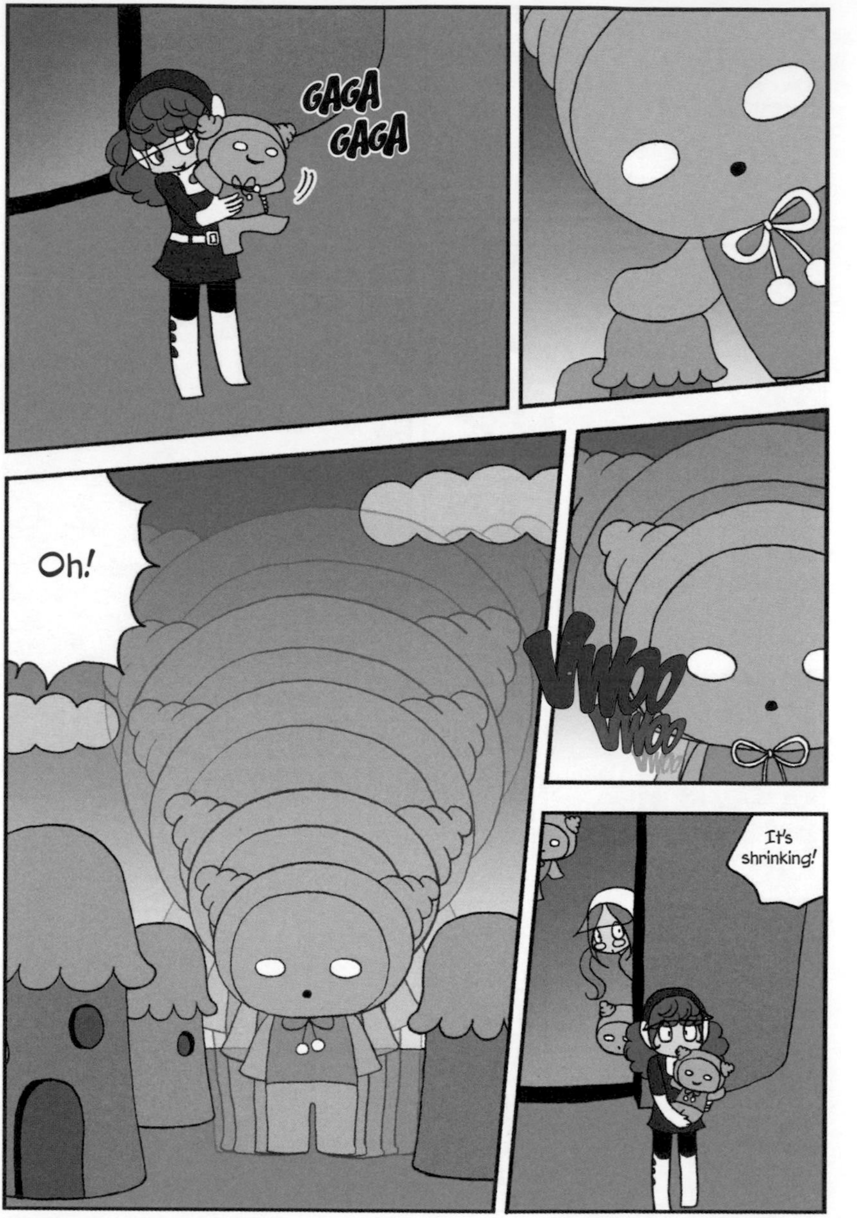
GAGA
GAGA
VWOO
VWOO
It's shrinking!
Oh!

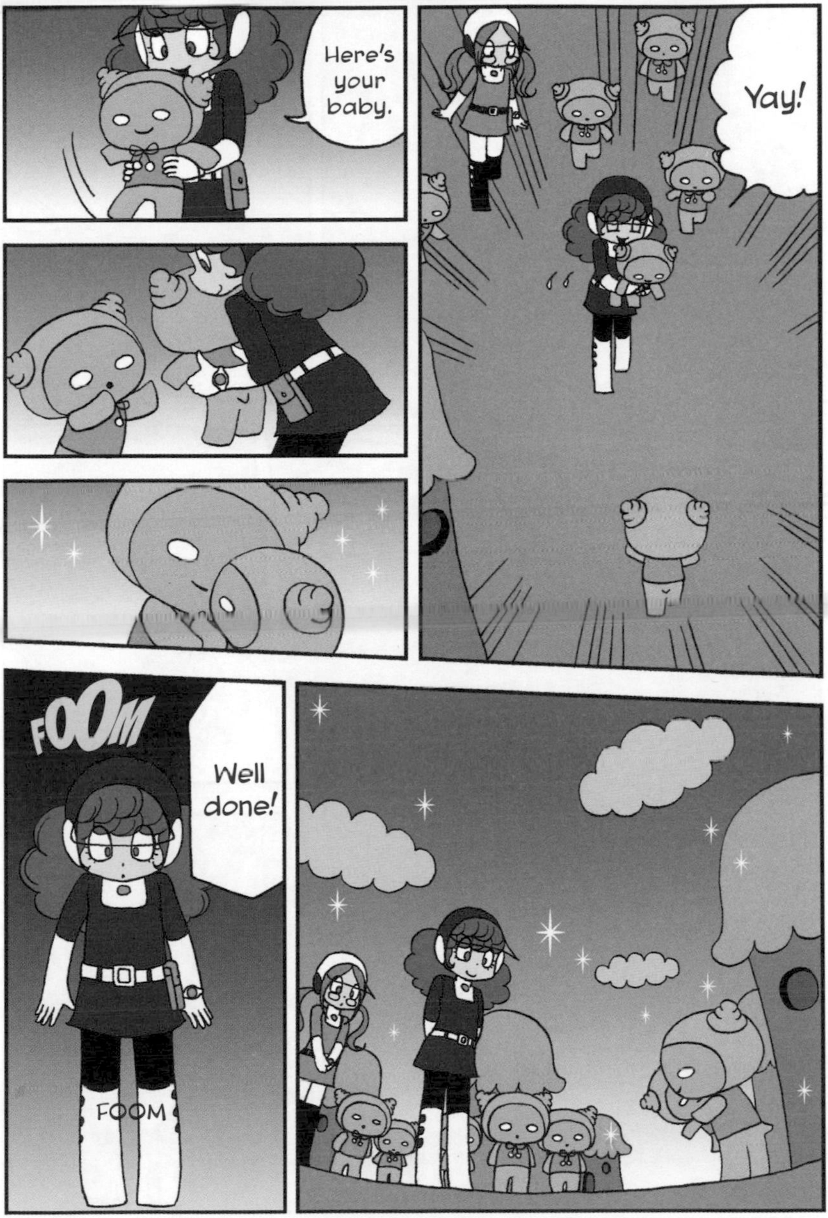
Yay!
Here's your baby.
FOOM
Well done!
FOOM

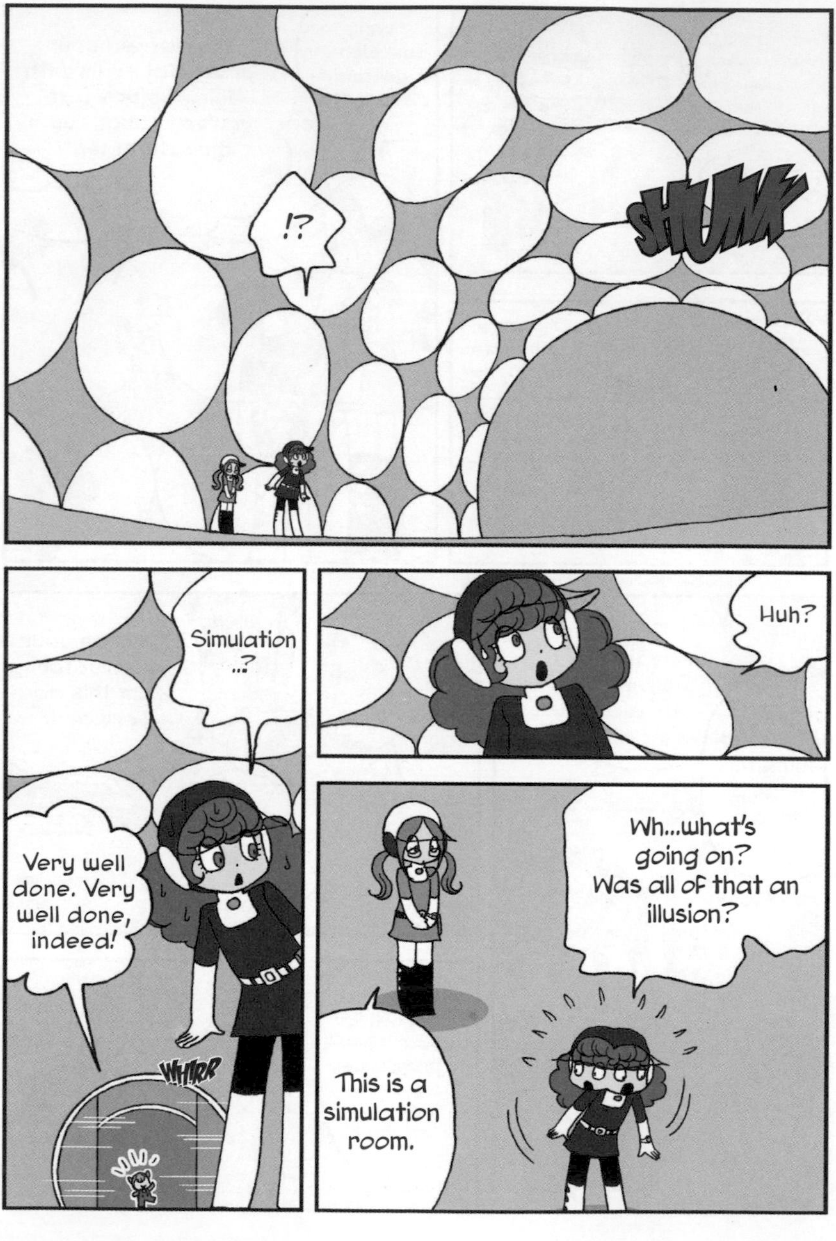
SHUNK
!?
Huh?
Wh...what's going on? Was all of that an illusion?
This is a simulation room.
Simulation ...?
Very well done. Very well done, indeed!
WHIRR

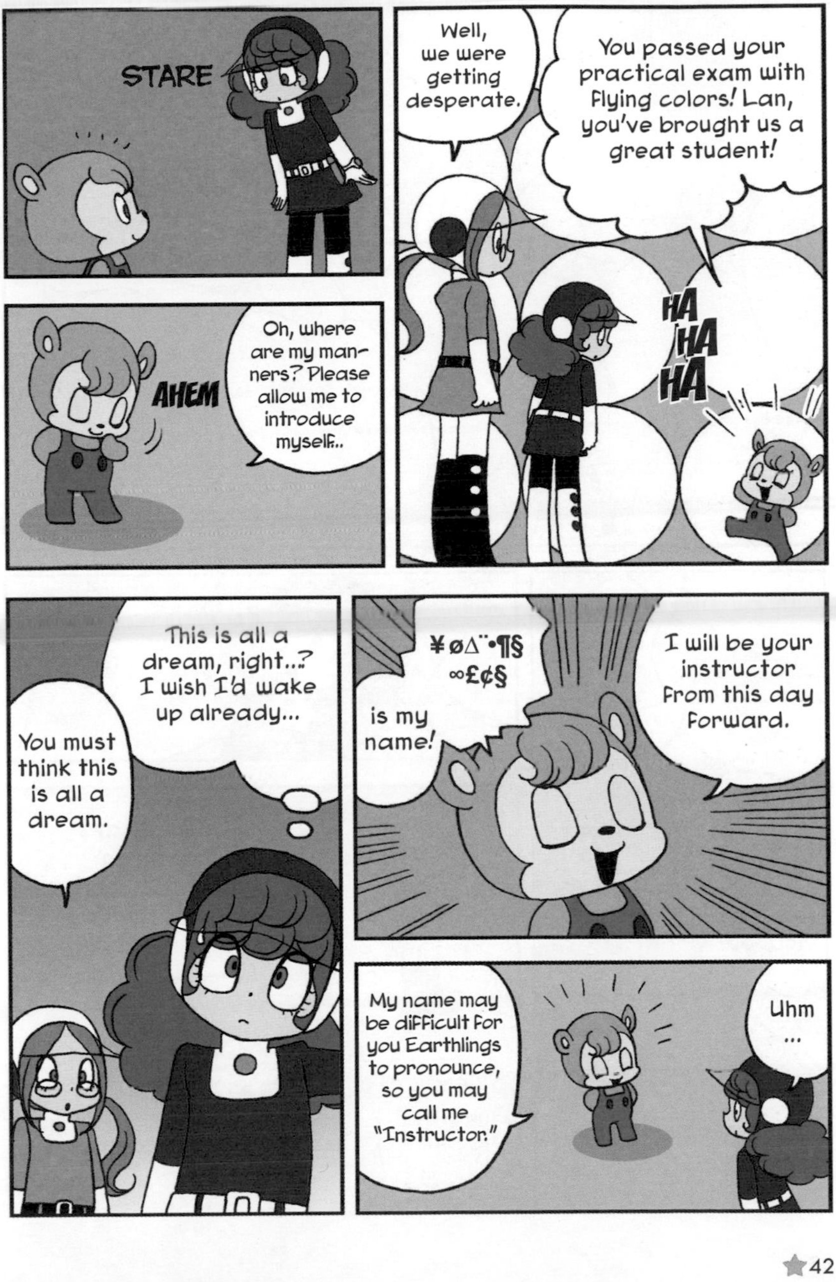
You passed your practical exam with flying colors! Lan, you've brought us a great student!
Well, we were getting desperate.
HA HA HA
STARE
Oh, where are my man-ners? Please allow me to introduce myself...
AHEM
I will be your instructor from this day forward.
¥øΔ¨•¶§ ∞£¢§
is my name!
Uhm ...
My name may be difficult for you Earthlings to pronounce, so you may call me "Instructor."
This is all a dream, right...? I wish I'd wake up already...
You must think this is all a dream.

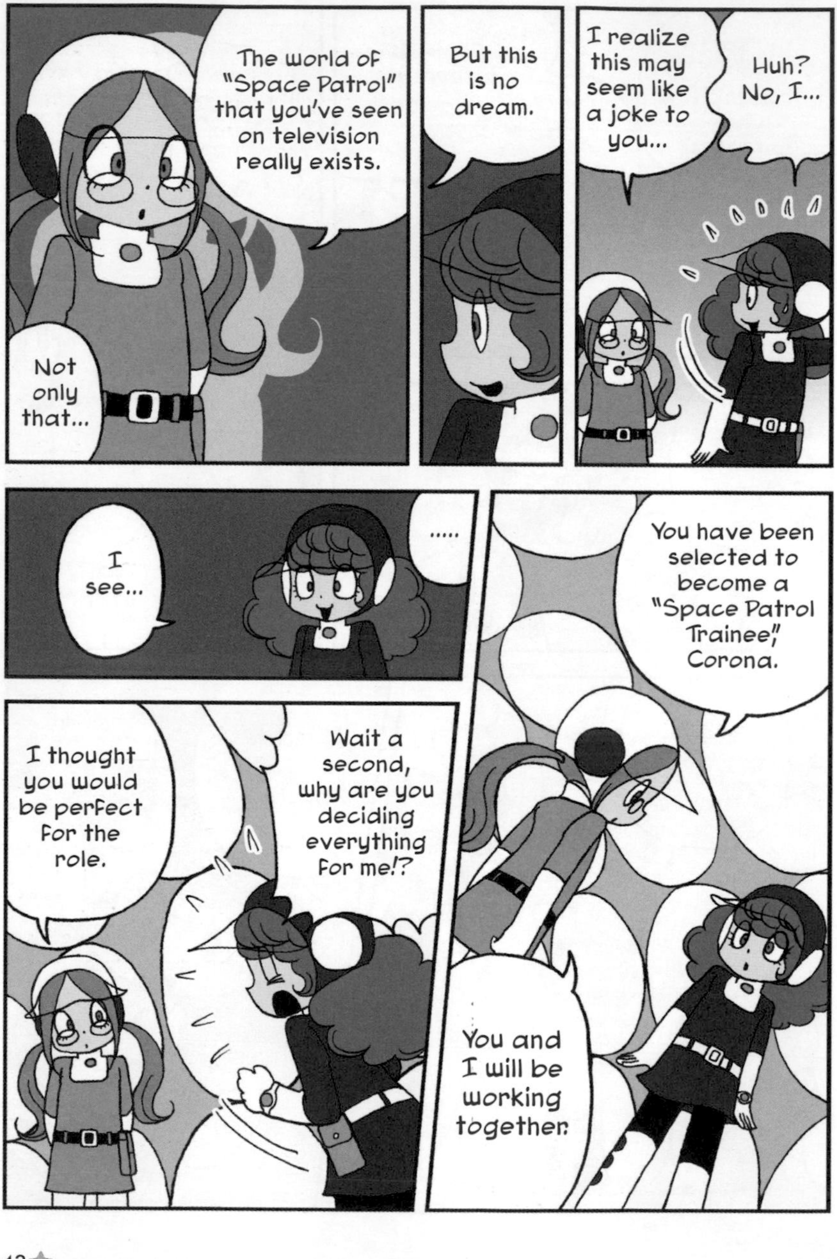
Huh? No, I...
I realize this may seem like a joke to you...
But this is no dream.
The world of "Space Patrol" that you've seen on television really exists.
Not only that...
You have been selected to become a "Space Patrol Trainee," Corona.
You and I will be working together.
.....
I see...
Wait a second, why are you deciding everything for me!?
I thought you would be perfect for the role.

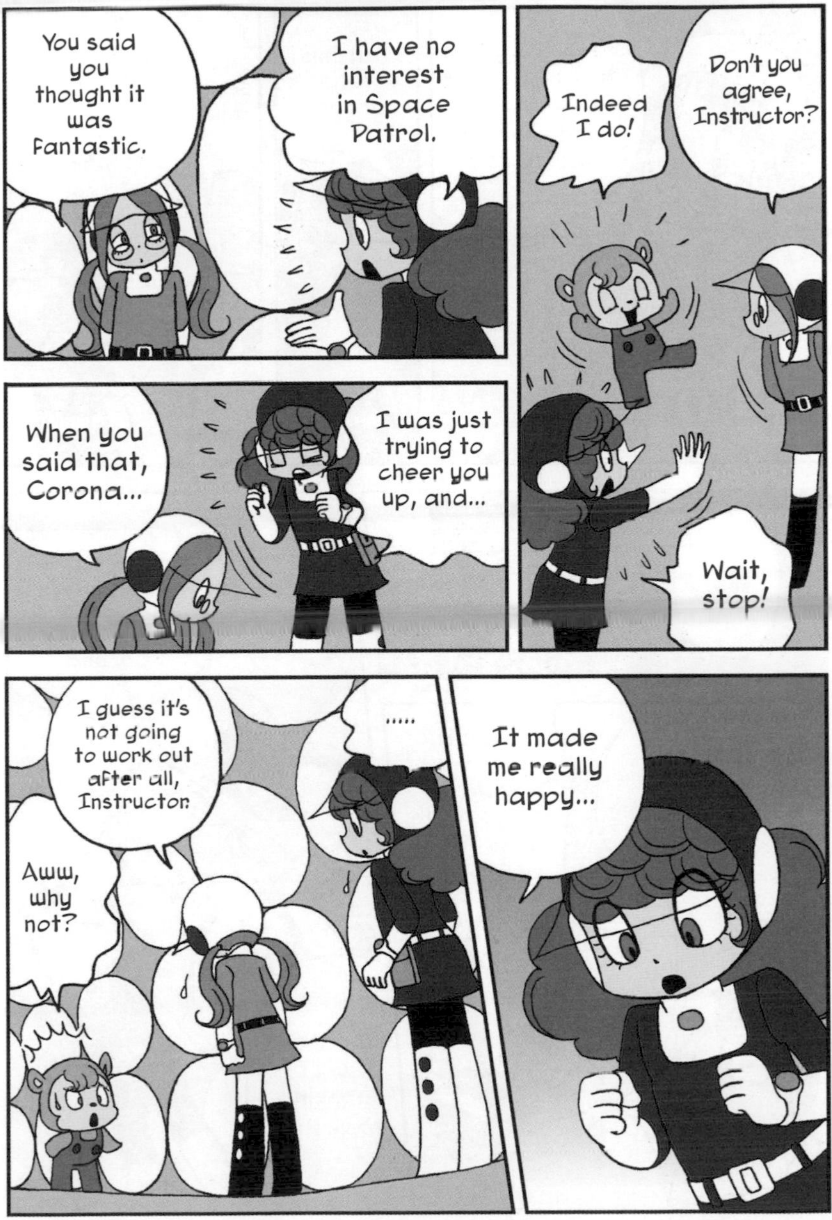
Don't you agree, Instructor?
Indeed I do!
Wait, stop!
I have no interest in Space Patrol.
You said you thought it was fantastic.
I was just trying to cheer you up, and...
When you said that, Corona...
It made me really happy...
.....
I guess it's not going to work out after all, Instructor.
Aww, why not?

I wasn't lying when I said that... but...
Then you agree!!
We're all set!
Wait a second ...
We can discuss the details later.
Hurry, Instructor!
Oh, right... Lan Tsukishima, Corona Hoshino...
I hereby grant you official authoriza-tion...
You two are now Space Patrol Trainees!!
Do your best to preserve the peace and order of the universe!
Roger!!
SNAP
STUMBLE

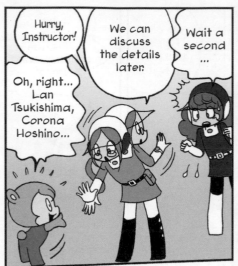

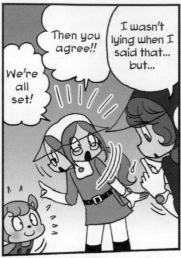

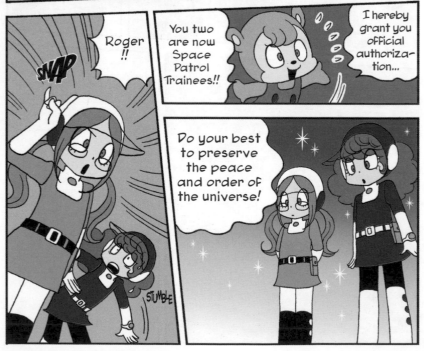

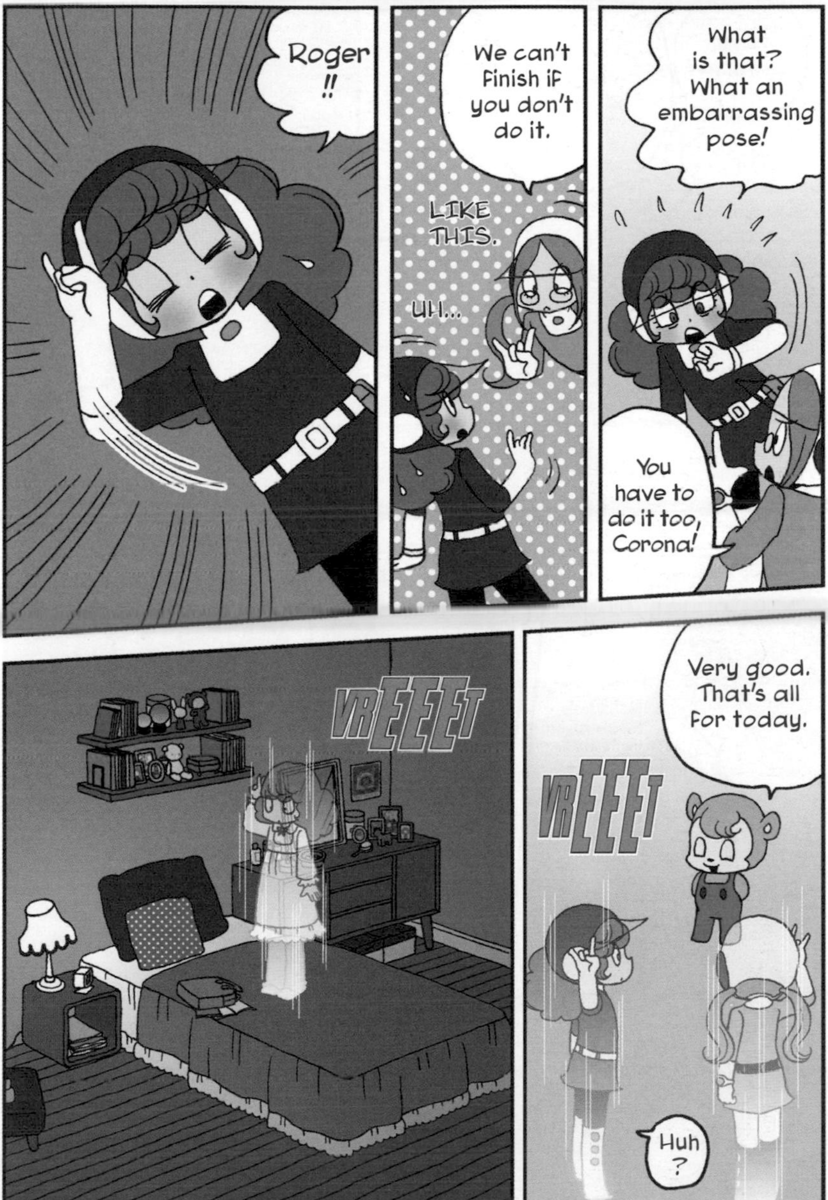
What is that? What an embarrassing pose!
You have to do it too, Corona!
We can't finish if you don't do it.
LIKE THIS.
UH...
Roger!!
Very good. That's all for today.
VREEEET
Huh?
VREEEET

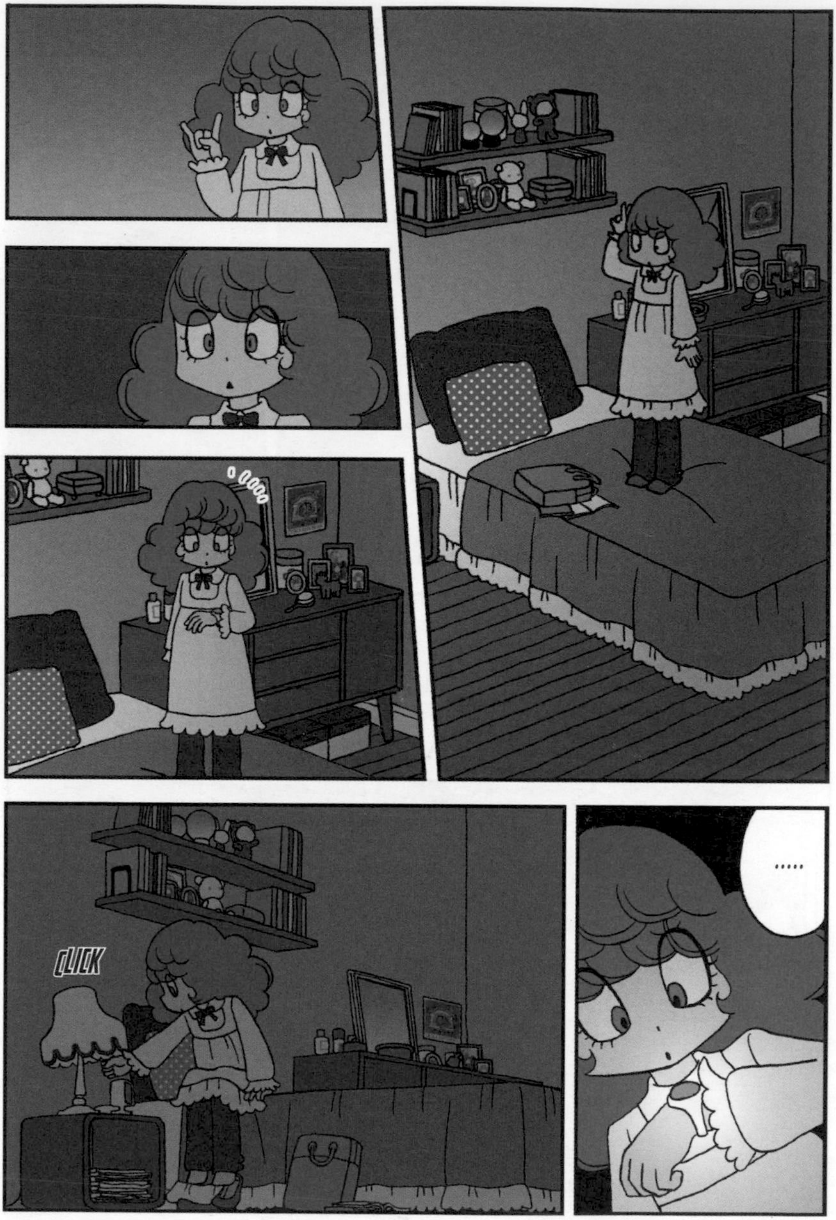
......
CLICK

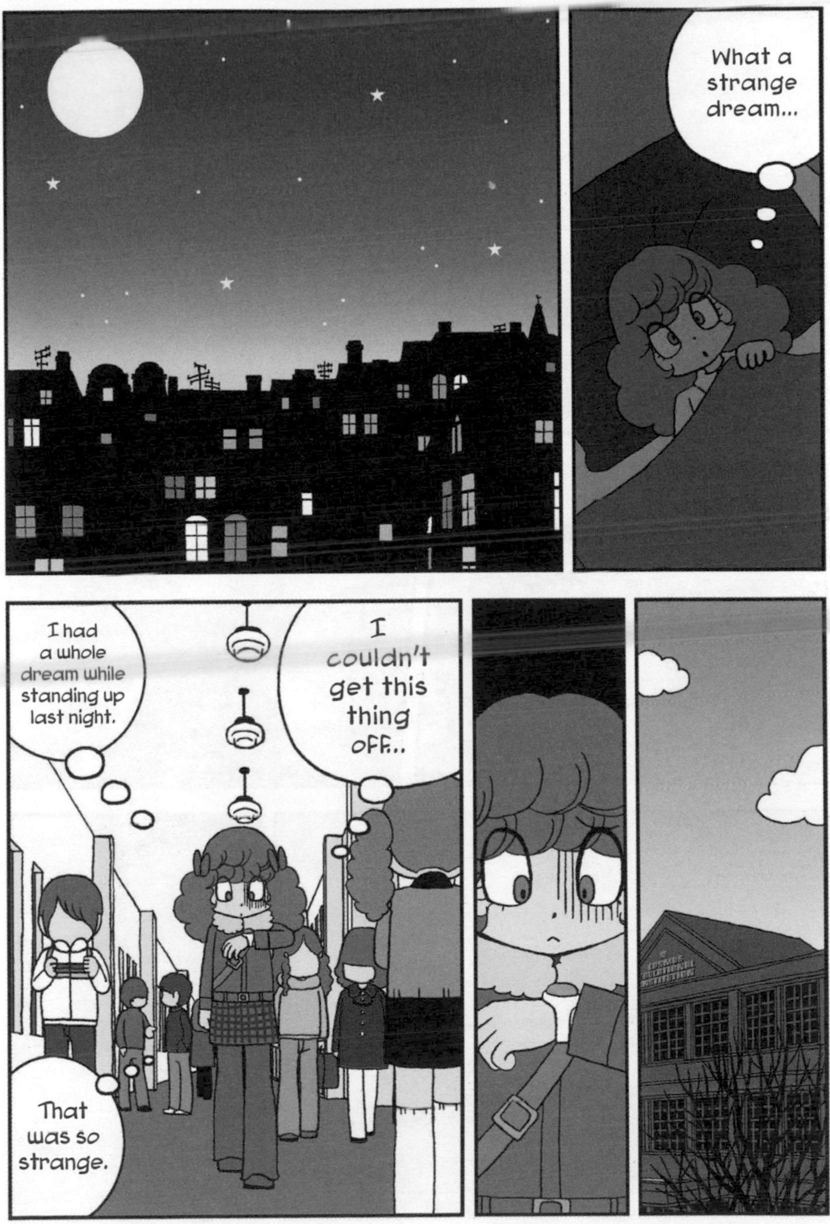
What a strange dream...
I couldn't get this thing off...
I had a whole dream while standing up last night.
That was so strange.

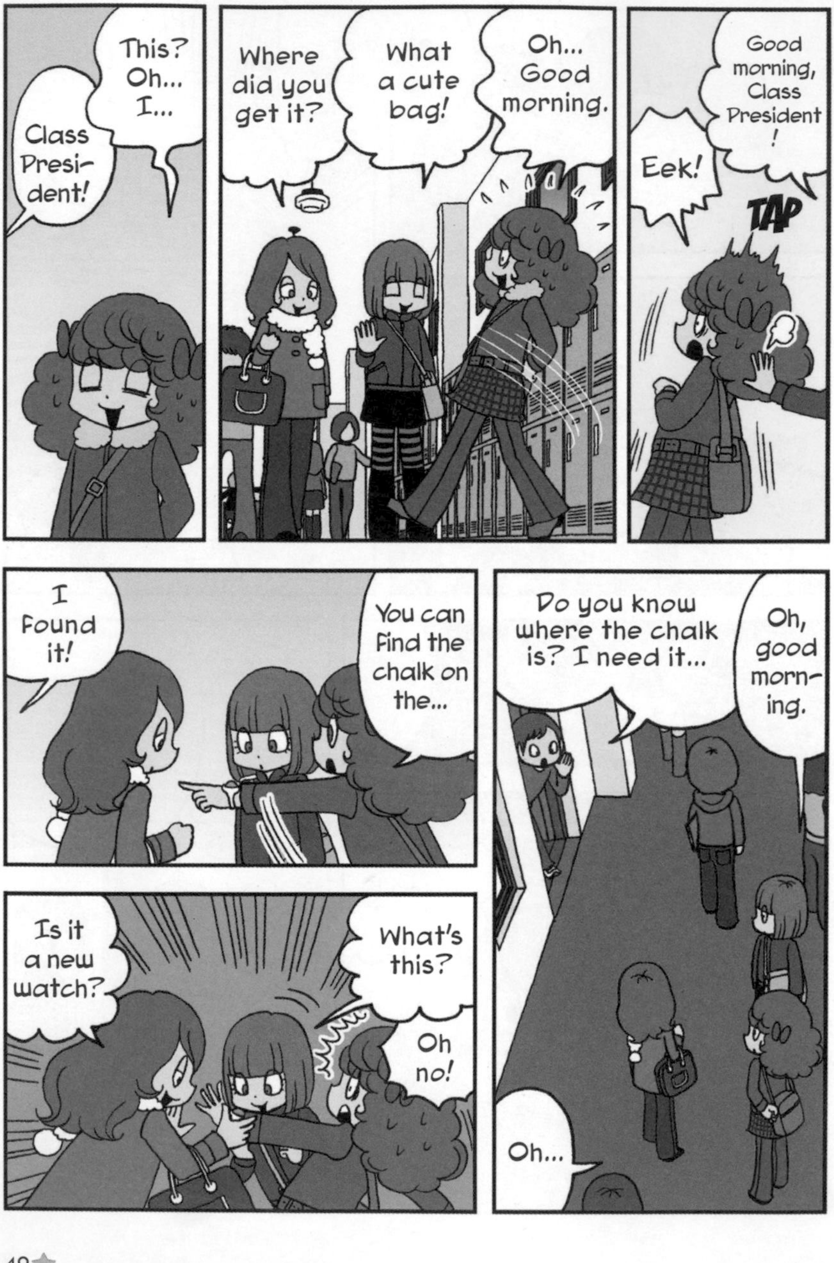
Good morning, Class President!
Eek!
TAP
Oh... Good morning.
What a cute bag!
Where did you get it?
This? Oh... I...
Class President!
Oh, good morning.
Do you know where the chalk is? I need it...
Oh...
You can find the chalk on the...
I found it!
What's this?
Is it a new watch?
Oh no!

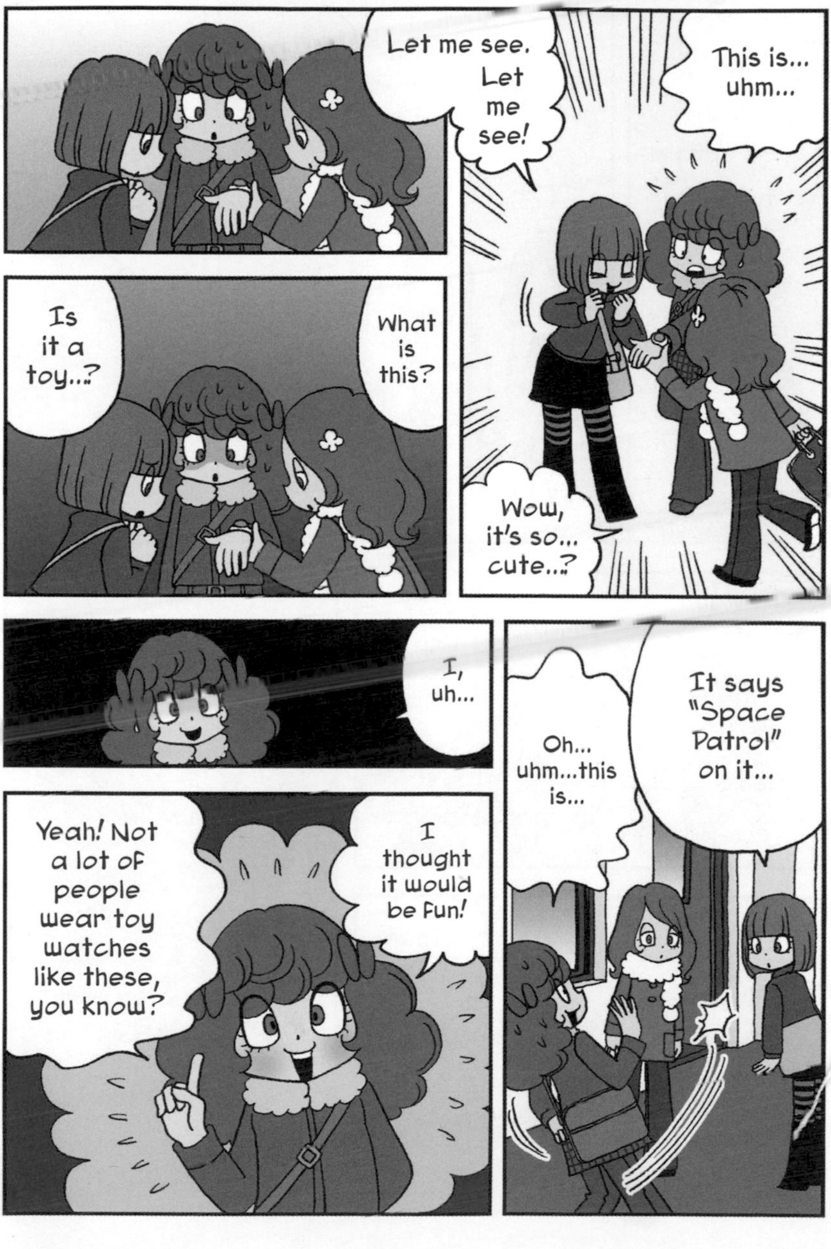
This is... uhm...
Wow, it's so... cute...?
Let me see. Let me see!
What is this?
Is it a toy...?
It says "Space Patrol" on it...
Oh... uhm...this is...
I, uh...
I thought it would be fun!
Yeah! Not a lot of people wear toy watches like these, you know?

That's so Funny!
HAHAHAHA
I can't be seen wearing this!
How do I get it off!?
You can't remove your Space Receiver.
The only way you can get it off is by quitting the Space Patrol.
Good morning, Corona.

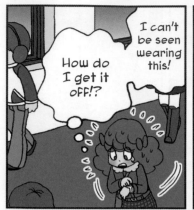

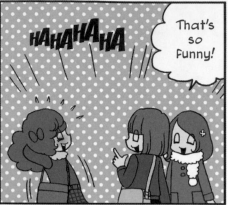

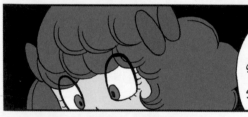

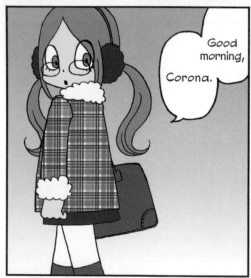

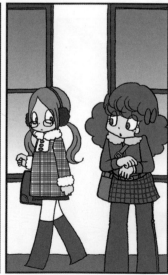

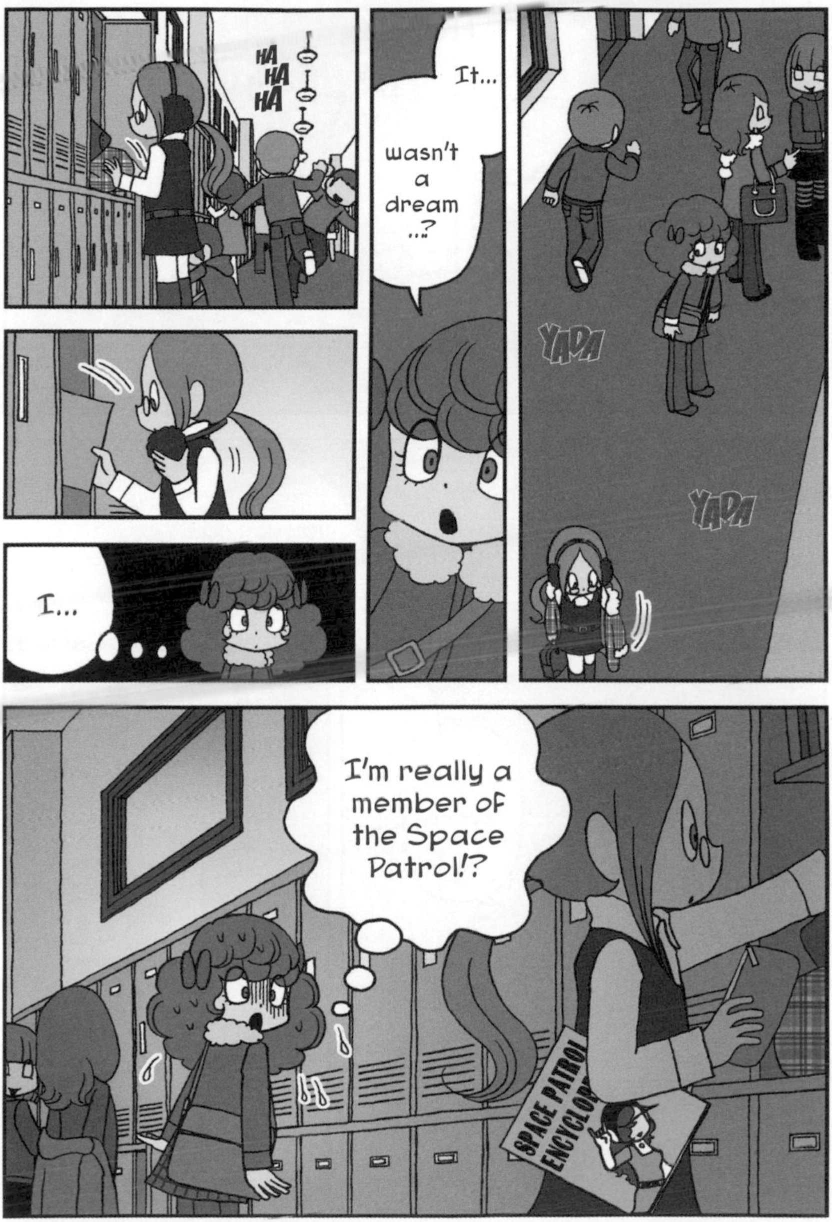
YADA
YADA
It...
wasn't a dream ...?
HA HA HA
I...
I'm really a member of the Space Patrol!?
SPACE PATROL ENCYCLOP

SWANS IN SPACE

CHAPTER 2
STRONG DETERMINATION

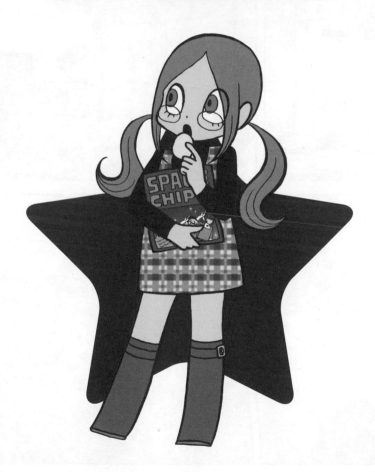

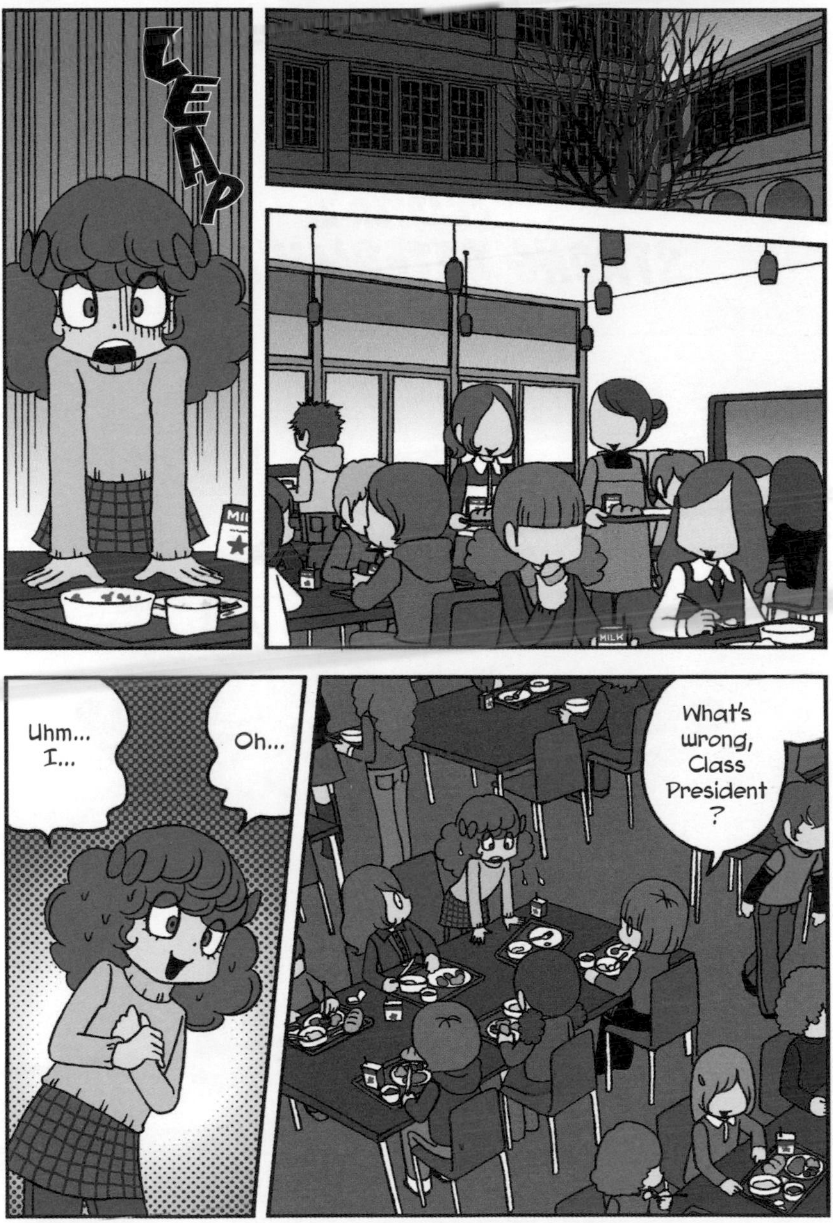
MILK
LEAP
What's wrong, Class President?
Oh...
Uhm... I...

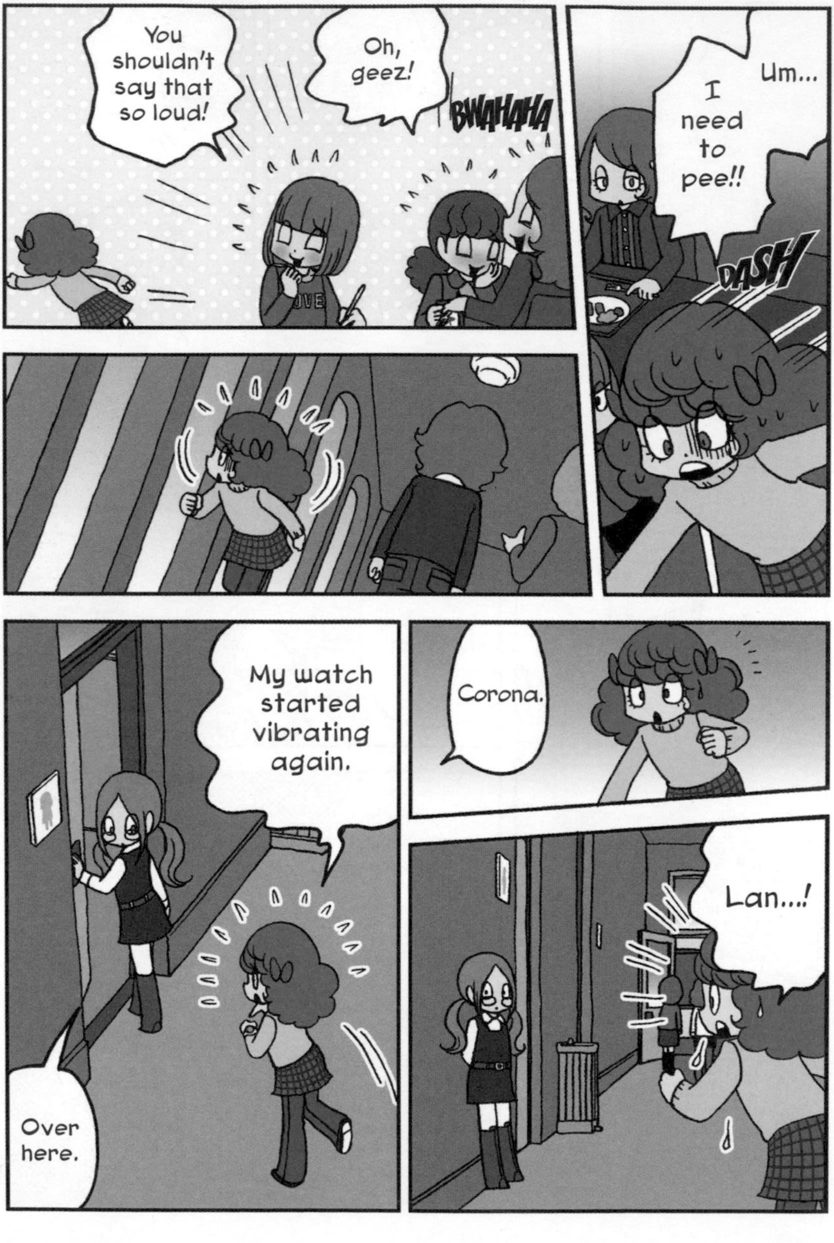
Um...
I need to pee!!
DASH
Oh, geez!
BWAHAHA
You shouldn't say that so loud!
Corona.
Lan...!
My watch started vibrating again.
Over here.

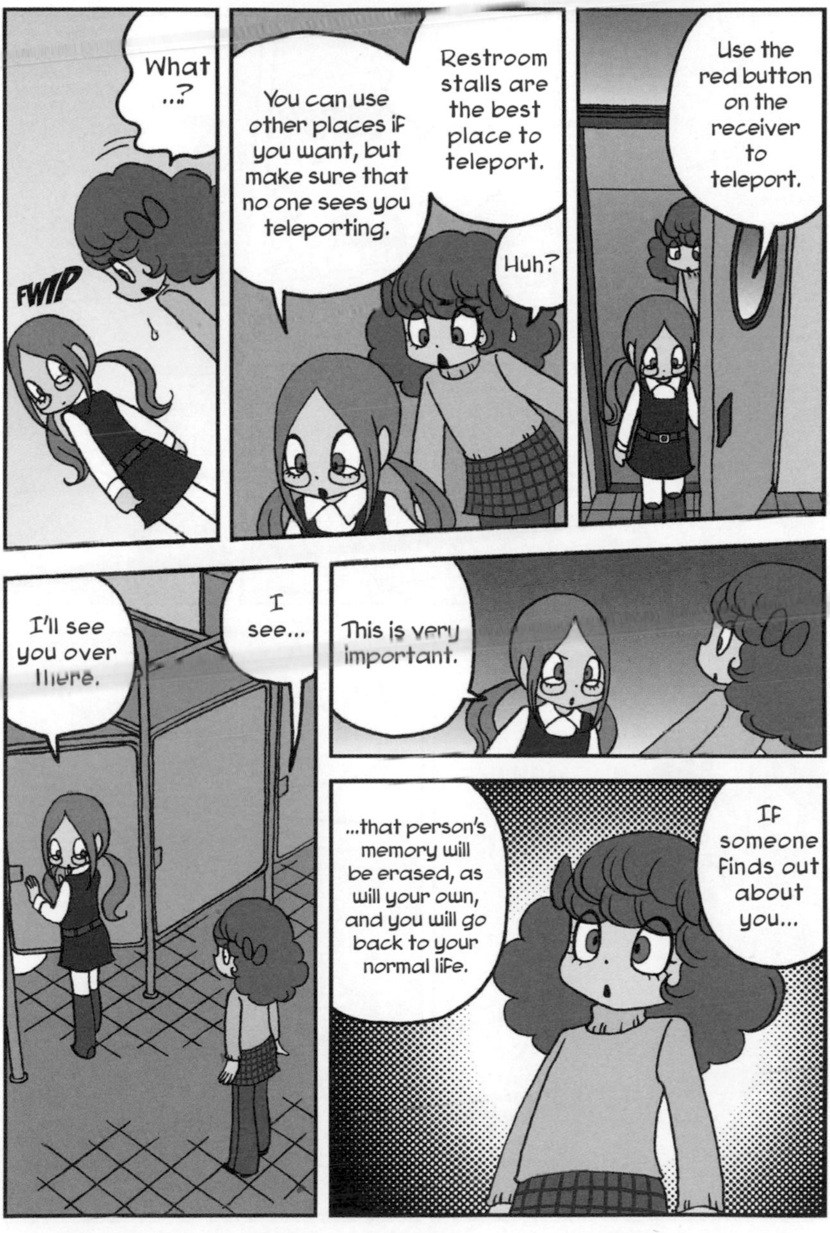
Use the red button on the receiver to teleport.
Restroom stalls are the best place to teleport.
You can use other places if you want, but make sure that no one sees you teleporting.
Huh?
What ...?
FWIP
This is very important.
If someone finds out about you...
...that person's memory will be erased, as will your own, and you will go back to your normal life.
I see...
I'll see you over there.

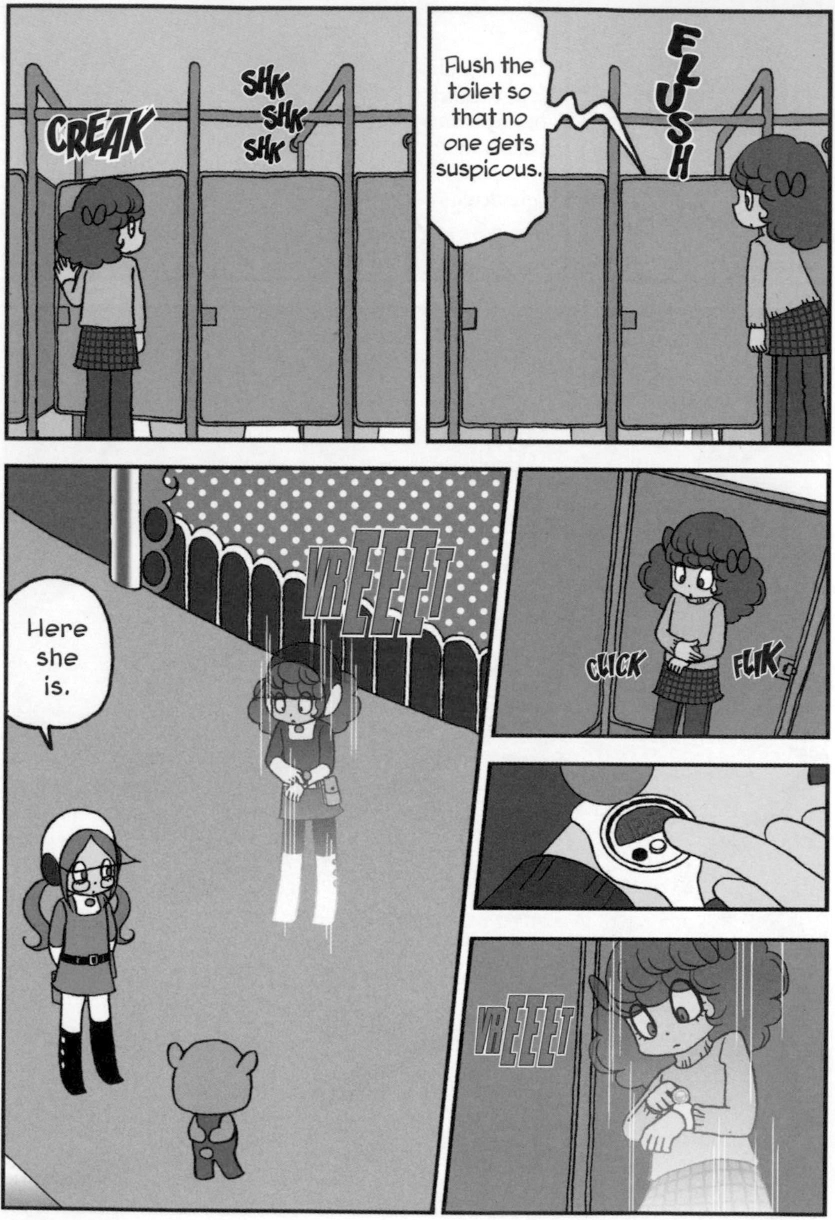
Flush the toilet so that no one gets suspicous.
FLUSH
SHK
SHK
SHK
CREAK
FLIK
CLICK
VREEEET
VREEEET
Here she is.

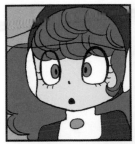

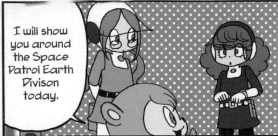

I will show you around the Space Patrol Earth Divison today.

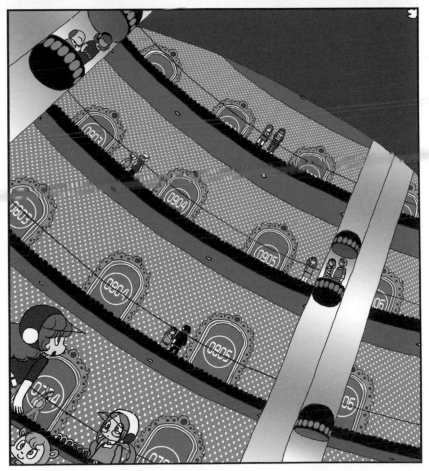

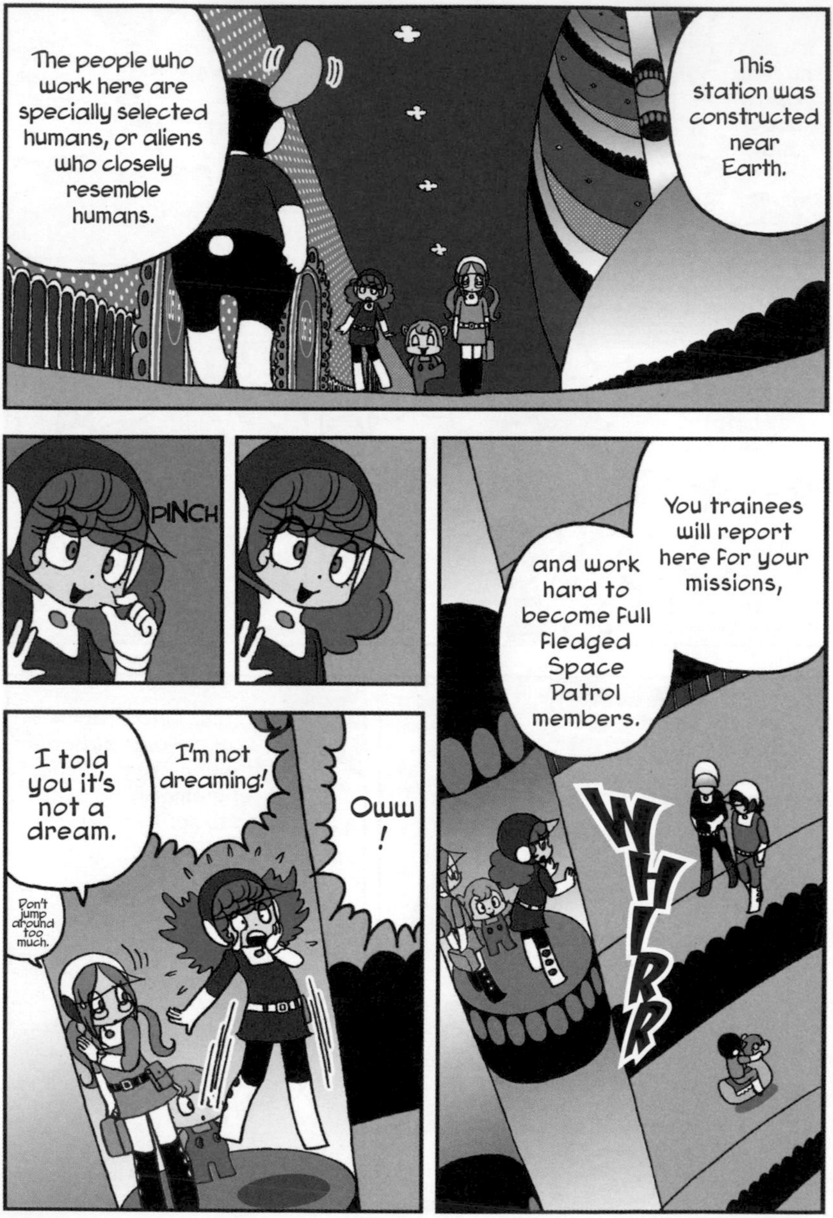
This station was constructed near Earth.
The people who work here are specially selected humans, or aliens who closely resemble humans.
You trainees will report here for your missions,
and work hard to become full fledged Space Patrol members.
WHIRR
PINCH
Oww!
I'm not dreaming!
I told you it's not a dream.
Don't jump around too much.

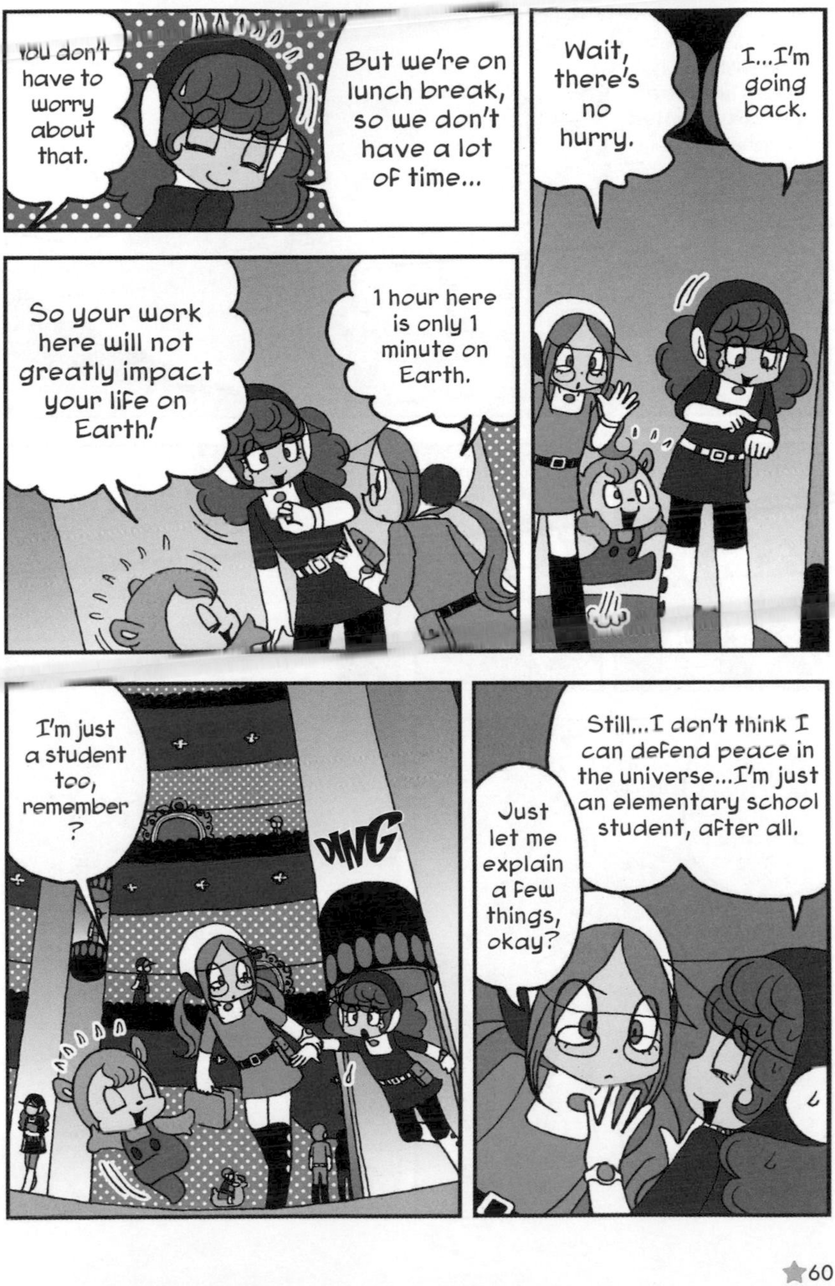
I...I'm going back.
Wait, there's no hurry.
But we're on lunch break, so we don't have a lot of time...
You don't have to worry about that.
1 hour here is only 1 minute on Earth.
So your work here will not greatly impact your life on Earth!
Still...I don't think I can defend peace in the universe...I'm just an elementary school student, after all.
Just let me explain a few things, okay?
I'm just a student too, remember?
DING

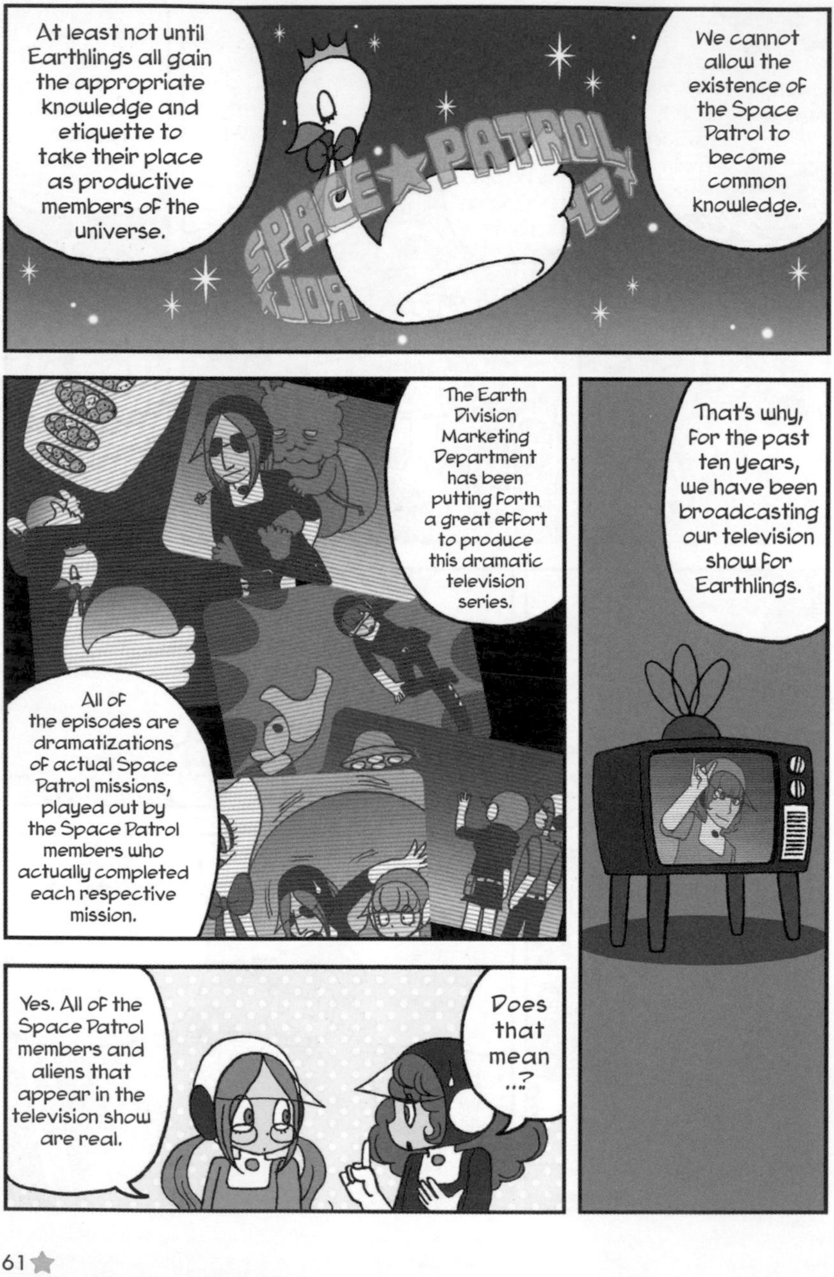
We cannot allow the existence of the Space Patrol to become common knowledge.
At least not until Earthlings all gain the appropriate knowledge and etiquette to take their place as productive members of the universe.
SPACE★PATROL
That's why, for the past ten years, we have been broadcasting our television show for Earthlings.
The Earth Division Marketing Department has been putting forth a great effort to produce this dramatic television series.
All of the episodes are dramatizations of actual Space Patrol missions, played out by the Space Patrol members who actually completed each respective mission.
Does that mean ...?
Yes. All of the Space Patrol members and aliens that appear in the television show are real.

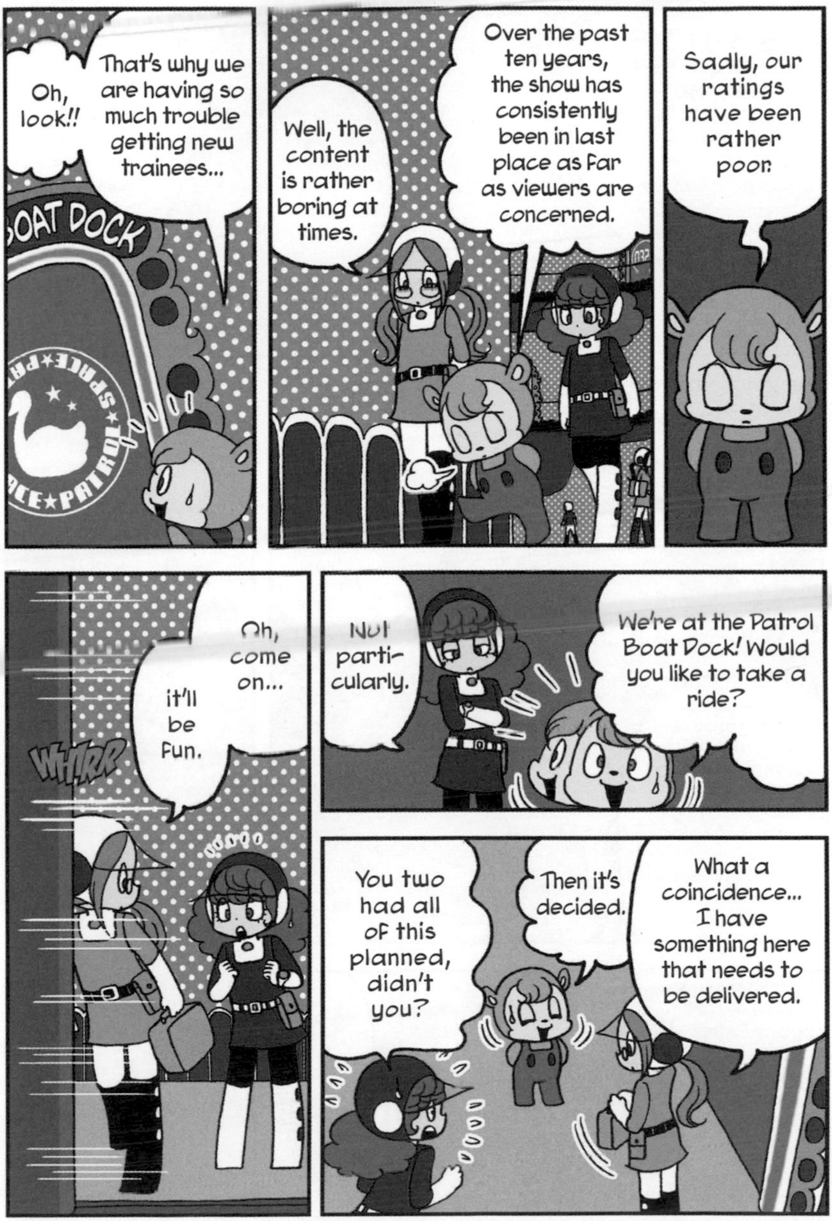

Sadly, our ratings have been rather poor.
Over the past ten years, the show has consistently been in last place as far as viewers are concerned.
Well, the content is rather boring at times.
That's why we are having so much trouble getting new trainees...
Oh, look!!
BOAT DOCK
SPACE PATROL
We're at the Patrol Boat Dock! Would you like to take a ride?
Not particularly.
What a coincidence... I have something here that needs to be delivered.
Then it's decided.
You two had all of this planned, didn't you?
Oh, come on...
it'll be fun.
WHIRR

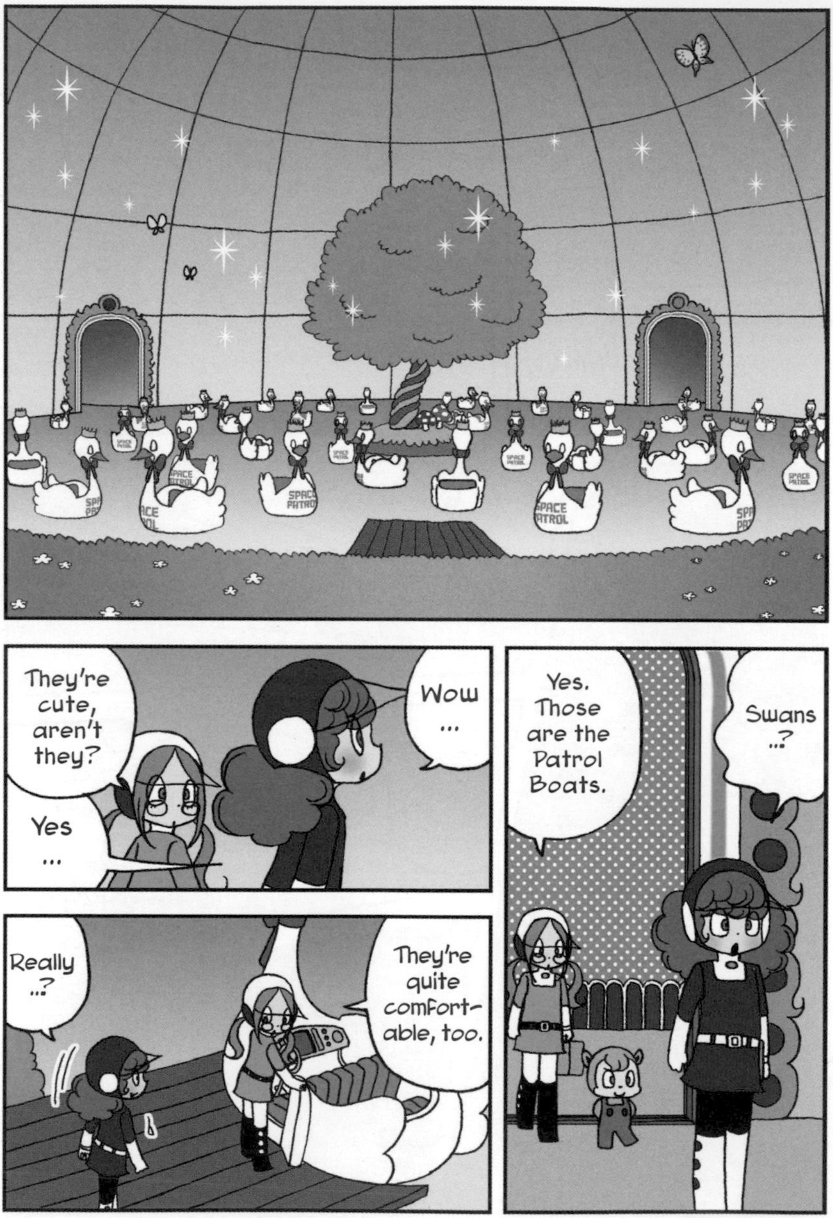
Swans ..?
Yes. Those are the Patrol Boats.
Wow ...
They're cute, aren't they?
Yes ...
They're quite comfort-able, too.
Really ..?
SPACE PATROL

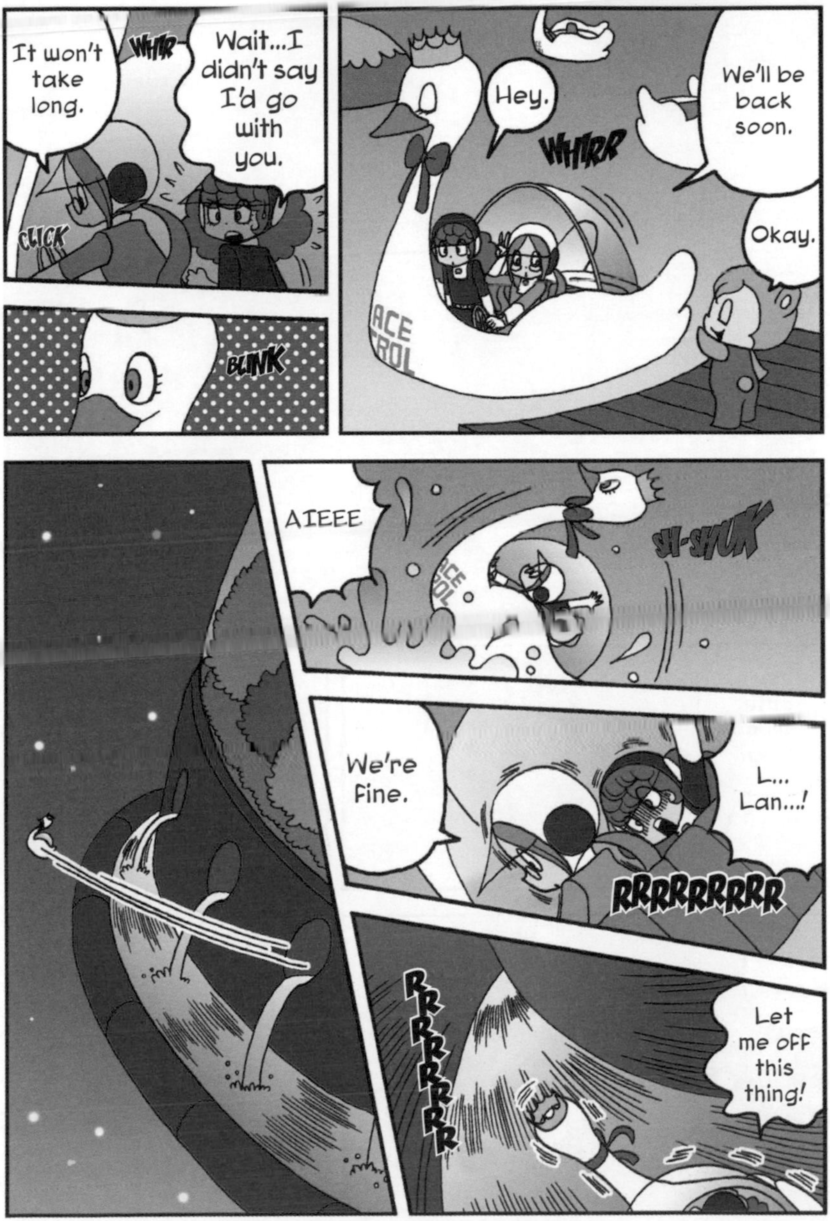
We'll be back soon.
Hey.
WHIRR
Okay.
Wait...I didn't say I'd go with you.
WHIR
It won't take long.
CLICK
BLINK
AIEEE
SH-SHUK
L... Lan...!
We're fine.
RRRRRRRRR
Let me off this thing!
RRRRRRRR

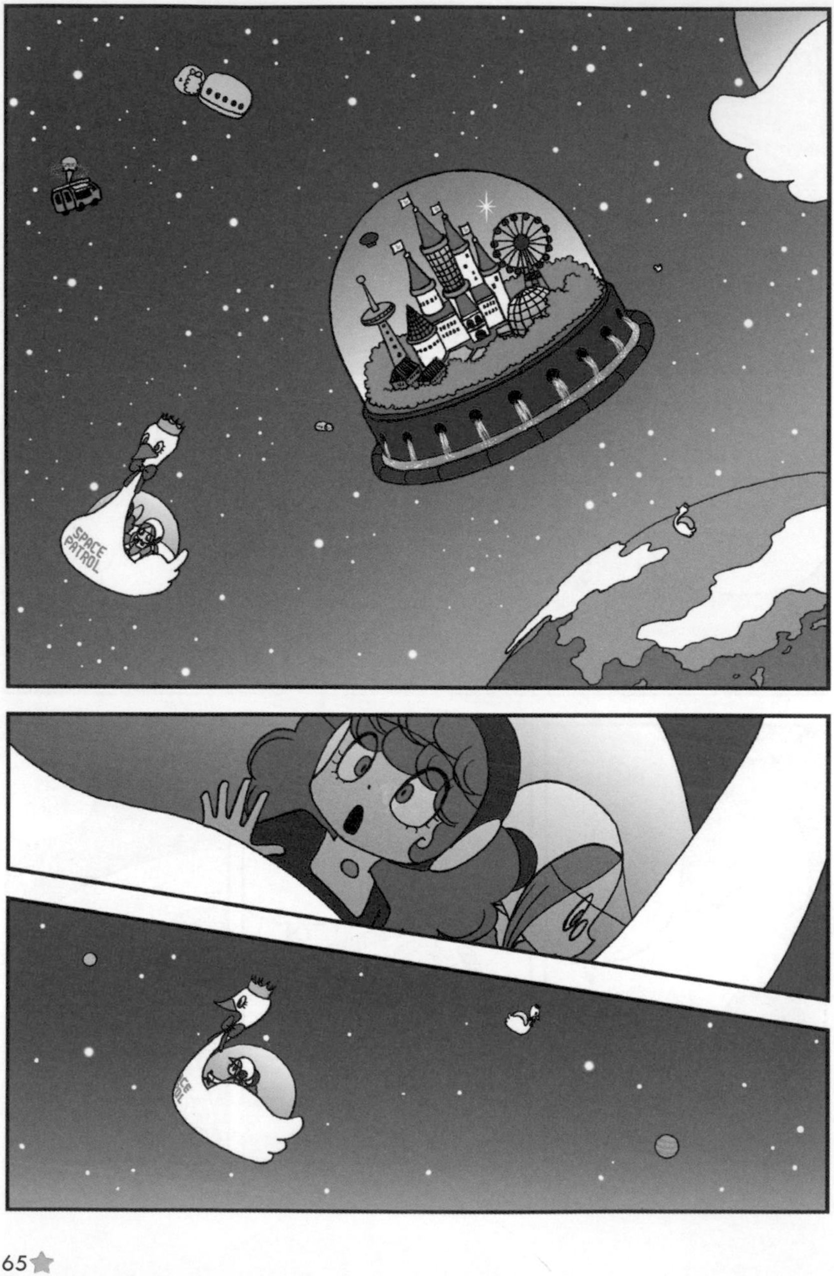
SPACE
PATROL

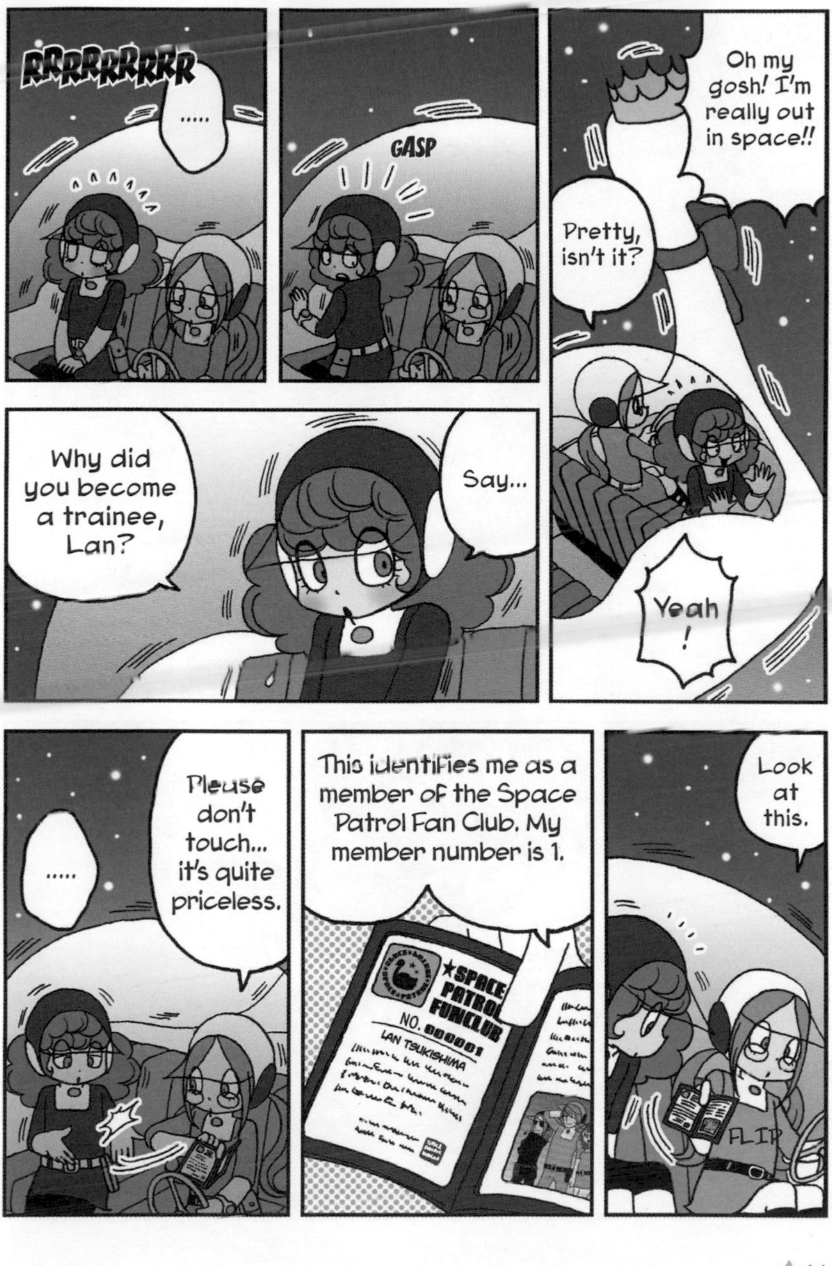
Oh my gosh! I'm really out in space!!
Pretty, isn't it?
Yeah!
GASP
RRRRRRRRR
.....
Say...
Why did you become a trainee, Lan?
Look at this.
FLIP
This identifies me as a member of the Space Patrol Fan Club. My member number is 1.
★SPACE PATROL FUNCLUB
NO. 000001
LAN TSUKISHIMA
Please don't touch... it's quite priceless.
.....

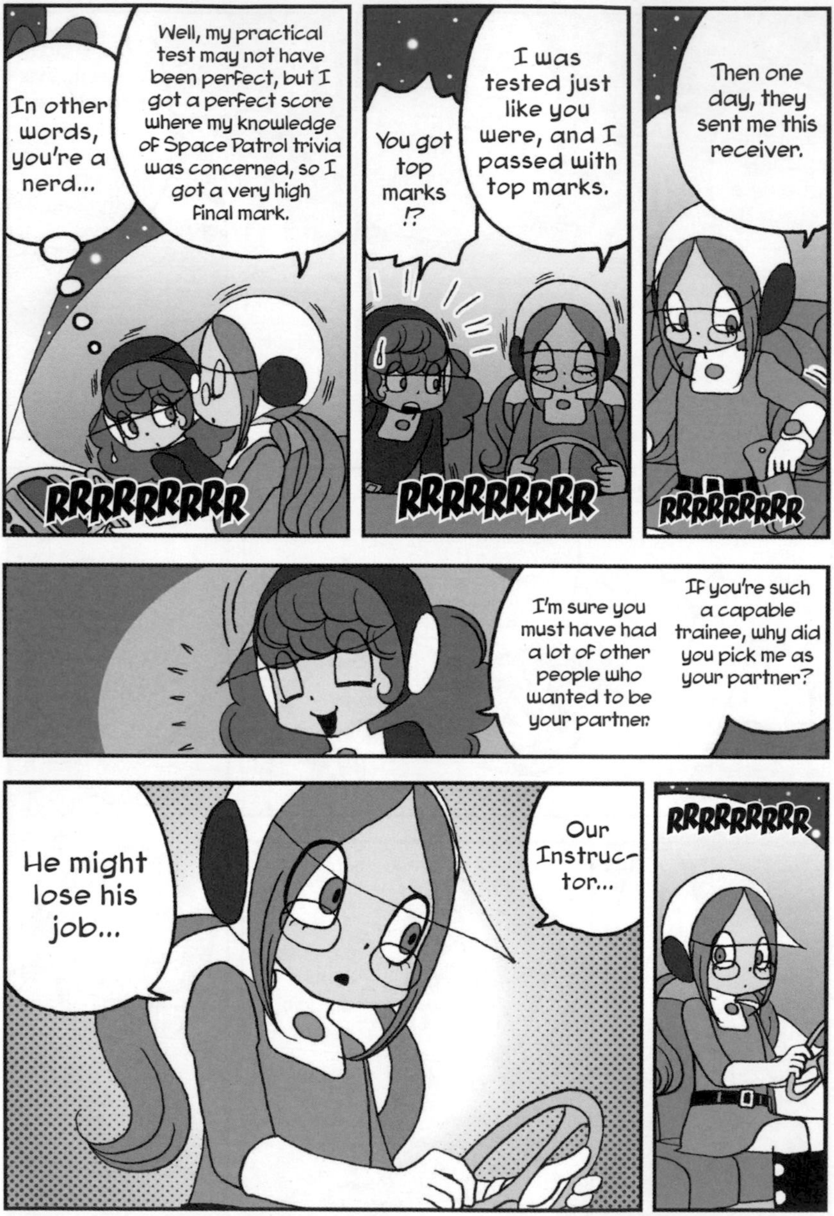
Then one day, they sent me this receiver.
RRRRRRRRR
I was tested just like you were, and I passed with top marks.
You got top marks!?
RRRRRRRRR
Well, my practical test may not have been perfect, but I got a perfect score where my knowledge of Space Patrol trivia was concerned, so I got a very high final mark.
In other words, you're a nerd...
RRRRRRRRR
If you're such a capable trainee, why did you pick me as your partner?
I'm sure you must have had a lot of other people who wanted to be your partner.
RRRRRRRRR
Our Instructor...
He might lose his job...

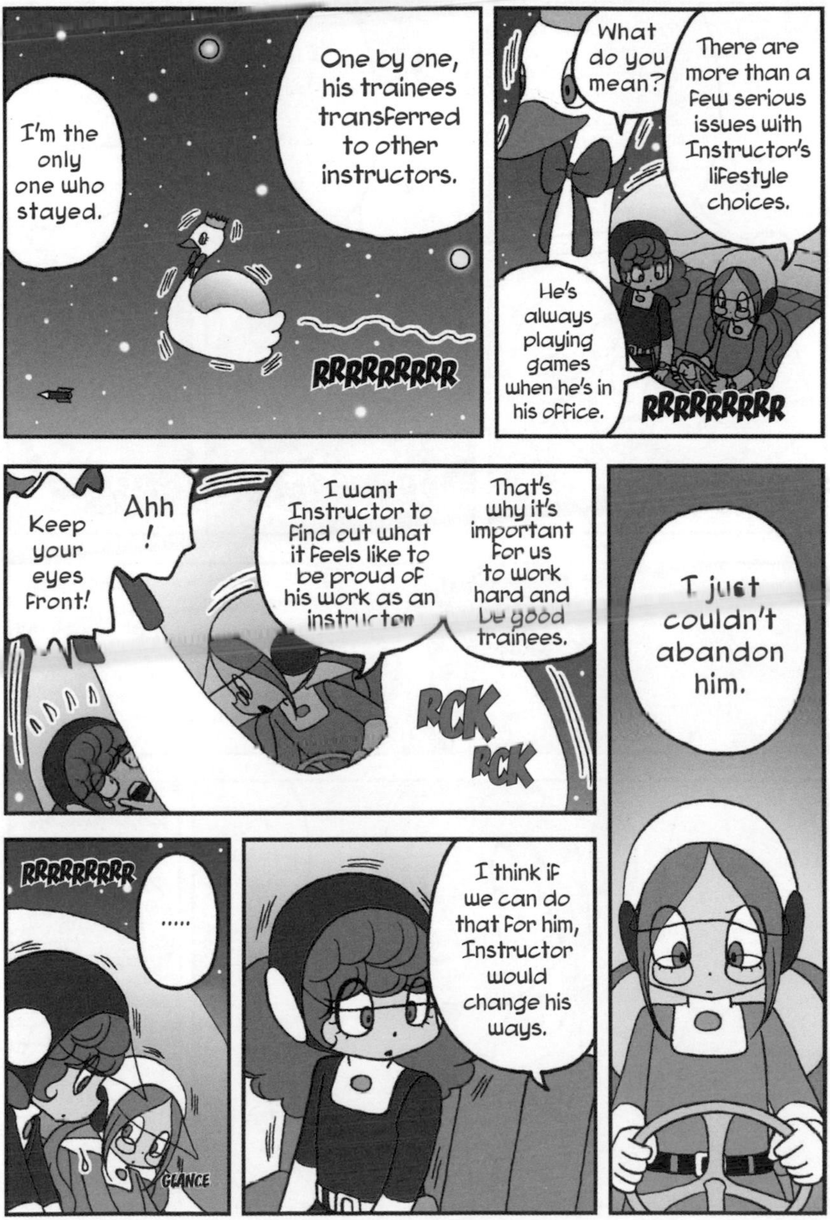
What do you mean?
There are more than a few serious issues with Instructor's lifestyle choices.
He's always playing games when he's in his office.
RRRRRRRRR
One by one, his trainees transferred to other instructors.
I'm the only one who stayed.
RRRRRRRRR
I just couldn't abandon him.
That's why it's important for us to work hard and be good trainees.
I want Instructor to find out what it feels like to be proud of his work as an instructor.
Ahh!
Keep your eyes front!
RCK
RCK
I think if we can do that for him, Instructor would change his ways.
RRRRRRRRR
.....
GLANCE

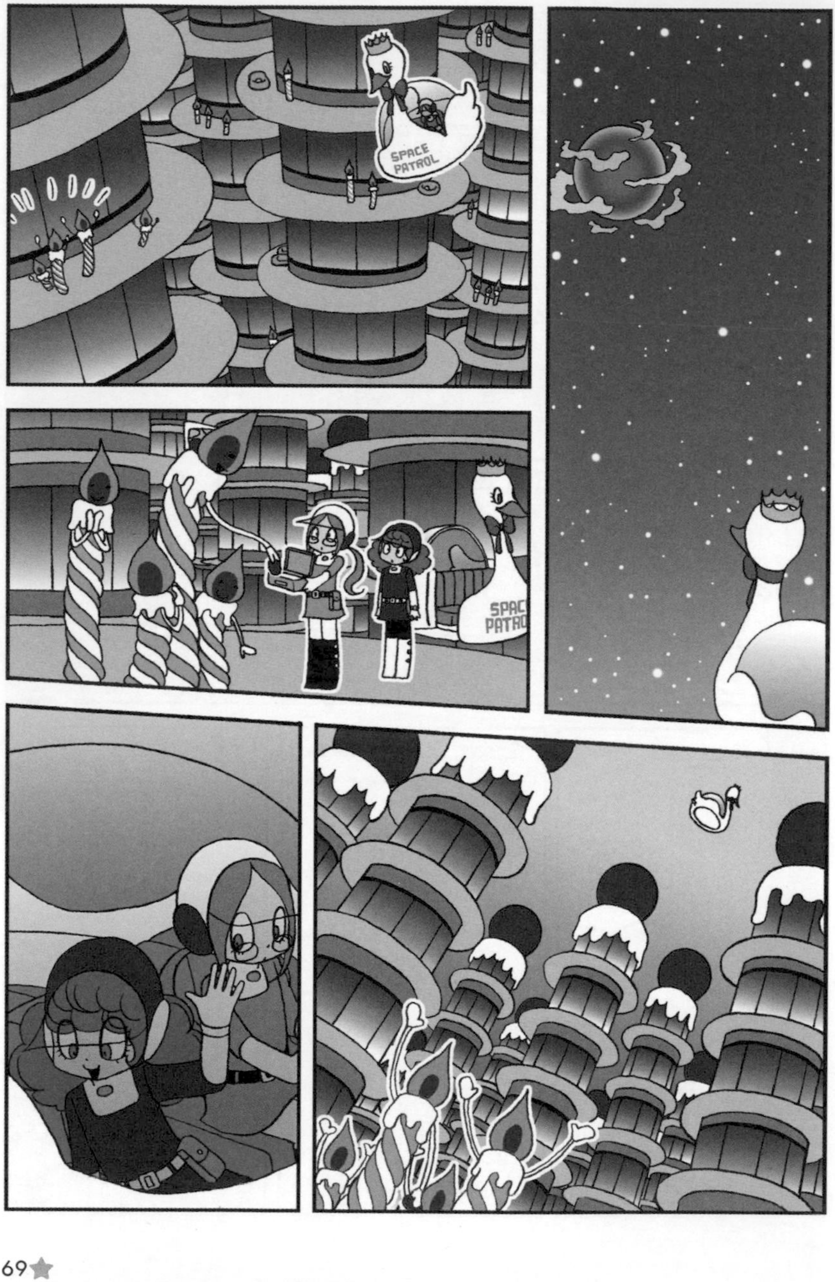
SPACE PATROL
SPACE PATROL

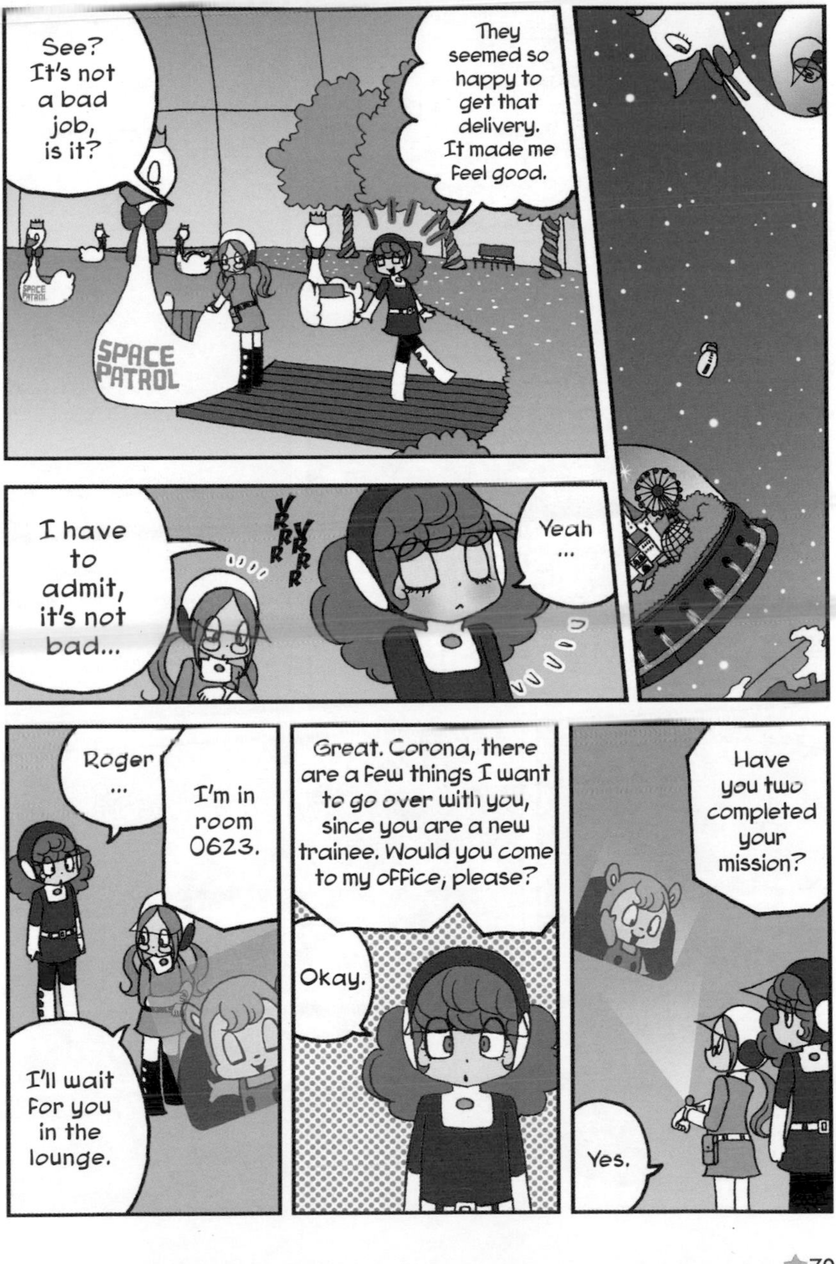
They seemed so happy to get that delivery. It made me feel good.
See? It's not a bad job, is it?
SPACE PATROL
SPACE PATROL
Yeah ...
VRRR VRRR
I have to admit, it's not bad...
Have you two completed your mission?
Yes.
Great. Corona, there are a few things I want to go over with you, since you are a new trainee. Would you come to my office, please?
Okay.
I'm in room 0623.
Roger ...
I'll wait for you in the lounge.

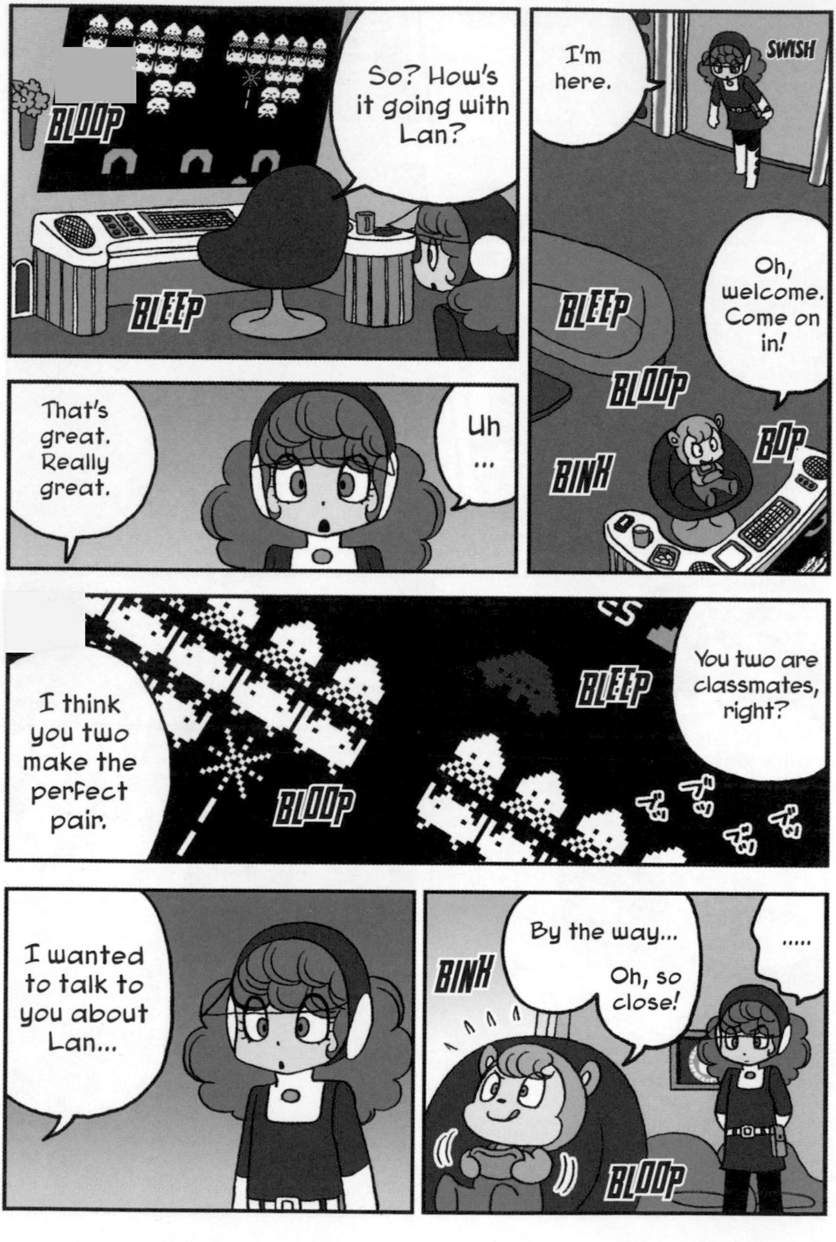
I'm here.
SWISH
Oh, welcome. Come on in!
BLEEP
BLOOP
BOP
BINK
So? How's it going with Lan?
BLOOP
BLEEP
Uh ...
That's great. Really great.
You two are classmates, right?
BLEEP
BLOOP
I think you two make the perfect pair.
.....
By the way...
Oh, so close!
BINK
BLOOP
I wanted to talk to you about Lan...

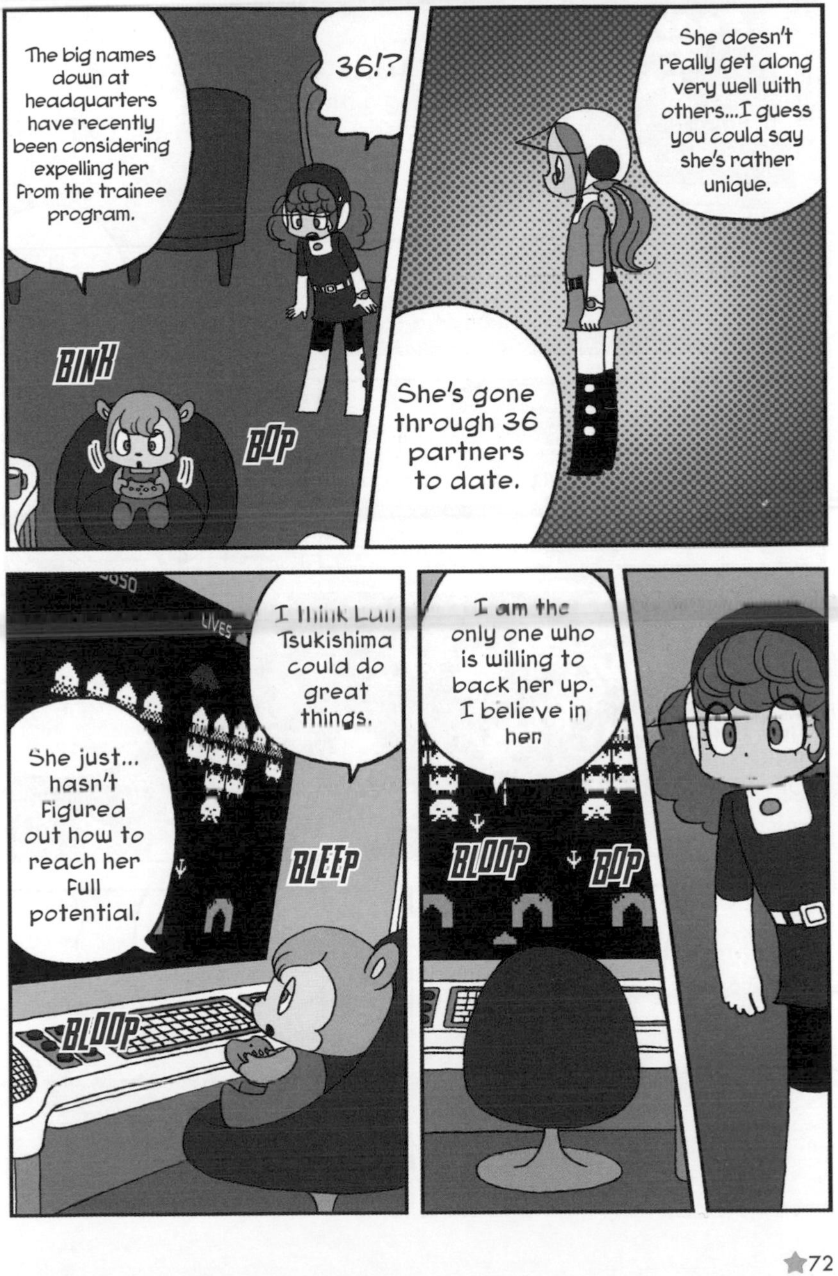
She doesn't really get along very well with others...I guess you could say she's rather unique.
She's gone through 36 partners to date.
36!?
The big names down at headquarters have recently been considering expelling her from the trainee program.
BINK
BOP
BLOOP
BOP
I am the only one who is willing to back her up. I believe in her
I think Luna Tsukishima could do great things.
She just... hasn't figured out how to reach her full potential.
BLEEP
BLOOP

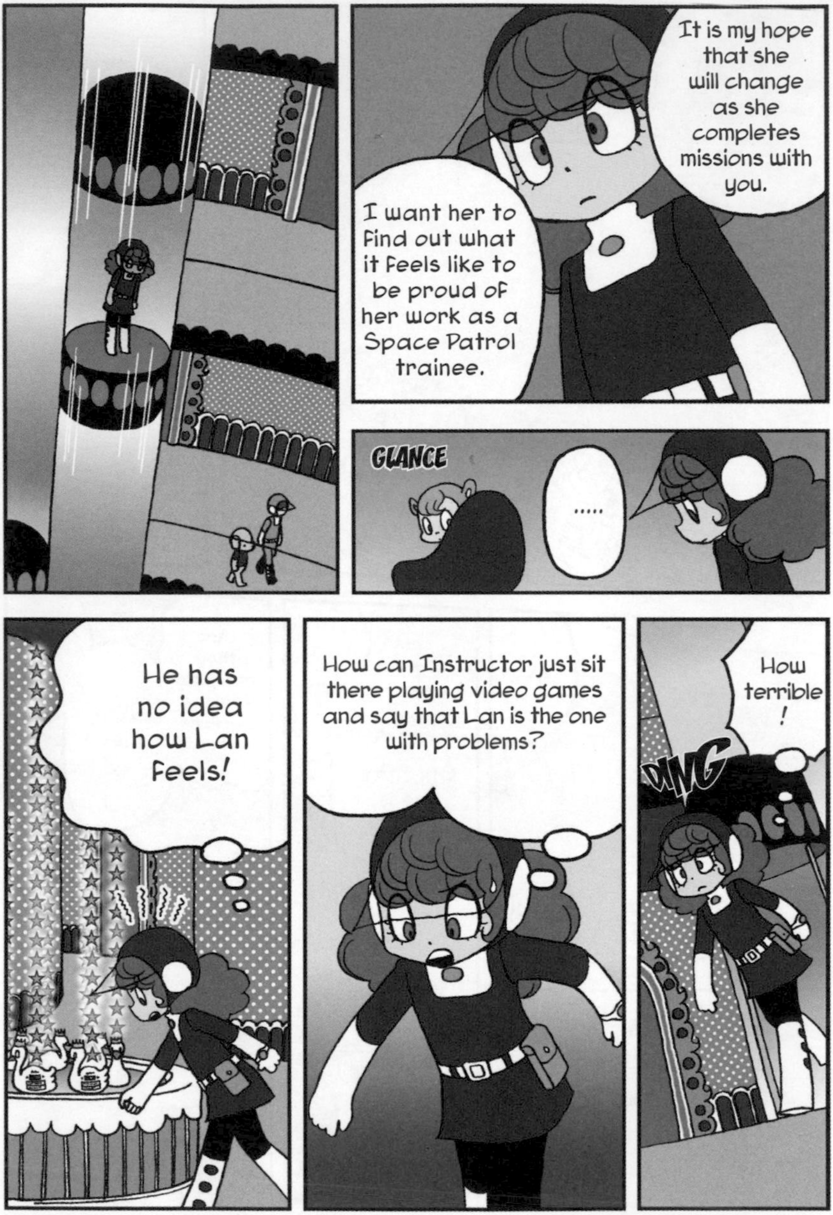
It is my hope that she will change as she completes missions with you.
I want her to find out what it feels like to be proud of her work as a Space Patrol trainee.
.....
GLANCE
How terrible!
DING
How can Instructor just sit there playing video games and say that Lan is the one with problems?
He has no idea how Lan feels!

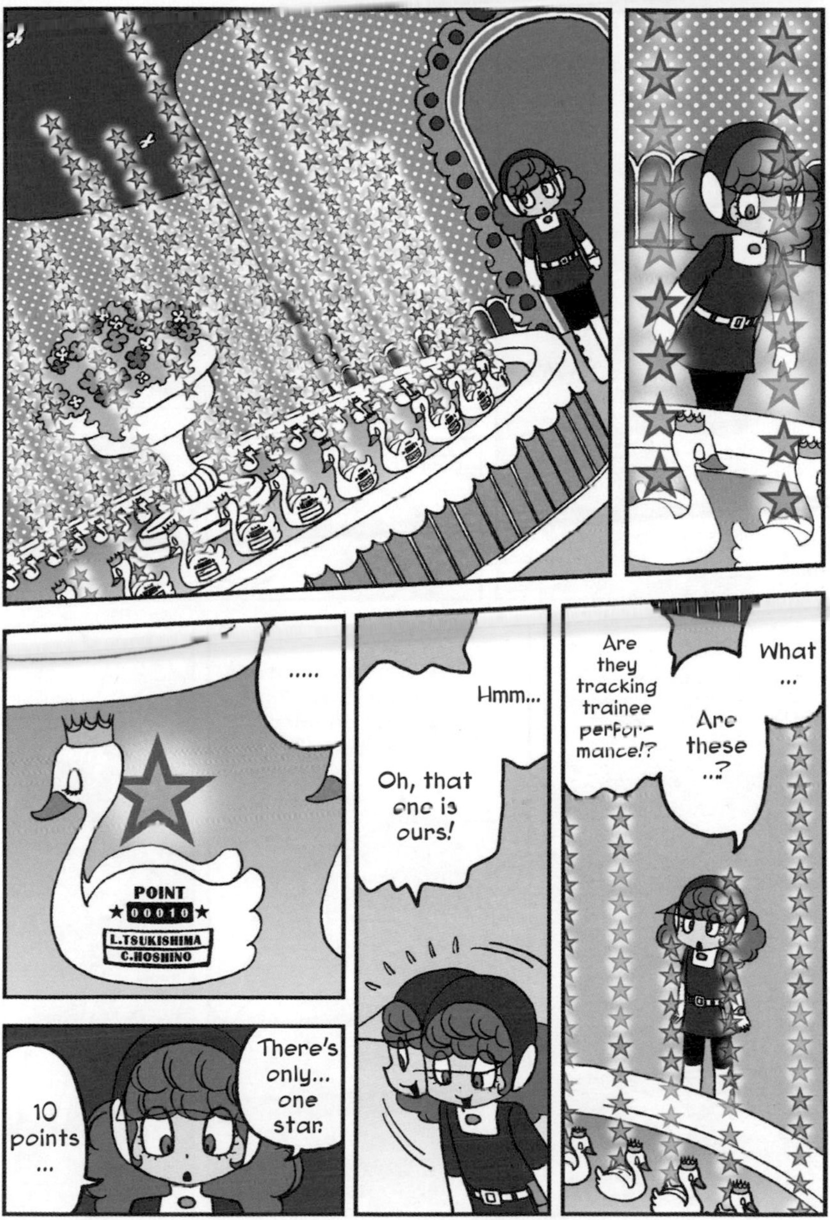
What ...
Are these ...?
Are they tracking trainee performance!?
Hmm...
Oh, that one is ours!
.....
POINT
00010
L.TSUKISHIMA
C.HOSHINO
There's only... one star.
10 points ...

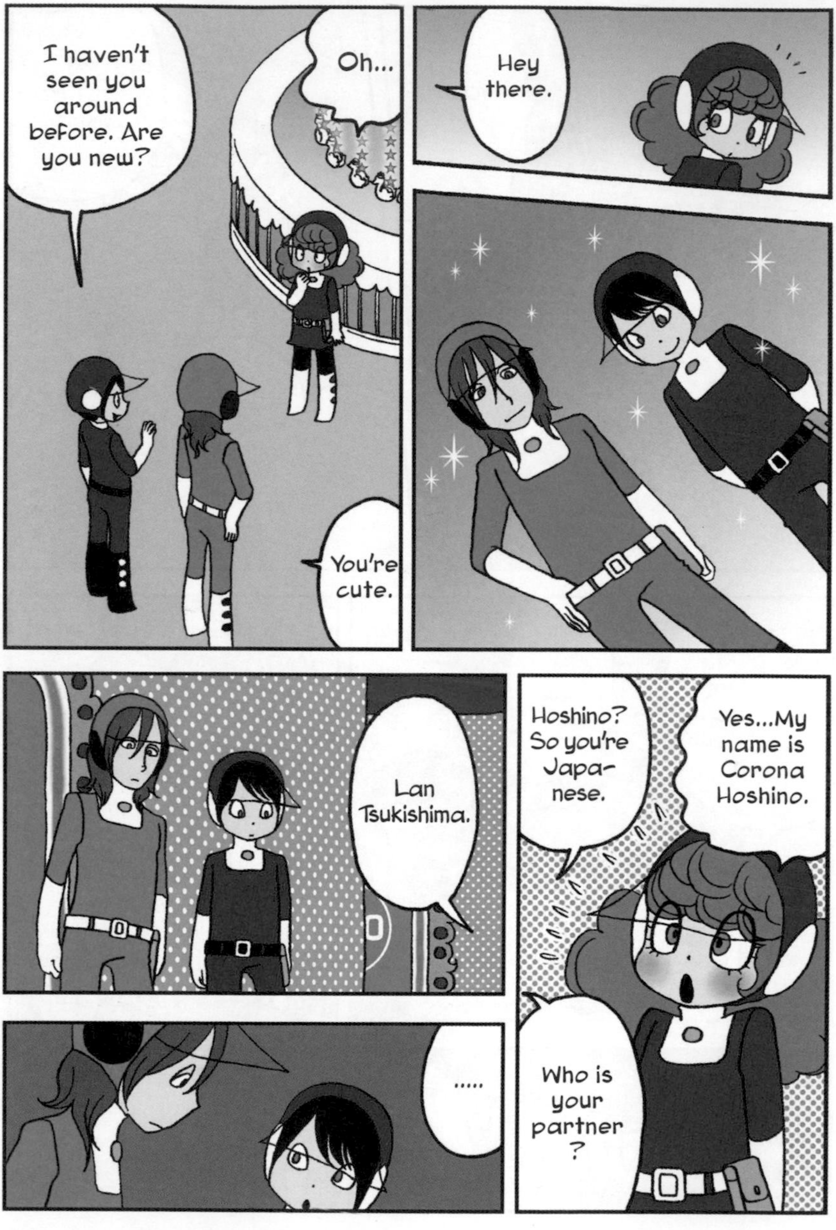
Hey there.
Oh...
I haven't seen you around before. Are you new?
You're cute.
Yes...My name is Corona Hoshino.
Hoshino? So you're Japa-nese.
Who is your partner?
Lan Tsukishima.
.....

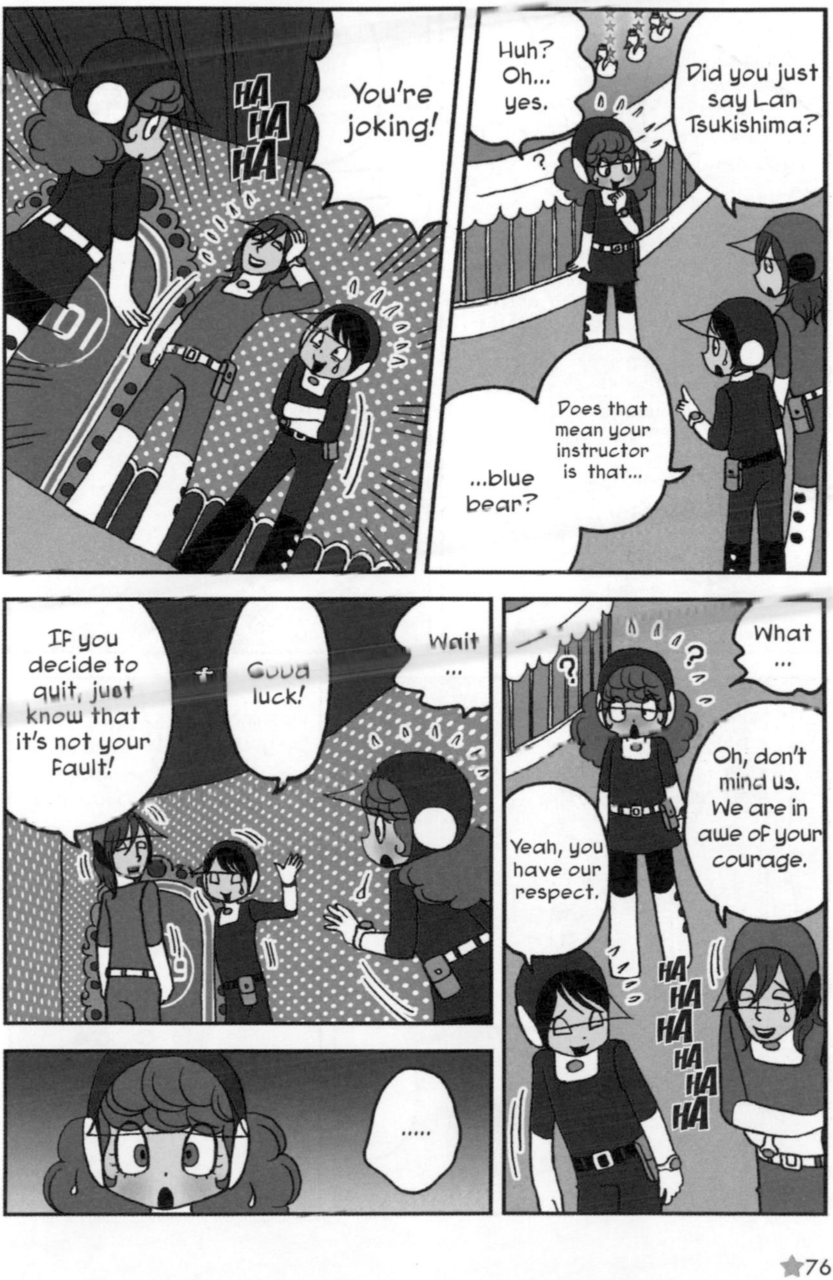
Did you just say Lan Tsukishima?
Huh? Oh... yes.
Does that mean your instructor is that...
...blue bear?
You're joking!
HA HA HA
What ...
Oh, don't mind us. We are in awe of your courage.
Yeah, you have our respect.
HA HA HA HA HA HA
Wait ...
Good luck!
If you decide to quit, just know that it's not your fault!
.....

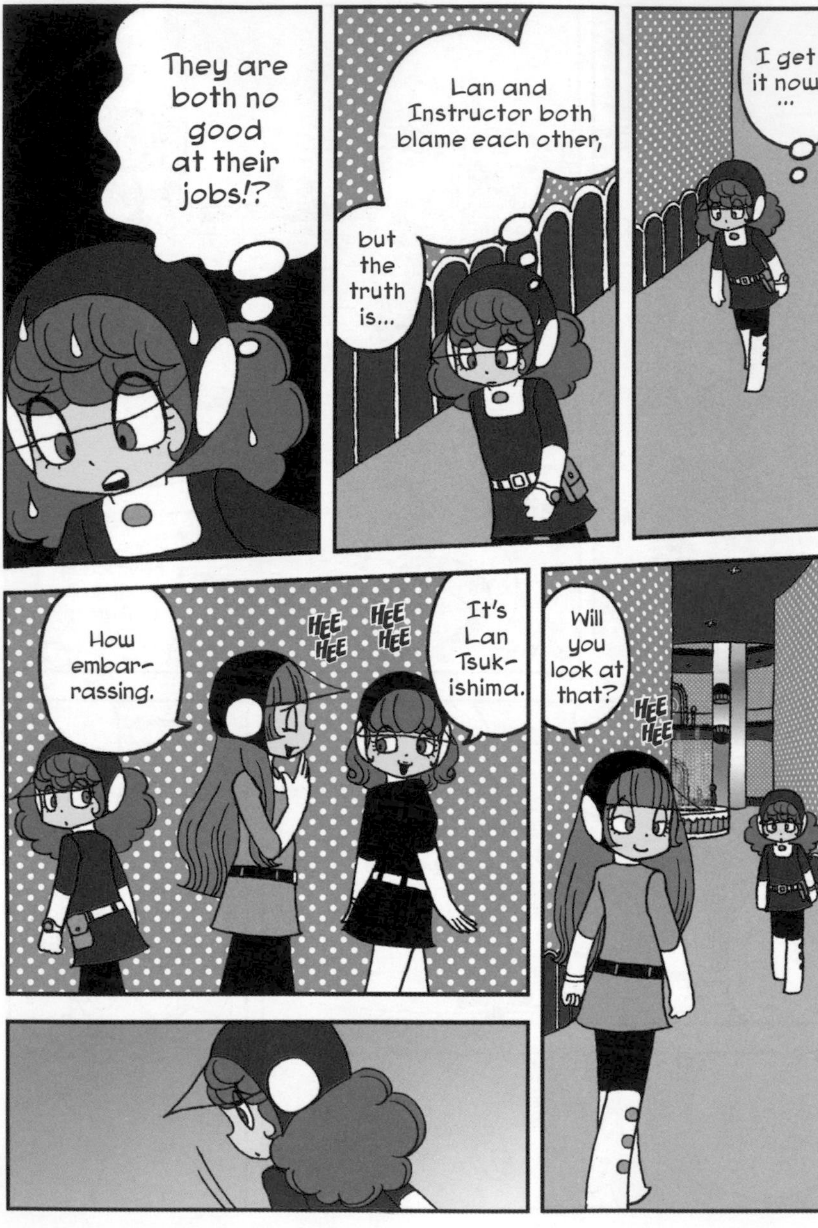
I get it now ...
Lan and Instructor both blame each other,
but the truth is...
They are both no good at their jobs!?
Will you look at that?
HEE HEE
It's Lan Tsuk-ishima.
HEE HEE
HEE HEE
How embar-rassing.

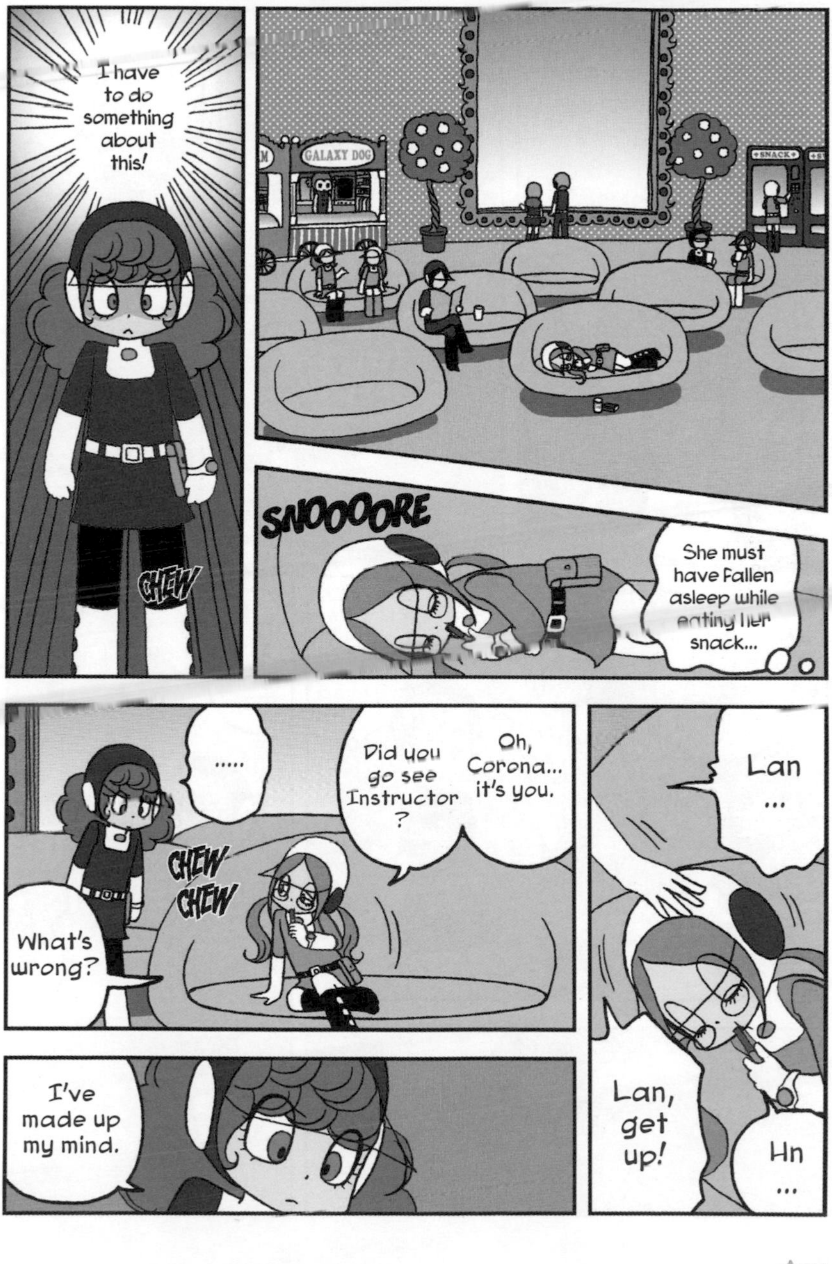
GALAXY DOG
SNACK
SNOOOORE
She must have fallen asleep while eating her snack...
I have to do something about this!
CHEW
Lan ...
Lan, get up!
Hn ...
Oh, Corona... it's you.
Did you go see Instructor ?
.....
CHEW CHEW
What's wrong?
I've made up my mind.

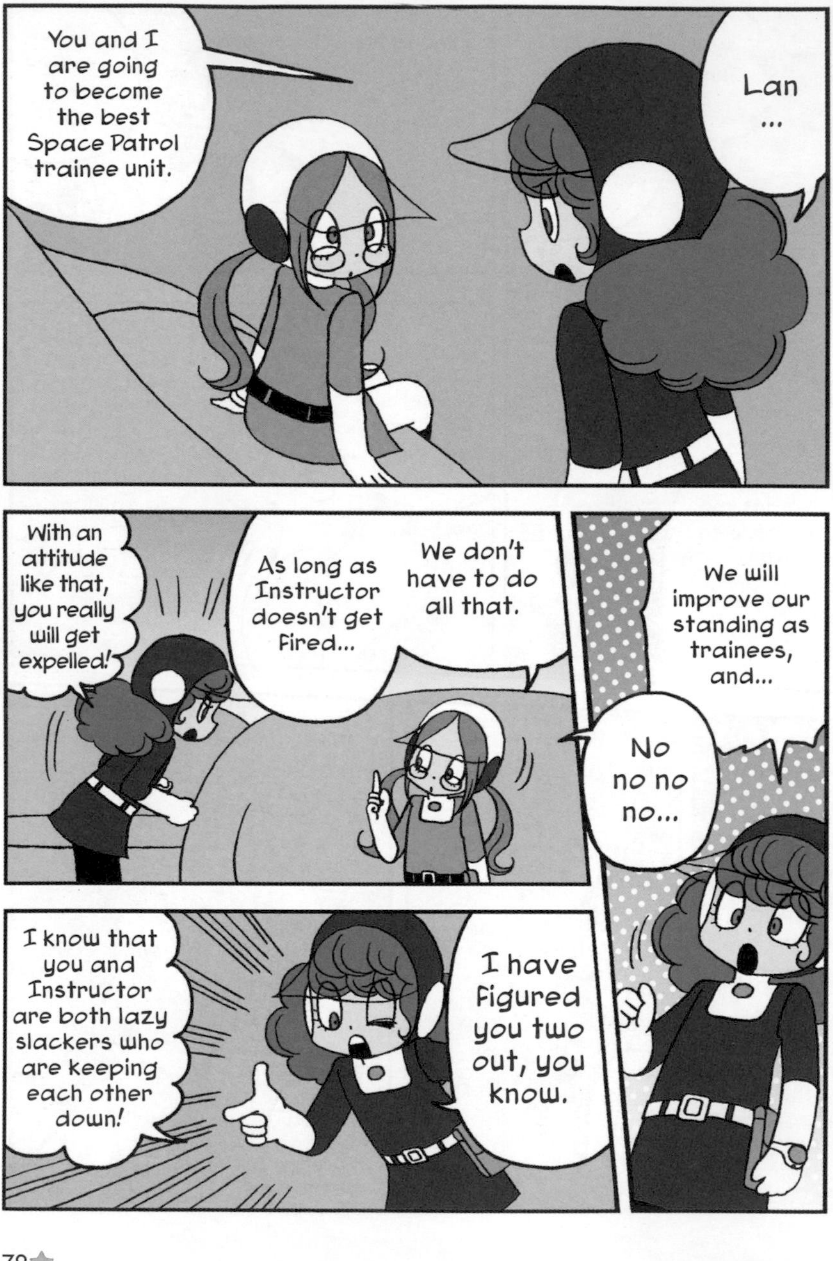
Lan ...
You and I are going to become the best Space Patrol trainee unit.
We will improve our standing as trainees, and...
No no no no...
We don't have to do all that.
As long as Instructor doesn't get fired...
With an attitude like that, you really will get expelled!
I have figured you two out, you know.
I know that you and Instructor are both lazy slackers who are keeping each other down!

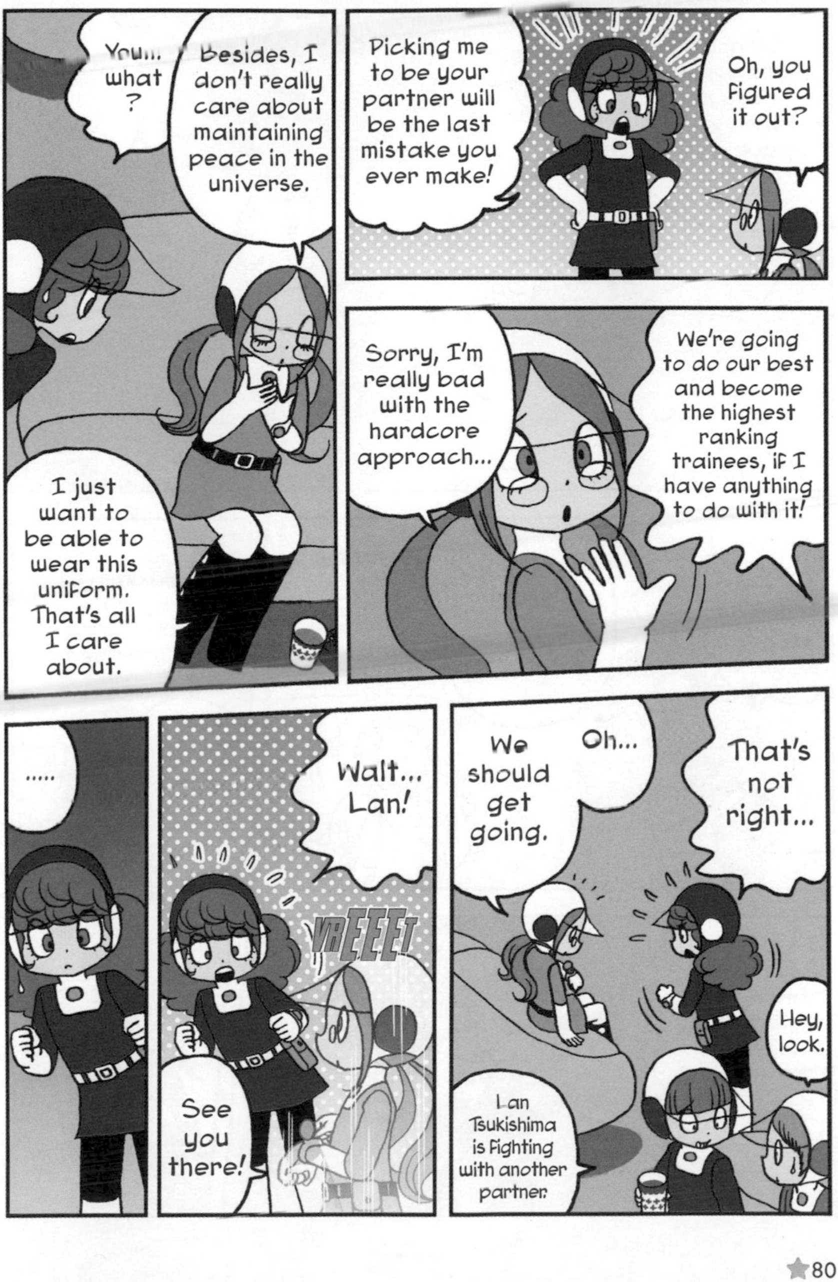
Oh, you figured it out?
Picking me to be your partner will be the last mistake you ever make!
We're going to do our best and become the highest ranking trainees, if I have anything to do with it!
Sorry, I'm really bad with the hardcore approach...
Besides, I don't really care about maintaining peace in the universe.
You... what?
I just want to be able to wear this uniform. That's all I care about.
That's not right...
Oh...
We should get going.
Hey, look.
Lan Tsukishima is fighting with another partner.
Walt... Lan!
VREEET
See you there!
.....

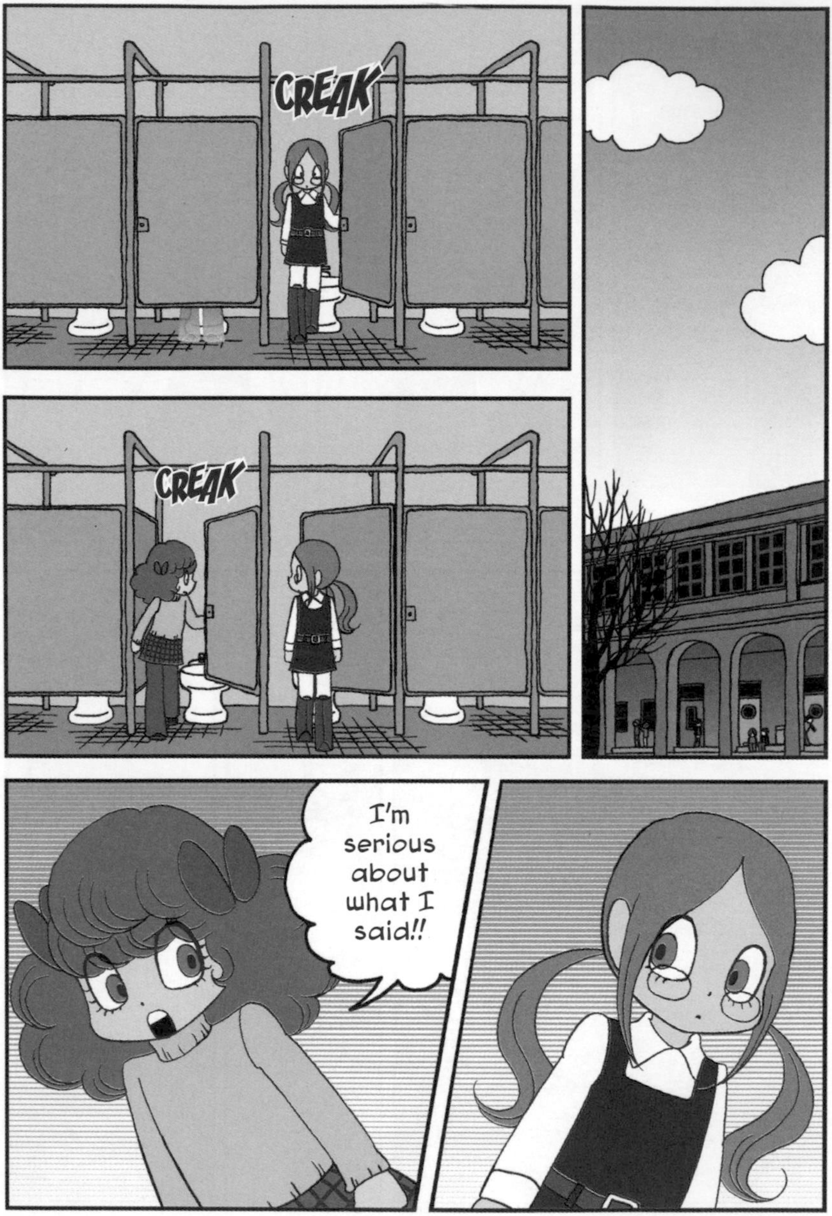
CREAK
CREAK
I'm serious about what I said!!

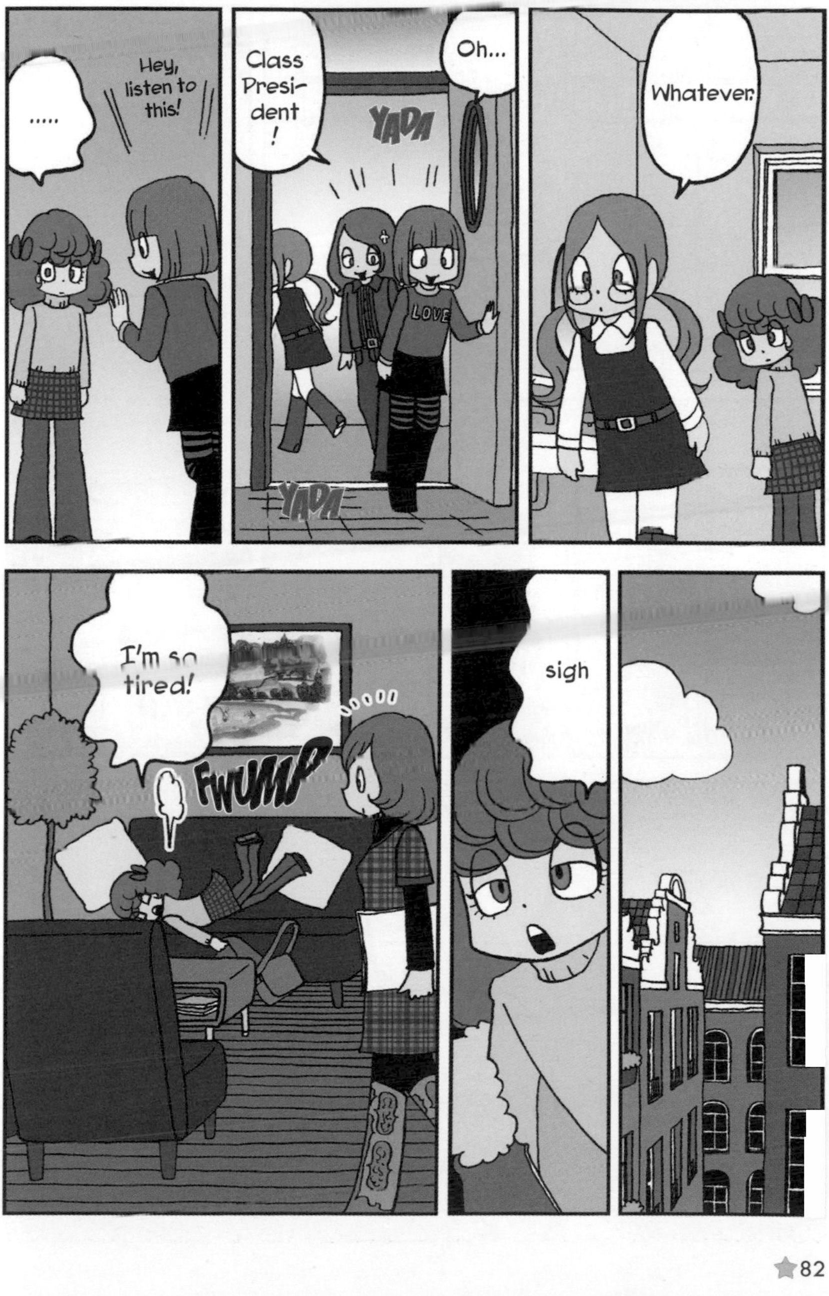
Whatever.
Oh...
YADA
Class President!
YADA
Hey, listen to this!
.....
sigh
I'm so tired!
FWUMP

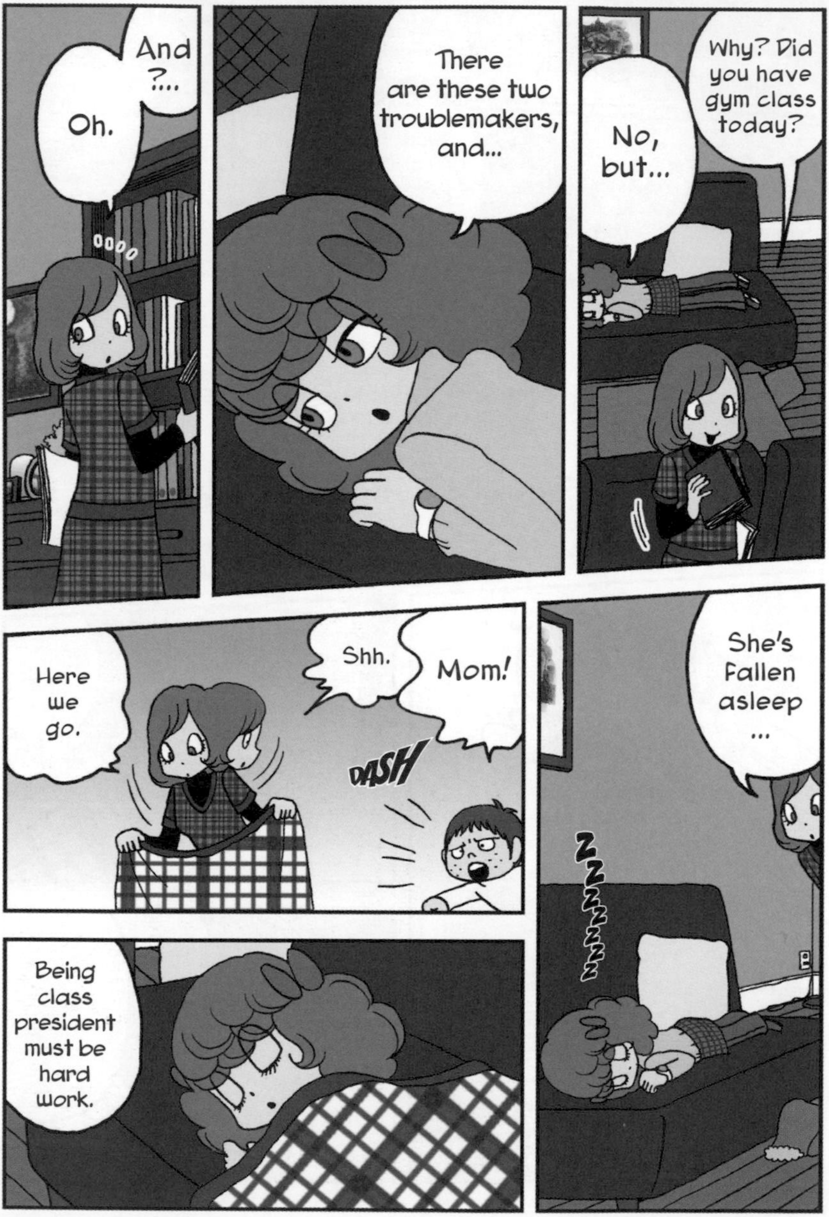

Why? Did you have gym class today?
No, but...
There are these two troublemakers, and...
And ?....
Oh.
She's fallen asleep ...
ZZZZZZZ
Mom!
Shh.
Here we go.
DASH
Being class president must be hard work.

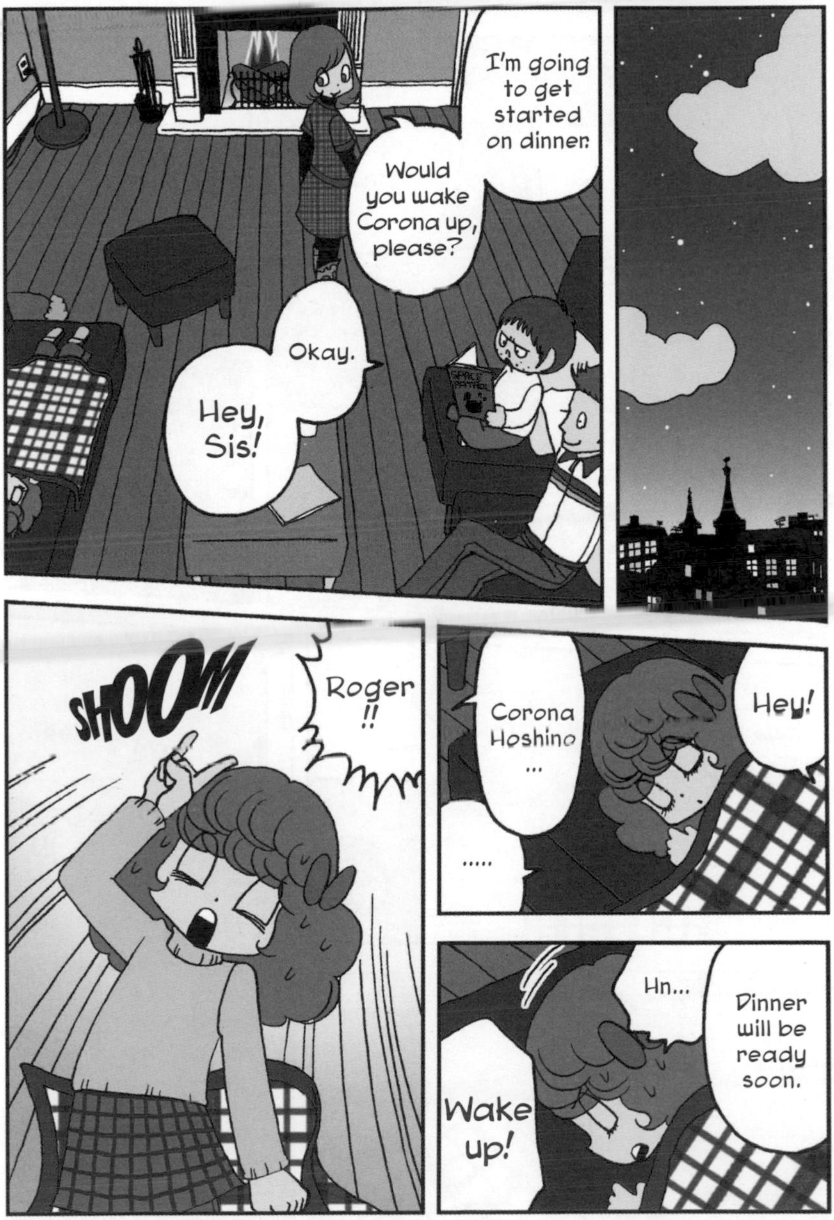
I'm going to get started on dinner.
Would you wake Corona up, please?
Okay.
Hey, Sis!
Hey!
Corona Hoshino ...
.....
Dinner will be ready soon.
Hn...
Wake up!
Roger !!
SHOOM

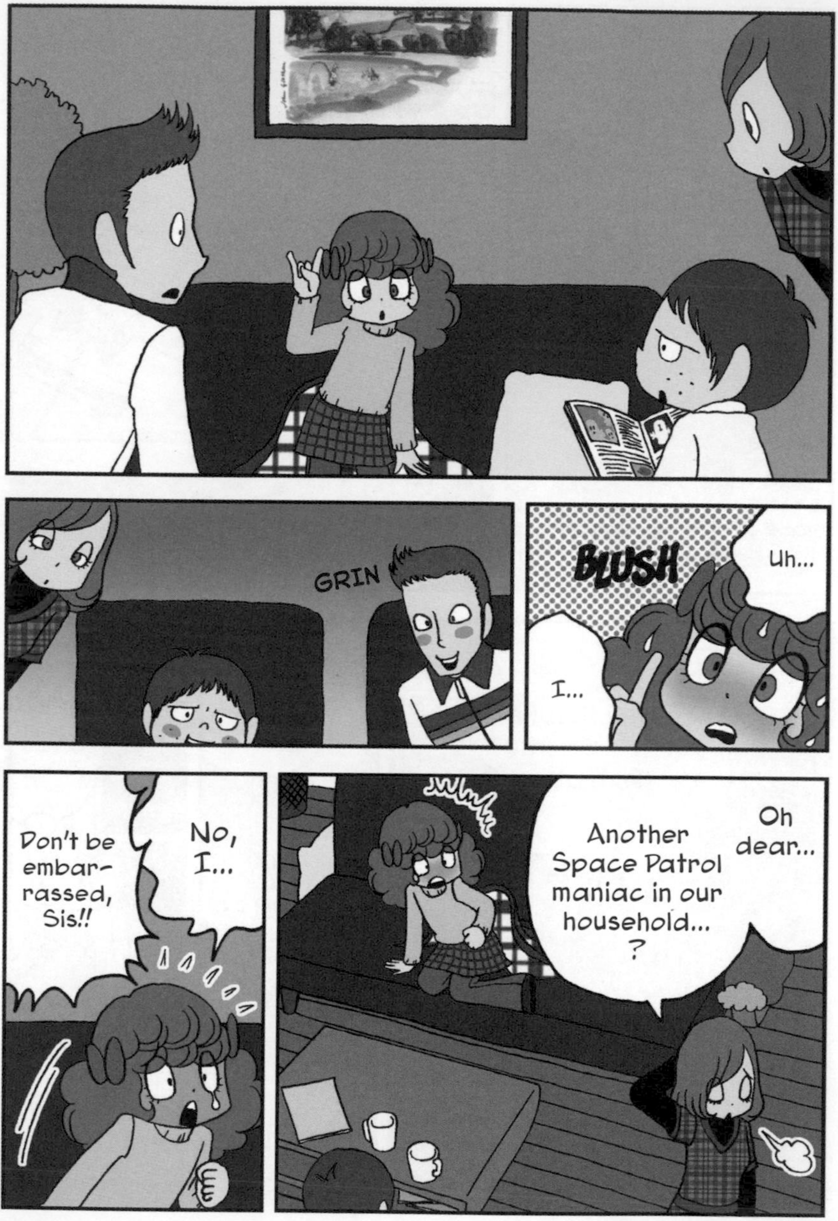
BLUSH
Uh...
I...
GRIN
Oh dear...
Another Space Patrol maniac in our household... ?
No, I...
Don't be embarrassed, Sis!!

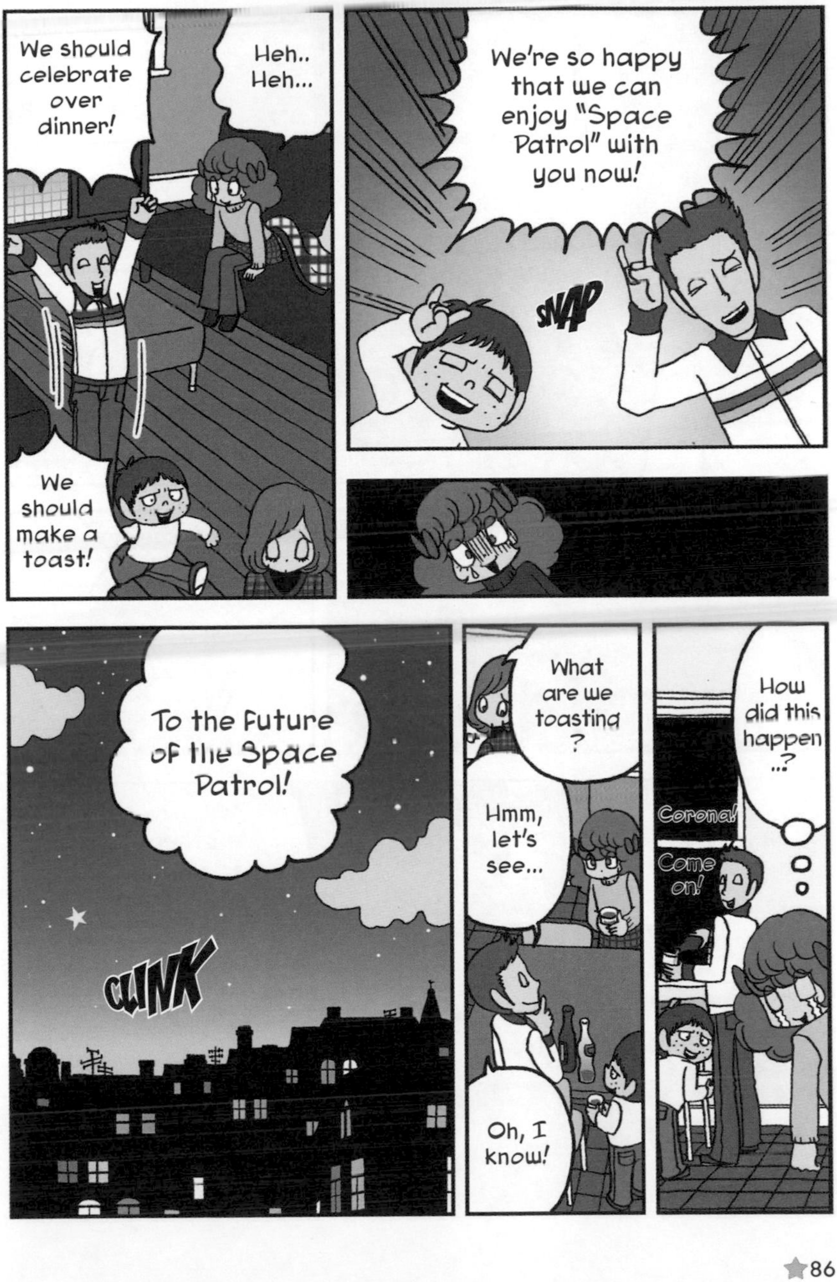
We're so happy that we can enjoy "Space Patrol" with you now!
SNAP
Heh.. Heh...
We should celebrate over dinner!
We should make a toast!
How did this happen ..?
Corona!
Come on!
What are we toasting ?
Hmm, let's see...
Oh, I know!
To the future of the Space Patrol!
CLINK

SWANS IN SPACE

CHAPTER 3
CORONA HUSTLE

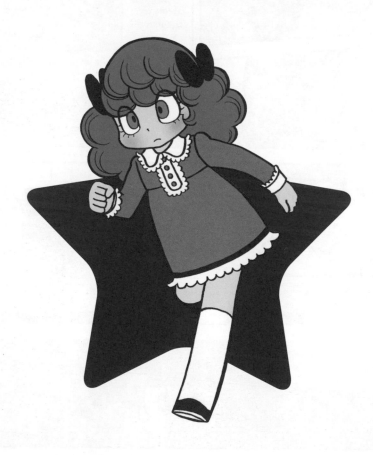

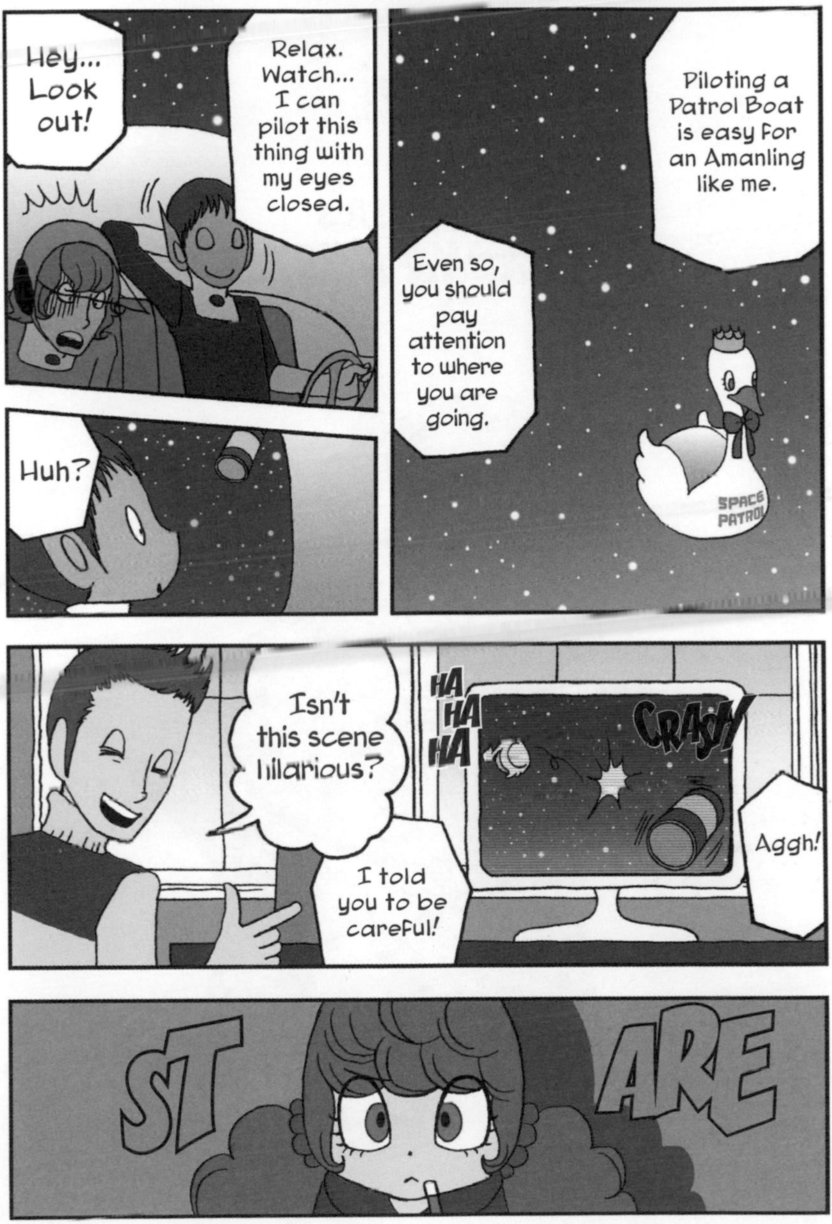
Hey... Look out!
Relax. Watch... I can pilot this thing with my eyes closed.
Piloting a Patrol Boat is easy for an Amanling like me.
Even so, you should pay attention to where you are going.
SPACE PATROL
Huh?
Isn't this scene hilarious?
HA HA HA
CRASH
Aggh!
I told you to be careful!
ST ARE

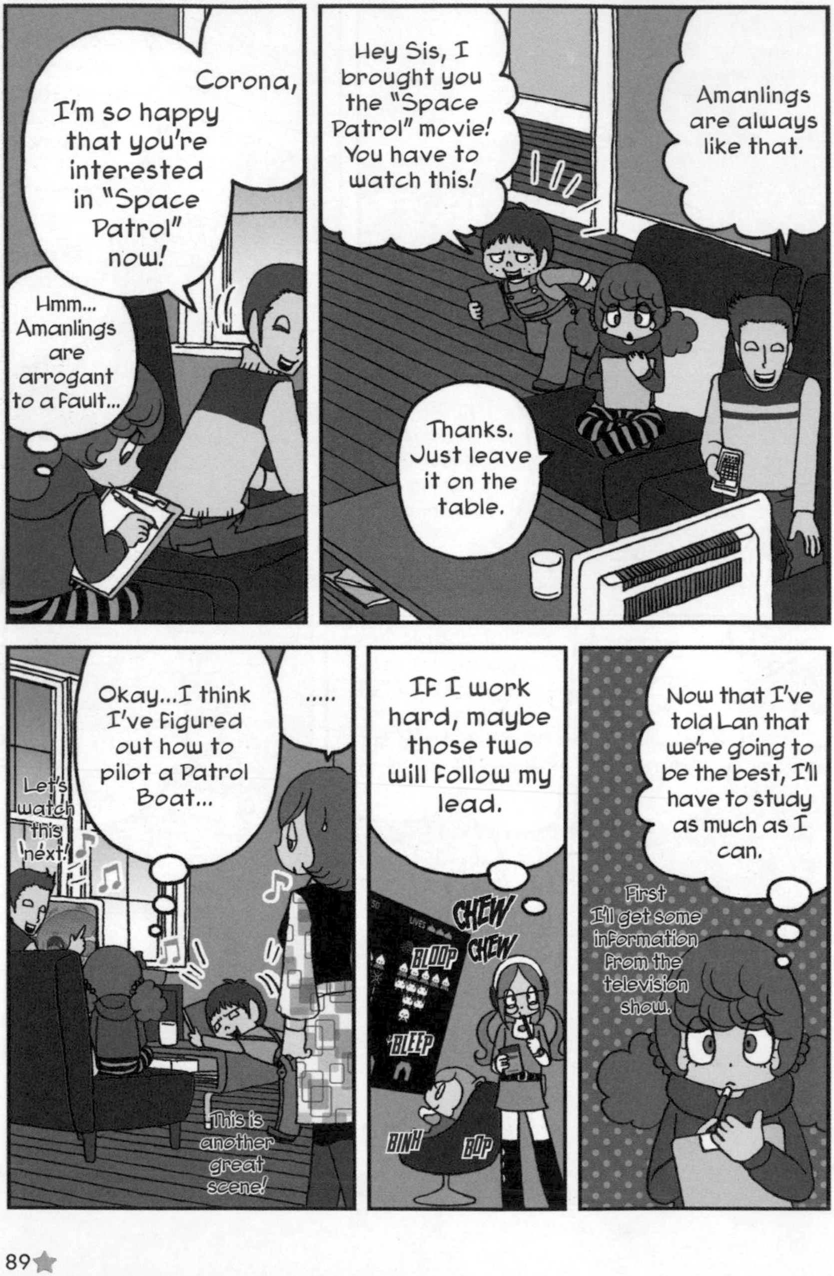
Amanlings are always like that.
Hey Sis, I brought you the "Space Patrol" movie! You have to watch this!
Thanks. Just leave it on the table.
Corona, I'm so happy that you're interested in "Space Patrol" now!
Hmm... Amanlings are arrogant to a fault...
Now that I've told Lan that we're going to be the best, I'll have to study as much as I can.
First I'll get some information from the television show.
If I work hard, maybe those two will follow my lead.
CHEW
CHEW
BLOOP
BLEEP
BINK
BOP
.....
Okay...I think I've figured out how to pilot a Patrol Boat...
Let's watch this next!
This is another great scene!

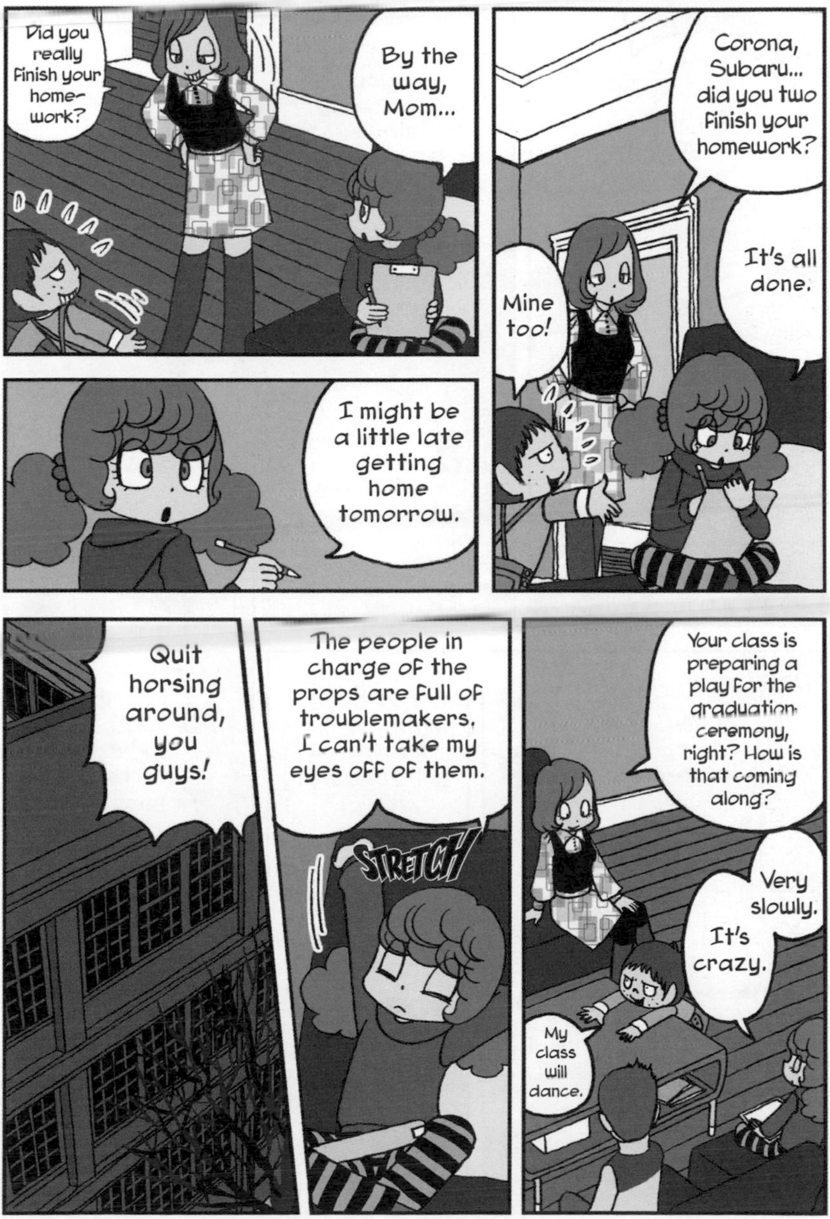
Corona, Subaru... did you two finish your homework?
It's all done.
Mine too!
By the way, Mom...
Did you really finish your home-work?
I might be a little late getting home tomorrow.
Your class is preparing a play for the graduation ceremony, right? How is that coming along?
Very slowly.
It's crazy.
My class will dance.
The people in charge of the props are full of troublemakers. I can't take my eyes off of them.
STRETCH
Quit horsing around, you guys!

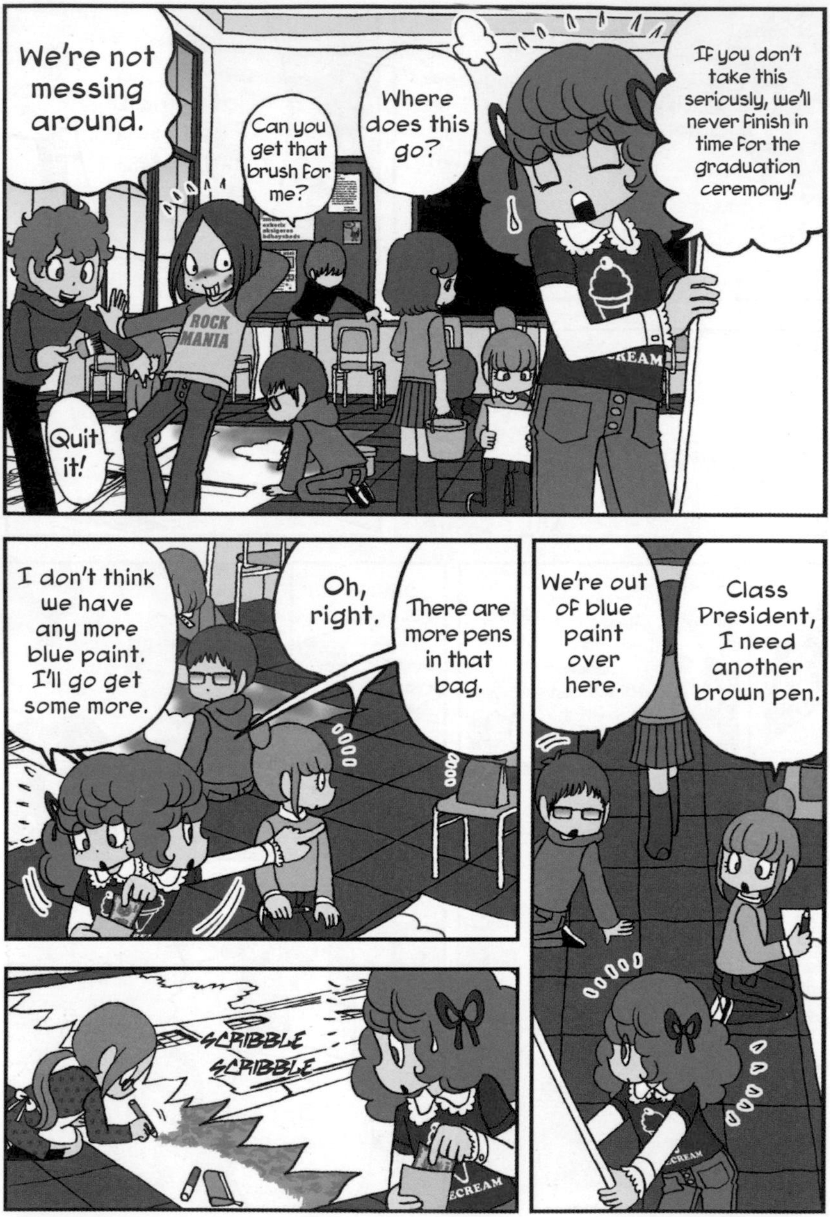
If you don't take this seriously, we'll never finish in time for the graduation ceremony!
Where does this go?
Can you get that brush for me?
We're not messing around.
ROCK MANIA
Quit it!
Class President, I need another brown pen.
We're out of blue paint over here.
There are more pens in that bag.
Oh, right.
I don't think we have any more blue paint. I'll go get some more.
SCRIBBLE
SCRIBBLE

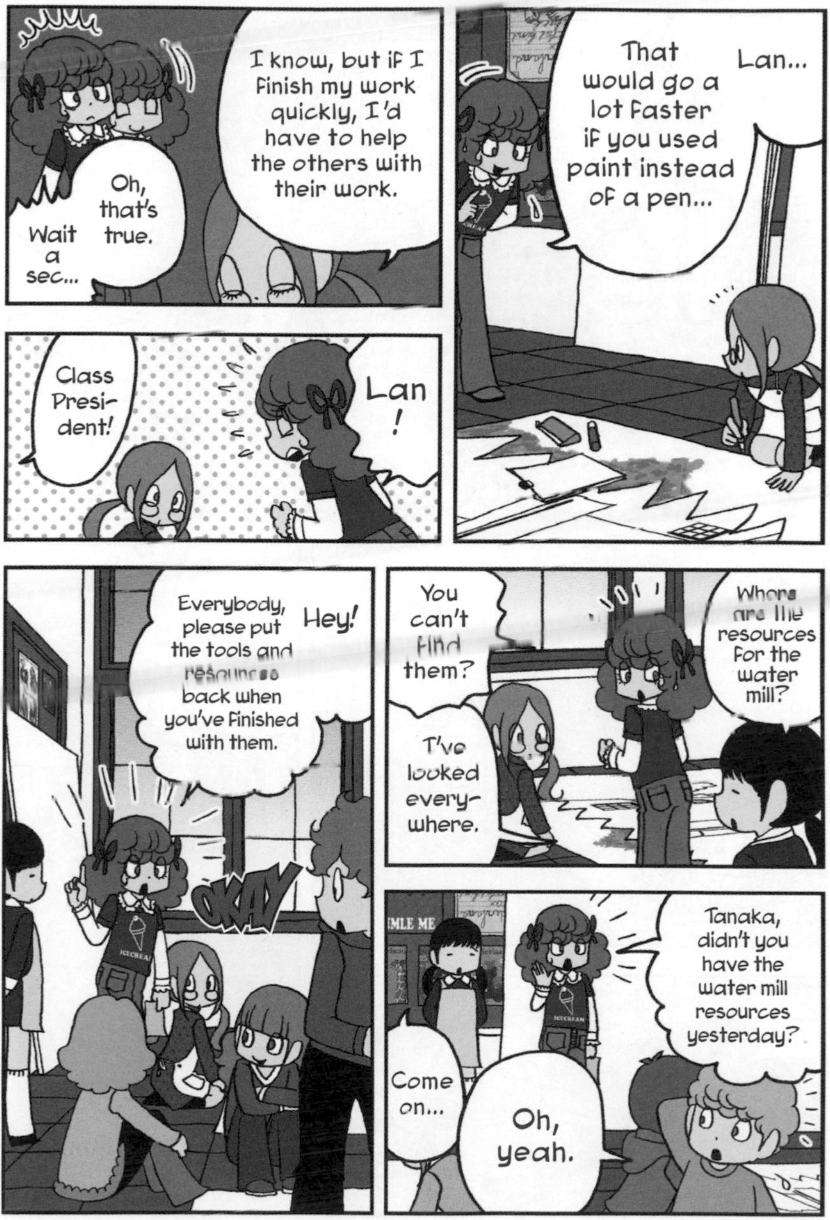
Lan...
That would go a lot faster if you used paint instead of a pen...
I know, but if I finish my work quickly, I'd have to help the others with their work.
Oh, that's true.
Wait a sec...
Lan!
Class President!
Where are the resources for the water mill?
You can't find them?
I've looked everywhere.
Tanaka, didn't you have the water mill resources yesterday?
Oh, yeah.
Come on...
Hey!
Everybody, please put the tools and resources back when you've finished with them.
OKAY

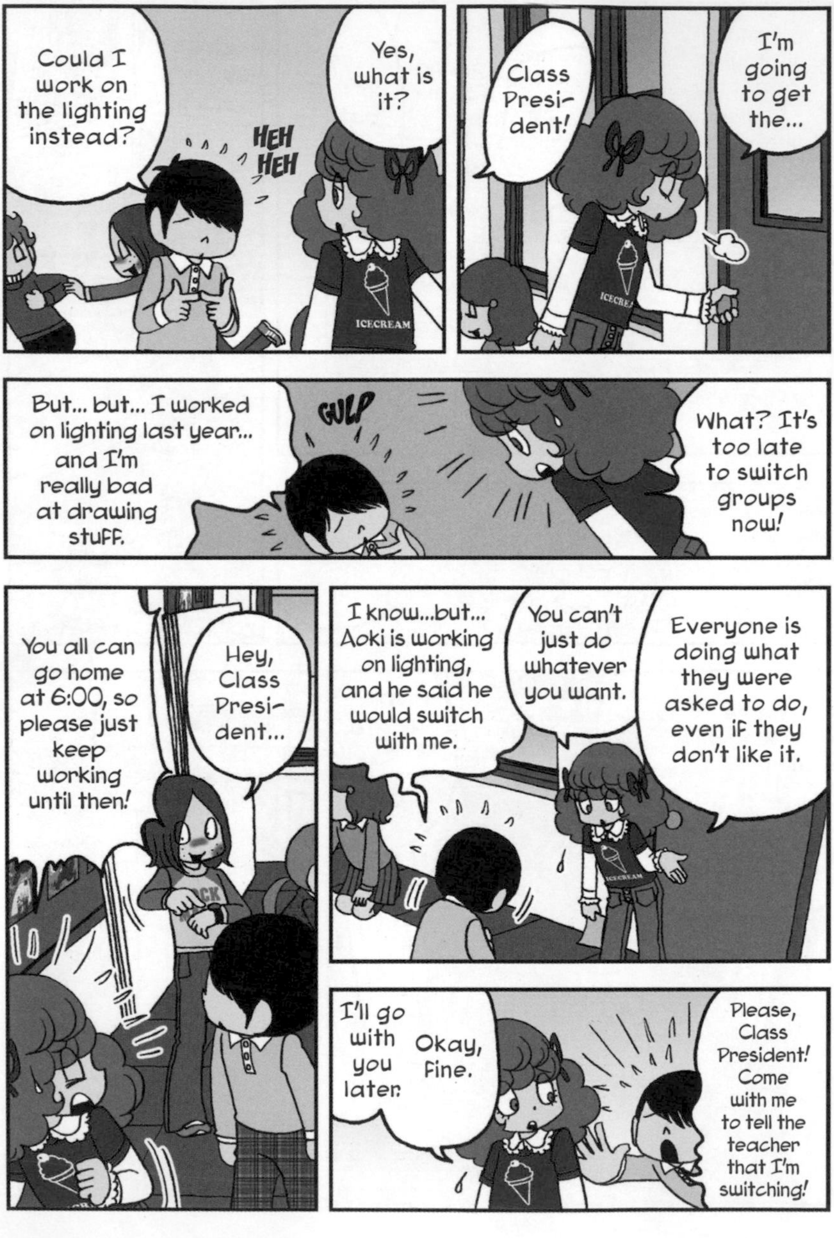
I'm going to get the...
Class President!
Yes, what is it?
HEH HEH
Could I work on the lighting instead?
What? It's too late to switch groups now!
GULP
But... but... I worked on lighting last year... and I'm really bad at drawing stuff.
Everyone is doing what they were asked to do, even if they don't like it.
You can't just do whatever you want.
I know...but... Aoki is working on lighting, and he said he would switch with me.
Please, Class President! Come with me to tell the teacher that I'm switching!
Okay, fine.
I'll go with you later.
Hey, Class President...
You all can go home at 6:00, so please just keep working until then!

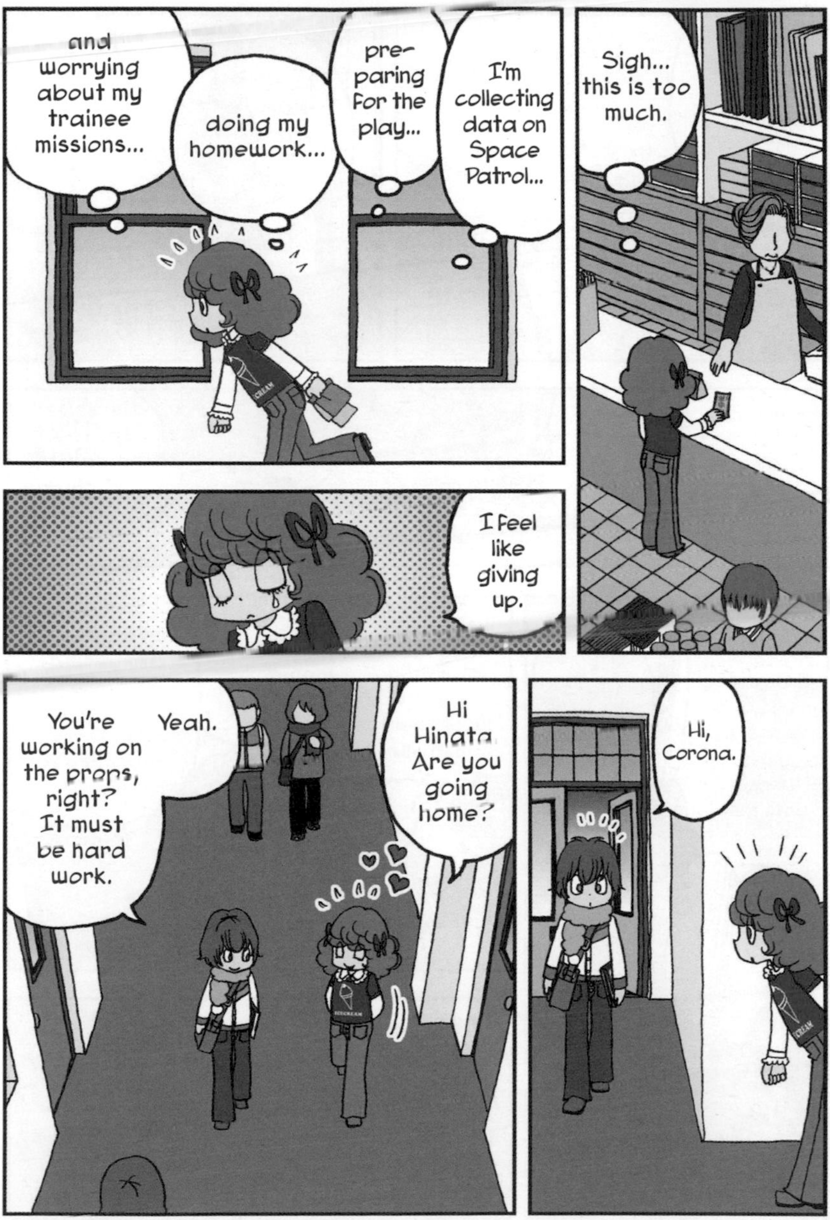
Sigh... this is too much.
I'm collecting data on Space Patrol...
pre-paring for the play...
doing my homework...
and worrying about my trainee missions...
I feel like giving up.
Hi, Corona.
Hi Hinata. Are you going home?
Yeah.
You're working on the props, right? It must be hard work.

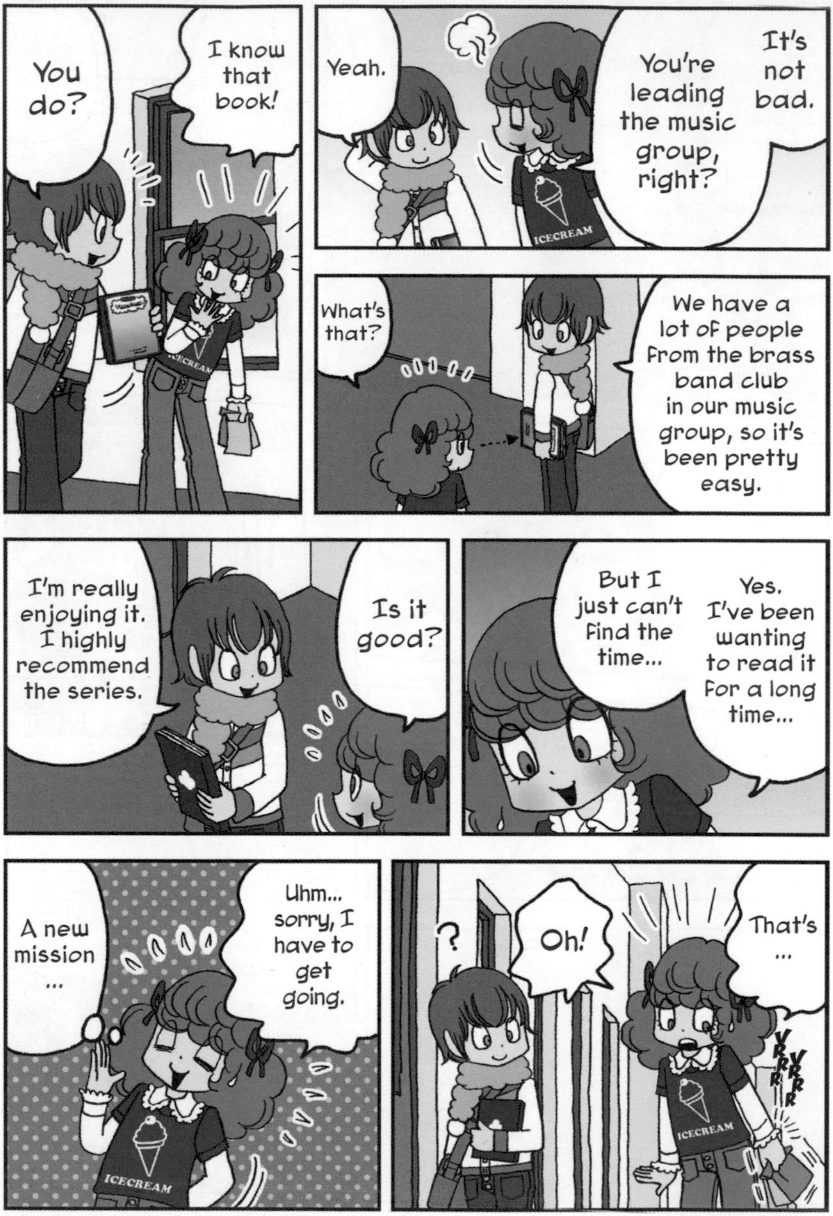
It's not bad.
You're leading the music group, right?
Yeah.
We have a lot of people from the brass band club in our music group, so it's been pretty easy.
What's that?
I know that book!
You do?
Yes. I've been wanting to read it for a long time...
But I just can't find the time...
Is it good?
I'm really enjoying it. I highly recommend the series.
That's ...
Oh!
?
VRRR VRRR
Uhm... sorry, I have to get going.
A new mission ...

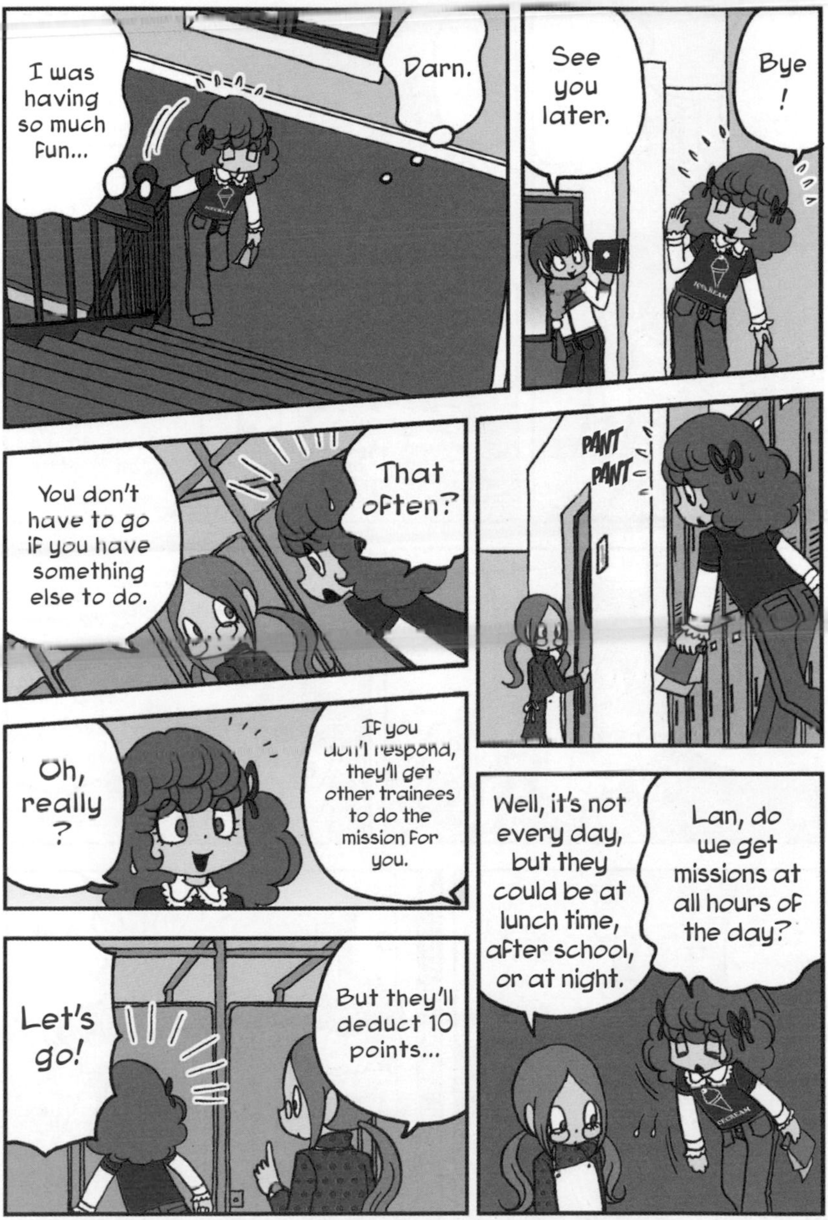

Bye!
See you later.
Darn.
I was having so much fun...
PANT PANT
Lan, do we get missions at all hours of the day?
Well, it's not every day, but they could be at lunch time, after school, or at night.
That often?
You don't have to go if you have something else to do.
If you don't respond, they'll get other trainees to do the mission for you.
Oh, really?
But they'll deduct 10 points...
Let's go!

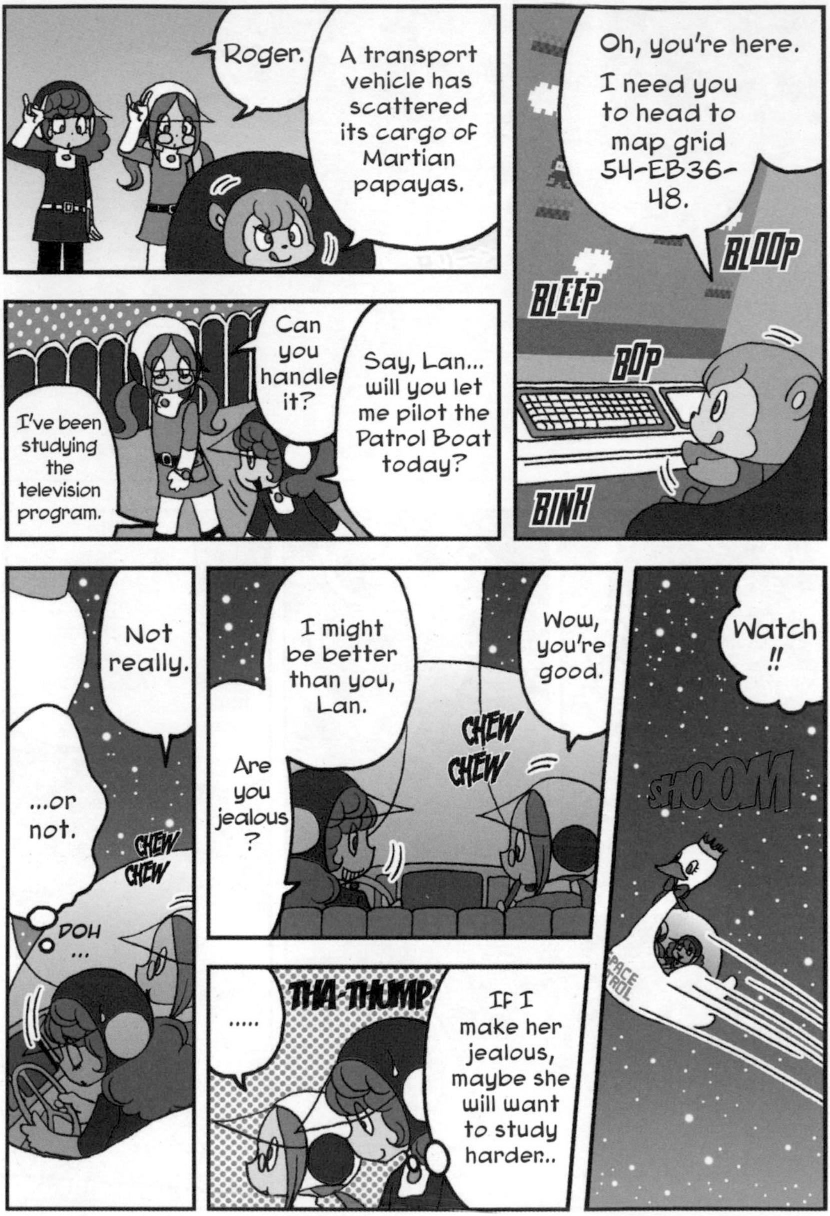
Oh, you're here.
I need you to head to map grid 54-EB36-48.
BLOOP
BLEEP
BOP
BINK
A transport vehicle has scattered its cargo of Martian papayas.
Roger.
Say, Lan... will you let me pilot the Patrol Boat today?
Can you handle it?
I've been studying the television program.
Watch !!
SHOOM
Wow, you're good.
I might be better than you, Lan.
CHEW CHEW
Are you jealous ?
If I make her jealous, maybe she will want to study harder...
THA-THUMP
.....
Not really.
...or not.
CHEW CHEW
DOH ...

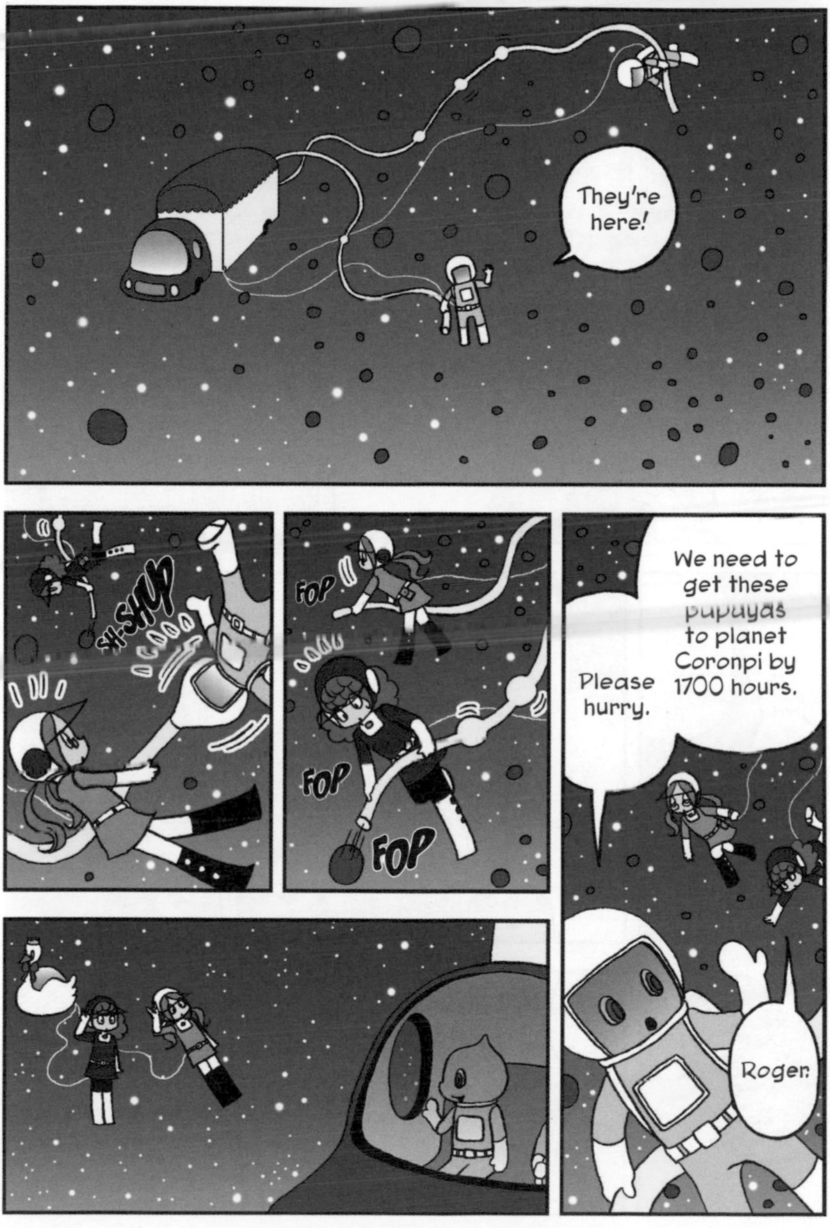
They're here!
We need to get these papayas to planet Coronpi by 1700 hours.
Please hurry.
Roger.
FOP
FOP
FOP
SH-SHUP

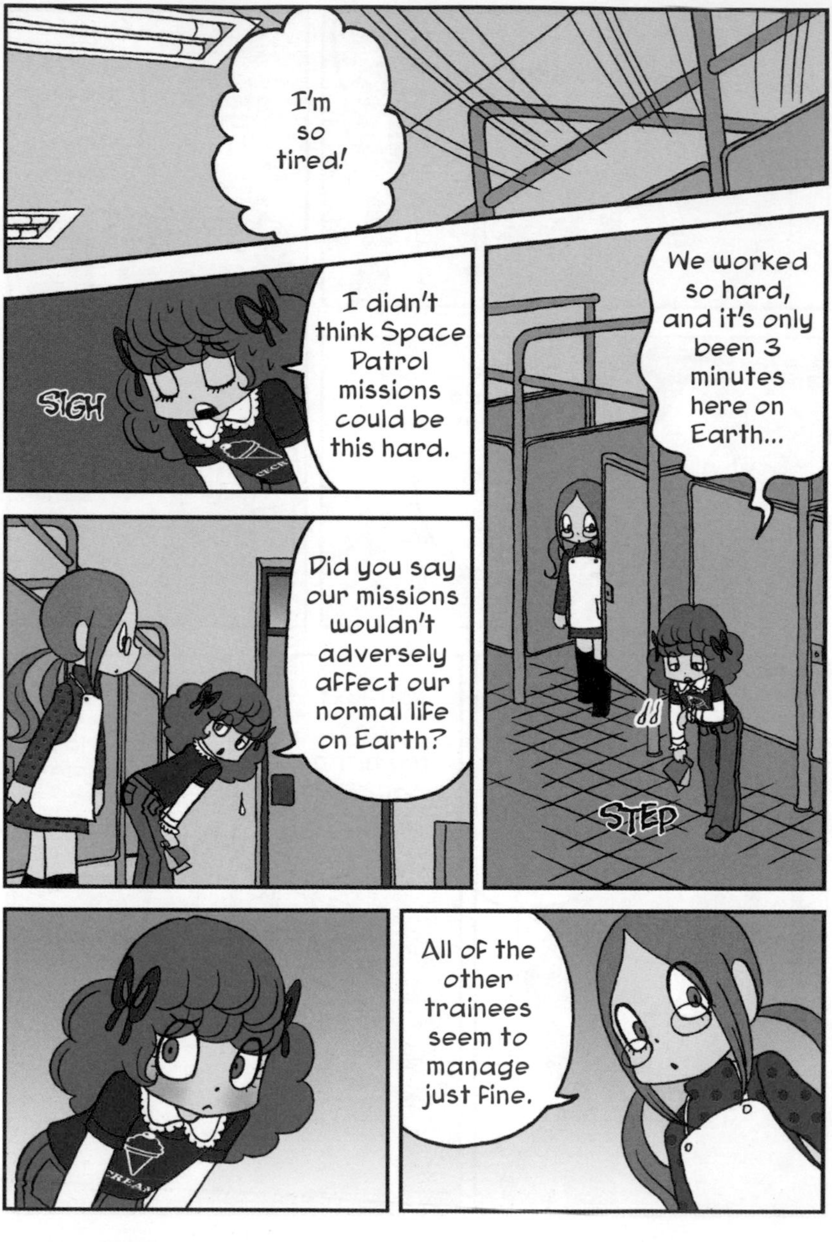
I'm so tired!
We worked so hard, and it's only been 3 minutes here on Earth...
STEP
I didn't think Space Patrol missions could be this hard.
SIGH
Did you say our missions wouldn't adversely affect our normal life on Earth?
All of the other trainees seem to manage just fine.

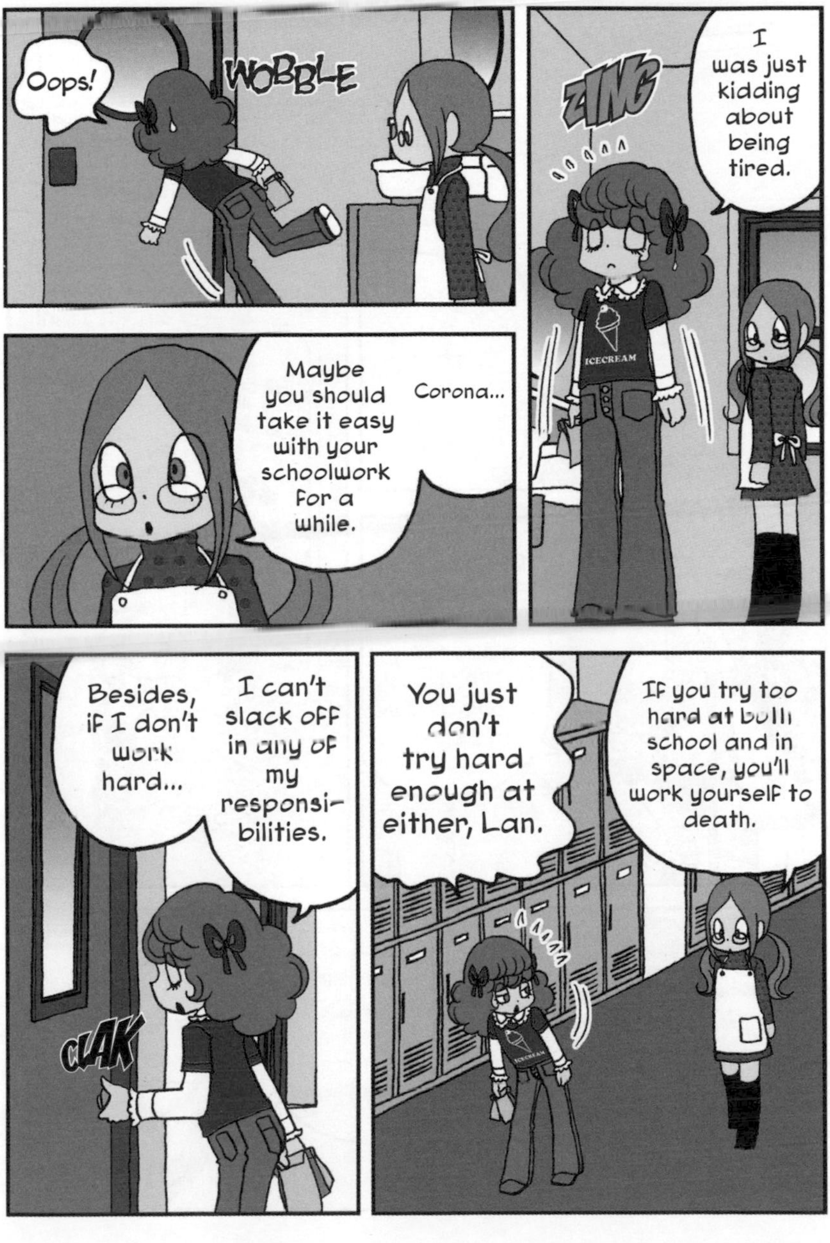
ZING
I was just kidding about being tired.
WOBBLE
Oops!
Corona...
Maybe you should take it easy with your schoolwork for a while.
If you try too hard at both school and in space, you'll work yourself to death.
You just don't try hard enough at either, Lan.
I can't slack off in any of my responsi-bilities.
Besides, if I don't work hard...
CLAK

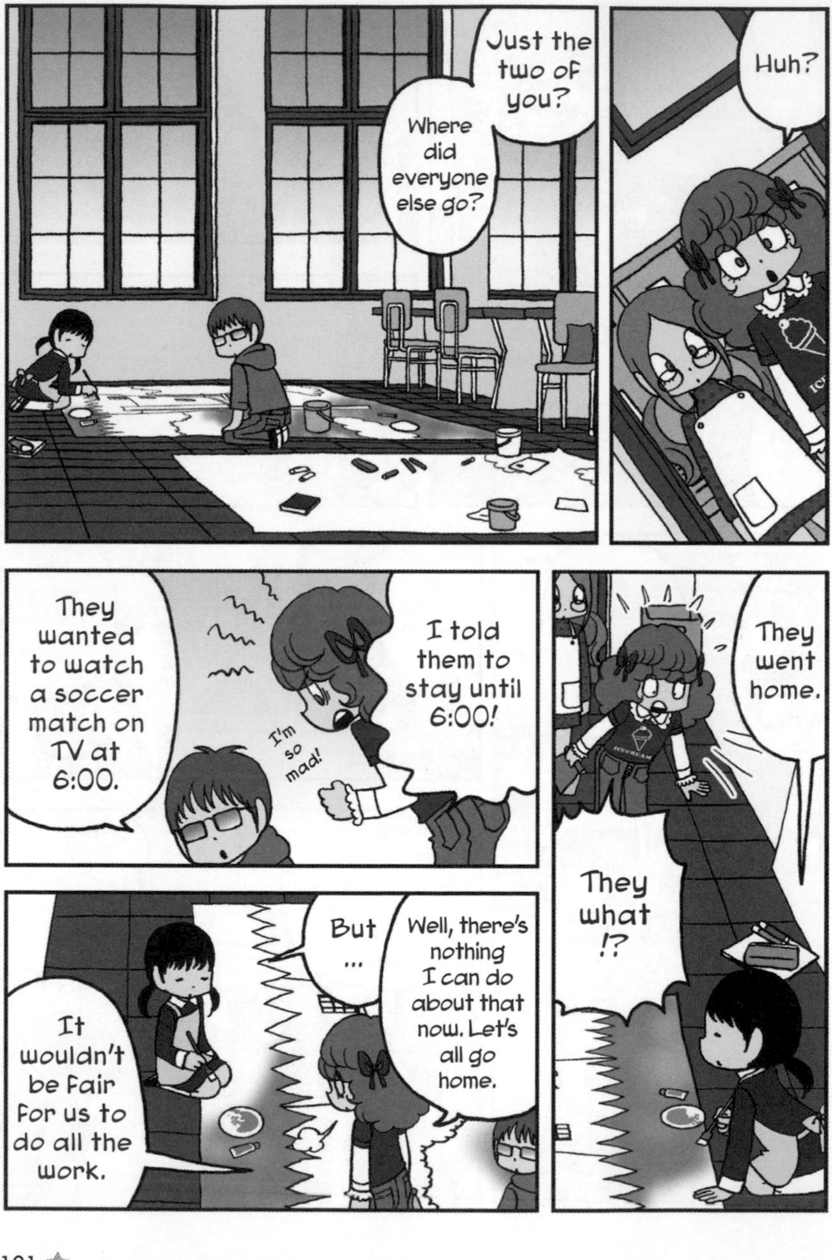
Huh?
Just the two of you?
Where did everyone else go?
They went home.
They what!?
I told them to stay until 6:00!
I'm so mad!
They wanted to watch a soccer match on TV at 6:00.
Well, there's nothing I can do about that now. Let's all go home.
But ...
It wouldn't be fair for us to do all the work.

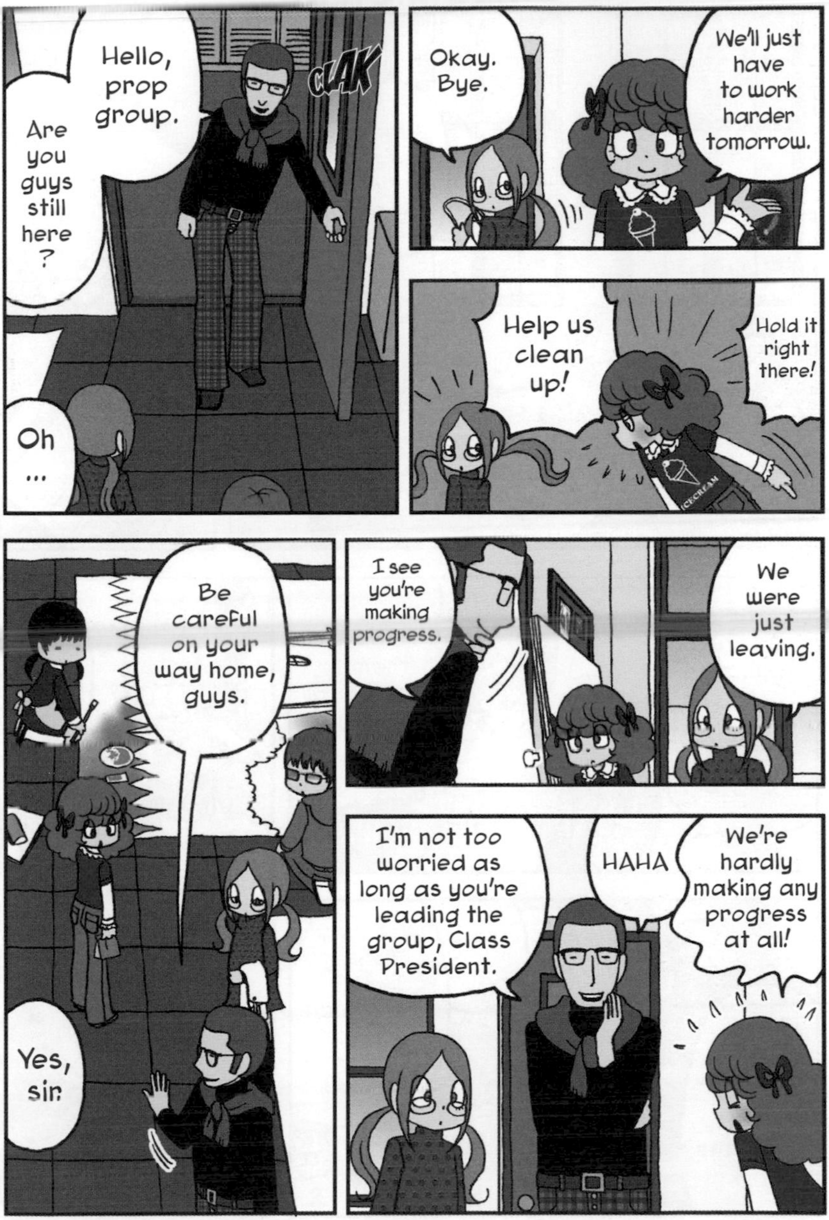
We'll just have to work harder tomorrow.
Okay. Bye.
Hold it right there!
Help us clean up!
CLAK
Hello, prop group.
Are you guys still here?
Oh ...
We were just leaving.
I see you're making progress.
We're hardly making any progress at all!
HAHA
I'm not too worried as long as you're leading the group, Class President.
Be careful on your way home, guys.
Yes, sir.

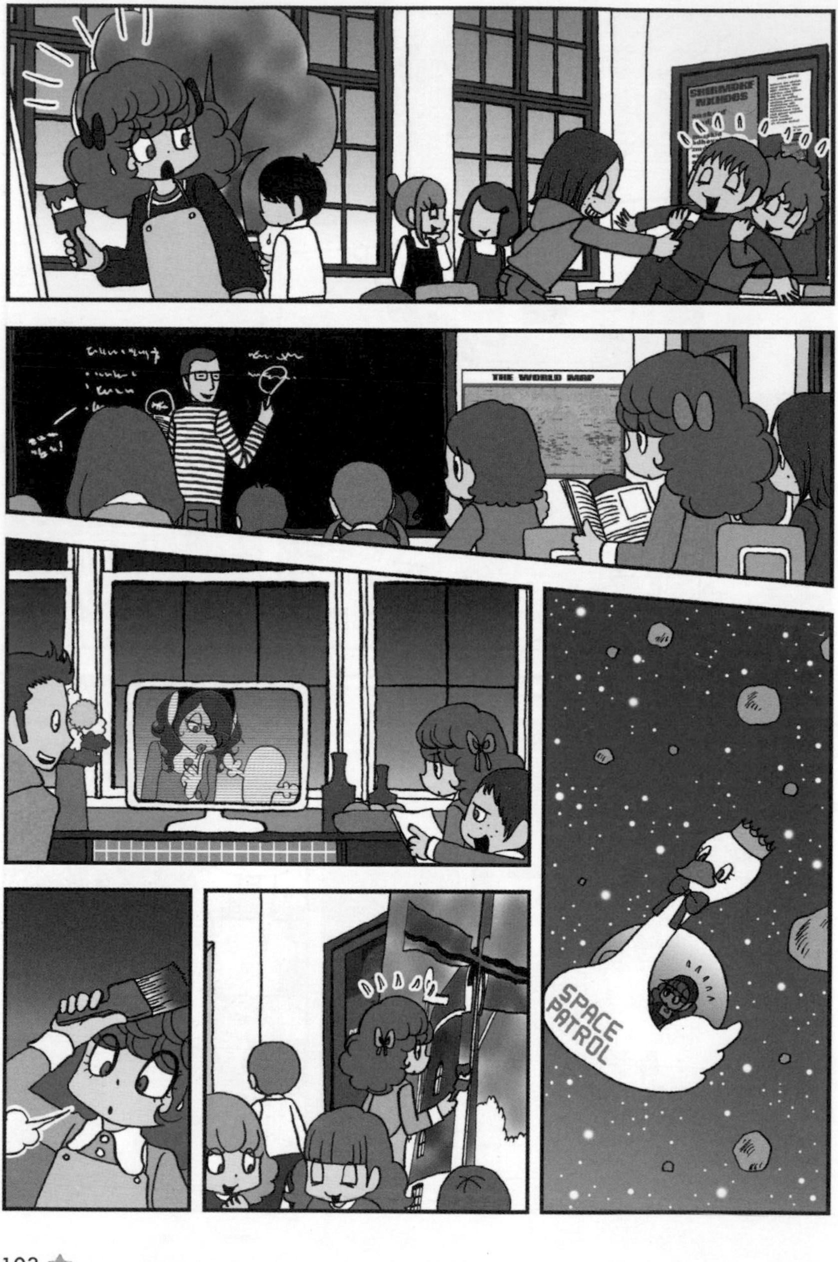
THE WORLD MAP
SPACE PATROL

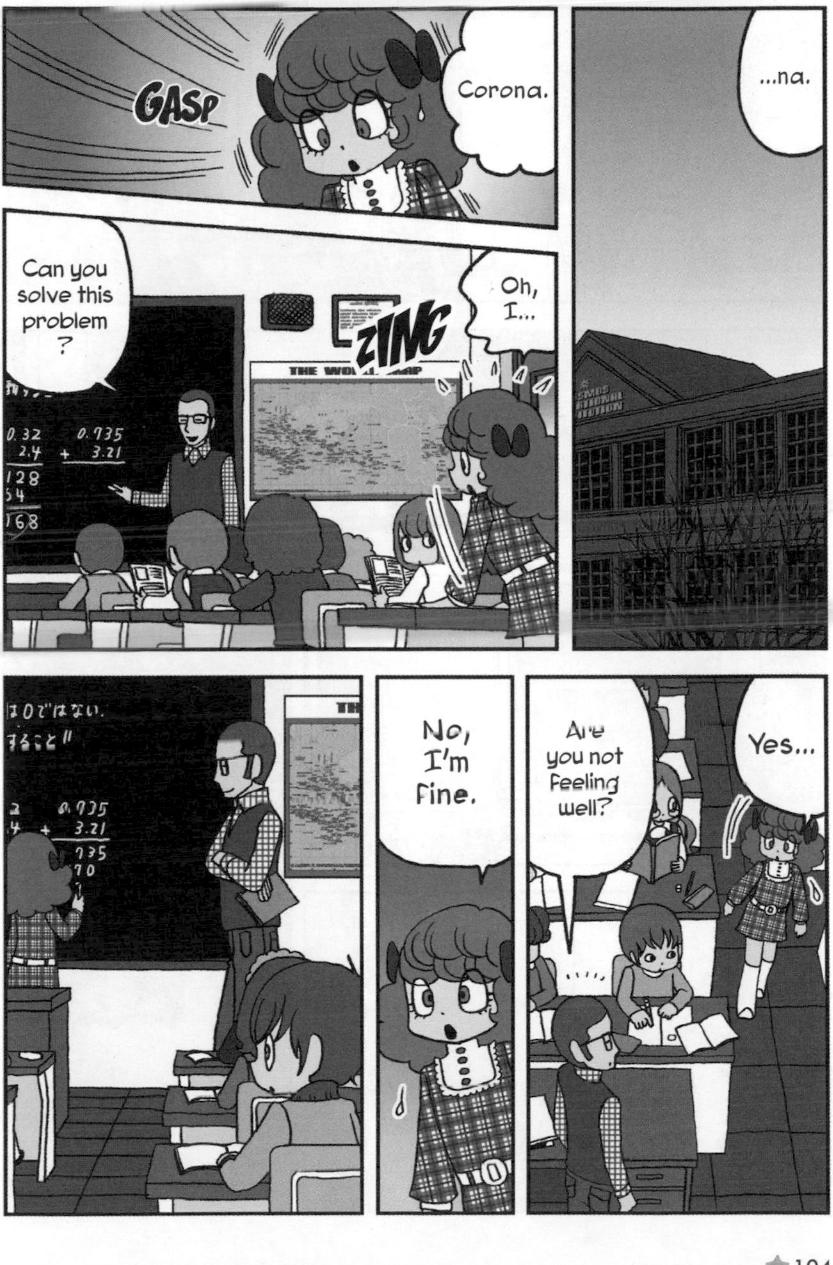
...na.
Corona.
GASP
Oh, I...
ZING
Can you solve this problem?
Yes...
Are you not feeling well?
No, I'm fine.

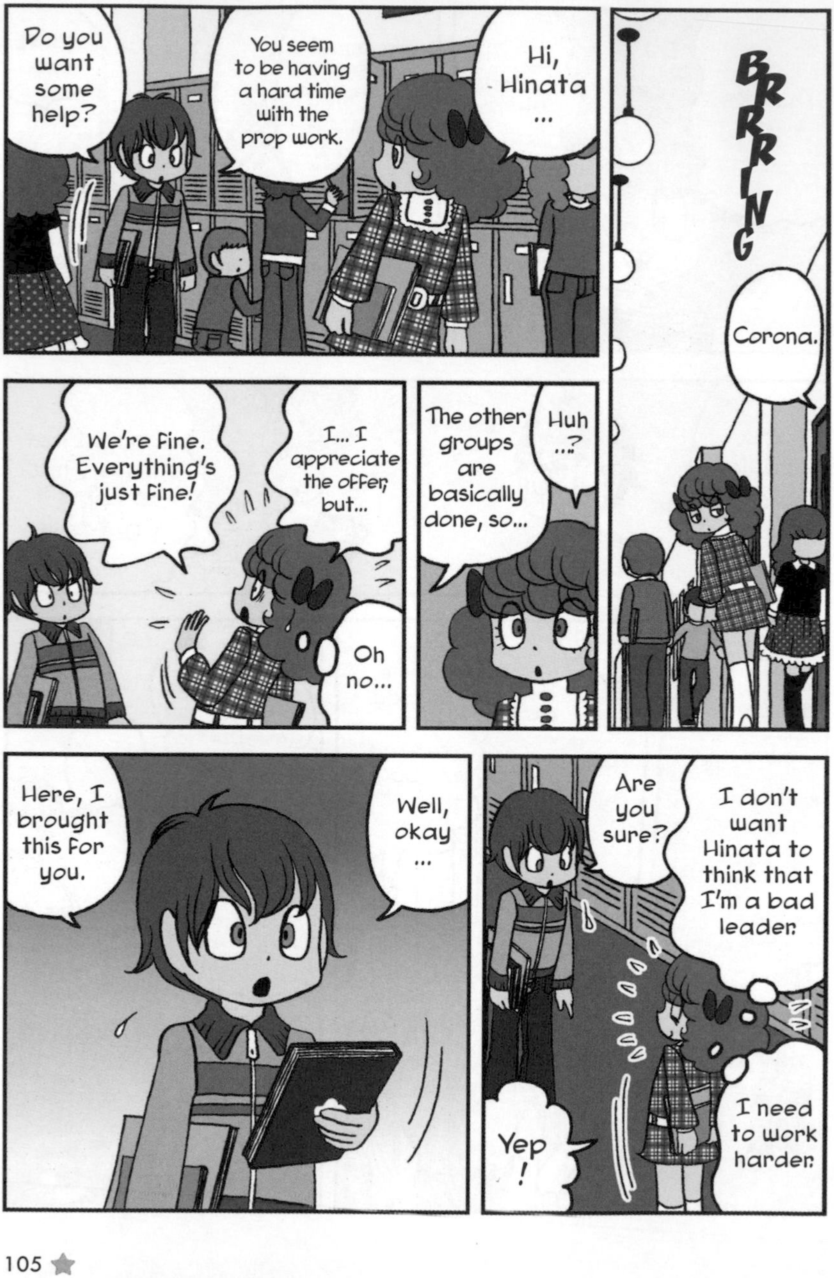
BRRRING
Corona.
Hi, Hinata ...
You seem to be having a hard time with the prop work.
Do you want some help?
Huh ...?
The other groups are basically done, so...
I... I appreciate the offer, but...
We're fine. Everything's just fine!
Oh no...
I don't want Hinata to think that I'm a bad leader.
Are you sure?
I need to work harder.
Yep !
Well, okay ...
Here, I brought this for you.

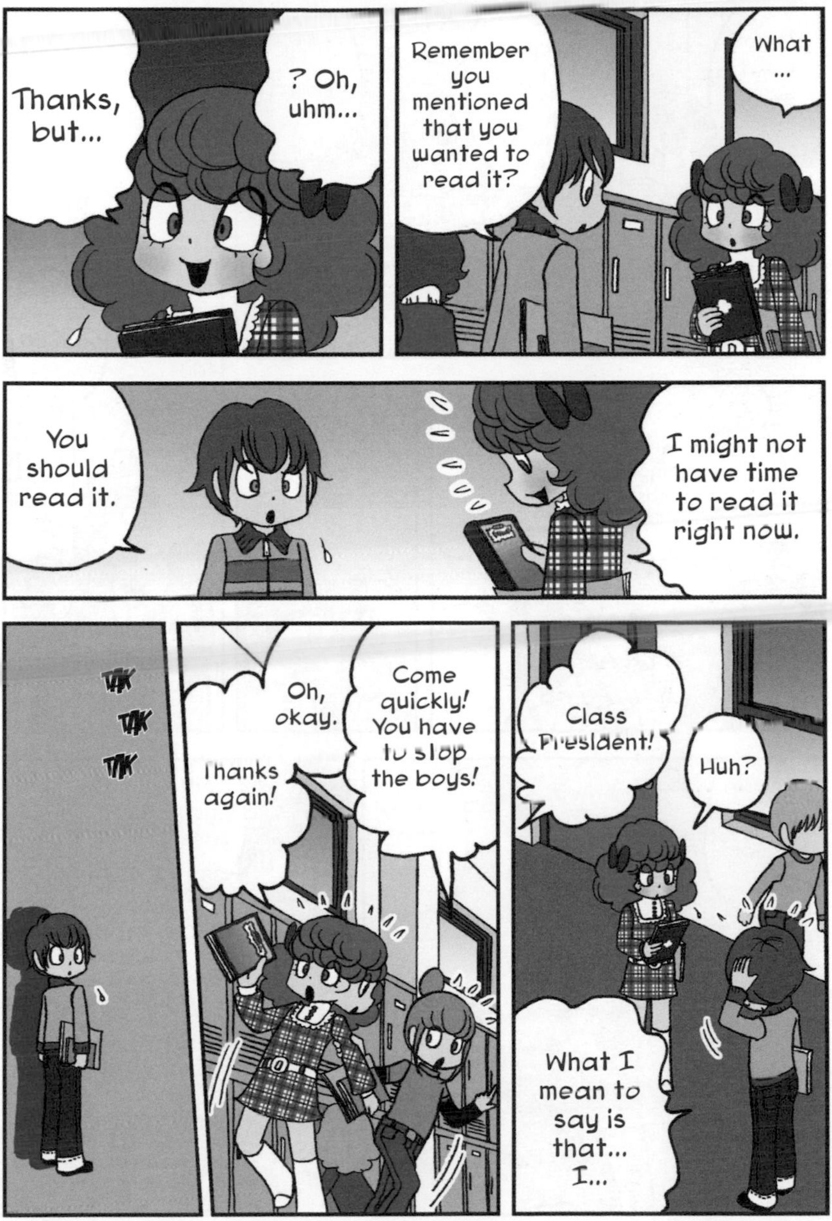
What ...
Remember you mentioned that you wanted to read it?
? Oh, uhm...
Thanks, but...
I might not have time to read it right now.
You should read it.
Class President!
Huh?
What I mean to say is that... I...
Come quickly! You have to stop the boys!
Oh, okay.
Thanks again!
TAK
TAK
TAK

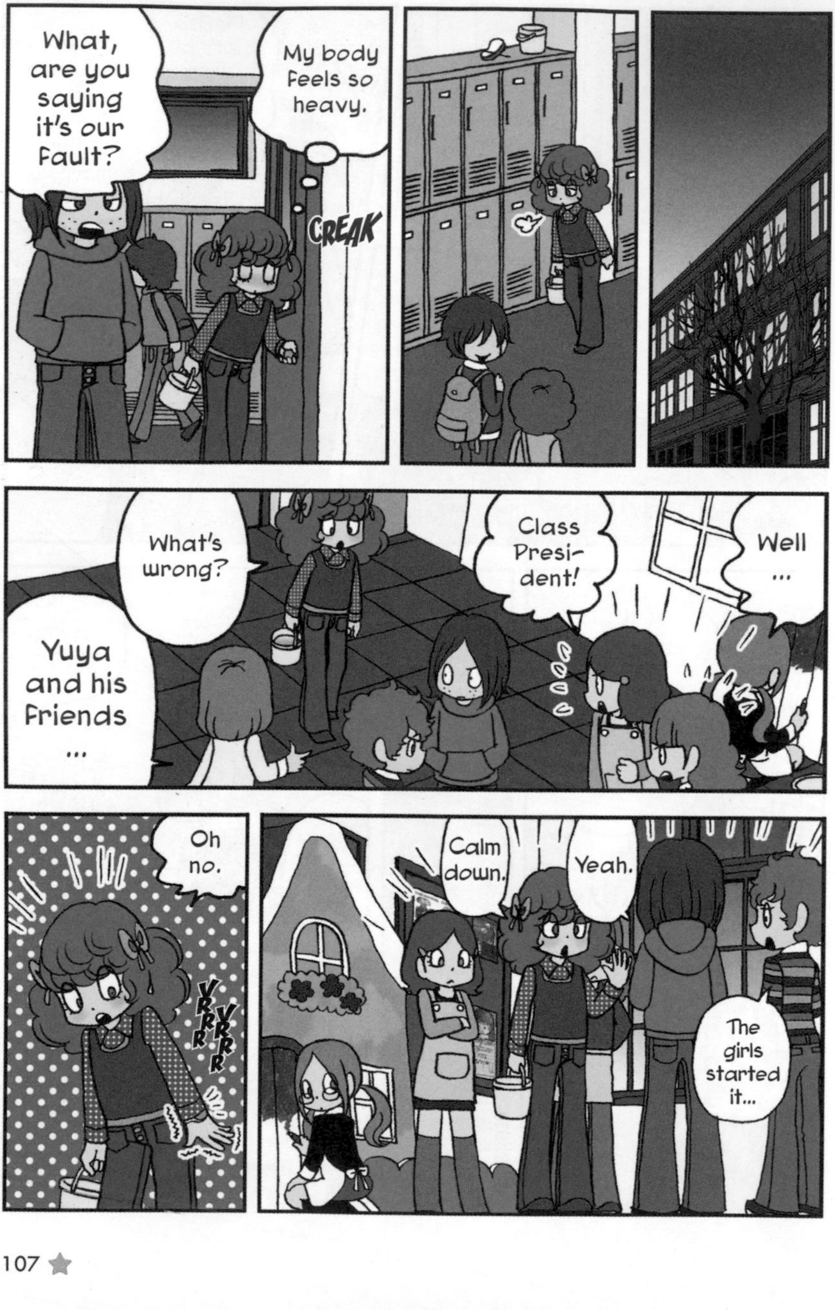
My body feels so heavy.
What, are you saying it's our fault?
CREAK
Well ...
Class President!
What's wrong?
Yuya and his friends ...
Yeah.
Calm down.
The girls started it...
Oh no.
VRRR VRRR

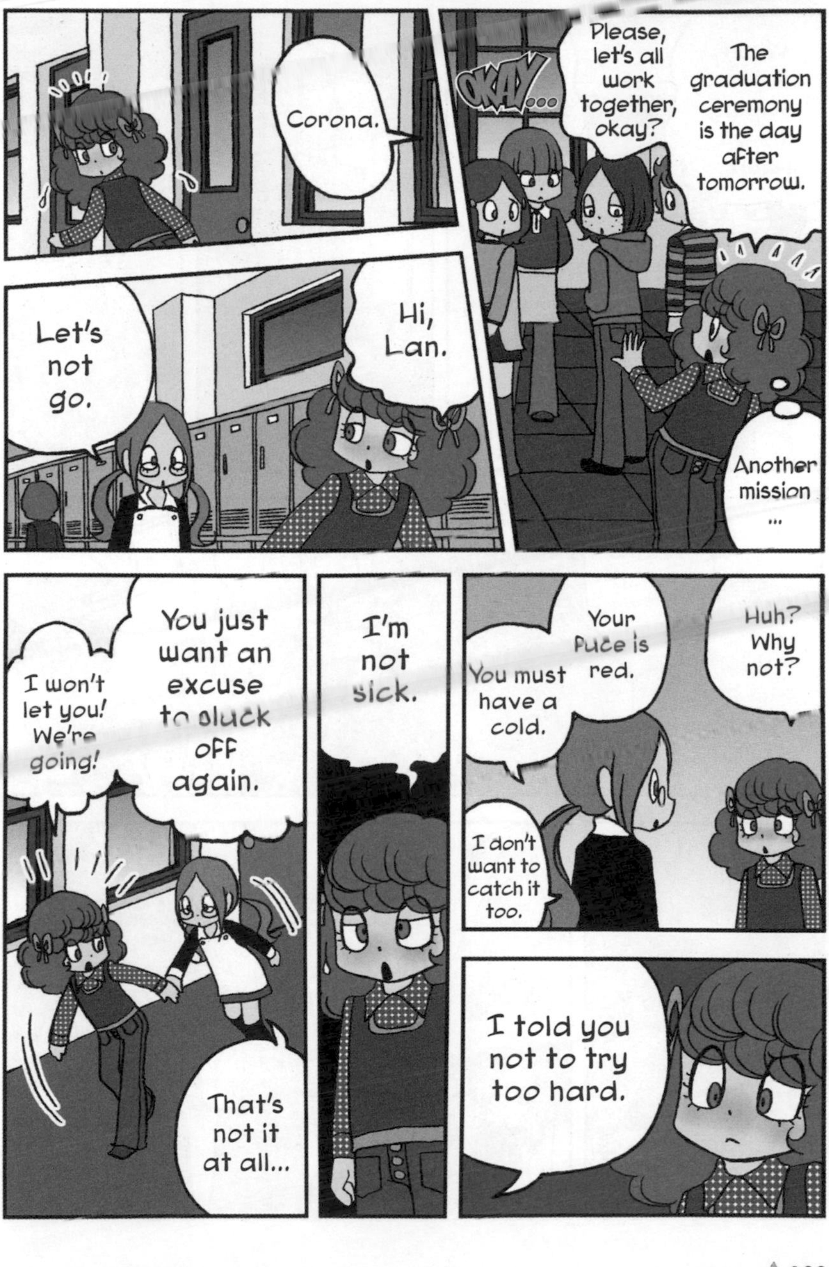
The graduation ceremony is the day after tomorrow.
Please, let's all work together, okay?
OKAY...
Another mission ...
Corona.
Hi, Lan.
Let's not go.
Huh? Why not?
Your face is red.
You must have a cold.
I don't want to catch it too.
I told you not to try too hard.
I'm not sick.
You just want an excuse to slack off again.
I won't let you! We're going!
That's not it at all...

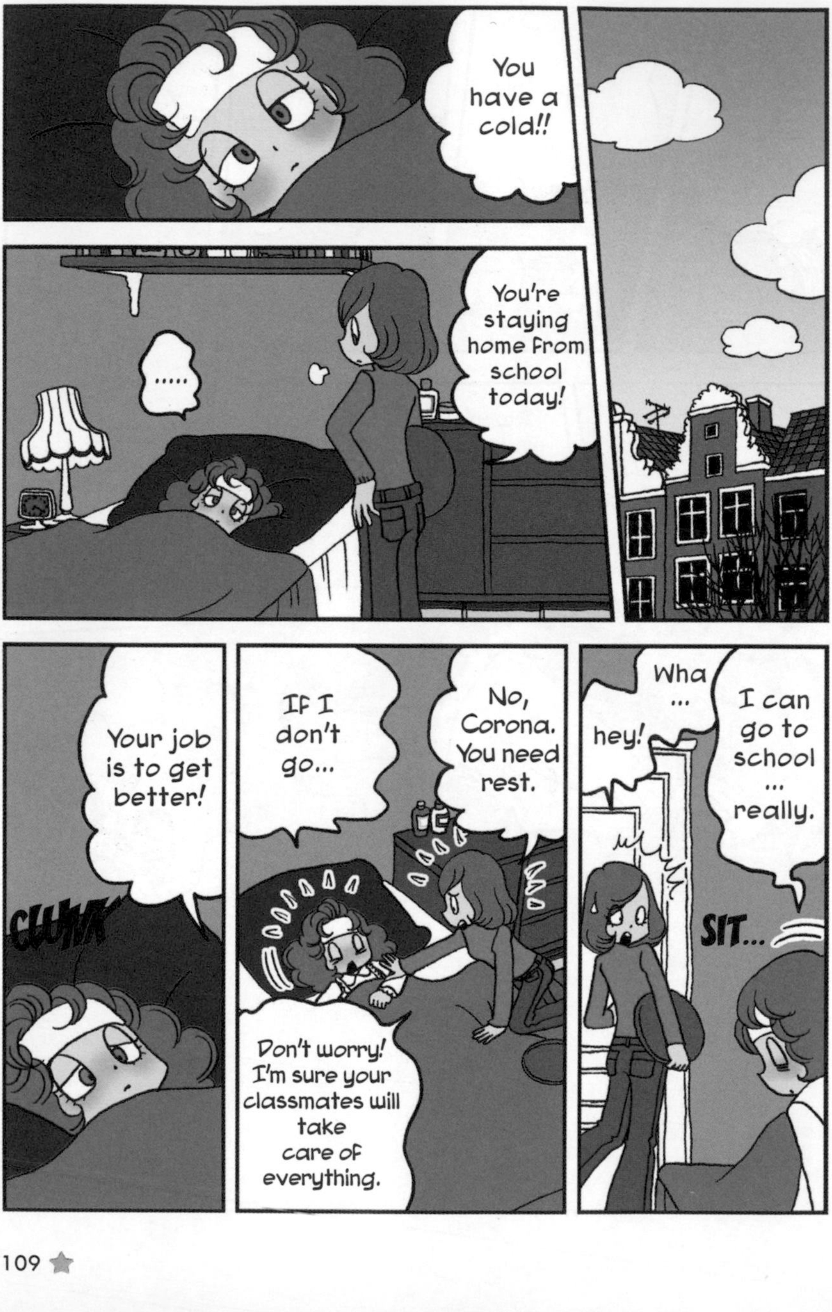
You have a cold!!
You're staying home from school today!
......
I can go to school ... really.
Wha ... hey!
SIT...
No, Corona. You need rest.
If I don't go...
Don't worry! I'm sure your classmates will take care of everything.
Your job is to get better!

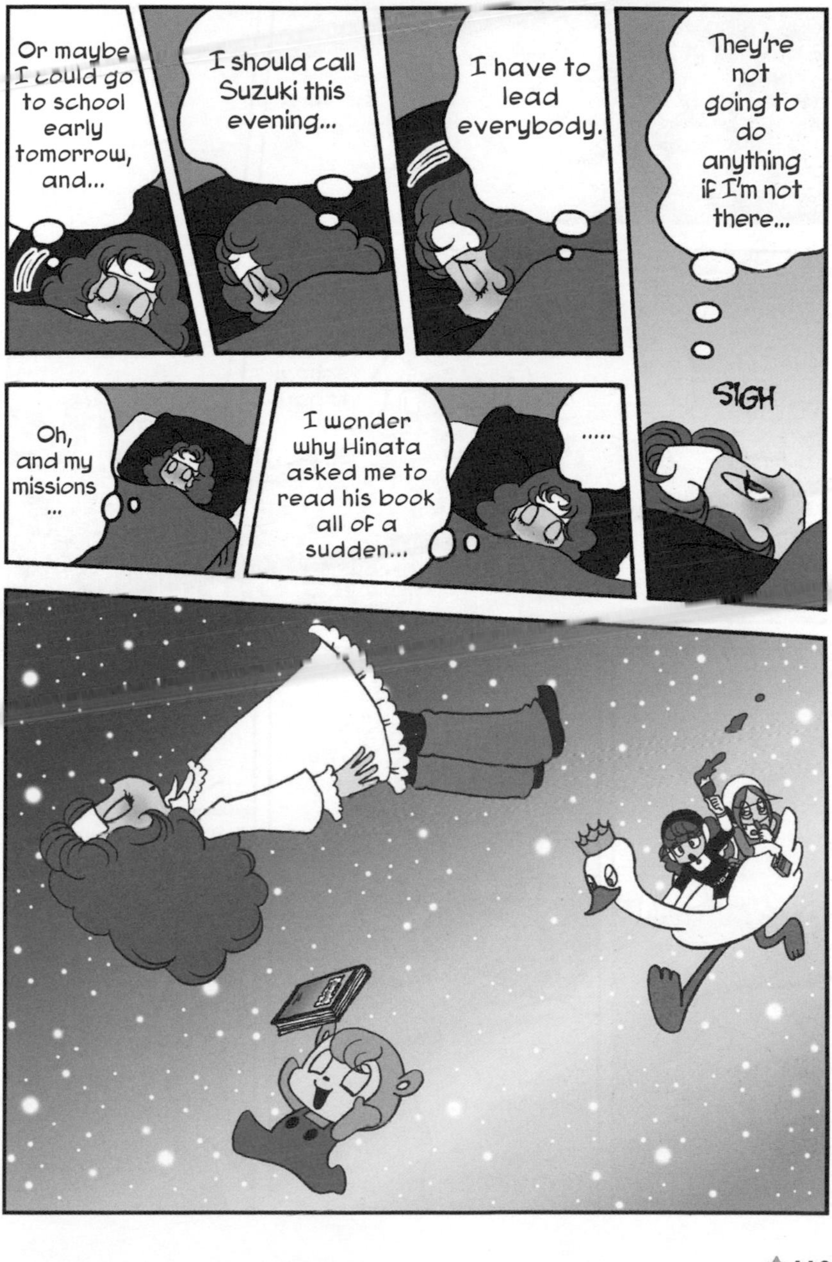
They're not going to do anything if I'm not there...
SIGH
I have to lead everybody.
I should call Suzuki this evening...
Or maybe I could go to school early tomorrow, and...
.....
I wonder why Hinata asked me to read his book all of a sudden...
Oh, and my missions ...

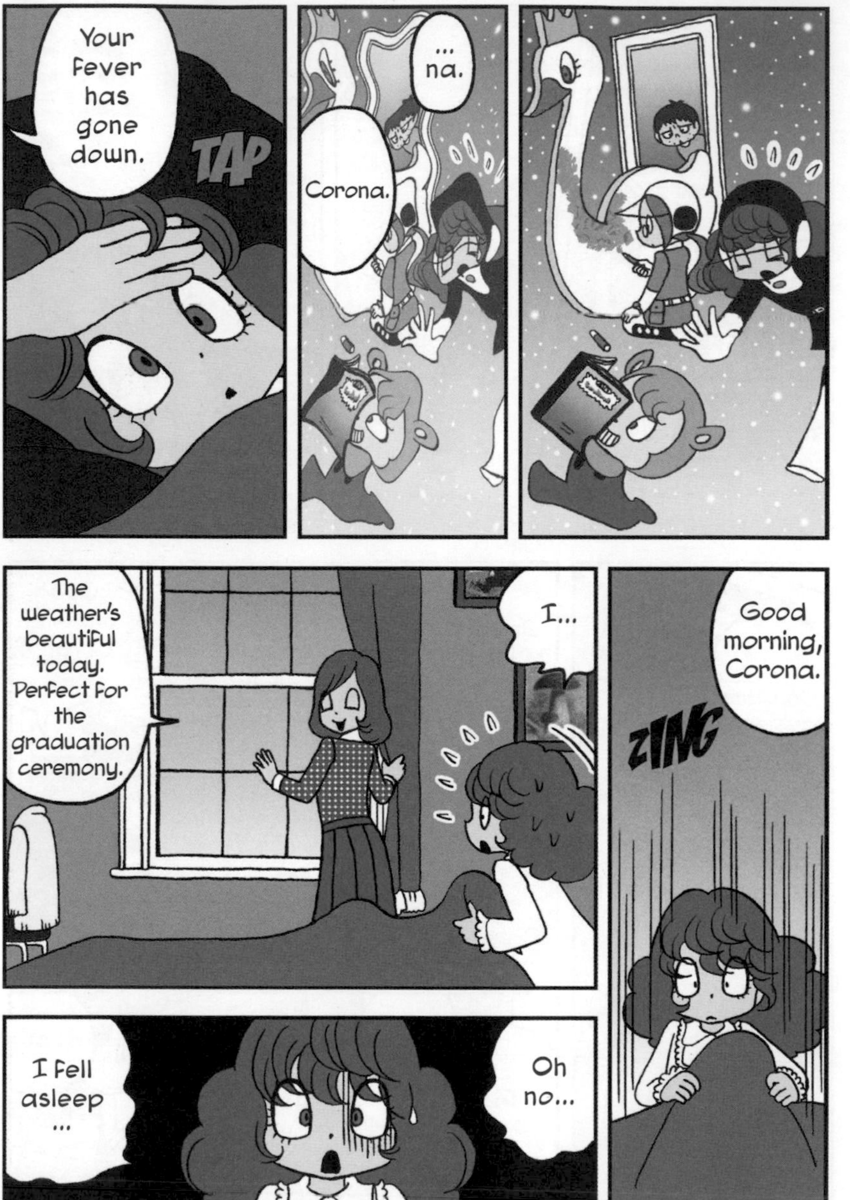
... na.
Corona.
Your fever has gone down.
TAP
Good morning, Corona.
ZING
I...
The weather's beautiful today. Perfect for the graduation ceremony.
Oh no...
I fell asleep ...

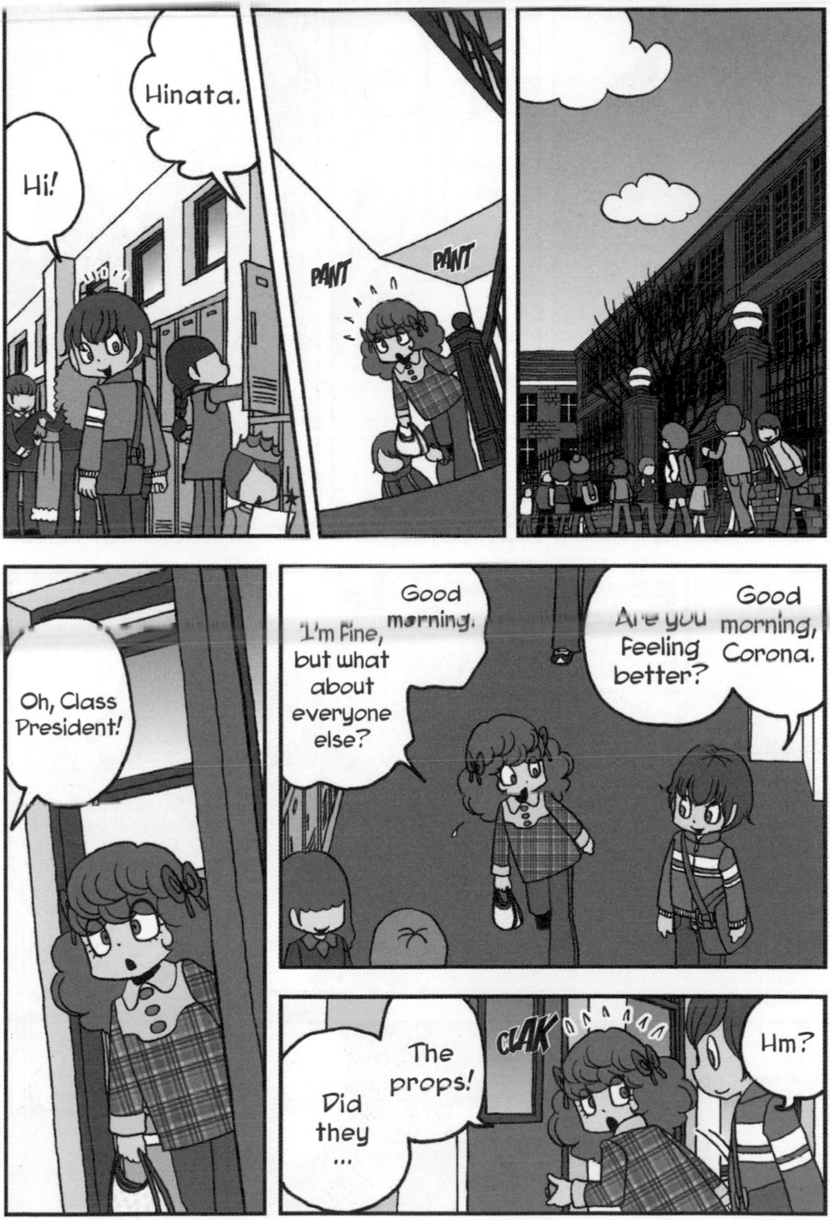
PANT
PANT
Hinata.
Hi!
Good morning, Corona.
Are you feeling better?
Good morning.
I'm fine, but what about everyone else?
Hm?
CLAK
The props!
Did they ...
Oh, Class President!

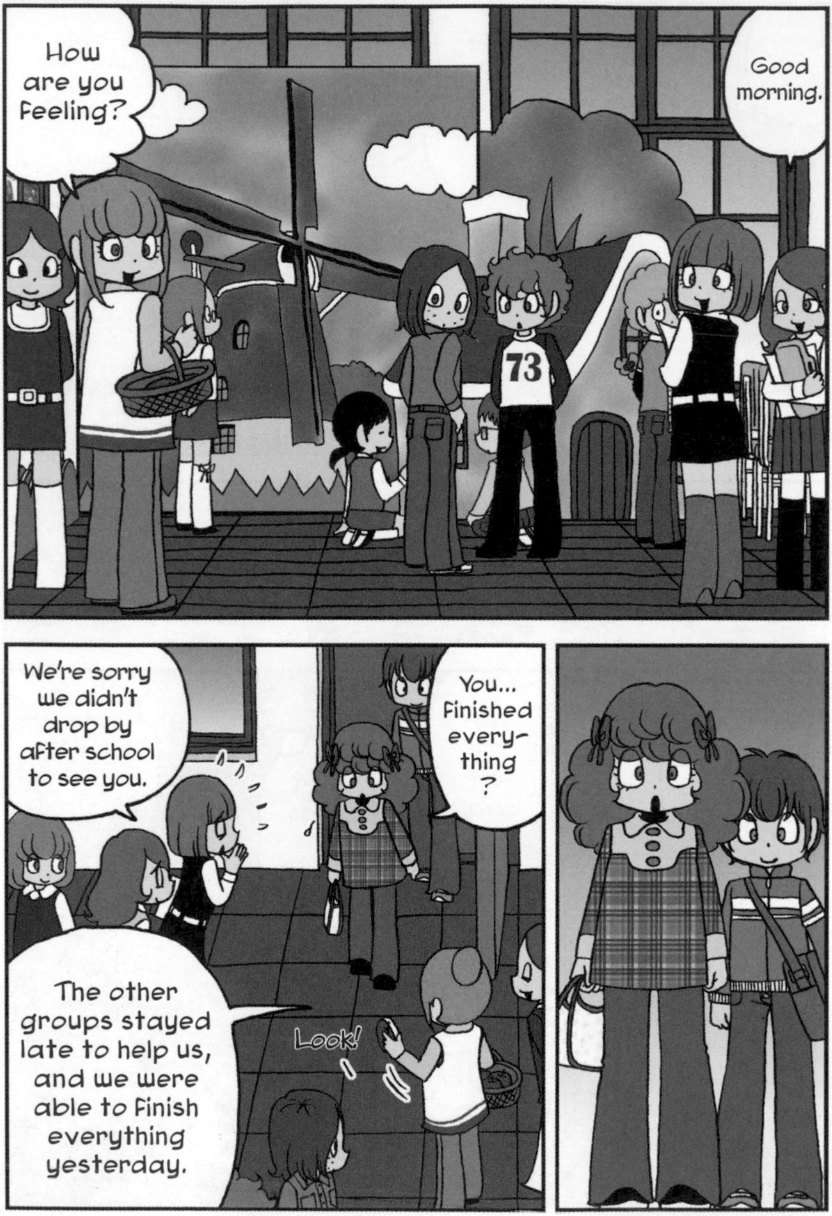
Good morning.
How are you feeling?
You... finished everything?
We're sorry we didn't drop by after school to see you.
The other groups stayed late to help us, and we were able to finish everything yesterday.
Look!

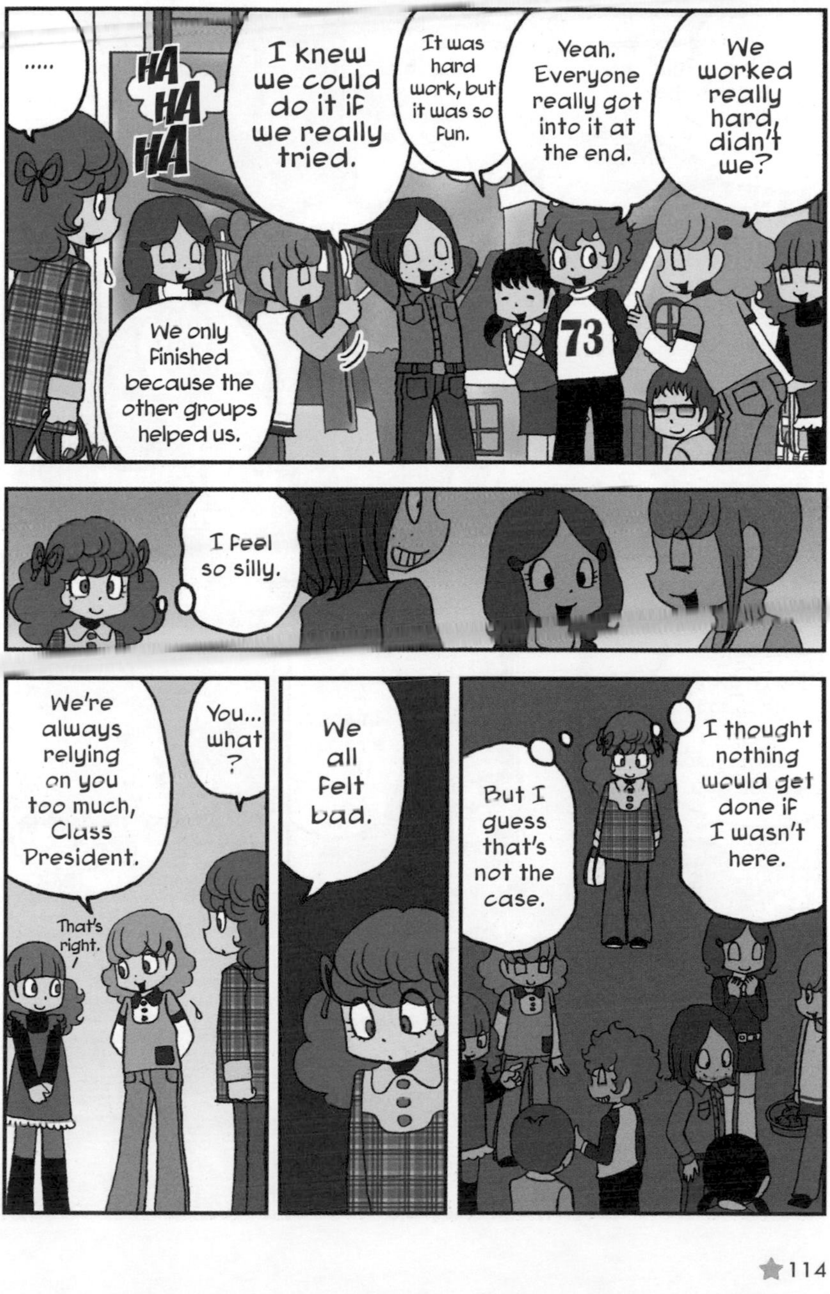
We worked really hard, didn't we?
Yeah. Everyone really got into it at the end.
It was hard work, but it was so fun.
I knew we could do it if we really tried.
HA HA HA
.....
We only finished because the other groups helped us.
I feel so silly.
I thought nothing would get done if I wasn't here.
But I guess that's not the case.
We all felt bad.
You... what?
We're always relying on you too much, Class President.
That's right.

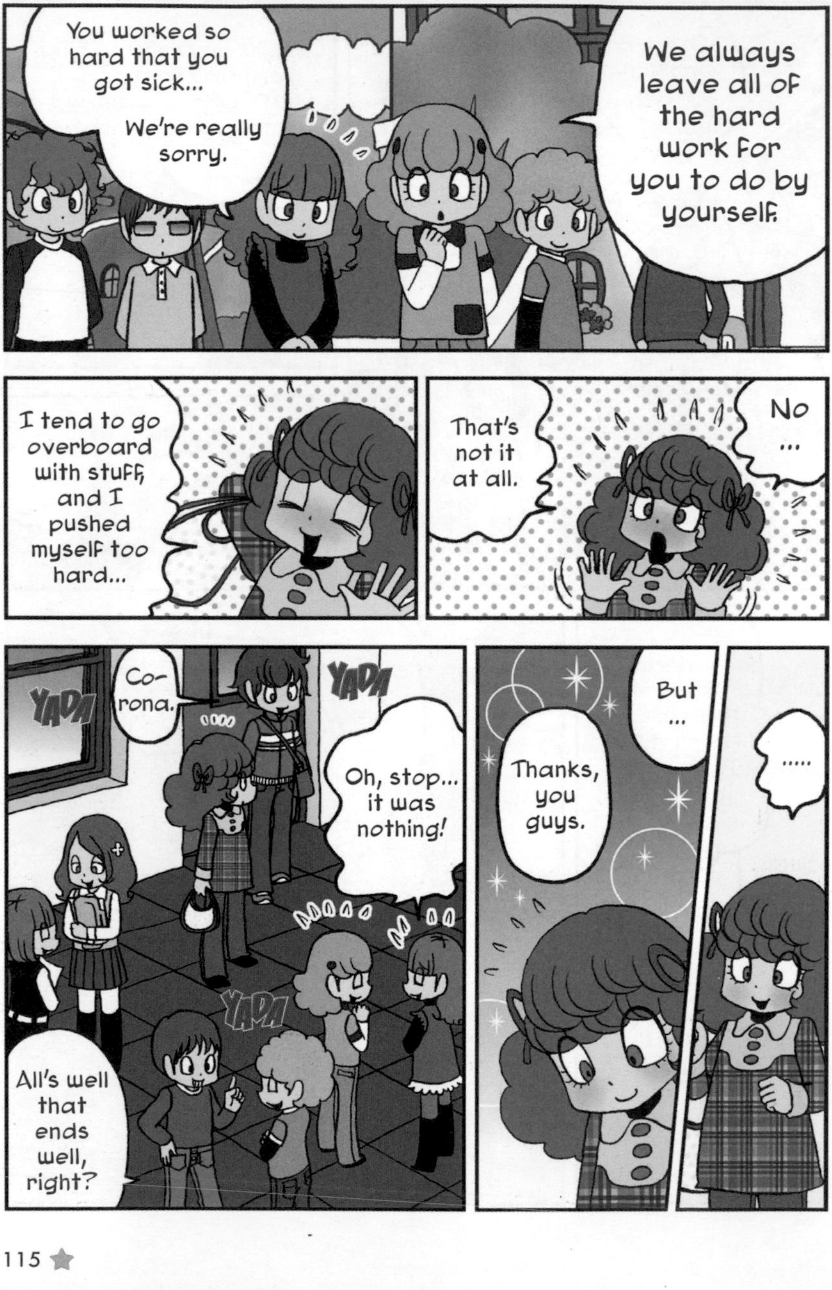

We always leave all of the hard work for you to do by yourself.
You worked so hard that you got sick...
We're really sorry.
No ...
That's not it at all.
I tend to go overboard with stuff, and I pushed myself too hard...
.....
But ...
Thanks, you guys.
YADA
Co-rona.
YADA
Oh, stop... it was nothing!
YADA
All's well that ends well, right?

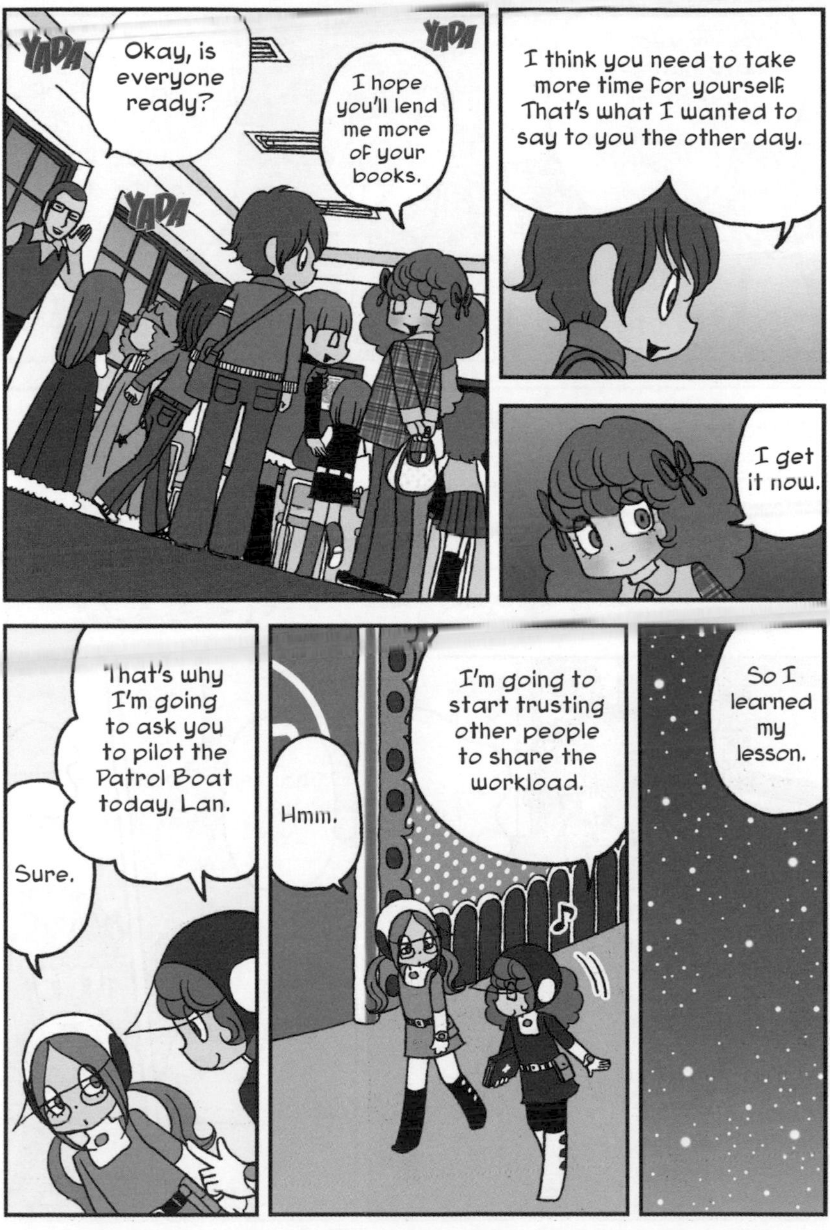
I think you need to take more time for yourself. That's what I wanted to say to you the other day.
I get it now.
YADA
I hope you'll lend me more of your books.
Okay, is everyone ready?
YADA
YADA
So I learned my lesson.
I'm going to start trusting other people to share the workload.
Hmm.
That's why I'm going to ask you to pilot the Patrol Boat today, Lan.
Sure.

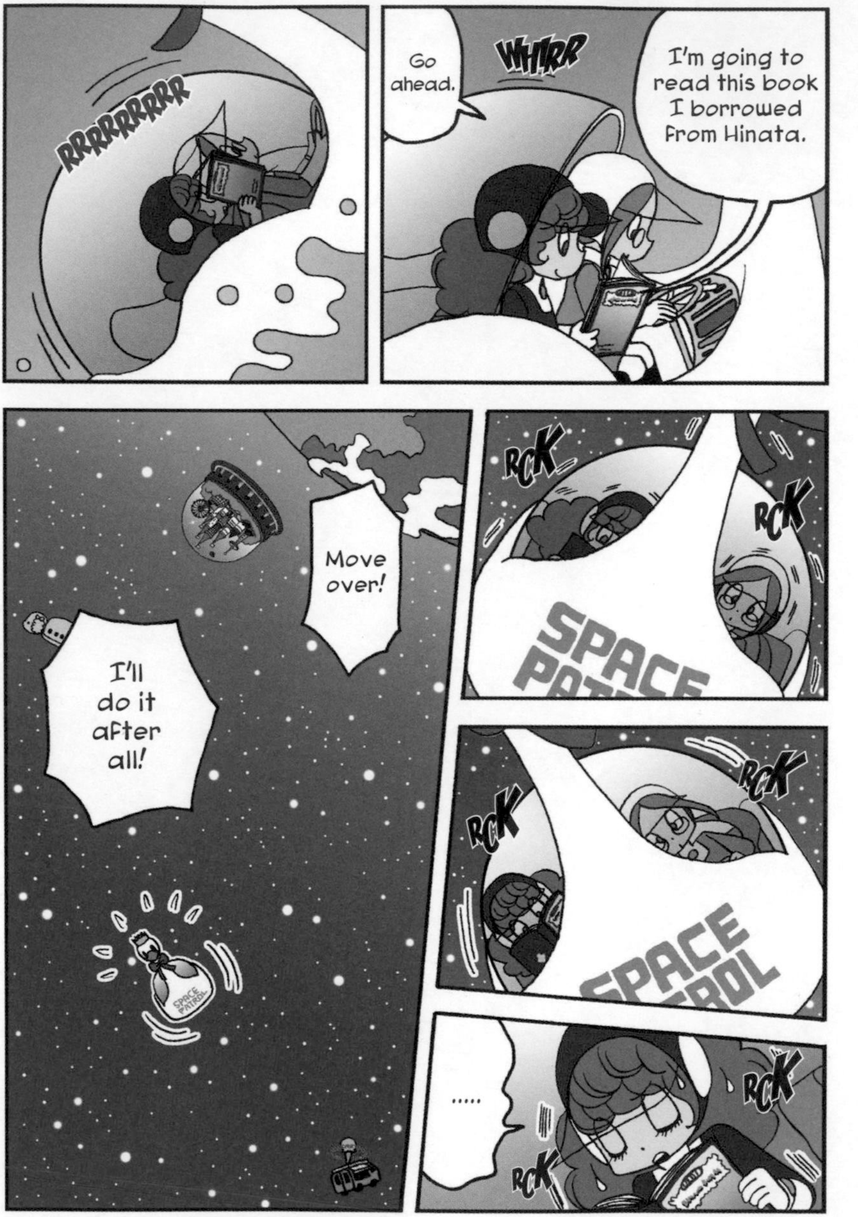
I'm going to read this book I borrowed from Hinata.
WHIRR
Go ahead.
RRRRRRRRR
RCK
RCK
SPACE PATROL
RCK
RCK
SPACE PATROL
RCK
.....
RCK
Move over!
I'll do it after all!
SPACE PATROL

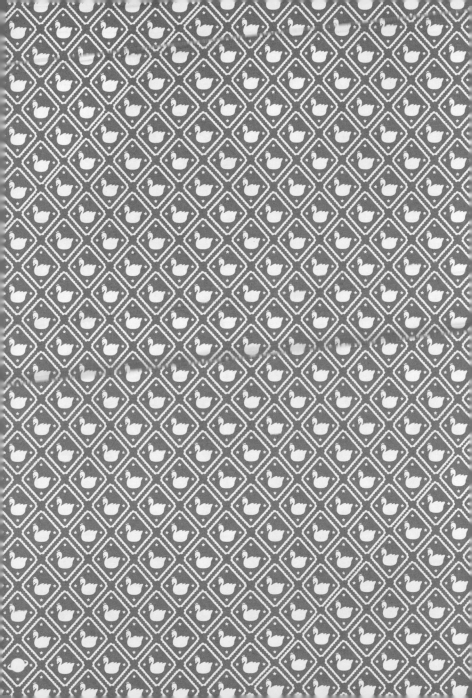

SWANS IN SPACE

CHAPTER 4
MY CHILD, NUMBER ONE IN SPACE

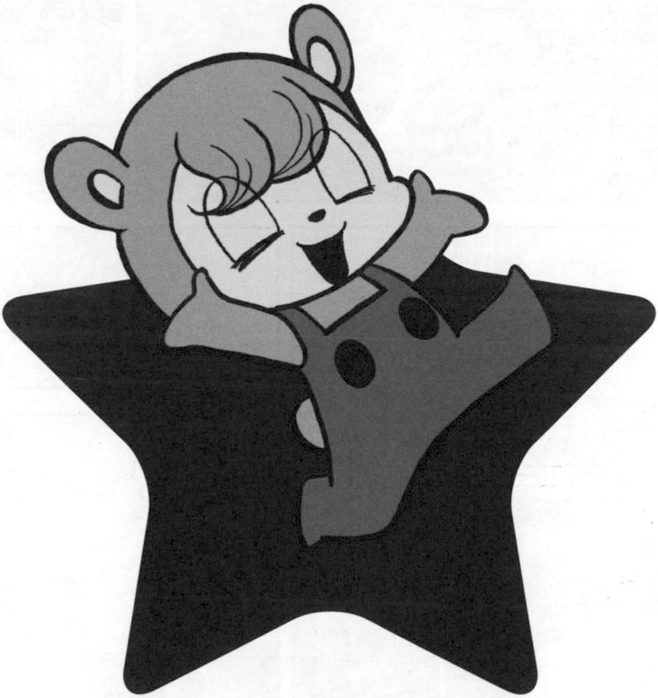

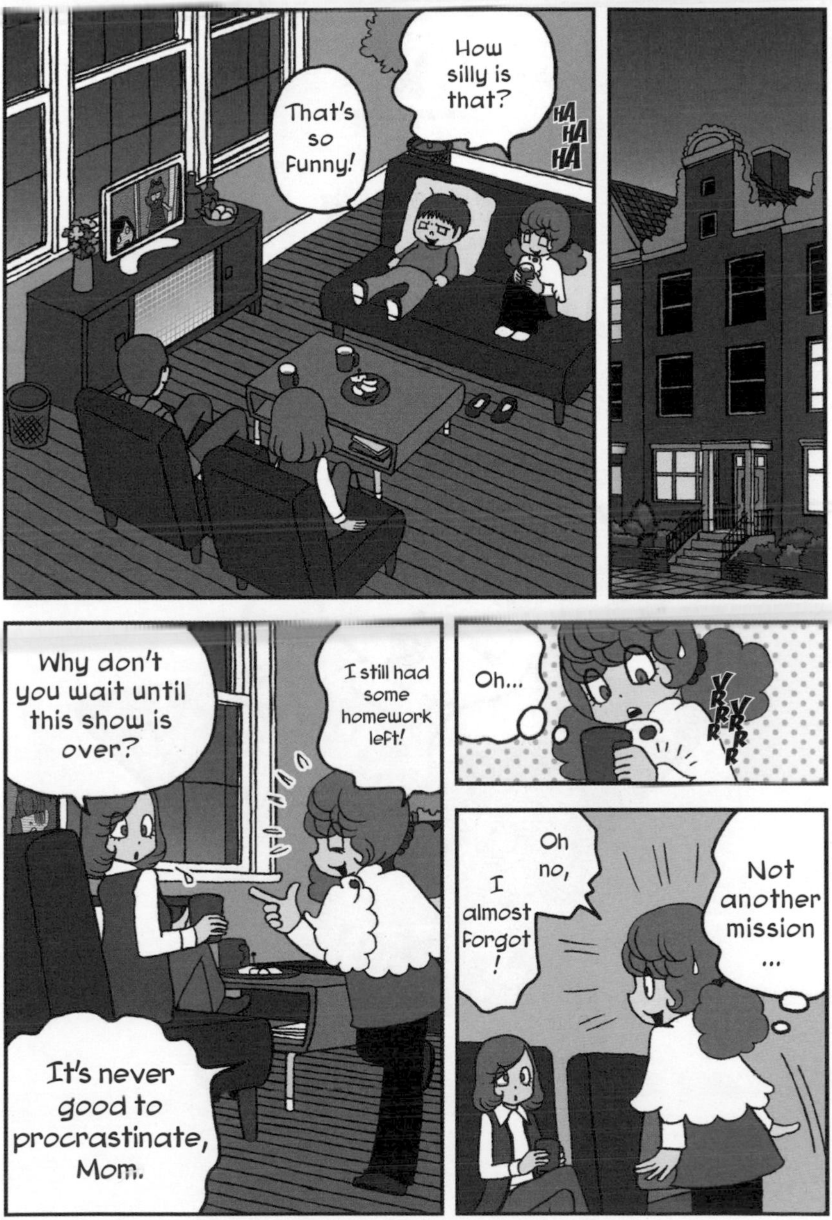
HA HA HA
How silly is that?
That's so funny!
Oh...
VRRR VRRR
Not another mission ...
Oh no, I almost forgot!
I still had some homework left!
Why don't you wait until this show is over?
It's never good to procrastinate, Mom.

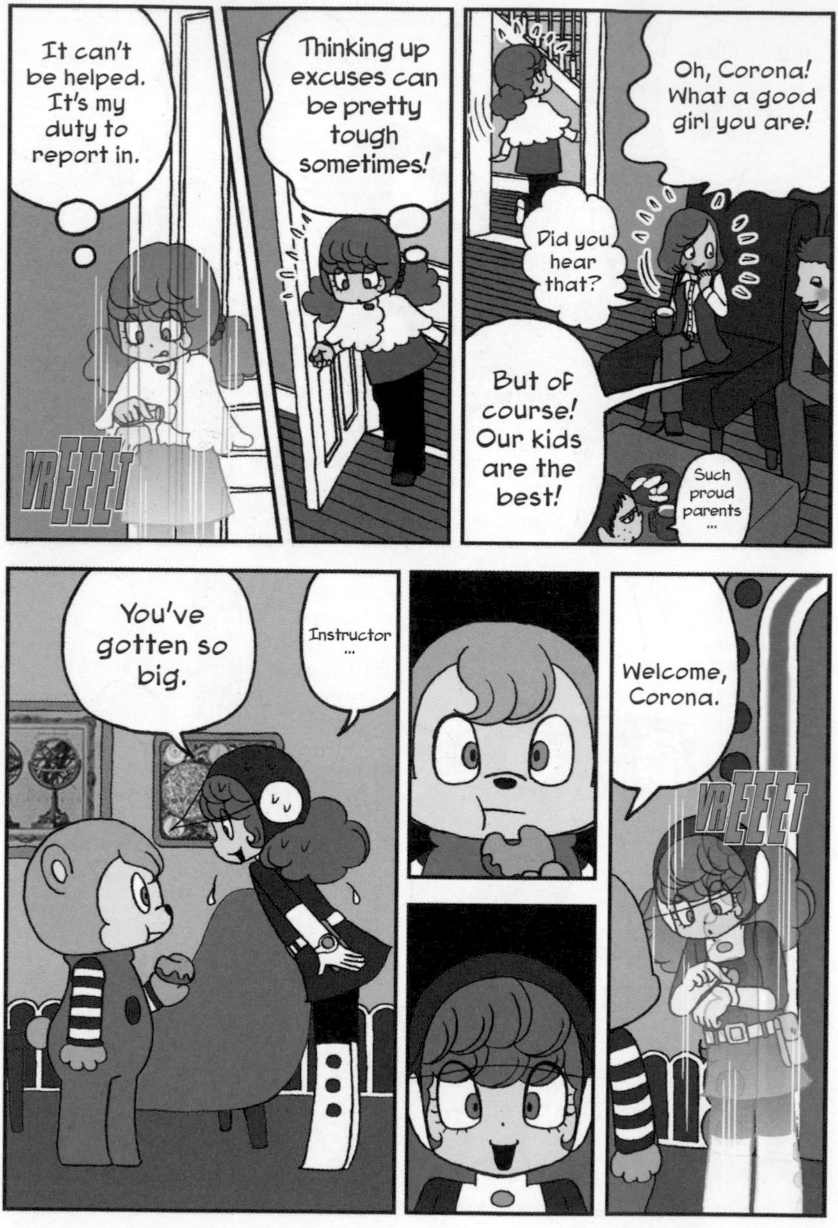
Oh, Corona! What a good girl you are!
Did you hear that?
But of course! Our kids are the best!
Such proud parents ...
Thinking up excuses can be pretty tough sometimes!
It can't be helped. It's my duty to report in.
VREEEET
Welcome, Corona.
VREEEET
Instructor ...
You've gotten so big.

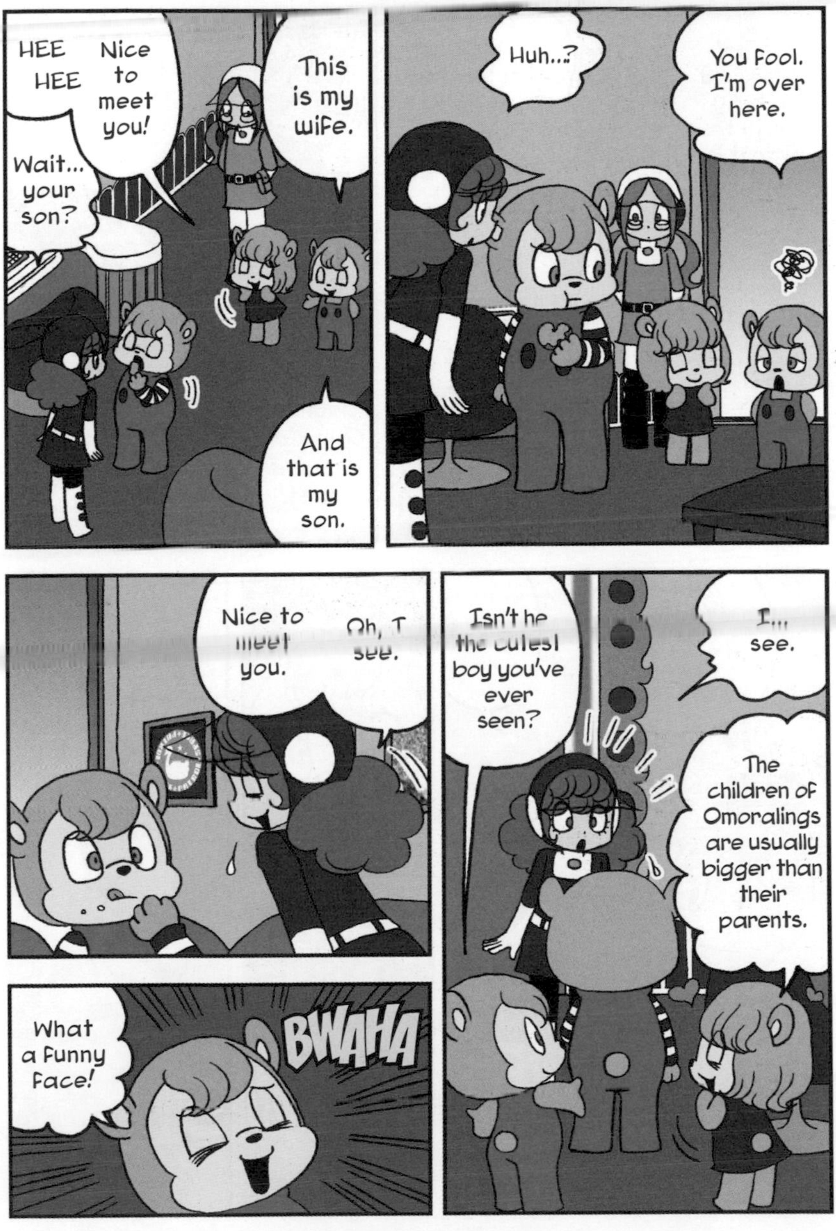
You fool. I'm over here.
Huh...?
This is my wife.
Nice to meet you!
HEE HEE
Wait... your son?
And that is my son.
I... see.
Isn't he the cutest boy you've ever seen?
The children of Omoralings are usually bigger than their parents.
Oh, I see.
Nice to meet you.
BWAHA
What a funny face!

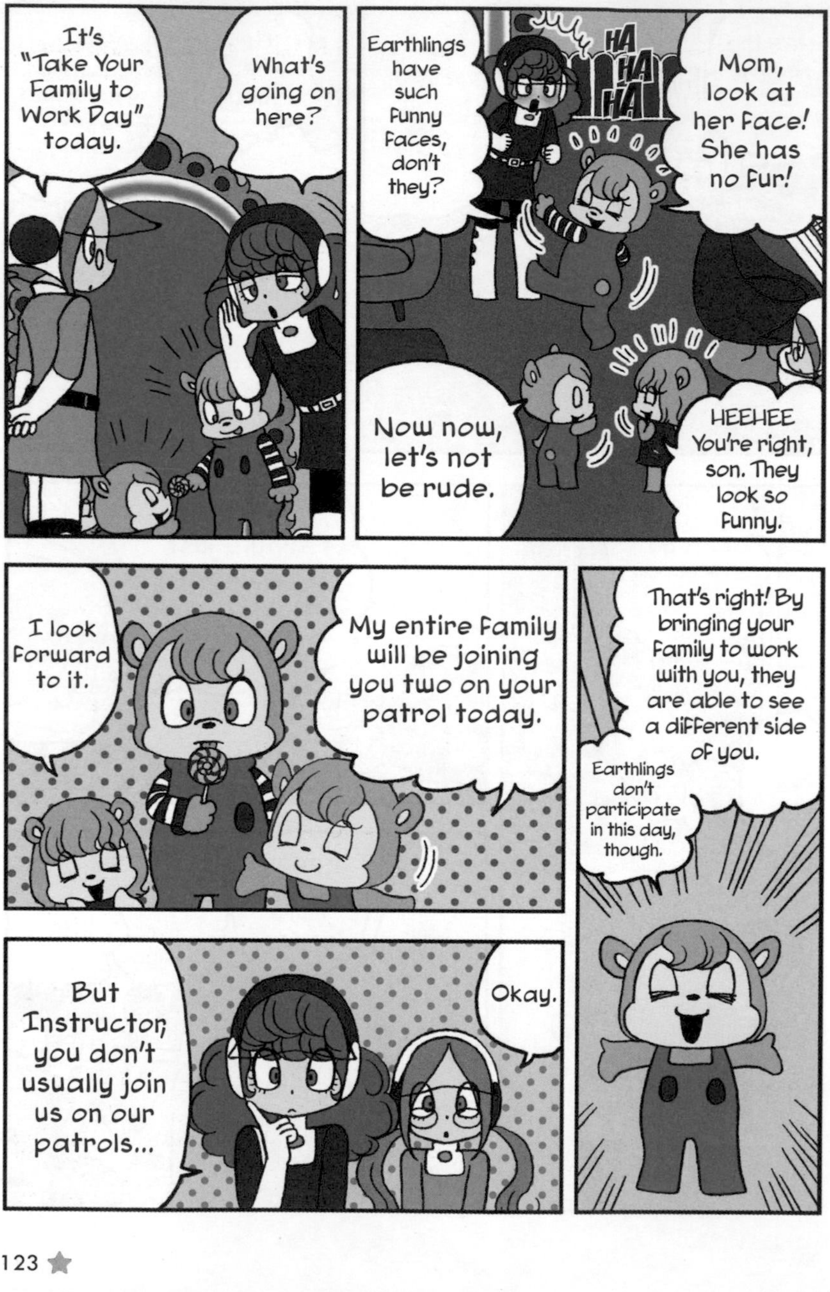
Mom, look at her face! She has no fur!
HA HA HA
Earthlings have such funny faces, don't they?
HEEHEE You're right, son. They look so funny.
Now now, let's not be rude.
What's going on here?
It's "Take Your Family to Work Day" today.
That's right! By bringing your family to work with you, they are able to see a different side of you.
Earthlings don't participate in this day, though.
My entire family will be joining you two on your patrol today.
I look forward to it.
Okay.
But Instructor, you don't usually join us on our patrols...

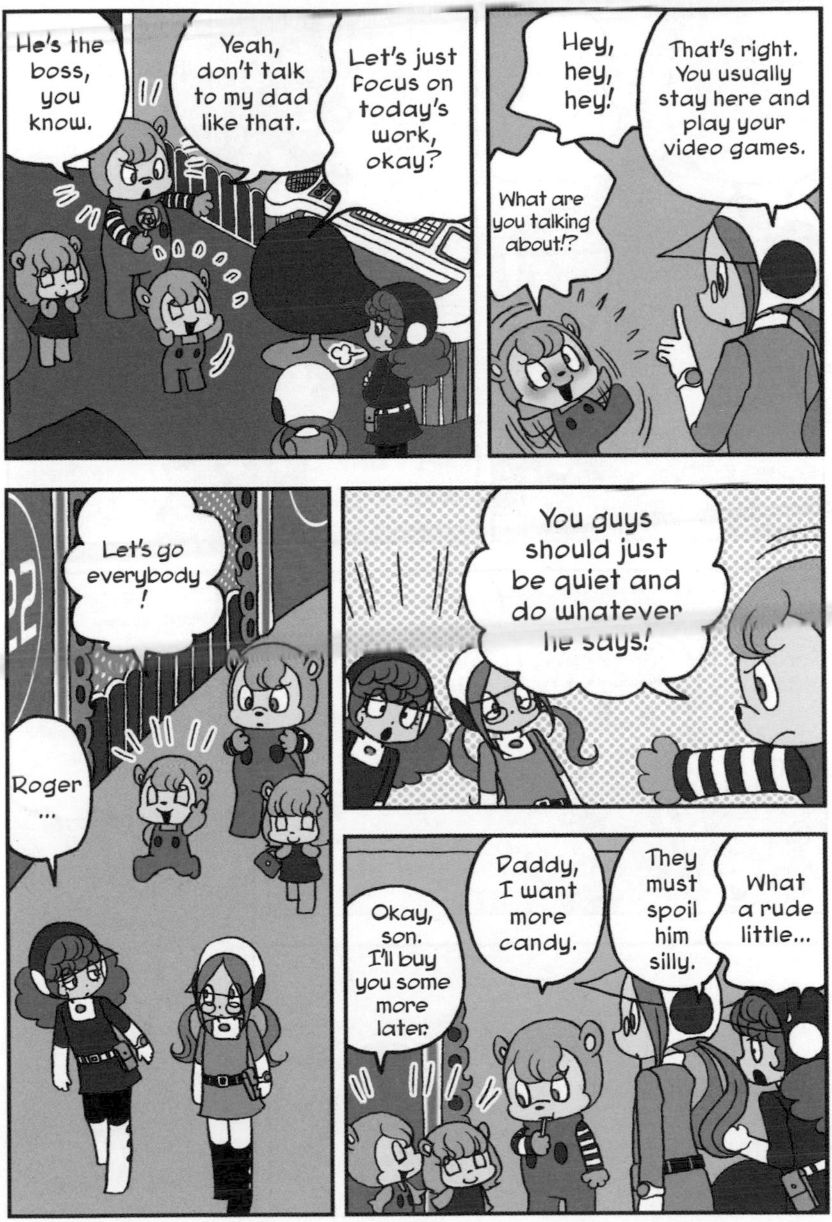
That's right. You usually stay here and play your video games.
Hey, hey, hey!
What are you talking about!?
Let's just focus on today's work, okay?
Yeah, don't talk to my dad like that.
He's the boss, you know.
You guys should just be quiet and do whatever he says!
What a rude little...
They must spoil him silly.
Daddy, I want more candy.
Okay, son. I'll buy you some more later.
Let's go everybody!
Roger ...

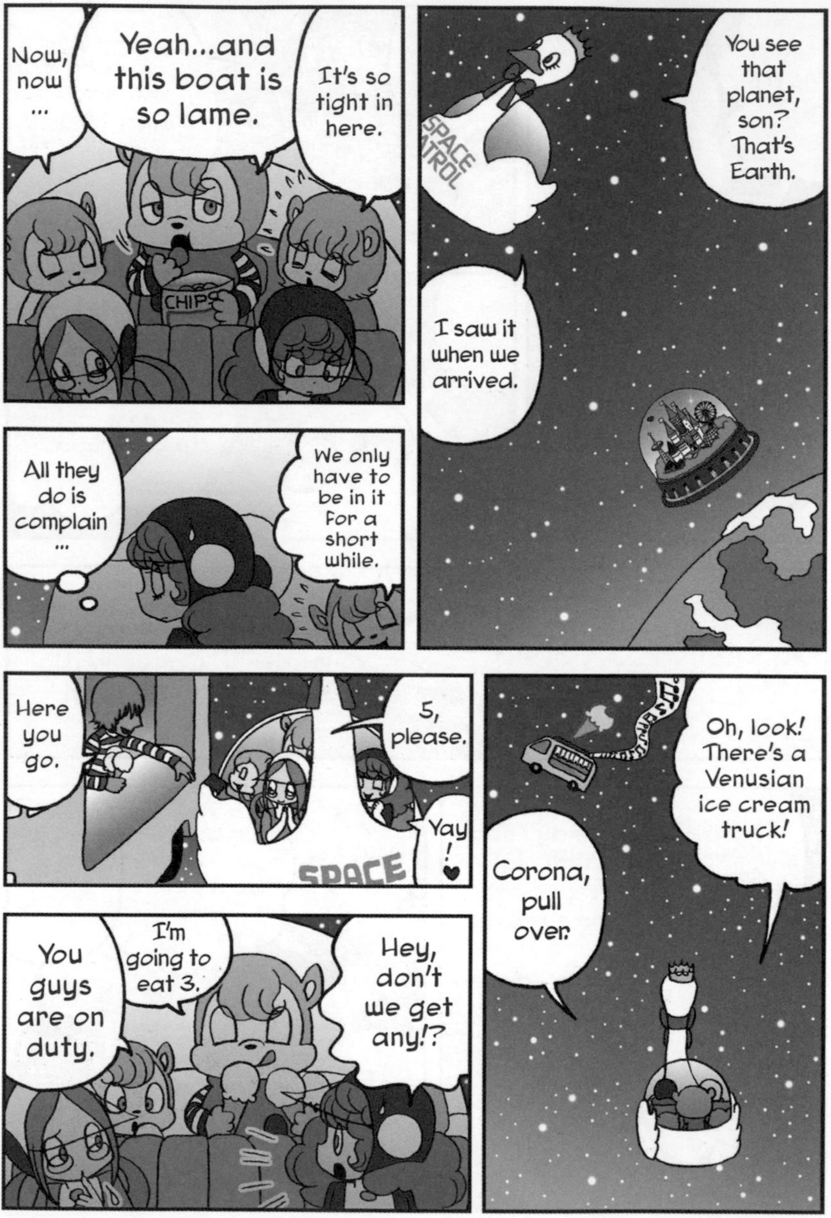
You see that planet, son? That's Earth.
I saw it when we arrived.
It's so tight in here.
Yeah...and this boat is so lame.
Now, now ...
CHIPS
We only have to be in it for a short while.
All they do is complain ...
Oh, look! There's a Venusian ice cream truck!
Corona, pull over.
5, please.
Here you go.
Yay! ♥
Hey, don't we get any!?
I'm going to eat 3.
You guys are on duty.

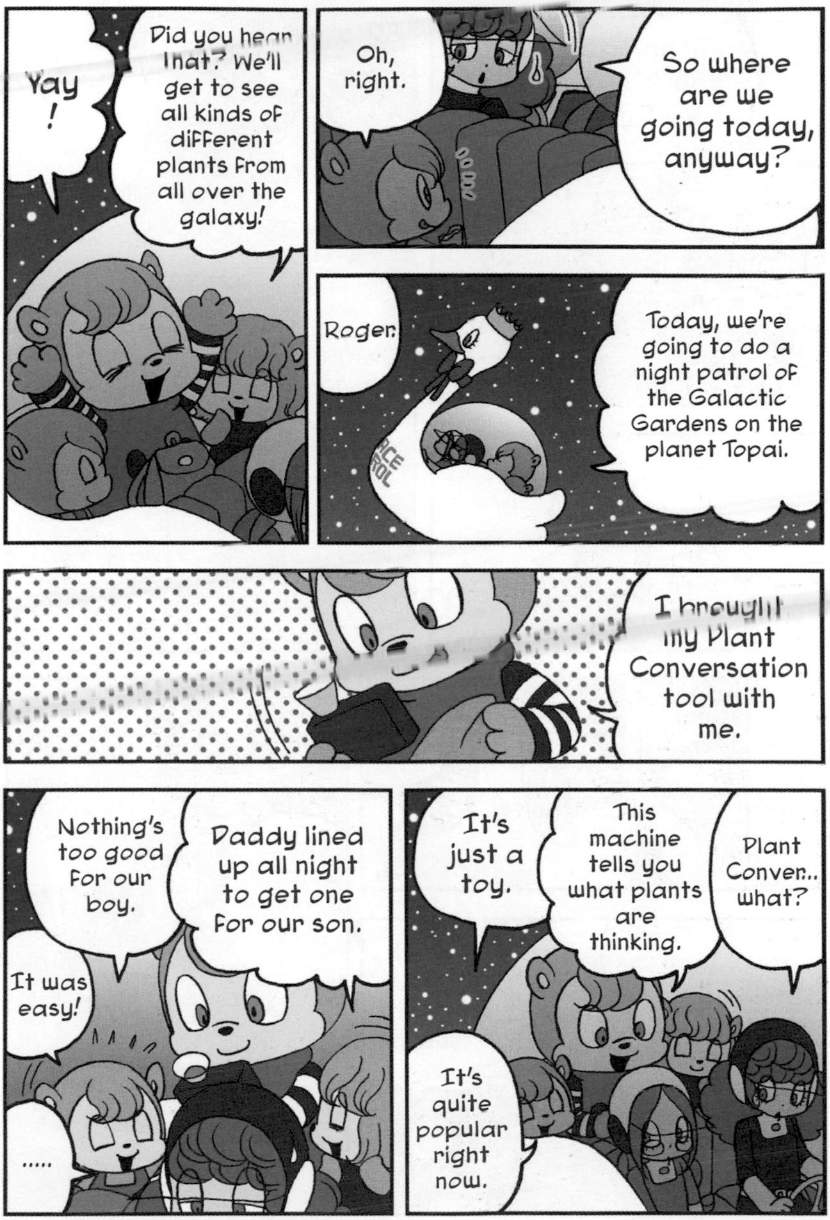
So where are we going today, anyway?
Oh, right.
Today, we're going to do a night patrol of the Galactic Gardens on the planet Topai.
Roger.
Did you hear that? We'll get to see all kinds of different plants from all over the galaxy!
Yay!
I brought my Plant Conversation tool with me.
Plant Conver... what?
This machine tells you what plants are thinking.
It's just a toy.
It's quite popular right now.
Daddy lined up all night to get one for our son.
Nothing's too good for our boy.
It was easy!
.....

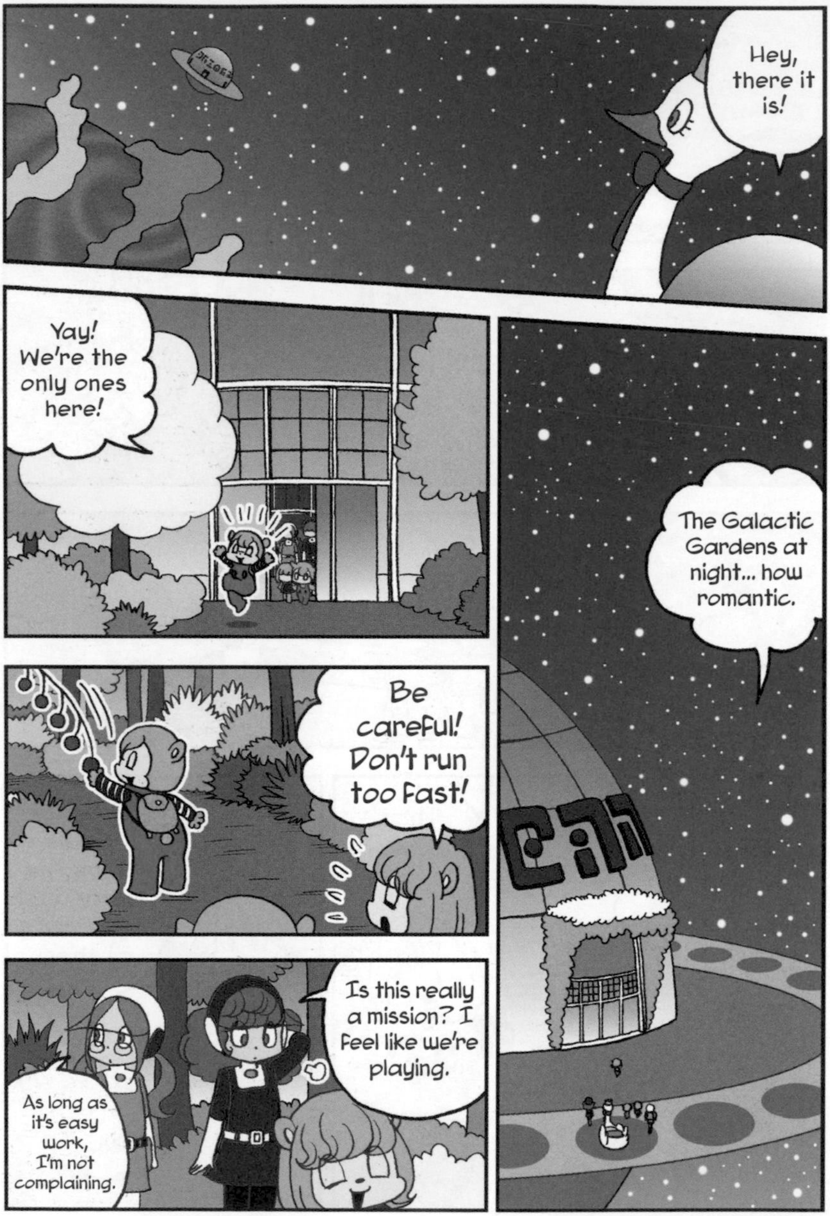
Hey, there it is!
The Galactic Gardens at night... how romantic.
Yay! We're the only ones here!
Be careful! Don't run too fast!
Is this really a mission? I feel like we're playing.
As long as it's easy work, I'm not complaining.

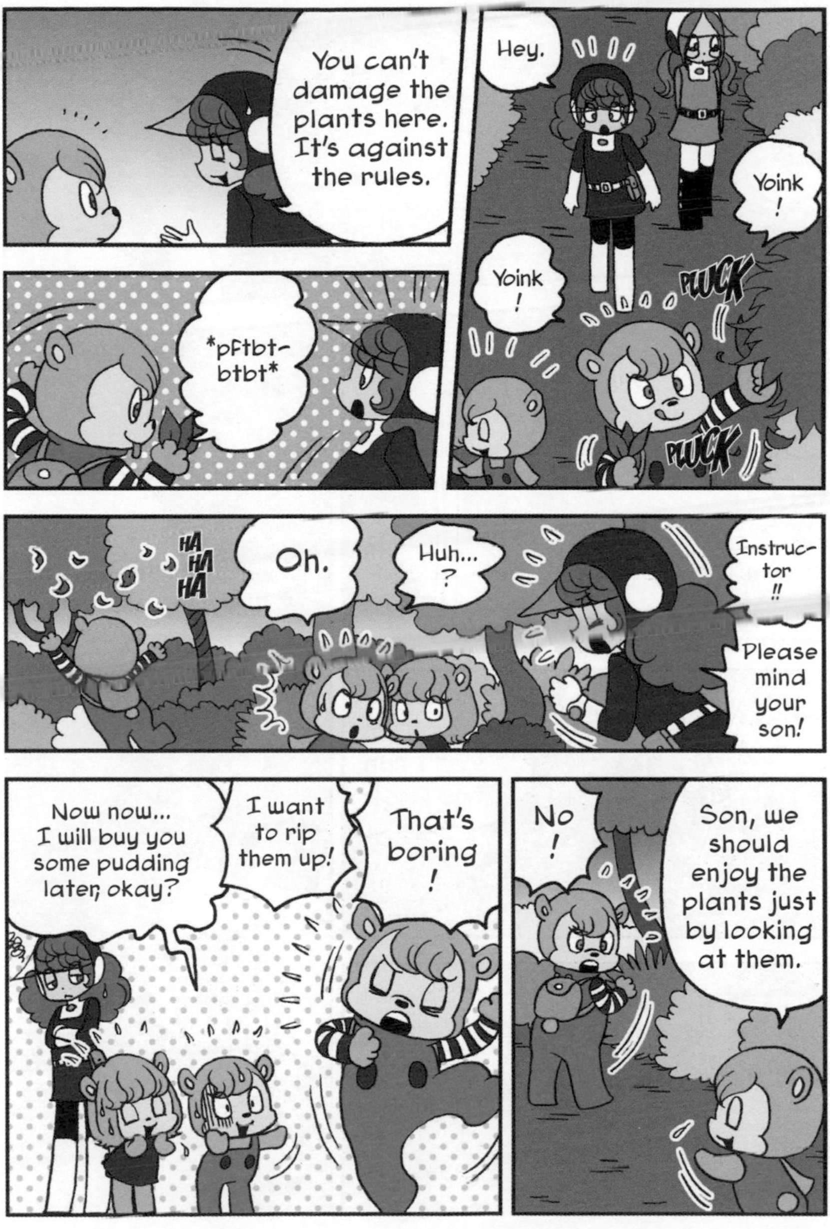
Hey.
Yoink!
Yoink!
PLUCK
PLUCK
You can't damage the plants here. It's against the rules.
pftbt-btbt
Instructor!!
Please mind your son!
Huh...?
Oh.
HA HA HA
Son, we should enjoy the plants just by looking at them.
No!
That's boring!
I want to rip them up!
Now now... I will buy you some pudding later, okay?

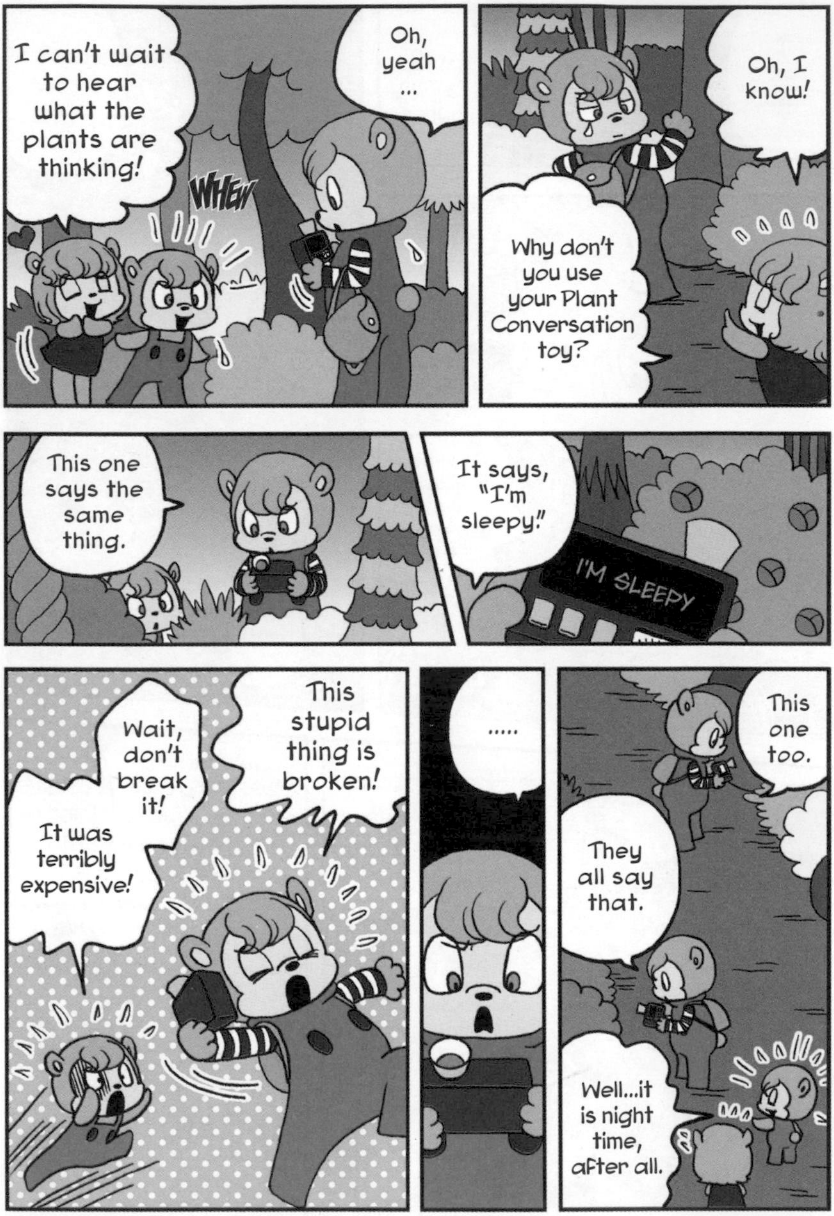
Oh, I know!
Why don't you use your Plant Conversation toy?
Oh, yeah ...
I can't wait to hear what the plants are thinking!
WHEW
It says, "I'm sleepy."
I'M SLEEPY
This one says the same thing.
This one too.
They all say that.
Well...it is night time, after all.
.....
This stupid thing is broken!
Wait, don't break it!
It was terribly expensive!

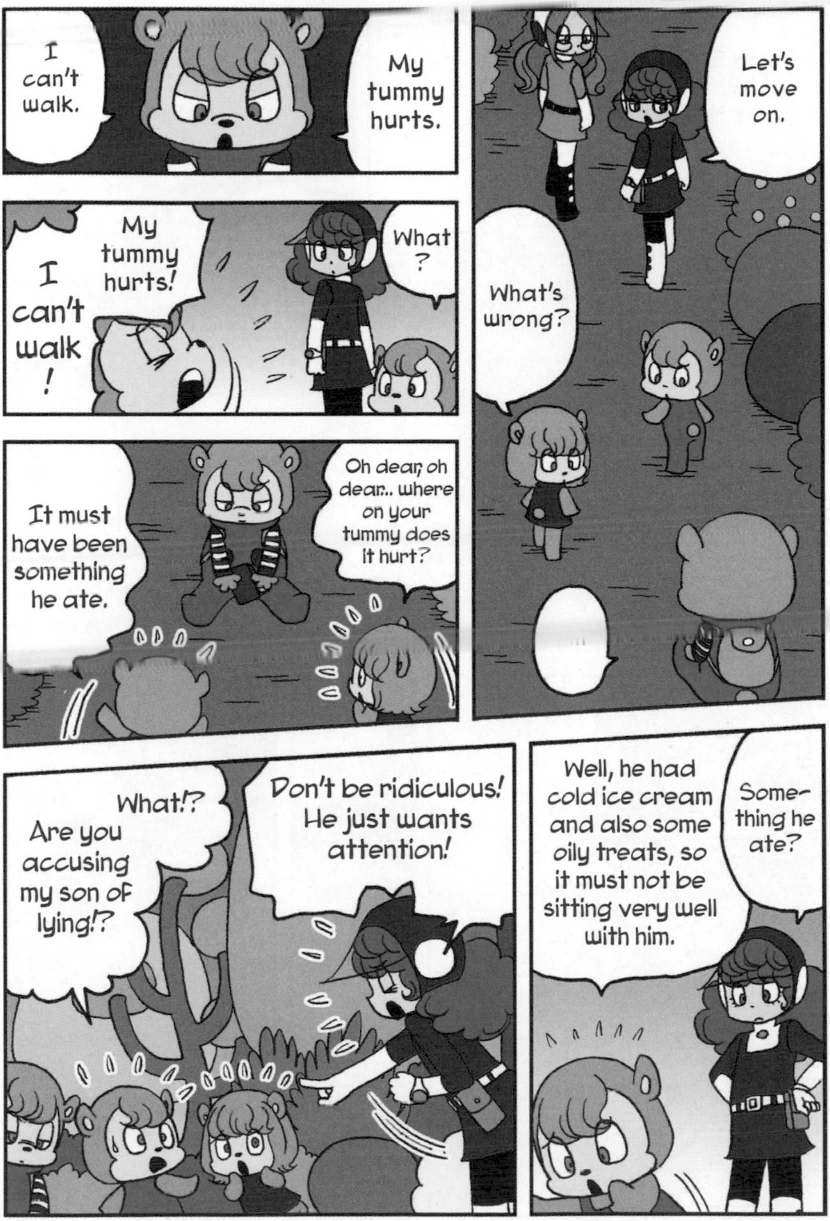

Let's move on.
What's wrong?
My tummy hurts.
I can't walk.
What?
My tummy hurts!
I can't walk!
Oh dear, oh dear... where on your tummy does it hurt?
It must have been something he ate.
Some-thing he ate?
Well, he had cold ice cream and also some oily treats, so it must not be sitting very well with him.
Don't be ridiculous! He just wants attention!
What!? Are you accusing my son of lying!?

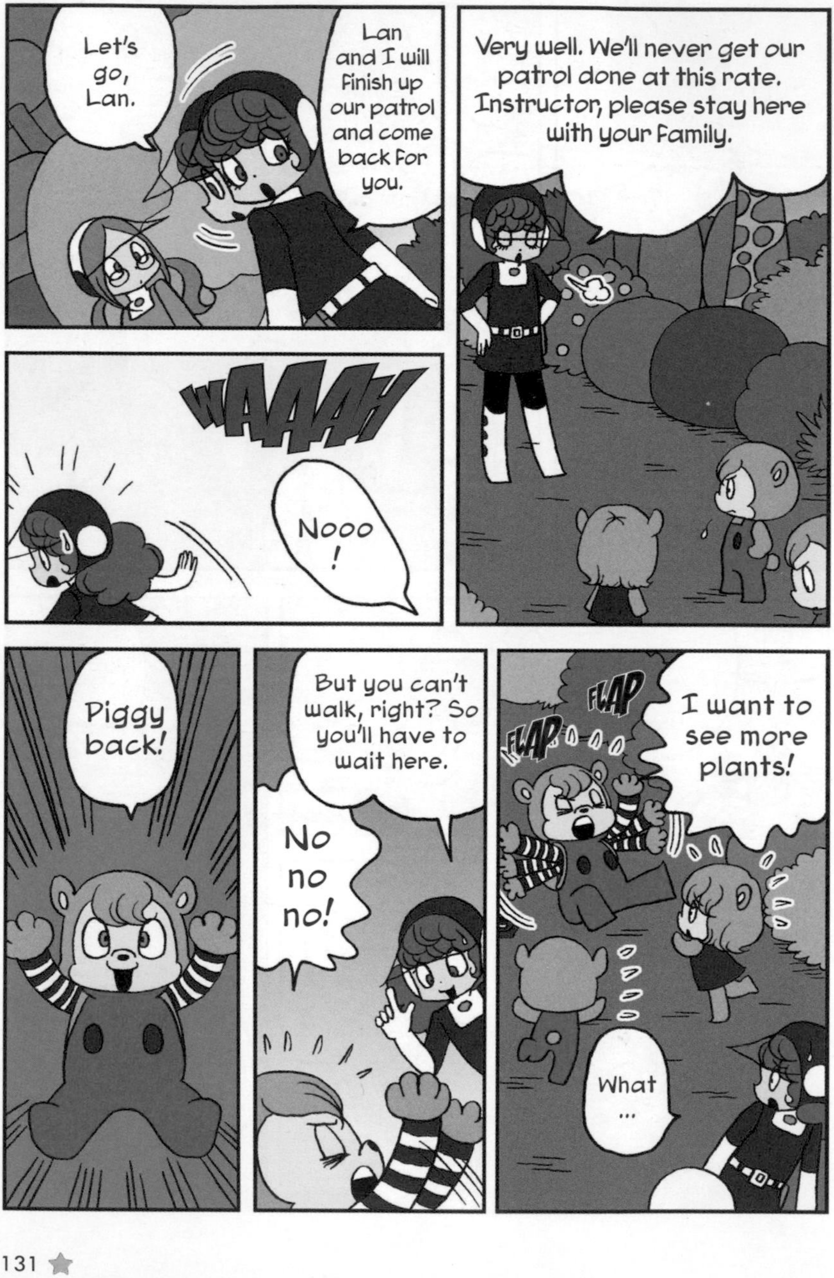
Very well. We'll never get our patrol done at this rate. Instructor, please stay here with your family.
Lan and I will finish up our patrol and come back for you.
Let's go, Lan.
WAAAH
Nooo!
I want to see more plants!
FLAP
FLAP
What...
But you can't walk, right? So you'll have to wait here.
No no no!
Piggy back!

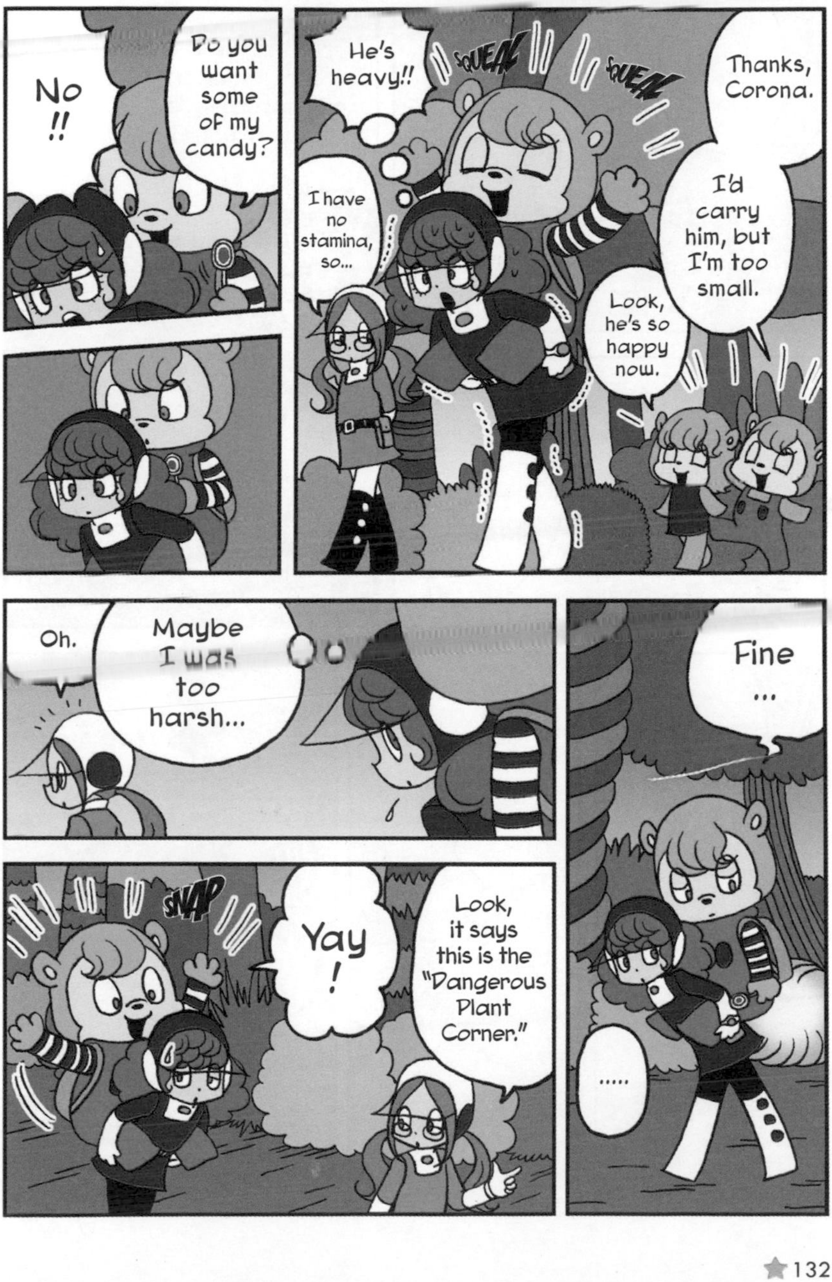
Thanks, Corona.
SQUEAL
I'd carry him, but I'm too small.
SQUEAL
He's heavy!!
Look, he's so happy now.
I have no stamina, so...
Do you want some of my candy?
No !!
Fine ...
.....
Maybe I was too harsh...
Oh.
Look, it says this is the "Dangerous Plant Corner."
Yay !
SNAP

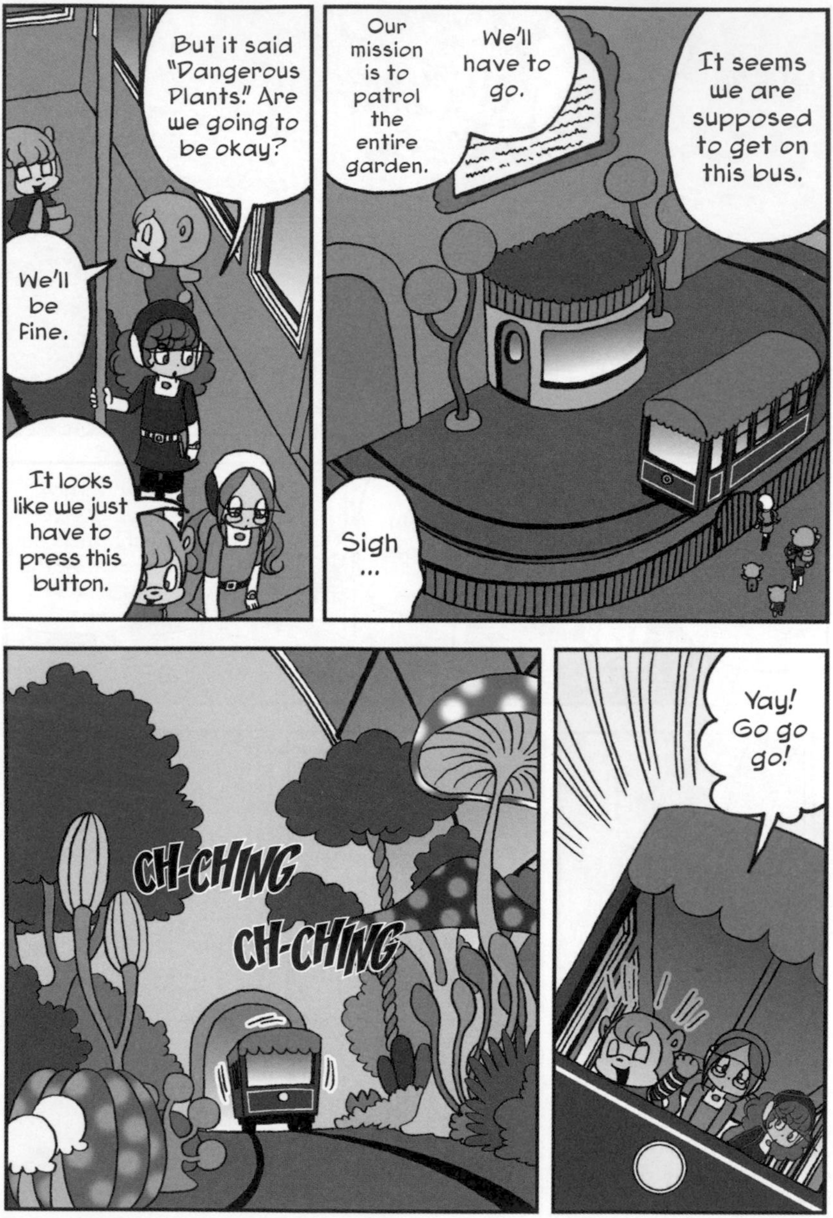
It seems we are supposed to get on this bus.
We'll have to go.
Our mission is to patrol the entire garden.
Sigh ...
But it said "Dangerous Plants." Are we going to be okay?
We'll be fine.
It looks like we just have to press this button.
Yay! Go go go!
CH-CHING
CH-CHING

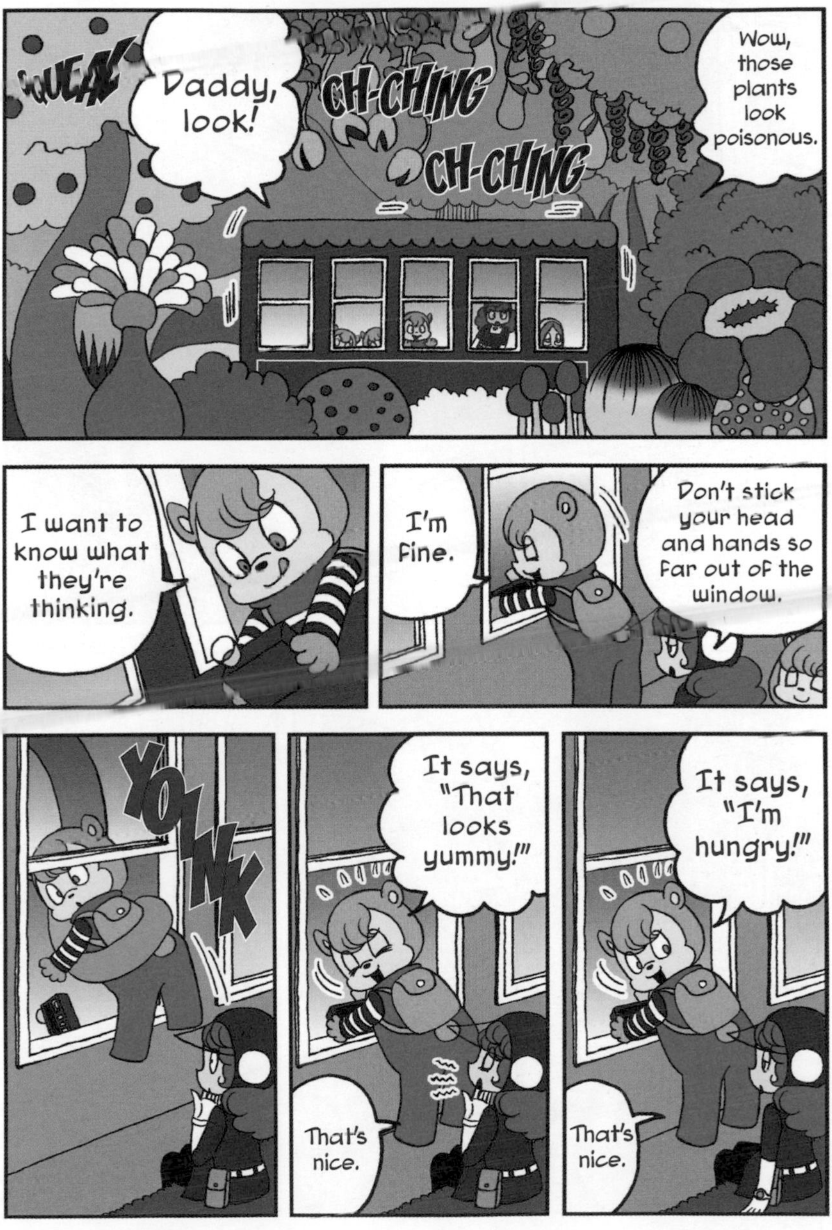
Wow, those plants look poisonous.
CH-CHING
Daddy, look!
SQUEAK
CH-CHING
Don't stick your head and hands so far out of the window.
I'm fine.
I want to know what they're thinking.
It says, "I'm hungry!"
That's nice.
It says, "That looks yummy!"
That's nice.
YOINK

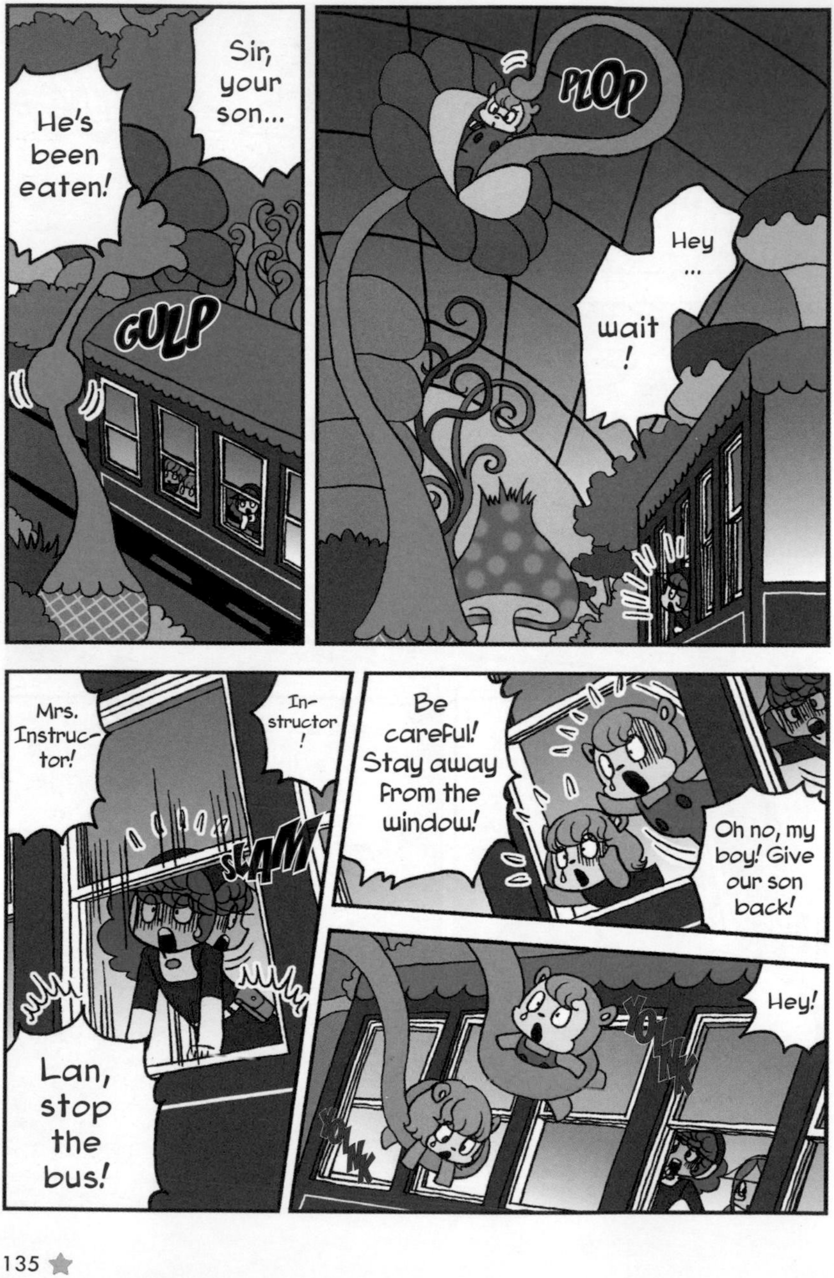
PLOP
Hey ... wait!
Sir, your son...
He's been eaten!
GULP
Oh no, my boy! Give our son back!
Be careful! Stay away from the window!
Hey!
YOINK
YOINK
In-structor!
Mrs. Instruc-tor!
SLAM
Lan, stop the bus!

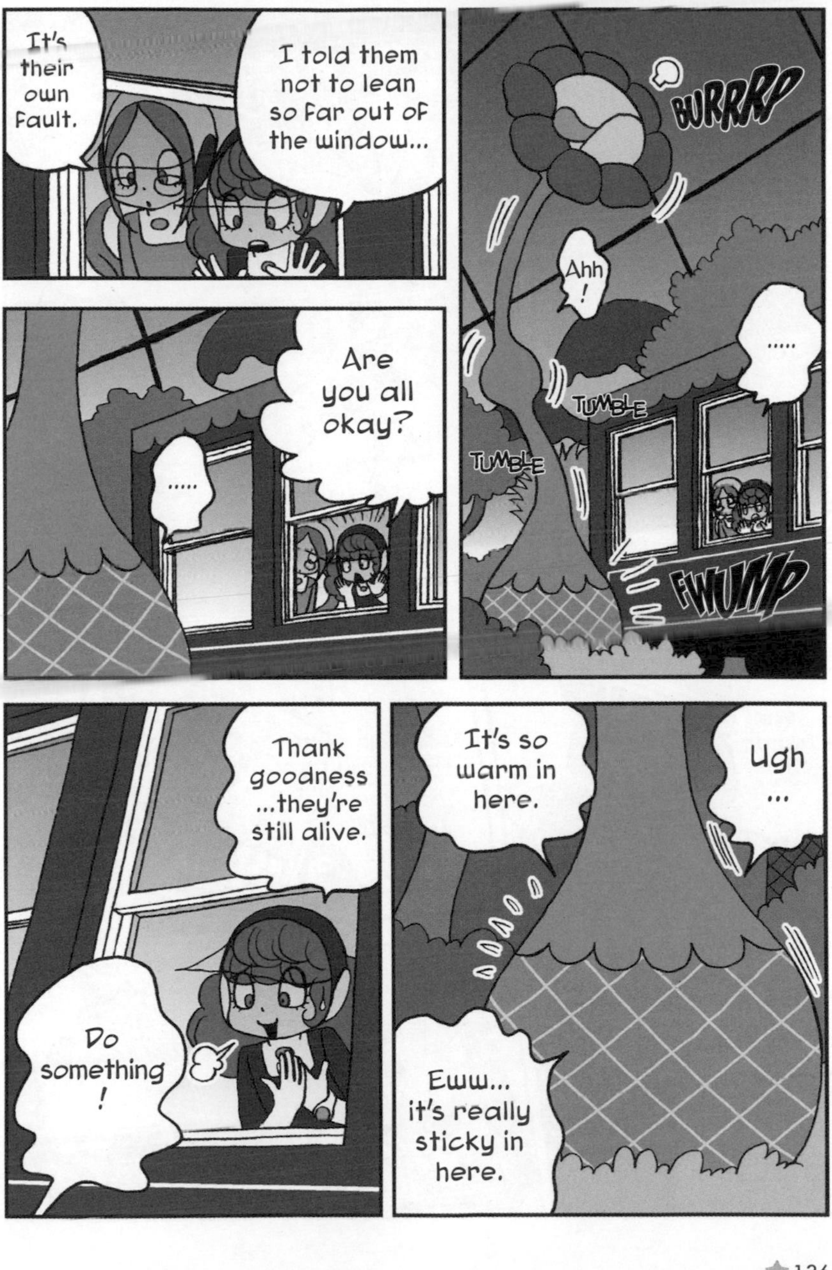
BURRRP
Ahh!
.....
TUMBLE
TUMBLE
FWUMP
I told them not to lean so far out of the window...
It's their own fault.
Are you all okay?
.....
Ugh...
It's so warm in here.
Eww... it's really sticky in here.
Thank goodness ...they're still alive.
Do something!

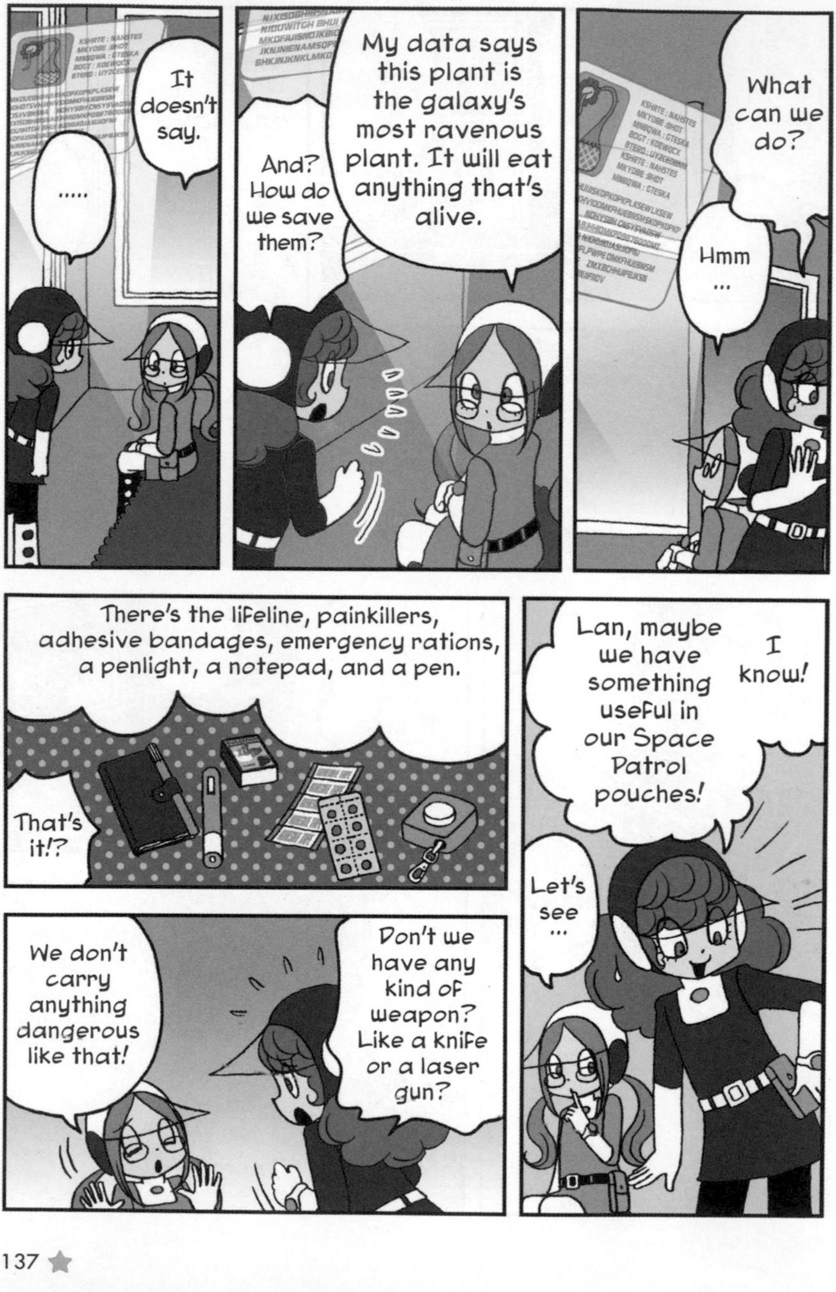
What can we do?
Hmm ...
My data says this plant is the galaxy's most ravenous plant. It will eat anything that's alive.
And? How do we save them?
It doesn't say.
.....
I know!
Lan, maybe we have something useful in our Space Patrol pouches!
Let's see ...
There's the lifeline, painkillers, adhesive bandages, emergency rations, a penlight, a notepad, and a pen.
That's it!?
Don't we have any kind of weapon? Like a knife or a laser gun?
We don't carry anything dangerous like that!

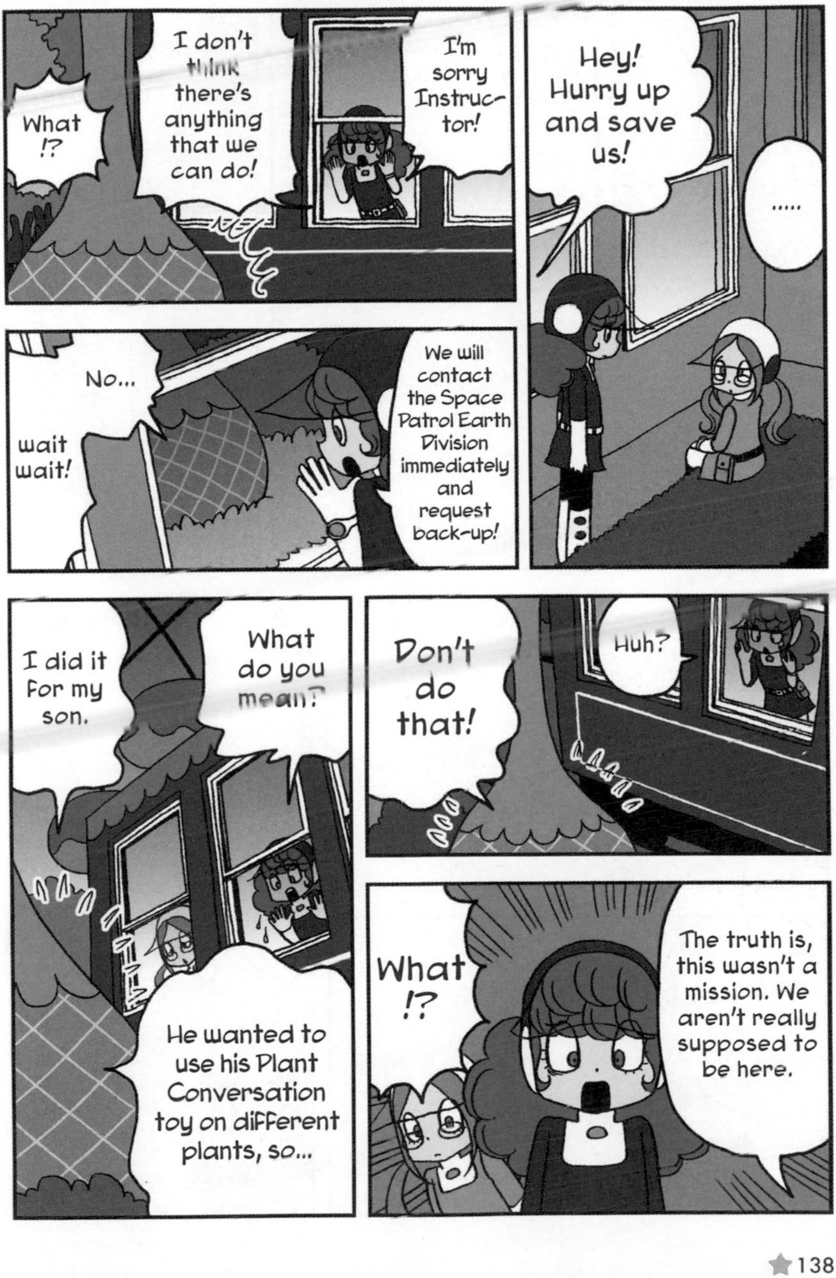

Hey! Hurry up and save us!
.....
I'm sorry Instructor!
I don't think there's anything that we can do!
What!?
We will contact the Space Patrol Earth Division immediately and request back-up!
No...
wait wait!
Huh?
Don't do that!
The truth is, this wasn't a mission. We aren't really supposed to be here.
What!?
What do you mean?
I did it for my son.
He wanted to use his Plant Conversation toy on different plants, so...

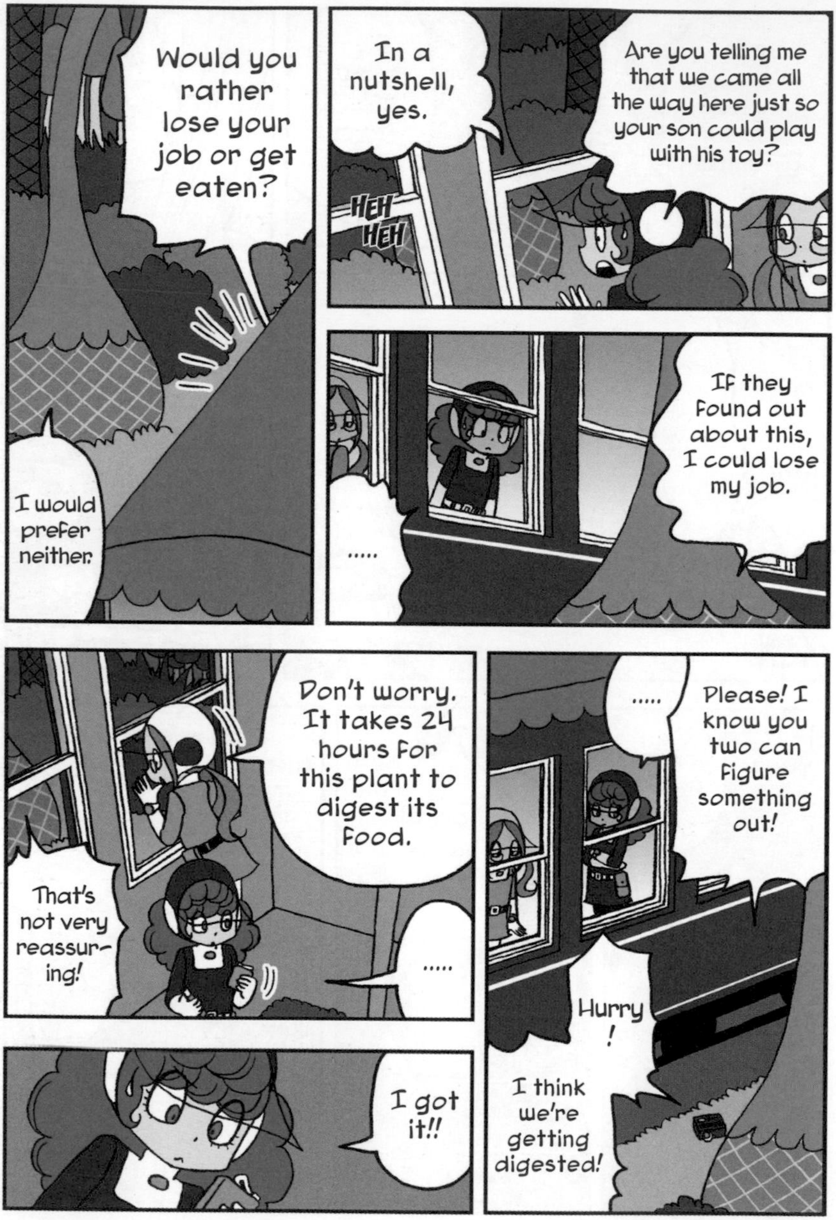

Are you telling me that we came all the way here just so your son could play with his toy?
In a nutshell, yes.
HEH HEH
If they found out about this, I could lose my job.
.....
Would you rather lose your job or get eaten?
I would prefer neither.
Please! I know you two can figure something out!
.....
Hurry!
I think we're getting digested!
Don't worry. It takes 24 hours for this plant to digest its food.
That's not very reassur-ing!
.....
I got it!!

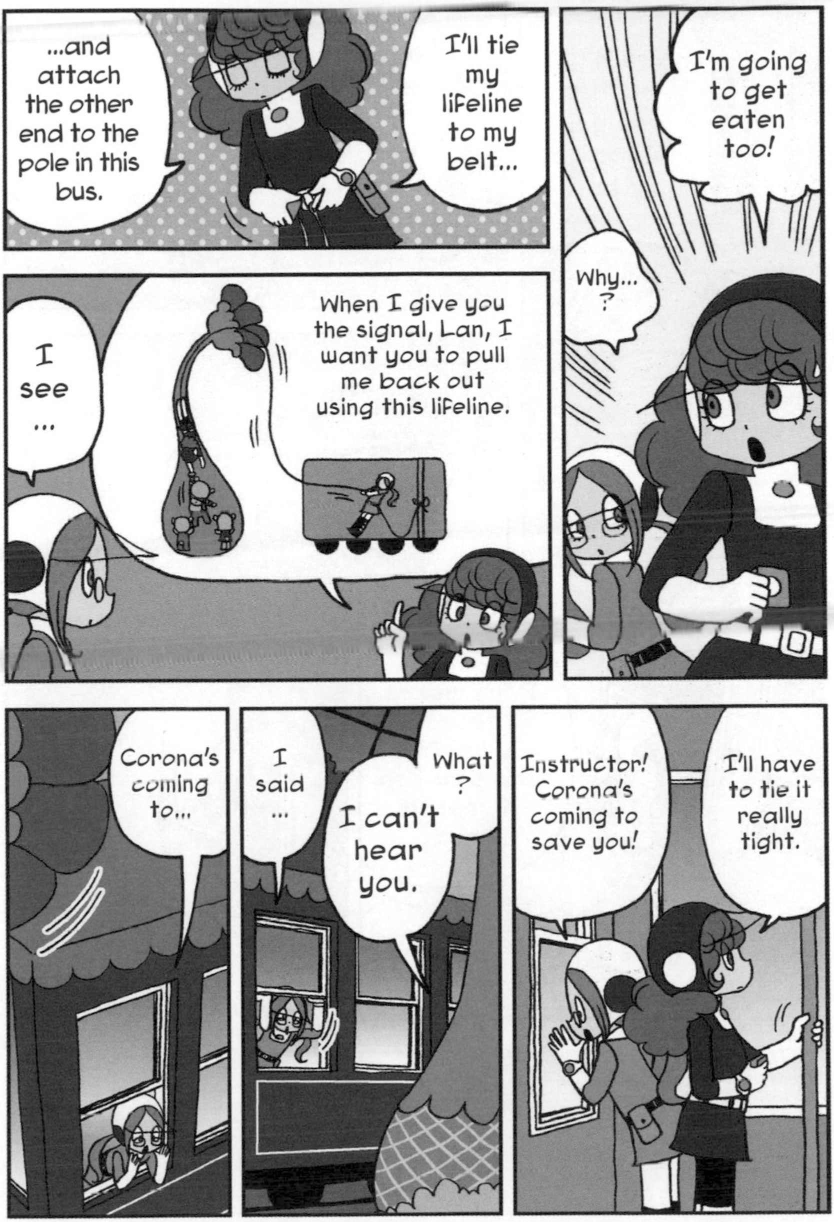
I'm going to get eaten too!
Why...?
I'll tie my lifeline to my belt...
...and attach the other end to the pole in this bus.
When I give you the signal, Lan, I want you to pull me back out using this lifeline.
I see...
I'll have to tie it really tight.
Instructor! Corona's coming to save you!
What?
I can't hear you.
I said...
Corona's coming to...

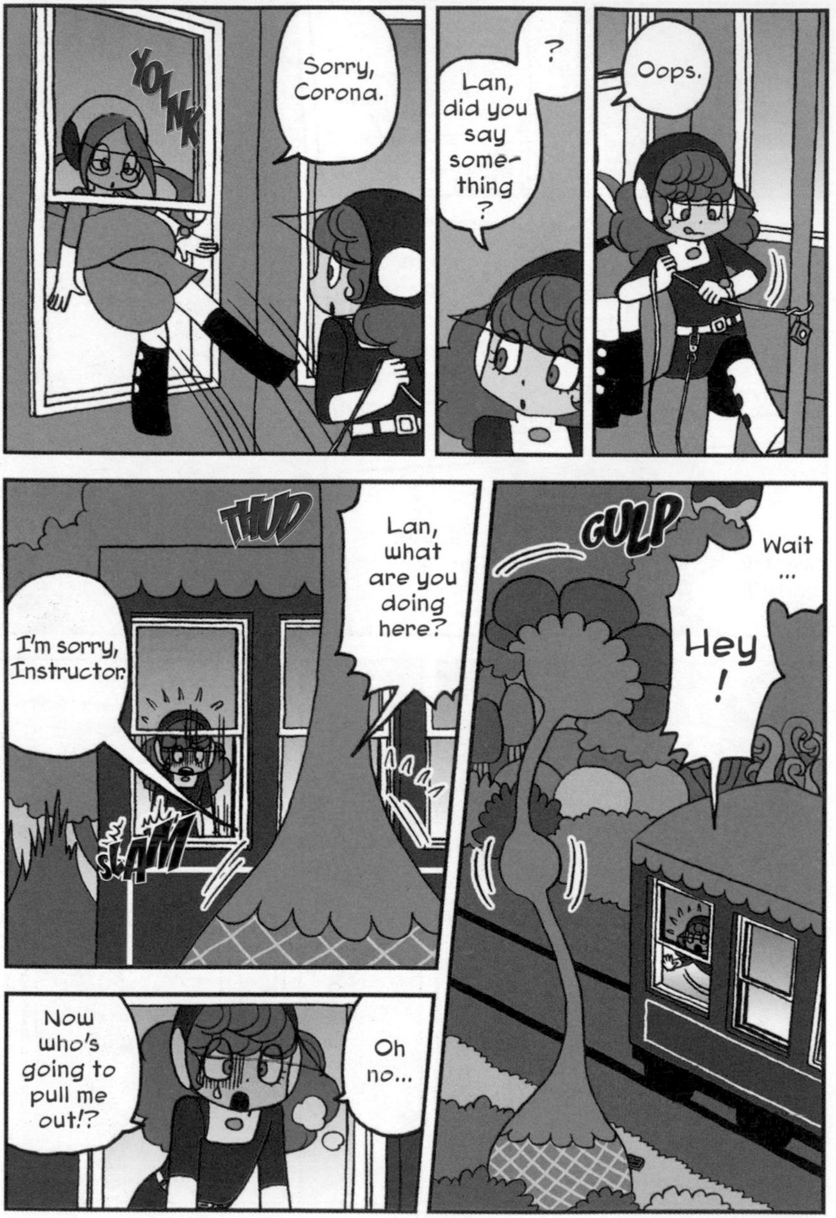
Oops.
?
Lan, did you say some-thing?
Sorry, Corona.
YOINK
Wait ...
Hey!
GULP
Lan, what are you doing here?
THUD
I'm sorry, Instructor.
SLAM
Oh no...
Now who's going to pull me out!?

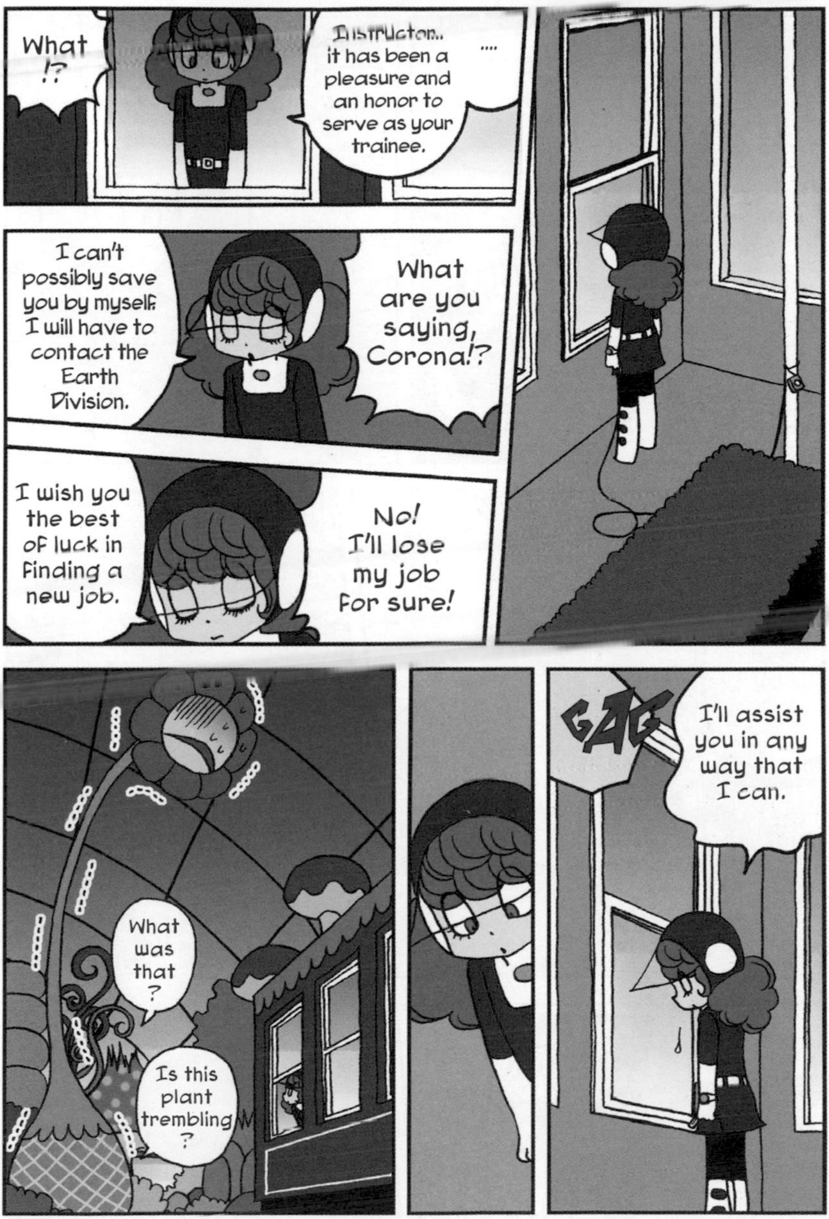
....
Instructor.. it has been a pleasure and an honor to serve as your trainee.
What!?
What are you saying, Corona!?
I can't possibly save you by myself. I will have to contact the Earth Division.
No! I'll lose my job for sure!
I wish you the best of luck in finding a new job.
I'll assist you in any way that I can.
GAG
What was that?
Is this plant trembling?

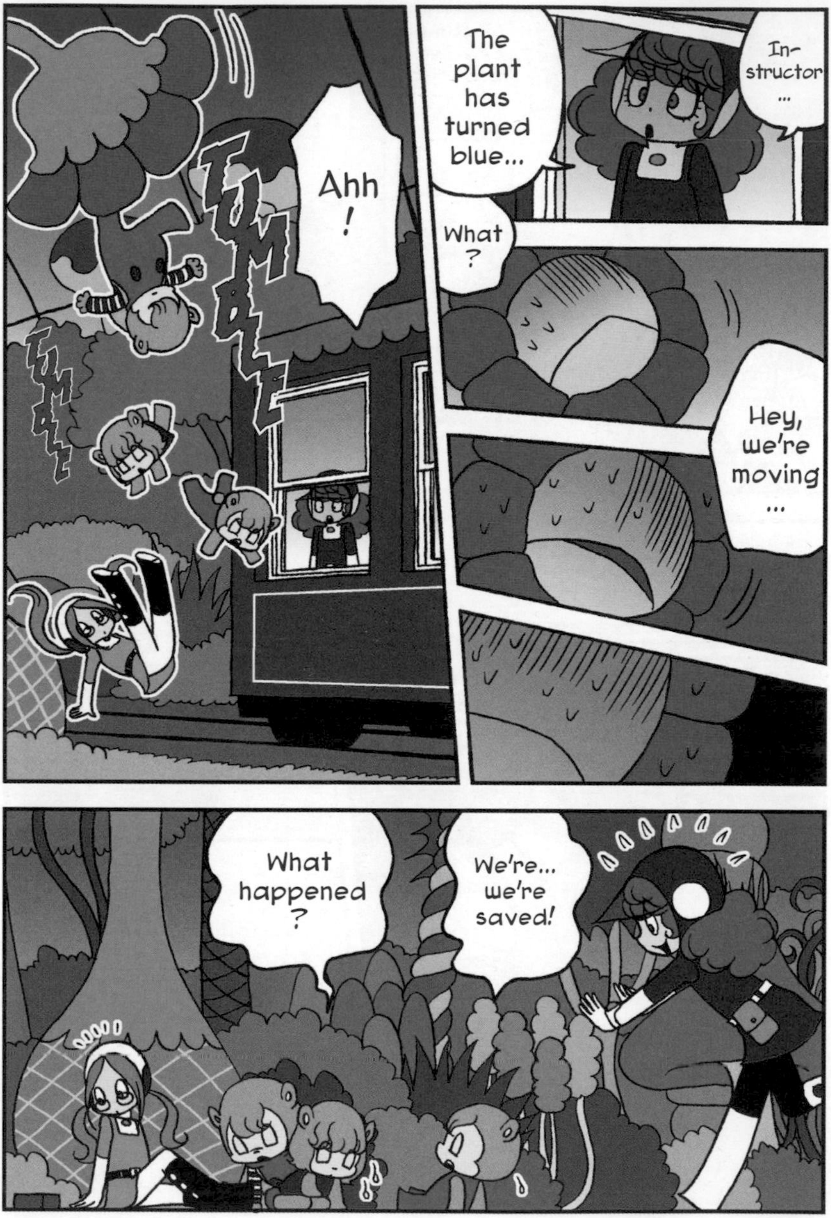
In-structor...
The plant has turned blue...
What?
Hey, we're moving...
Ahh!
TUMBLE
TUMBLE
We're... we're saved!
What happened?

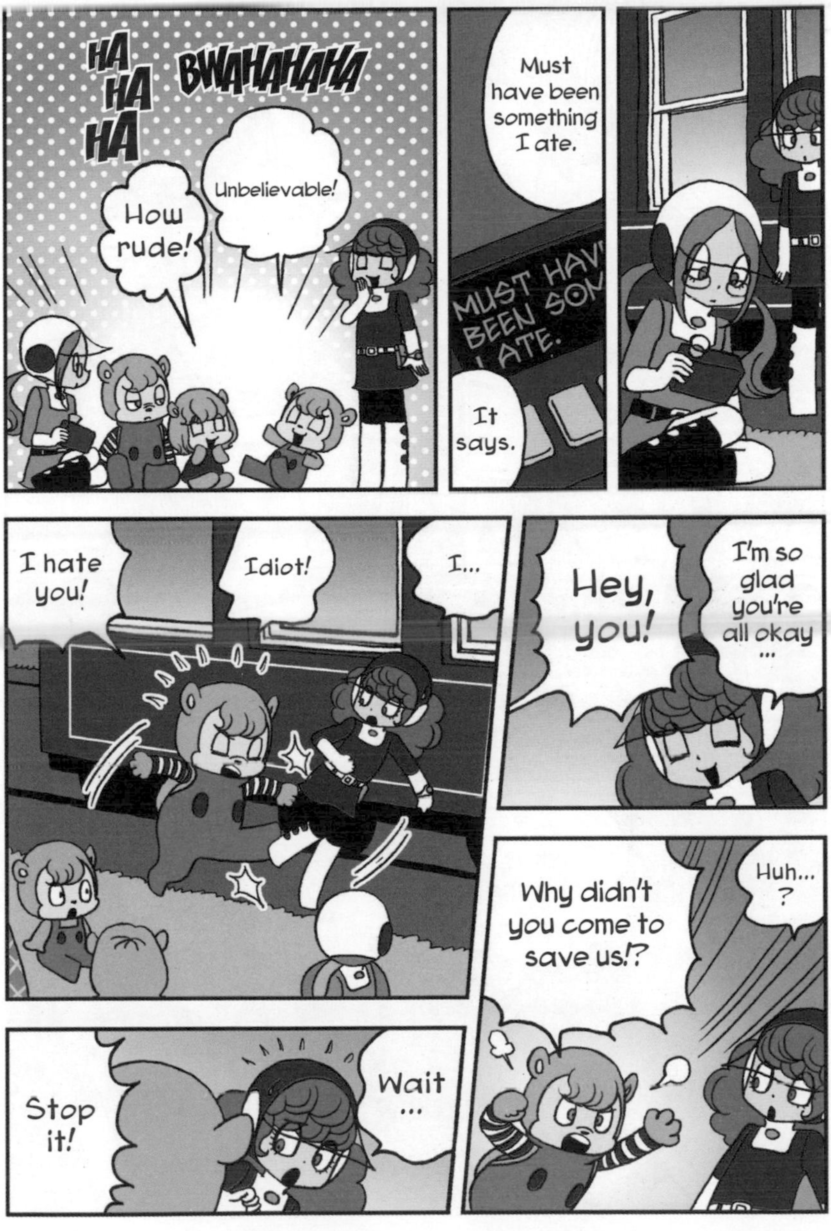
Must have been something I ate.
It says.
HA HA HA
BWAHAHAHA
Unbelievable!
How rude!
I'm so glad you're all okay ...
Hey, you!
Huh... ?
Why didn't you come to save us!?
I...
Idiot!
I hate you!
Wait ...
Stop it!

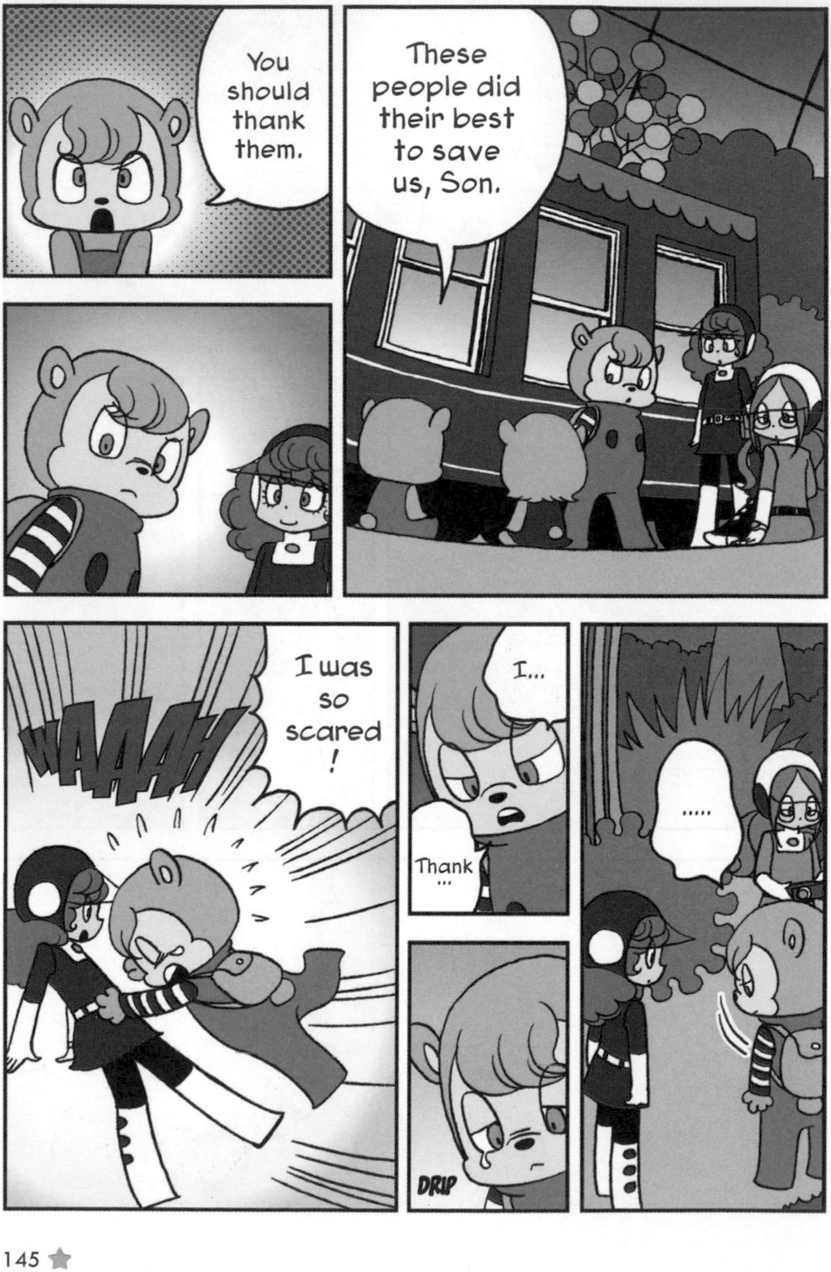
These people did their best to save us, Son.
You should thank them.
......
I...
Thank ...
DRIP
I was so scared!
WAAAH

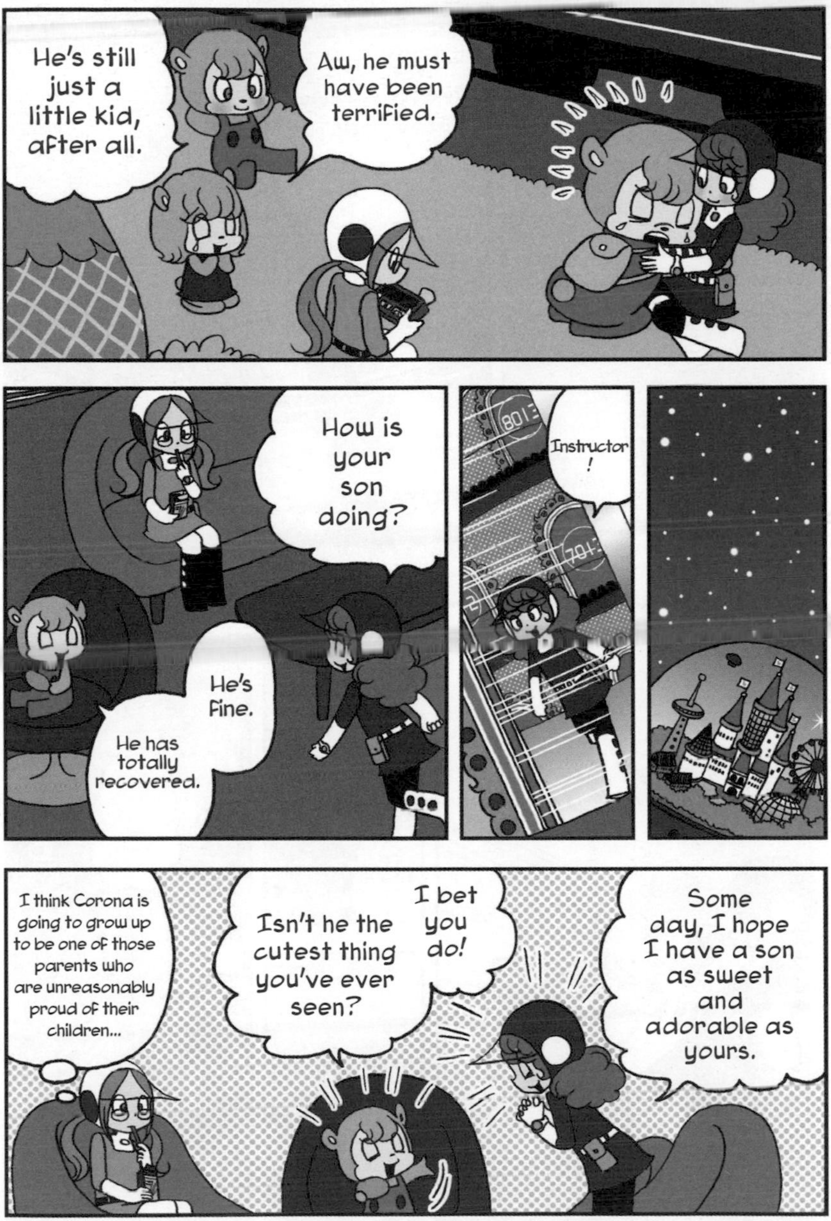
Aw, he must have been terrified.
He's still just a little kid, after all.
Instructor!
How is your son doing?
He's fine.
He has totally recovered.
Some day, I hope I have a son as sweet and adorable as yours.
I bet you do!
Isn't he the cutest thing you've ever seen?
I think Corona is going to grow up to be one of those parents who are unreasonably proud of their children...

FUN EXTRAS!

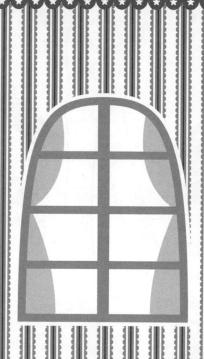

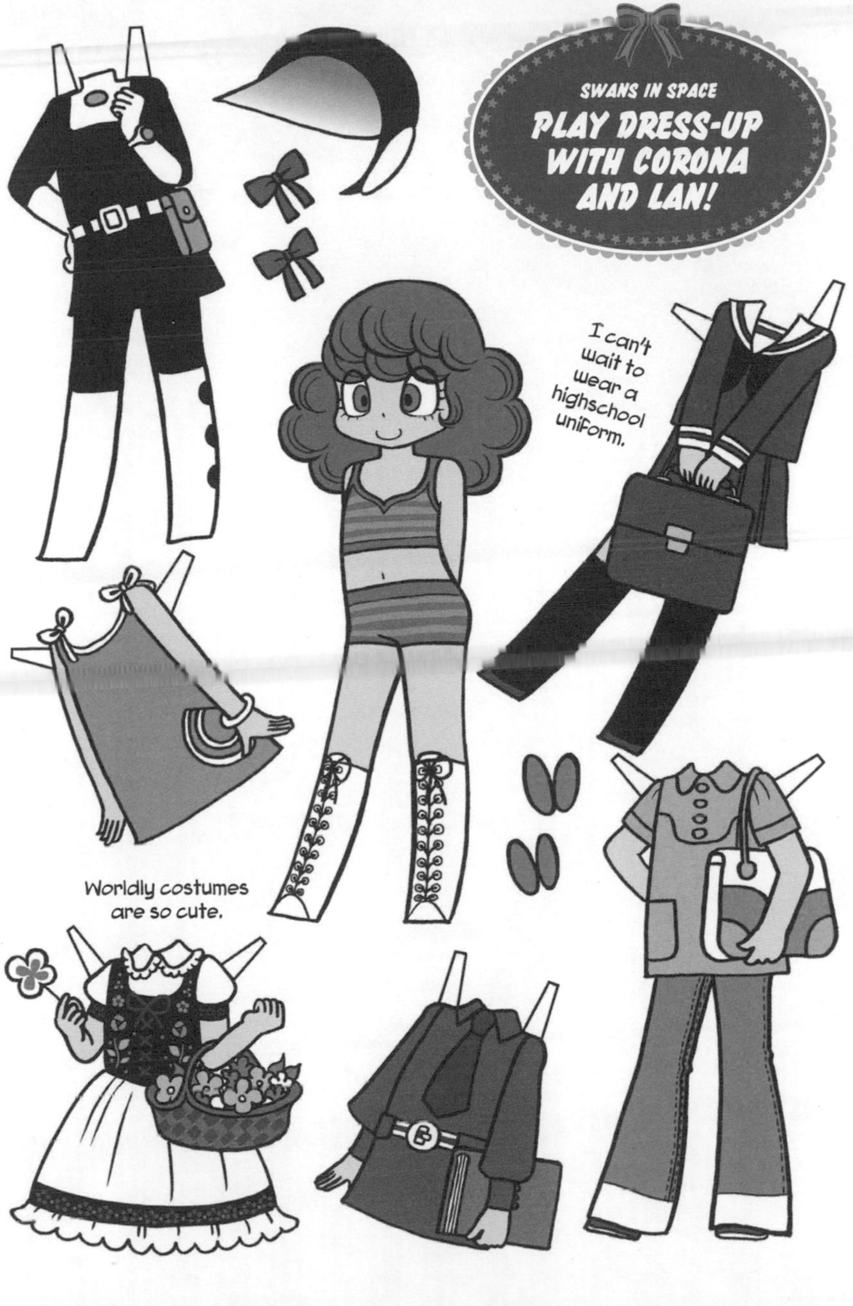
SWANS IN SPACE
PLAY DRESS-UP WITH CORONA AND LAN!
I can't wait to wear a highschool uniform.
Worldly costumes are so cute.

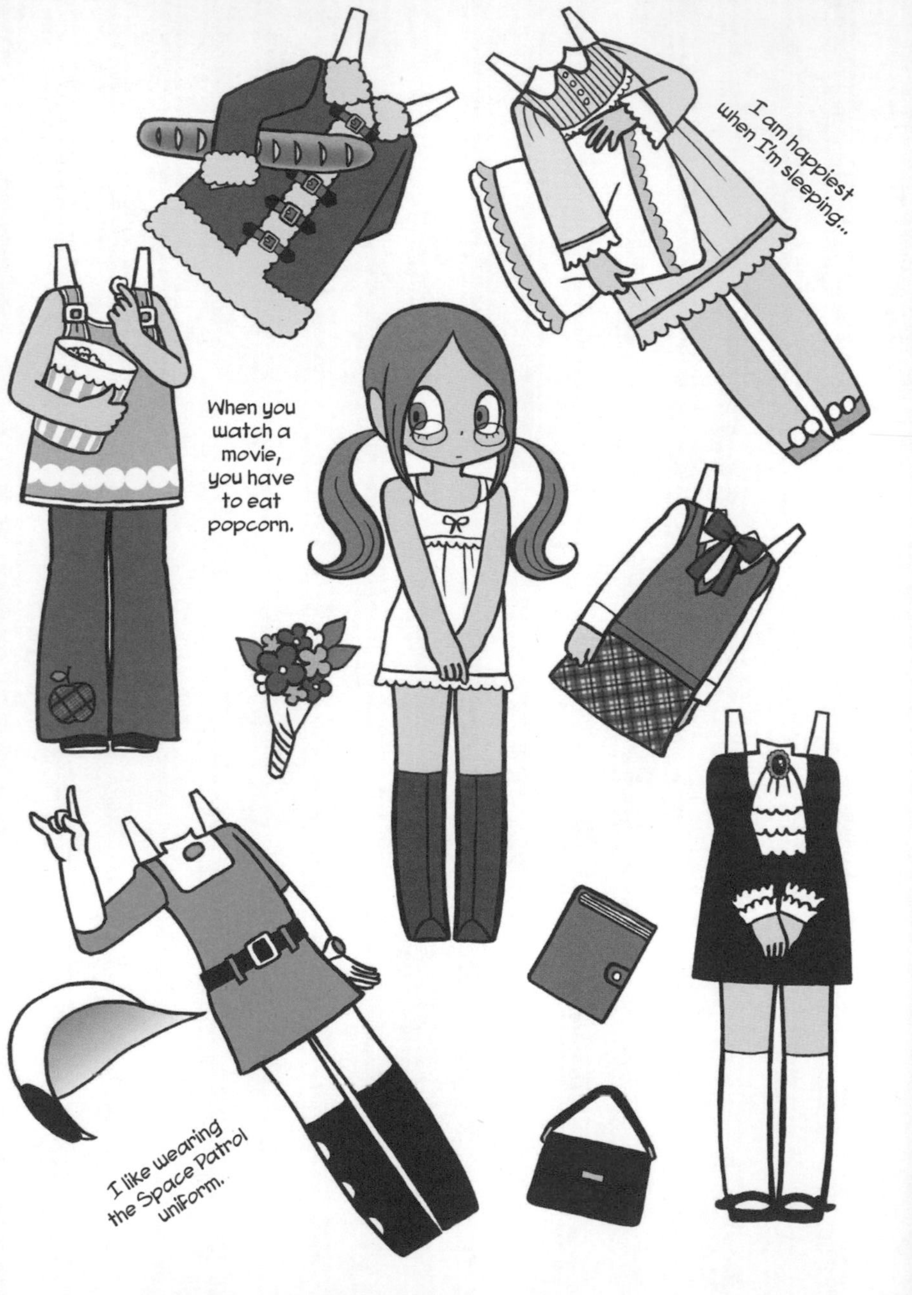
I am happiest when I'm sleeping...
When you watch a movie, you have to eat popcorn.
I like wearing the Space Patrol uniform.

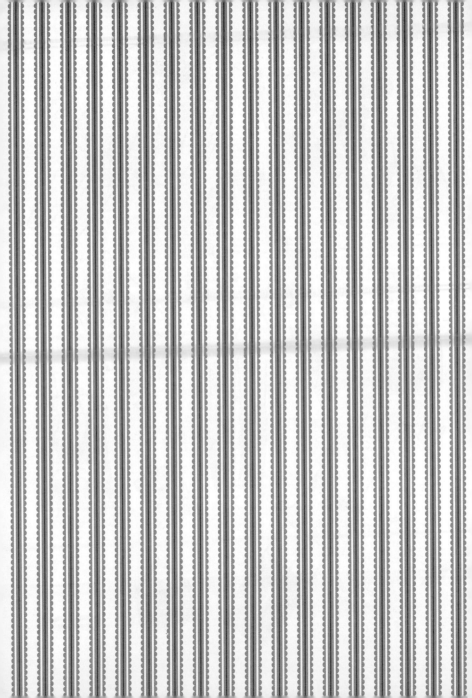

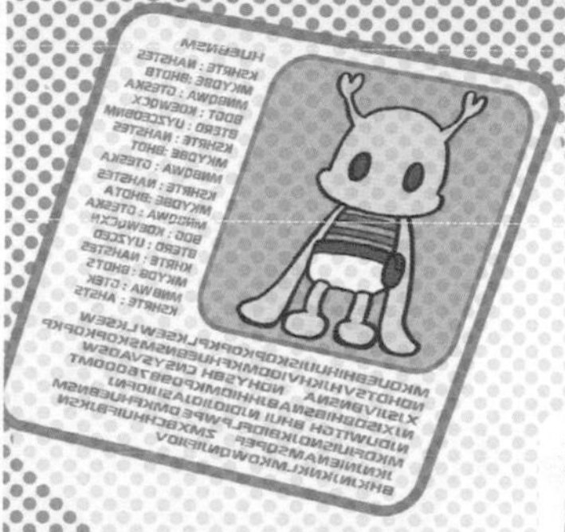

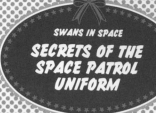

SWANS IN SPACE

SECRETS OF THE SPACE PATROL UNIFORM

Once equipped, the Space Patrol uniform provides an invisible force field which allows its wearer to perform their work unhindered in the potentially harsh environments of space and other planets.

Space Receiver

When summoned for a mission, the Space Receiver allows its wearer to instantly teleport from Earth to the Earth Division space station. It can also be used as a database and a video communication device.

Brooch

Trainees wear turquoise blue brooches, but will get red brooches instead once they graduate and become Space Patrol officers.

Earphones

Allows Space Patrol personnel to understand and fluently communicate with beings from other planets.

Pouch Contents

Notepad, pen, penlight, lifeline, adhesive bandages, painkillers, and emergency rations.

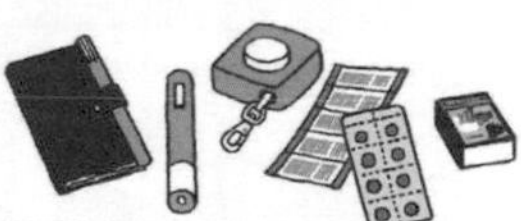

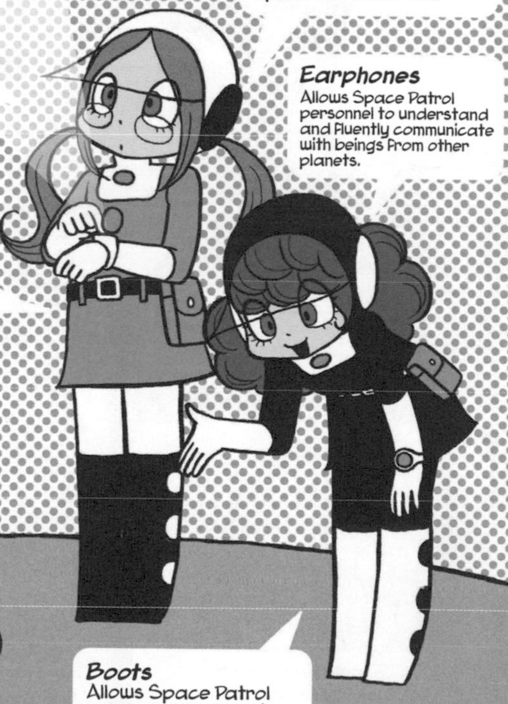

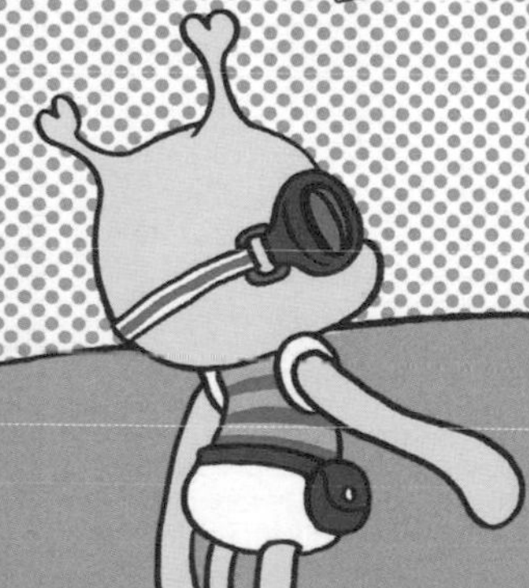

Boots

Allows Space Patrol personnel to move freely in zero-gravity environments.

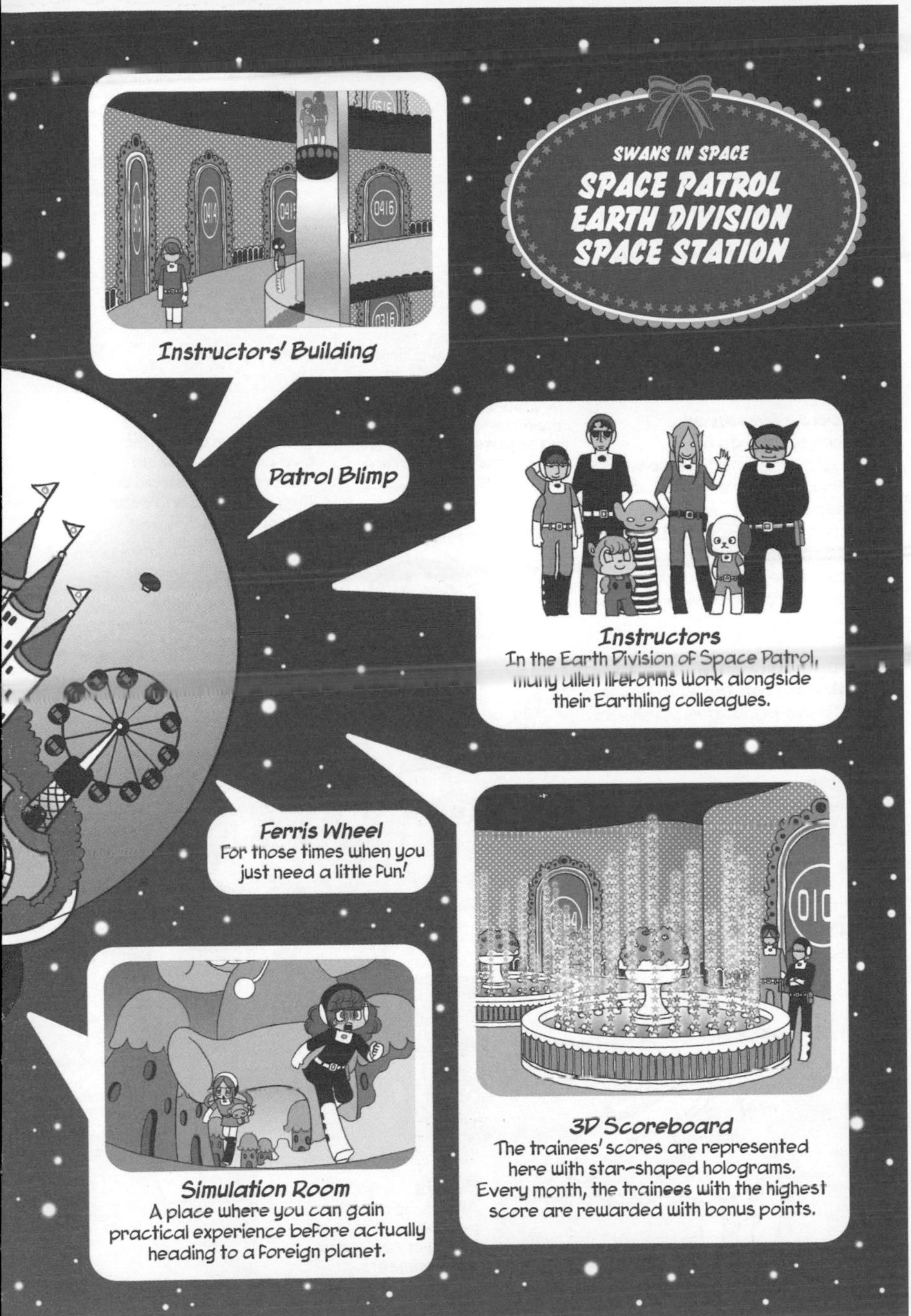
SWANS IN SPACE
SPACE PATROL EARTH DIVISION SPACE STATION
Instructors' Building
Patrol Blimp
Instructors
In the Earth Division of Space Patrol, many alien lifeforms work alongside their Earthling colleagues.
Ferris Wheel
For those times when you just need a little fun!
3D Scoreboard
The trainees' scores are represented here with star-shaped holograms. Every month, the trainees with the highest score are rewarded with bonus points.
Simulation Room
A place where you can gain practical experience before actually heading to a foreign planet.

Dining Hall

Located one floor above the lounge, the dining hall is only open to Space Patrol officers and staff.

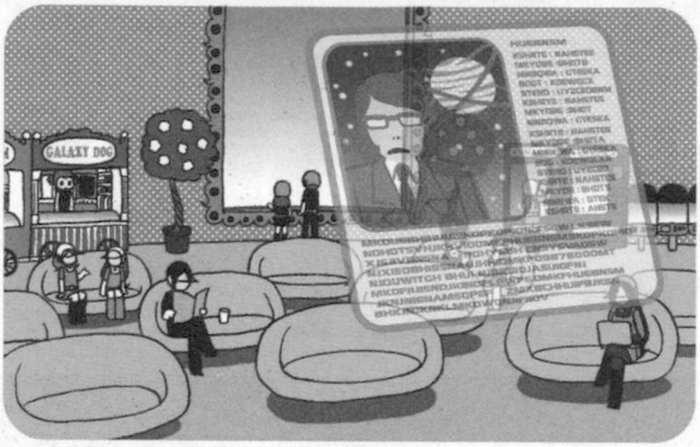
GALAXY DOG

Lounge

A place to relax between missions. The vendor kiosks offer a variety of juices and snacks, as well as a number of items that are useful to have on patrol.

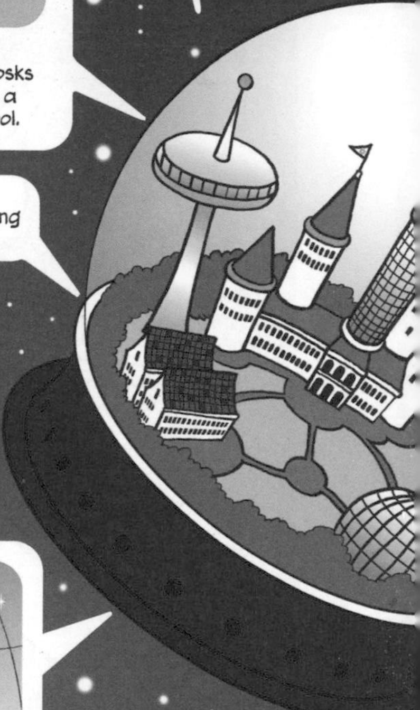

Dormitory Tower

This is where people stay during long missions or for training camps.

Interplanetary Shuttles for Aliens

Instructor commutes to work every day on one of these.

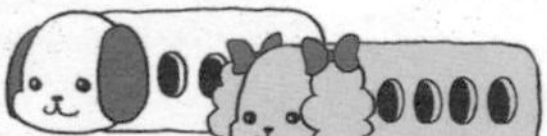

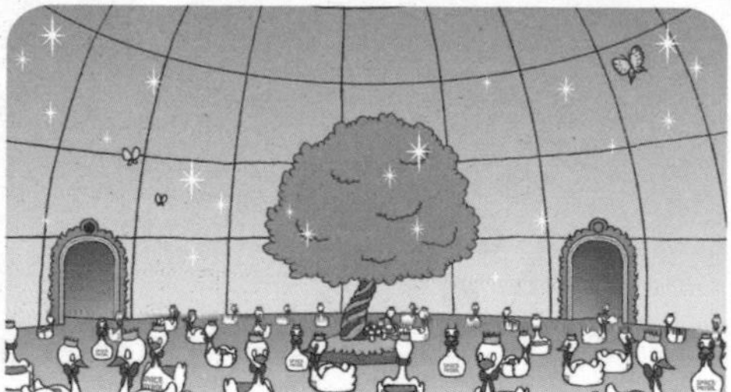
SPACE PATROL

Garden

The environmental settings in the garden are similar to Earth's various climates, which allows a collection of flora from Earth to be raised here. There is also a greenhouse in the garden where plants from different planets are kept for experiments.

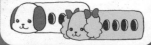

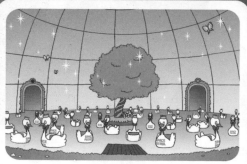

Boat Dock

The Patrol Boats used by Space Patrol officers and trainees can be found here. Each team has its own designated boat.

COMING SOON:

SWANS in SPACE

VOLUME 2

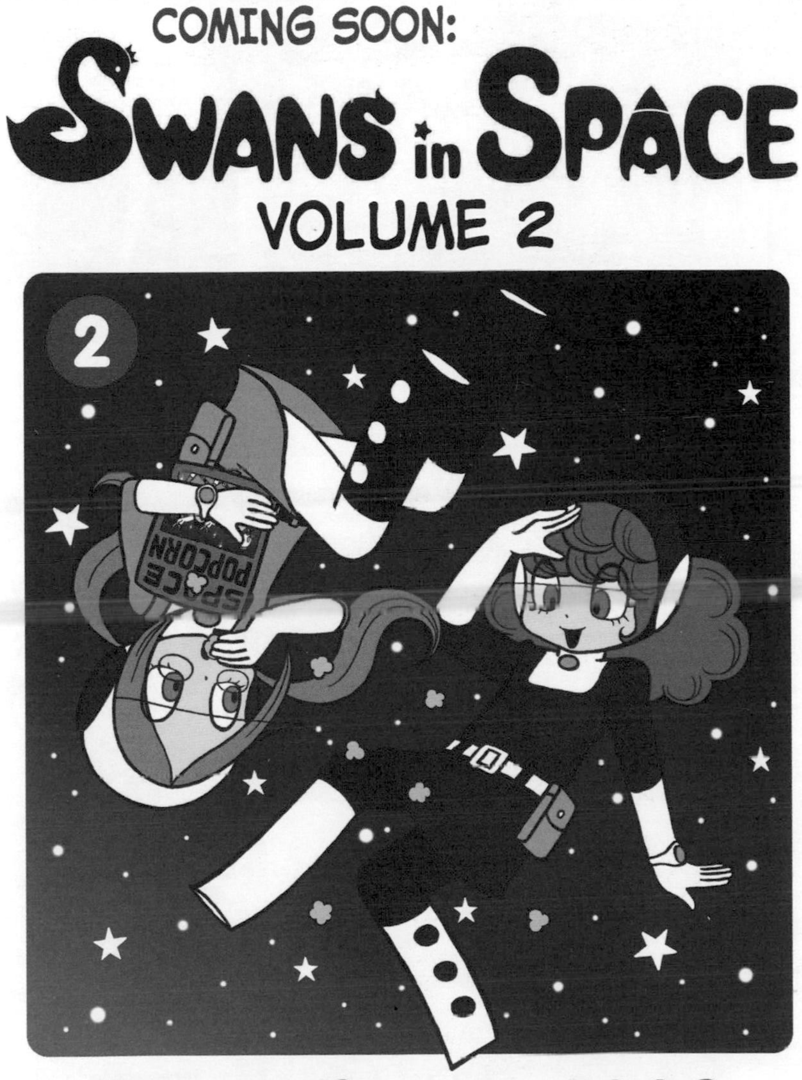
2
SPACE POPCORN

ARRIVING OCTOBER 2009

SWANS IN SPACE Vol.2
ISBN: 978-1-897376-94-2

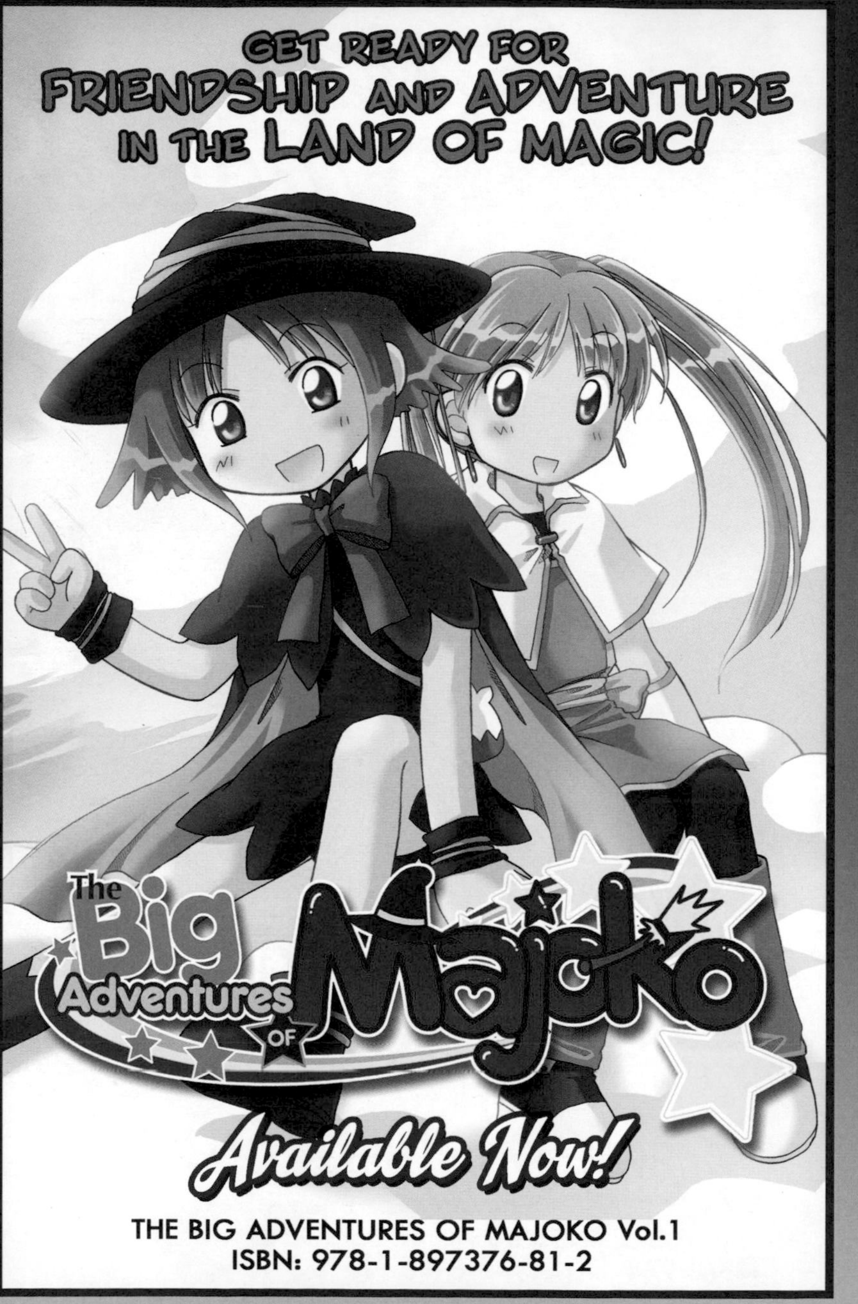
GET READY FOR
FRIENDSHIP AND ADVENTURE
IN THE LAND OF MAGIC!
The Big Adventures of Majoko
Available Now!
THE BIG ADVENTURES OF MAJOKO Vol.1
ISBN: 978-1-897376-81-2

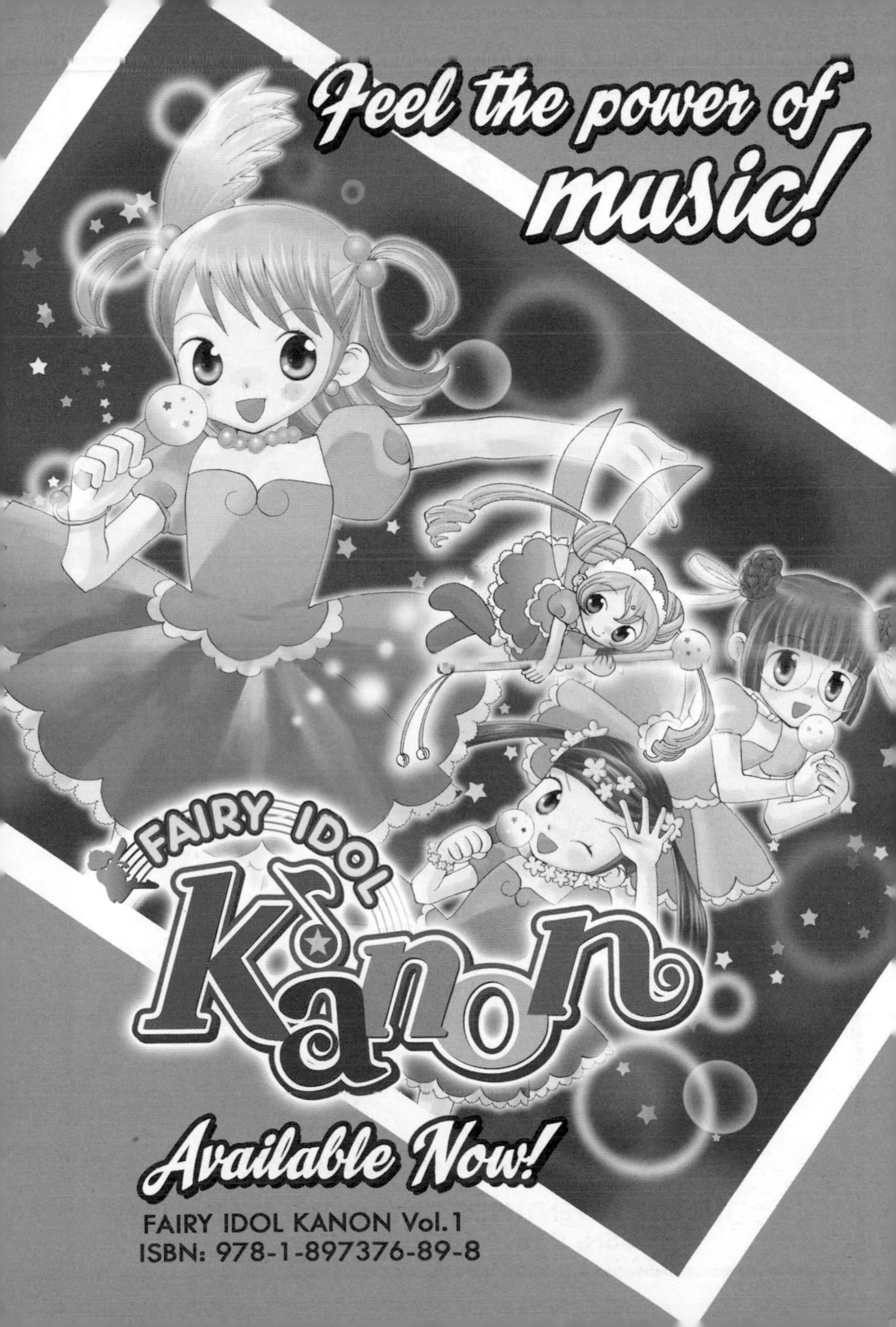
Feel the power of music!
FAIRY IDOL
Kanon
Available Now!
FAIRY IDOL KANON Vol.1
ISBN: 978-1-897376-89-8

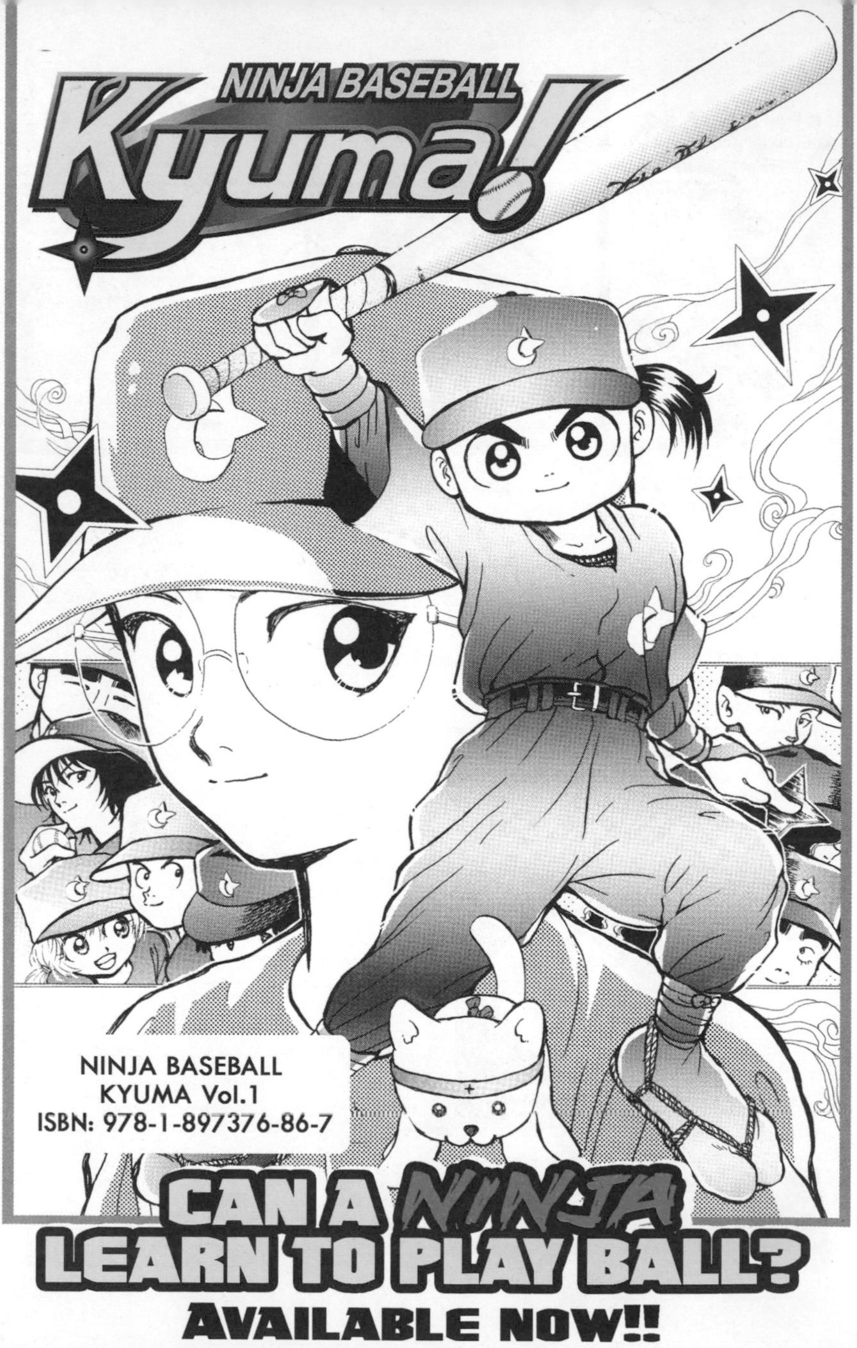
NINJA BASEBALL
Kyuma!
NINJA BASEBALL
KYUMA Vol.1
ISBN: 978-1-897376-86-7

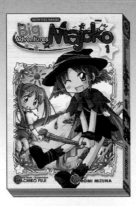

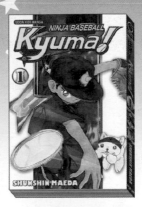

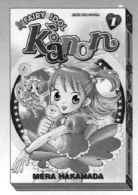

THE BIG ADVENTURES OF MAJOKO

Vol.1 *(On sale now!)*
ISBN: 978-1-897376-81-2

Vol.2 *(JUL 2009)*
ISBN: 978-1-897376-82-9

Vol.3 *(NOV 2009)*
ISBN: 978-1-897376-83-6

NINJA BASEBALL KYUMA

Vol.1 *(On sale now!)*
ISBN: 978-1-897376-86-7

Vol.2 *(SEP 2009)*
ISBN: 978-1-897376-87-4

Vol.3 *(FEB 2010)*
ISBN: 978-1-897376-88-1

FAIRY IDOL KANON

Vol.1 *(On sale now!)*
ISBN: 978-1-897376-89-8

Vol.2 *(AUG 2009)*
ISBN: 978-1-897376-90-4

Vol.3 *(JAN 2010)*
ISBN: 978-1-897376-91-1

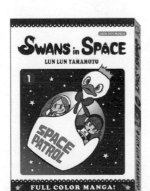

SWANS IN SPACE

Vol.1 *(JUN 2009)*
ISBN: 978-1-897376-93-5

Vol.2 *(OCT 2009)*
ISBN: 978-1-897376-94-2

Vol.3 *(APR 2010)*
ISBN: 978-1-897376-95-9

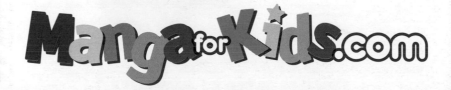

SWANS IN SPACE

SWANS in SPACE

Story & Art: Lun Lun Yamamoto

Translation: M. Kirie Hayashi
Lettering: Ben Lee
English Logo Design: Hanna Chan

UDON STAFF
Chief of Operations: Erik Ko
Project Manager: Jim Zubkavich
Managing Editor: Matt Moylan
Marketing Manager: Stacy King

UCHU NO SWAN Vol.1 © Lun Lun Yamamoto
All rights reserved.

Original Japanese edition published by POPLAR Publishing Co., Ltd. Tokyo
English translation rights arranged directly with POPLAR Publishing Co., Ltd.

No part of this publication may be reproduced, stored in retrieval system, or
transmitted in any form or by any means, electronic, mechanical photocopying,
recording, or otherwise, without the prior written permission of the Publisher.

English edition of SWANS IN SPACE Vol. 1
©2009 UDON Entertainment Corp.

Any similarities to persons living or dead is purely coincidental.

English language version produced and published by
UDON Entertainment Corp.
P.O. Box 5002, RPO MAJOR MACKENZIE
Richmond Hill, Ontario, L4S 0B7, Canada

www.udonentertainment.com

First Printing: June 2009
ISBN-13: 978-1-897376-93-5
ISBN-10 : 1-897376-93-6
Printed in Canada

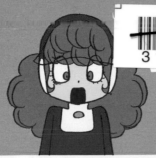

This is the BACK of the book!

Swans in Space is a comic book created in Japan, where comics are called **manga**. Manga is read from right-to-left, which is backwards from the normal books you know. This means that you will find the first page where you expect to find the last page! It also means that each page begins in the top right corner.

START HERE!

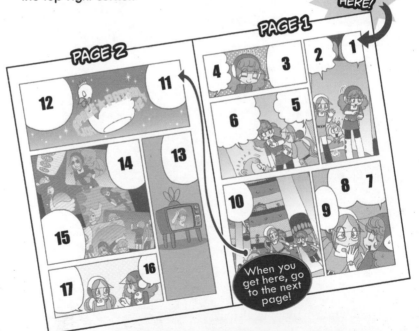

When you get here, go to the next page!

Now head to the other end of the book and enjoy **Swans in Space!**

P9-DDS-941

3 1122 01

Cook Memorial P

COOK MEMORIAL LIBRARY
413 N. MILWAUKEE AVE.
LIBERTYVILLE, ILLINOIS 60048

JUN 1 3 2011